Billy the Kid

"He's deep as well water and damn near as cold."

Falcon tried once more to get Billy to listen to reason.
"Kid, this group you're set on joining is nothing more than
a bunch of vigilantes, and being a vigilante is just one short
step from the owl hoot trail."

"We're not vigilantes, Falcon," the Kid said. "We're
Regulators, and we're gonna regulate that gang right out
of Lincoln County."

"Whatever you call yourselves, Kid, doesn't matter. If you
ride with these men, it's going to set you on a course that
can only lead to your death."

"You got it wrong, Falcon. All of us Regulators swore an
oath to arrest, not to execute, the wrongdoers, and bring
them to Lincoln for a trial."

"Kid, no matter what they say these men are out for
blood. I count you as a friend, and I hope you'll reconsider
riding with them."

"They're my friends, too, Falcon, and I swore an oath
of allegiance."

Falcon sighed. "Then so be it, Kid." He stuck out his
hand. "Good luck."

Without a backward glance, the Kid stormed out. Falcon
sat, helplessly watching a good man throw his life away . . .
with no chance at all of coming out of this fracas alive.

BOOK YOUR PLACE ON OUR WEBSITE
AND MAKE THE
READING CONNECTION!

We've created a customized website just for our very special readers, where you can get the inside scoop on everything that's going on with Zebra, Pinnacle and Kensington books.

When you come online, you'll have the exciting opportunity to:

- View covers of upcoming books

- Read sample chapters

- Learn about our future publishing schedule (listed by publication month *and author*)

- Find out when your favorite authors will be visiting a city near you

- Search for and order backlist books from our online catalog

- Check out author bios and background information

- Send e-mail to your favorite authors

- Meet the Kensington staff online

- Join us in weekly chats with authors, readers and other guests

- Get writing guidelines

- AND MUCH MORE!

Visit our website at
http://www.pinnaclebooks.com

SONG OF EAGLES

William W. Johnstone

Pinnacle Books
Kensington Publishing Corp.
http://www.williamjohnstone.com

I would rather be remembered by a song than a victory.
Alexander Smith, *Dreamthorp,* 1863

One

Bonito, Arizona, 1877

Henry McCarty, known locally as Kid Antrim, looked over his cards and smiled. Though his stated age was seventeen, the gesture, along with his wispy, brown hair, short stature, and baby soft skin made him look no more than fourteen.

"You gonna fold them worthless cards or bet, Windy?" the Kid asked.

Frank P. "Windy" Cahill narrowed his eyes and glared at the Kid. "I think you're bluffin', runt." He watched carefully to see what effect his words would have on the younger man.

The Kid grinned, showing bucked upper teeth. It was a trait which would become his trademark in later years. Even though he was furious inside at the insult, he hid his killing rage behind a cheerful, smiling façade. Many men were going to die with that smile being the last thing they saw on this earth.

"I can see why you're such a good blacksmith, Windy," the Kid said. He inclined his head at Cahill's more than ample paunch, which hung over his belt. "You're damn near as big as the horses you shoe, and twice as fat."

The Kid leaned forward and pointed his finger at the pile of money in the middle of the table. "Now, you can call me names all night, but that don't matter none a'tall. What matters is, are you gonna call my bet or fold?"

"Call." Cahill snarled and threw a twenty dollar double eagle gold coin onto the stack of money. He grinned through blackened, grimy teeth and spread his cards on the table. "Two pair, aces over queens. Read 'em and weep, Kid."

"That's a mighty good hand, Windy."

As the man laughed and leaned forward to rake in the pot, Kid Antrim added softly, "But not good enough to win. I got three deuces."

Cahill leaned back, scowling as the Kid raked in his winnings. "Deuces are a lot like me, Windy," he said. "They ain't exactly big cards, but they sure do get the job done, 'specially when you got plenty of 'em."

Miles Leslie Wood, proprietor of the local hotel where the Kid usually ate his meals, sat across the table in a chair next to Cahill. He frowned and stubbed his cigar out with an impatient gesture. "Cut the crap, Kid, and deal."

The Kid riffled the cards a few times and began to deal them out. As he got to Wood, he hesitated. "The way you been losing tonight, Miles, I would'a thought you'd want me to deal slower 'stead of faster. That way you might be able to stay in the game a mite longer."

"Damn, but you got a smart mouth on you, Kid," Cahill growled from across the table. "Maybe somebody ought'a shut it for you."

The Kid never looked up from his dealing. His lips curled in a smile that didn't reach his cold, blue eyes. "You are welcome to try any time, Windy. But you got to promise me you won't fall on me, 'cause with as much lard as you're carrying it might be fatal."

With a yell, the blacksmith jumped up from his chair and lunged across the table at the Kid. His weight of two hundred and fifty pounds caused the table to collapse, scattering money and cards and drinks all over the floor.

Kid Antrim scrambled back just in time to avoid being crushed by the table. Mabel Adkins, proprietor of the Adkins Dance Hall where the poker game was being held, came from her usual place at the end of the bar and stood with her hands on her hips. "Kid, you better get the hell out of here 'fore Windy gets to his feet. He's liable to kill ya."

Kid Antrim stooped to pick up his pile of money. "He ain't gonna kill nobody. He's just full of hot air. That's why they call him Windy." He nodded at Adkins. "Night, Mabel. I'll see you next Saturday, and maybe escort you around the dance floor a time or two."

Adkins smiled, for the Kid had a way with the ladies. "Okay, Kid, now you get on outta here while you can still walk."

The Kid sauntered out the door of the dance hall, whistling a tune the other teamsters at Camp Grant had taught him, something about a darling Clementine.

He had just reached the middle of the dirt road that served as main street in Bonito when he heard Miles Wood call out from behind him, "Kid, look out!"

The Kid turned just in time to be barreled over by two hundred and fifty pounds of furious blacksmith. Cahill grabbed him in a bear hug and threw him to the ground, shouting incoherently with spittle spraying from his lips, "Gonna kill you . . . you little pimp!"

The Kid reared his head back and head-butted Cahill in the nose, breaking it and spreading it all over the huge man's face. "I ain't no pimp, you sonofabitch!"

They rolled a couple of times in the dusty street until coming to rest with Cahill on top. With blood streaming from his ruined nose, he wrapped his large hands around the Kid's throat and began to squeeze.

Within seconds the Kid's vision began to blur, and dark spots swam before his eyes. He knew the man was going to kill him. There was no doubt in his mind. He flailed futilely at Cahill's face, but his strength was failing and his blows had no effect.

As he thrust at the big man's gut, trying to push him away, his right hand fell on Cahill's Colt pistol. The Kid jerked the gun free and stuck it in Cahill's belly and pulled the trigger, blowing Cahill backward amid the roar of the pistol—to land sprawled, spread-eagled on his back, grasping his stomach and screaming in agony.

The Kid rolled to his knees, gasping for air, and vomited in the dirt next to where the blood-spattered pistol lay. As he heaved, he vowed never again to be caught without a pistol on his hip.

After he emptied his stomach, the Kid stood and walked toward the Aravaipa Creek that marked the boundary between Camp Grant and Bonito, to wash the blood off his hands and face.

When Cahill died the next morning, Miles Wood, local justice of the peace as well as hotel proprietor, conducted a coroner's inquest into the killing. A. M. "Gus" Gildea, a civilian scout at Camp Grant and a friend of Kid Antrim, was called as a witness to the fight.

The rail-thin cowboy turned his weather-beaten face to the jury of townspeople from the witness box. He leaned over the railing and looked for a spittoon, and when he found there was none shifted his chaw from one cheek to the other and swallowed it with a grimace. "There ain't no doubt in the matter. The boy plumb didn't have no choice. He had to use his equalizer," he said to the jury.

Wood asked from behind the judge's desk, "But isn't it true, Mr. Gildea, that the Kid didn't warn Mr. Cahill, that he just pulled the pistol and shot him without giving him a chance?"

Gildea, who had been one of the participants in the poker game, narrowed his eyes at Wood. "That's not the way it happened and you know it, Miles. You was just sore cause the Kid took all your money . . ."

Wood banged his gavel, shouting, "Objection. Not relevant testimony! Did the Kid warn Cahill before shootin' him down in cold blood or not? Just answer the question."

"No, you damn fool. The Kid couldn't say nothin' 'cause Cahill had him by the throat . . ."

The gavel banged again, cutting Gildea's testimony off mid-sentence. Wood turned to the jury. "Gentlemen of the jury, you have heard how a routine bar fight ended with the death of an honest citizen of our town. How do you find?"

The six men sitting in two rows at the side of the room leaned their heads together for a moment, speaking in low tones. Finally they all nodded and one stood up. "We find that the killing was criminal and unjustifiable, and that Henry Antrim, alias the Kid, is guilty thereof."

The next morning, while the Kid was eating breakfast in his hotel, Wood walked up to his table and arrested him.

"I've got to take you in, Kid. The jury found you guilty of murder."

The Kid looked up from his eggs and bacon, took a final drink of his coffee, and said, "I never figured you for such a sore loser, Miles."

The Kid offered no resistance as Wood escorted him across Aravaipa Creek to the post guardhouse at Camp Grant, where he was incarcerated.

Two nights later, during a dance and dinner at Captain G. C. Smith's quarters, two or three shots were heard. Captain Smith ordered the officer of the day, Lieutenant Benny Cheever of the Sixth Cavalry, out to investigate.

He returned five minutes later and snapped off a smart salute. "Sir, the shots you heard were fired by the sentry at the guardhouse at a man who escaped."

"Who was it, soldier?" the irritated captain asked, embarrassed at this news being uttered in front of his guests.

"I believe it was Kid Antrim, sir."

"How could this happen, Cheever?"

The lieutenant called the captain aside, "The sentry thinks one of the soldiers on the base aided the prisoner, sir."

The captain nodded, "Well, look into it, but keep it quiet. I don't want anyone else to know he had help, especially from a soldier under my command, understand?"

"Yes, sir."

Kid Antrim had seized the fastest horse he could find—"Cashaw," a racing pony belonging to John Murphey. About a week later, the pony was returned by a traveler who told Murphey that the Kid asked him to return the animal to its rightful owner.

The Kid made his way from Silver City to Mesilla, New Mexico, then joined up with a young man his age named Tom O'Keefe. They rode together through the Organ Mountains and across the Tularosa Basin, then tried to cross the northern portion of the Guadalupe Mountains.

On the second day of their trip through the mountains, they were climbing an old Indian trail when O'Keefe suddenly reined in. "Hey, Kid, look down there." He pointed down the side of the mountain to a glimmering pool of water at the bottom of the canyon below them. "I don't know 'bout you, Kid, but I'm might near outta water."

The Kid shook his canteen, finding it bone dry. "Yeah, me, too. I'll climb down there and get us filled up whilst you stay here with the horses."

He took both canteens and climbed down the rocky, steep, cliff wall to the water. He was about to return when sounds of gunfire reached him. "Goddamn," he muttered, remembering stories he and O'Keefe had been told about travelers in this region being attacked by roving bands of renegade Apaches.

Taking cover behind rocks and brush, the Kid made his way back up to where he had left O'Keefe and the horses. There was no sign of O'Keefe, horses, bedrolls, or rations.

Keeping himself hidden until nightfall, the Kid resumed his journey on foot. It took him two days of hard walking through the mountains and down Rocky Arroyo until he came upon a barren ranch, with a wind and sun-bleached cabin and barn. A hand-lettered sign at the front gate read Jones.

Heiskell Jones, his wife, Barbara, and their ten children lived there. Barbara, known locally as Ma'am Jones, heard the Kid outside and found him staggering up to their cabin. She grabbed him just before he fell, and half carried him into the kitchen. She removed his boots, finding he wore no socks and his feet were raw and swollen.

"How long's it been since you ate, boy?"

"It's been more'n three days, ma'am."

Mrs. Jones heated some milk on the wood-burning stove and took it over to where the boy sat hunched under a blanket with his feet in hot water.

"I don't like milk," he said.

"Drink it. Later you may have some food, but not now. It's bad for you to eat before you've rested a little."

There was no reply.

"Do you want me to hold your nose and pour it down you?"

He took the cup. When he tasted the milk he made a wry face, but he drank.

"Now I'm going to put you to bed. You're worn out, and need sleep."

"I can sleep right here."

"You can sleep better in a bed."

The next day the Kid introduced himself as Billy Bonney. This was the first time he'd used this alias. He wanted to protect the Jones family from any reprisals for harboring a known fugitive. He told the Jones's eldest son, John, about his experiences with the Apaches while he and John were shooting target practice out behind the barn.

"How well do you shoot with your left hand?" John asked.

"Not so good," the Kid replied. "Sometimes I hit, but if I was in a jackpot I'd use my right."

When the Kid was sufficiently recovered John lent him a horse, and he was again on his way, headed toward John Chisum's South Spring River Ranch in Lincoln County, New Mexico, where he'd been told he might hire on as a range cowboy. At the time no one in the Jones family could have guessed Billy Bonney would become a central figure in the Territory's deadliest range war.

Two

Falcon MacCallister reined his horse Diablo to a halt a few hundred yards from the Chisum South Spring River Ranch house. It was an impressive edifice, the size of a small fort and made of native stone from the area, with very little wood showing.

Probably necessary, Falcon thought, *considering Chisum pried this land right from the hands of the Mescalero Apaches.* He pulled a cheroot from his coat pocket, struck a lucifer on his pant leg, and lighted it. Crossing his leg over his saddle horn, he mentally reviewed what his father had told him about Chisum. . . .

In 1868, John S. Chisum established himself at Bosque Grande, in the eastern portion of Lincoln County, New Mexico. As many Texans did at the time, he brought a herd of cattle with him from Texas. Never one short on courage, Chisum claimed two hundred miles up and down the Pecos Valley, calling it his "by right of discovery." The land had not yet been opened to settlers, and so Chisum "squatted" on it and made good his claim by his own means—usually by hiring men expert in the use of Colonel Colt's weapons.

La Placita del Rio Bonito was soon Americanized, called Lincoln, and was designated the county seat. Chisum himself—however many armed men might ride for him—never carried a gun, often remarking that "a six-shooter will get you into more trouble than it will get you out of." Before long he was considered the most powerful man in Lincoln County.

Before his death last year, Jamie Ian MacCallister had told Falcon if he was ever in this area to look Chisum up. They were old friends who "had rode the river together" when they were younger.

Falcon pitched his cigar in the dirt and spurred Diablo toward the ranch house. As he rode he kept his hands out in plain sight, for he knew he made a dangerous first impression on strangers and didn't want Chisum's men to take alarm. He stood well over six feet in height, had wheat-colored blond hair and cold, pale-blue eyes. His shoulders were so wide and his muscles so developed that his typical attire—black suits with crisp, ironed, white shirts and black silk kerchiefs around his neck—all had to be specially tailored to fit his massive frame. On his hips, tied down low, were a matched pair of Colt Peacemaker .45s, and behind his belt buckle was a two-shot derringer. A .44-40 caliber Winchester rifle was slung in a saddle boot within easy reach.

As he approached the ranch house, Falcon noted several cowboys in the area. The men all seemed to be heavily armed, with most carrying rifles or shotguns in addition to pistols on their hips. They wore their pistols tied down low, more like gunslicks instead of punchers. *Chisum looks like he's ready to go to war,* Falcon thought. *Kinda strange, since most of the Indians around this part of the country have been run off years ago.*

A tall, lanky man with mean-looking eyes stepped off the porch, shucked a shell into the chamber of his Henry, and called to Falcon, "Howdy, mister. What can I do for you?"

Falcon kept his hands on his reins and pulled his mount to a stop. "I'm Falcon MacCallister. I'm here to see John Chisum."

"Yeah? And what might your business be with Mr. Chisum?"

Falcon removed his Stetson and sleeved sweat off his forehead. "No business. I just came to give him my regards. He and my father used to ride together."

"Your father's name?"

"Jamie Ian MacCallister."

"Wait right here and I'll see if Mr. Chisum wants to talk to you."

"Is it all right if I water my horse? We been on the trail for some time, and he's a mite thirsty."

The man nodded and pointed to a horse trough next to the porch before disappearing into the house.

Falcon dismounted and walked his horse to the trough. While Diablo drank his fill, Falcon dipped his hands in the water and washed some of the trail dust off his face and hair.

The door opened and one of the broadest men he had ever seen stepped out on the porch. He smiled and held out his hand. "Howdy, Falcon. I'm John Chisum, and I'm pleased to meet you."

Chisum was a big man, standing over six feet tall. His chest and shoulders were wide as an axe-handle, and there was no fat on his body. He sported a large, handlebar moustache and muttonchop sideburns, and his face was dark and wrinkled as saddle leather, showing he had spent his entire life in the sun. He seemed genuinely glad to see Falcon.

"Come on in and light and sit, and let's talk."

He led Falcon into the house, which was wide and open with lots of windows to let in the sun. Falcon noticed all the windows had board shutters with gunports cut out of them, many showing evidence of bulletholes, as if they had been used for defense more than once.

Chisum's study walls were covered with dark wood paneling, and there were several filled bookcases and three gun cases with rifles, shotguns, and pistols arranged within.

Chisum waved Falcon to an overstuffed chair in front of a massive desk cut out of what appeared to be a solid chunk of oak. He stepped to a bar behind the desk and asked, "Bourbon okay?"

"That'll do just fine," Falcon answered. Falcon noticed the brand on the bottle of whiskey, which was a rather cheap one. It reminded him of another fact about Chisum his father had told—that the man, though as brave as they come and a good friend, was tight with a dollar, never paying for anything that he wasn't forced to. Falcon smiled to himself, remembering his father had also never been one to spend money unless absolutely necessary.

Chisum handed him a glass and held his up. "Here's to Jamie Ian MacCallister, the best man I ever rode with."

Falcon nodded and drank to his father.

Chisum sat behind his desk and leaned forward on his elbows. "How is Jamie nowadays? I haven't heard from that old beaver in . . ."—he scratched his chin and gazed at the ceiling as he thought—"why, it must be ten years or more."

"My father is dead, Mr. Chisum."

Chisum's face fell. "Oh, I'm sorry to hear that, Falcon. Please call me John. What happened?"

Falcon's face darkened. "He was backshot. Ambushed by someone who thought he was me."

Chisum frowned. Backshooting was about the lowest crime a man could commit in the West. "Why were the men after you, Falcon? You on the run from the law?"

"No, but it's a long story."

Chisum nodded. He poured them another glass of whiskey and sat back in his chair. He took a pair of long, black cigars from a humidor on his desk and handed one to Falcon. After he lighted them both, he took a sip of his bourbon and leaned back and put his boots on the desk. "I got time if you do, son."

Falcon took a deep drag of the cigar, blowing a cloud of pungent, blue smoke toward the ceiling. "It was just after my wife had been killed by Indians. Jamie found her body and buried her next to a river. I went to find it. . . ."

Falcon found Marie's grave and sat by it for a time, trying

to make some sense out of her death. He could not. Falcon had brought along a heavy hammer and a chisel, and after looking around for a proper stone, found one, muscled it into place, and began the laborious job of slowly chiseling her name into it.

He was intent upon his work, but didn't fail to occasionally check his surroundings, for this was still the Wild West despite all the moves toward civilization. And Falcon had been well-schooled by his father.

Falcon became aware that he was being watched. And not by Indians. He allowed himself a very small smile. He had never seen an Indian this clumsy. He continued his work on the stone, but only after furtively slipping the leather loops from the hammers of his pistols and checking to make sure his rifle was close at hand.

After concluding that his watchers were at least six strong, probably more, Falcon made several trips to his packs, ostensibly for a drink of water, but really to stuff his pockets full of cartridges for his rifle and pistols. Then he returned to work on the stone.

He worked and waited and wondered.

With the waters of the Blue River softly flowing not far away, Falcon heard the men when they made their rush toward him. He turned, dropped to one knee, and drew his right-hand pistol, all in one fluid motion.

"We want him alive!" Asa Pike shouted just as one of his men pointed a gun at Falcon.

Falcon shot the man in the chest and then threw himself to one side as the men rushed him. He drew his other pistol and opened fire; at nearly point-blank range, his fire was devastating.

The Jones brothers, Lloyd and Bob, were among the first to go down, both mortally wounded. Lloyd stumbled backward and lost his balance, finally tumbling over the side of the bank and falling into the river. Bob sat down hard, both hands holding his bullet-perforated belly.

Falcon had no time to observe what Bob did next; he was

in a fight for his life without having any idea why the men had attacked him.

The fight was over in less than a minute. The cool mountain air was acrid with lingering gunsmoke, mixed with the faint sounds of a couple of horses galloping away, the moaning of the wounded, and the silence of the dead.

Falcon quickly reloaded and, with a pistol in each hand, began warily walking among the wounded, kicking pistols away from the men and out of reach.

Falcon stood over one dying man and asked, "Why?"

" 'Cause you're a goddamn MacCallister, that's why," the man told him. Then he closed his eyes and died.

Falcon buried the dead far away from his wife's grave. He did not mark the shallow, mass grave. One attacker who had survived the fight had told Falcon who had led the ambush. Falcon had seen to the man's wounds as best he could with what he had, put him on a horse, and told him to go home, adding, "If I ever see you again, I'll shoot you on the spot."

"You'll not see me no more," the man said. "But Asa will be back. Bet on it."

"The man must be insane," Falcon said, then slapped the horse on the rump and sent him galloping.

Falcon spent the rest of the day finishing the marker for Marie's resting place. Then he tidied up the area and stood for a time by Marie's grave. Falcon put his hat on his head, walked to his horse, and rode away without looking back. He did not know where he was going. He was just riding. He headed west, toward Utah. Falcon wanted only to ride away his grief, to just be alone for a time and let the wind and the rain help cure the ache deep inside him.

He had no idea at the time that he was about to become one of the most wanted men west of the Mississippi River.

After getting himself a room in the small hotel in a tiny town in Utah, Falcon went down for a drink and something to eat. Much of the grief he'd been carrying had left him, but he was still not wanting company. He took his bottle and glass and went to a far corner of the saloon.

Two men walked in, one wearing a sheriff's badge, the other with a federal marshal's badge pinned to his suit coat. Falcon was not interested in them and paid them scant attention as they walked to the bar (strutted was more like it, he thought) and ordered whiskey. Falcon returned to his own whiskey and his sorrowful thoughts and ignored all others in the saloon.

But Falcon was his father's son—he could smell trouble, and the lawmen had it written all over them. To begin with, they were both small men, about five-six or -seven, and both walked as if they had something to prove—the bigger the man to prove it with, or on, the better.

Falcon was wondering where his dad was and how he was doing when he heard boots approaching his table. He looked up into the faces of the two star packers. Very unfriendly faces.

"Stand up," the federal marshal said.

"I beg your pardon?" Falcon questioned.

"Get on your feet, Lucas," the sheriff said.

"My name is not Lucas. It's Falcon MacCallister. And I am very comfortable sitting, thank you."

"I said get up, you thievin' son of a bitch!" the federal marshal demanded. "Lucas or MacCallister, it don't make no difference. You're still a horse thief and a rustler."

Falcon took a better look at the men. Definitely related. Probably brothers.

The sheriff pulled a leather-wrapped cosh from his back pocket and held it up threateningly. "Get up, you scum. Or I'll pound your head where you sit."

"That would be a real bad mistake, Sheriff," Falcon warned.

"You makin' threats agin my brother, boy?" the federal marshal asked.

Falcon was getting mad. He could feel his temper being unleashed. "My name is MacCallister. I'm from Valley, Colorado. I have done nothing wrong. Why don't you gentlemen take a seat and we'll talk about this?"

"Get up, you bastard!" the sheriff hollered. Then he took a swing at Falcon with the blackjack.

Falcon ducked the swing and grabbed the edge of the table, overturning it and knocking the two star packers sprawling on the floor. The federal marshal grabbed for his pistol, and Falcon kicked it out of his hand and then put his boot against the side of the man's jaw. The federal marshal kissed the floor, out cold.

The sheriff was struggling to get to his feet. Falcon helped him, sort of.

He reached down, grabbed a handful of the sheriff's shirt, and hit him on the side of the jaw with a powerful right fist. The sheriff's eyes rolled back into his head, and Falcon released the man. The sheriff sighed and joined his brother on the floor.

"Idiots," Falcon said, straightening his coat.

"Run, mister," a customer said. "Run for your life."

Falcon looked at the local. "Run? Why?"

" 'Cause when them two wakes up, they'll kill you for sure. Them's the Noonan brothers. They're both crazy. And they're Nance Noonan's brothers, both of 'em."

"Who the hell is Nance Noonan?"

"The he-coon of this part of the territory, son," an older man said. "And you're in his town. Nance Noonan owns everything and damn near everybody in this part of the territory. He owns the N Bar N ranch."

"He's right, mister," another local said. "Get gone from here as quick as you can. Pride ain't worth dyin' for. Not in my book, anyways."

"You do have a point," Falcon said.

"I'll saddle your horse whilst you pack your possibles," the local said. "Then ride, boy, ride. The name MacCallister don't mean nothin' to men like Nance Noonan . . ."

The federal marshal stirred and reached for his gun. "I'll kill you, you son of a bitch!"

Falcon palmed his gun and shot him, the .45 slug punching a hole in the center of the man's forehead.

"Git the hell up to your room and pack, son," Falcon was urged. "I'll throw a saddle on your horse."

Falcon was coming down the stairs with his bedroll, saddlebags, and rifle when Sheriff Butch Noonan rose to his boots and grabbed for his guns. Falcon lifted the Winchester .44-40, thumbed back the hammer, and drilled the man in the center of his chest.

"Oh, shit!" a citizen breathed.

"Ride, MacCallister, ride!" a man shouted. "Ride like Ole' Nick is after you, 'cause he damn shore is!"

Later, Falcon sat by a hat-size fire, frying his bacon, the coffee already made and the pot set off to one side on the circle of rocks. He knew he was in serious trouble, for even though the two brothers he'd killed back down the trail a ways had been no more than worthless bullies, they were still star packers. And one of them a federal lawman.

He'd have to stay on the run until this thing got straightened out; already he missed his kids something fierce.

He'd have to get word to his brothers in Valley, and they'd hire detectives to come in and ferret out the straight story of what had happened. Until then?

Falcon's laugh was void of humor. "I'm an outlaw on the run," he said. "Probably the richest outlaw in history, but on the run, nevertheless."

Falcon summed up his mood: "Crap!"

A hundred miles away, Jamie Ian MacCallister was buying supplies at a trading post on the North Platte when he heard the news about Falcon. To the eyes and mind of the new post owner, Jamie was just another rugged-looking old relic of a mountain man, not worth a dup of spit for anything.

Jamie bought his supplies, then had a drink and listened to the men talk. Falcon had killed two lawmen over in Utah Territory, a county sheriff and a deputy federal marshal.

But why had he killed them?

The men at the bar didn't know that, only that he had.

Falcon had left the little town riding a horse the color of dark sand—a big horse, for, like his father, Falcon was a big man. His packhorse was a gray.

Riding a horse the same color and approximately the same size as mine, and trailing a gray packhorse, just like mine, Jamie mused.

Jamie quietly left the trading post without notice and once more headed south. He stopped at Fort Fred Steele and told the commanding officer there what had really taken place at the Little Big Horn. The CO and his other officers listened intently as Jamie laid it all out, from beginning to end.

It was there that Jamie arranged for a wire to be sent to his kids in Valley. He knew that by now they would be worried sick.

Jamie pushed on toward home. He crossed the Divide, felt pretty sure he was in Colorado, and felt better. He was not that far from home. Well, maybe a week's riding.

About a day out of Valley, Jamie was humming an old war song that Kate used to sing when two hammer blows struck him in the back, almost knocking him out of the saddle. As he struggled to stay on the horse, he thought he heard a shout of triumph. Sundown took off like a bolt of lightning, the packhorse trailing.

When he got the big horse calmed down, Jamie managed to stuff handkerchiefs in the holes in his back. He knew he dared not leave the saddle. He'd never be able to get back on the deck if he did. Through waves of hot pain, he cut lengths of rope and tied himself in the saddle.

"All right, Sundown," Jamie gasped. "You know the way home. Take me to Kate."

Two of Jamie's great-grandsons spotted the slow-walking horse and the big man slumped unconscious in the saddle. When they realized who it was, they ran right down the middle of the main street, yelling and hollering at the top of their lungs. Matthew and Dr. Tom Prentiss came running up to Jamie and cut the ropes holding him on his horse.

The doctor took one look at the hideous wounds in his back and shook his head.

"Gather your kin, Matthew," he said.

Later, Matthew stepped into the doctor's outer office, a telegram in his hand. His brothers and sisters turned to him. Matthew's eyes were bright with anger. He held up the wire. "This is from a sheriff friend of mine over near the Utah line. Seems as though a posse of men from some ranch called the N Bar N, headed by several newly appointed deputy federal marshals, think they got lead into Falcon. Happened yesterday or the day before some miles north of here. What they done was they mistook Pa for Falcon."

Joleen said, "There'll be blood on the moon when Falcon hears of this."

"For a fact," Matthew said. "My friend is gonna send me more information as he gets it. How's Pa?"

"Dying," Ian said, then put his big hands on his face and wept openly.

Jamie Ian MacCallister, the man called Bear Killer, Man Who Is Not Afraid, Man Who Plays With Wolves, died on August the first, 1876, at eight o'clock in the morning. He was buried that afternoon, on a ridge overlooking the town of Valley. Overhead, circling and soaring high above the ridge, several eagles screamed.

The next day, James William Haywood, Jamie's grandson, opened Jamie's will in front of the family. He had read it the night before and was shocked right down to his boots at the enormity of Jamie's wealth.

"Your father," he told the gathering, "was more than likely the richest man in all of Colorado. He was worth millions of dollars. He drew up a map of all the places where he cached bags and boxes of gold and silver. During the wandering of your great-grandfather, the man called Silver Wolfe, he discovered a cave of Spanish treasure. He gave that to Jamie, and now Jamie is giving it to all of you. You children of Jamie and Kate MacCallister just might be the richest family in all of North America."

After the reading of the will, Jamie Ian met with Matthew in Falcon's Wild Rose Saloon and said, "Now, brother, you want to tell the truth about Falcon?"

"He's in Utah. He's going after Nance Noonan and those posse members. He's going to destroy the N Bar N and then burn down the town. Right down to the last brick and board."

"There were federal marshals in that posse."

"You think Falcon gives a damn about that?"

Jamie Ian sighed and shook his head. "I reckon not."

"Joleen summed it up the other day. There's gonna be blood on the moon before this is over."

The brothers walked out to stand on the boardwalk, looking up at the ridge where their mother and father and grandfather lay in peace.

"You think Pa would have done what Falcon is about to do?" Jamie Ian asked.

"It's exactly what Pa would have done."

Three

John Chisum took a final drag on his cigar and stared at Falcon through the cloud of smoke. After a moment he leaned forward and stubbed the butt out in a silver dish.

"That's a hell of a story, Falcon. I just can't believe old Jamie was backshot by those murdering cowards like that."

Falcon nodded. "Believe it, John." He drained his whiskey and said in a husky voice, "But they soon found out that those who called the dance had to pay the band."

"That's the way of it, all right." He stood and filled Falcon's empty glass and offered him another cigar.

"Thanks," Falcon said as he took the cigar and lighted it. "By the way, John, my father told me you had settled up here on the Pecos, but he never told me any details. How the hell did you get up here from Texas?"

"That's a hell of a story in its own right." Chisum filled his glass and sat back with a cigar in one hand and a glass in the other as he talked. "Back in . . . oh, sixty-seven I think it was, my brother Pitser and I brought my first herd of Jingle Bob cattle across the plains and through the buffalo hunting territory of the Comanches." He pointed the cigar at Falcon, a tight grin on his face. "They were some plenty hostile Injuns, let me tell you, an' could ride horses like no one I've ever seen."

Falcon nodded. "Yeah, I've had some dealings with them

myself, and my father always said they were the best warriors ever born."

Chisum's expression grew serious. "We lost some good boys on that first trip. We had to send scout riders ahead of the trail blazers to protect the herd from those devils, who were pretty numerous in the lower Pecos Valley at the time. More often than not the scouts didn't come back, or came back so shot up they couldn't work no more."

"Scouting is tough work, all right, especially in Indian territory. Takes a special breed of man to do it and survive."

Chisum wet his throat with bourbon and continued. "Well, the Jingle Bobs finally got here safely and we put them to grazing on the lands around our headquarters, which we set up at Bosque Grande, 'bout thirty-five miles northeast of Roswell, down on the Pecos itself. After a while, I left Pitser in charge and made some more trips back to Texas for more cattle."

"How many head you running now?"

"Oh, about a hundred thousand or so. Took us almost ten years to build up to that, 'cause of the Comanch. They finally died out or left after the buffalo were all killed, sometime around seventy-seven or seventy-eight."

"You ever marry, John?"

Chisum smiled. "Nope. Never felt no need, what with all my brothers and their wives and children around all the time. But enough about me. Tell me about how you went after Nance Noonan and his bunch."

Falcon shrugged. "That's a story for a different time and place. When I set out to right the wrong done to my father, I sent my kids back east so they could get proper schooling, so I'm kind'a at loose ends right now."

Chisum's face showed friendly concern. "Anything I can do? Do you need a job . . . money?"

"No, like I said, Jamie left all of his children with more money than we can ever spend." Falcon hesitated. "I was thinking more along the lines of investing in a saloon or gambling house. You know of any that might suit my needs?"

Chisum thought for a moment, then snapped his fingers. "You know, old Beaver Smith owns a saloon on the Pecos River, over at Fort Sumner. He might be willing to sell, or take in a partner."

"I'm not much one for partnering, but I'll sure go take a look at the place and see what I think."

Falcon stood and held out his hand. "Thanks for the whiskey, and the talk, John. I can see why my dad thought so much of you."

"Any time, Falcon. And I'm holding you to that promise to tell me what happened when you faced Nance Noonan and his gang. That's a story I can't wait to hear."

Chisum walked Falcon out to the front porch. "I'll tell the boys you're my friend and you're always welcome here at the South Spring. That way they won't hassle you when you come to visit."

As the two shook hands Chisum looked over MacCallister's shoulder and said, "Well I'll be jiggered. Looks like more company comin'."

Falcon turned to see a lone rider walking his horse up the dirt road toward the ranch house. The rider was a short man wearing a dirty black coat over a soiled and rumpled shirt that Falcon thought must have once been white. As the rider drew closer, Falcon turned to Chisum. "Hell, John. It looks like a kid on that horse. You taken to hiring boys now?"

Chisum chuckled. "Things aren't that bad yet, Falcon."

The rider reined his horse to a halt and sat, looking at the hard cases standing in front of the house with their rifles trained on him. He grinned and removed his hat, running his hands through light brown hair. His eyes crinkled as he smiled at Falcon and Chisum on the porch.

"One of you Mr. John Chisum?"

Chisum nodded and stepped forward. "Yeah, that's me. What can I do for you, young man?"

"My name's Billy Bonney. I heard you was lookin' to hire some men . . . men who know their way around a six-shooter."

Falcon noticed that though the lips smiled and the eyes narrowed in apparent good humor, there was something deep in the eyes that belied the grin. They were cold as well water on a frosty morning. As they flicked back and forth, sizing up the men with guns in the area, it was obvious they missed nothing. Falcon knew instinctively this was no mere boy, but a deadly man to be reckoned with.

Chisum gave a snort. "And you think that would be you, is that it?"

"Yes, sir." With a minimum of motion, Bonney slowly pulled his coat back and tucked it in his belt behind his back, letting his hands hang loose by his side. "If you have any doubts in the matter, I'd be right happy to show you with any of these galoots standing here."

Mack Monroe, one of the toughest looking hombres in the group of men, stepped forward. He was about five-foot eleven inches tall and must have weighed almost two hundred and fifty pounds. He stood in front of Bonney with his hands on his hips.

"I'm Mack Monroe, foreman of this here spread, an' you can show me how good you are, if you've got the guts." Without taking his eyes off the newcomer, he added, "You want I should throw this pup in the water trough, Boss?"

Bonney's eyes slowly looked Monroe up and down, then cut to Chisum. "If I kill this man, can I have his job, Mr. Chisum?" His face showed no fear whatsoever. In fact, he still had the boyish grin on his lips, as if taking a life was no more than a game to him.

Chisum rubbed his moustache, his own lips curled up in mirth at the *cojones* this boy was showing. He'd seen few men have the courage to face Monroe, with fists or with guns. "No, I'll have none of that, Mr. Bonney. If you kill him, I'll still be a man short even if I hire you."

Chisum walked to the porch rail and took a tin coffee mug and pitched it to one of the other hands. "Bob, on the count of three, throw this mug in the air. Monroe, you and Bonney can both draw down on it and we'll see if this kid has what it takes."

Falcon stood on the porch watching Bonney out of the corner of his eye and saw the young man's lips curl up in a sly smile at the mention of a shooting contest. "How good is Monroe, John?"

"He's the best I've got with a short gun, Falcon. Why?"

Falcon inclined his head at Bonney and said, where all could hear him. "I've got a hundred dollars says the kid takes him. Are you on?"

Chisum frowned suspiciously. "Do you know this man, Falcon?"

"Never seen him before in my life."

"Then why on earth would you risk a hundred dollars on him?"

"First of all, I'm a gambler, for a living and for fun. Second, look in his eyes and tell me what you see."

Chisum turned to stare for a moment at Bonney, and Falcon noticed the big man's smile falter. He was seeing the same thing Falcon was.

"Damned if you're not right, Falcon. No bet."

Monroe scowled and glanced at Falcon. "I'll take your bet, mister."

"You got a hundred dollars, cowboy?" Falcon asked.

Monroe pursed his lips, as if thinking. "I ain't gonna need it, 'cause I'm gonna beat this pup, but I've got a hand-tooled Mexican saddle that ought'a go for about that."

Falcon nodded. "Then you're on."

The cowboys all gathered around the two men after Bonney stepped down from his horse. There was almost noth-

ing punchers liked more than a contest, be it one of fisticuffs, riding broncs, or shooting at targets.

Several of the men were making small side bets, looking
nervously at Monroe as if they didn't want to get caught
betting against their foreman.

Finally all was ready, and Chisum counted to three. Bob
threw the cup in the air, and both Bonney and Monroe
grabbed iron.

Bonney's hand flashed upward with his Colt and fired
almost without aiming, before Monroe had even cleared
leather. The blast of the pistol was followed instantaneously
by the clang of a bullet blasting a hole in the cup, sending
it caroming off on a tangent.

When it reached its apex and began to fall, there was
another shot and another clang, making the cup dance in
the air once again.

"Goddamn," one of the punchers muttered, "he hit it
again whilst it was still in the air."

Monroe blushed a deep red, standing there with his pistol still half in his holster. He stared at Bonney, eyes hard
and face set.

Bonney had enough sense not to gloat. He holstered his
gun and turned, holding out his hand to Monroe. "Don't
take it to heart, Mr. Monroe. You and I both know shootin'
at somethin' that don't shoot back is easy. Things might'a
been different had we been facing another gunslick."

Monroe, mollified by Bonney's face-saving gesture,
grinned and took his hand. "You're all right, Bonney. And
one of the best shootists I've ever seen. I'd be right proud
to have you stand with me if it ever came to gunplay."

Falcon noticed how Bonney beat Chisum's best man and
then managed to cause the hostile crowd to turn their support to him, a total stranger. *Yep,* he thought, *there's more to
this boy than meets the eye. He's deep as well water, and damn
near as cold.*

Monroe stepped over to the porch and looked up at

Falcon. "I'll jest go get my saddle, mister, an' I'll bring it right over."

"I don't need another saddle, Mr. Monroe. But I'm going to be buying a gambling establishment in the near future. I'll call our bet even if you bring some of your friends in for the grand opening."

Monroe held a ham-sized hand up over the porch railing and shook with Falcon. "It's a deal. You just let me know when and where."

Chisum motioned Bonney to join him and Falcon on the porch. When he got there, Chisum said, "Mr. Bonney, I really don't need any more hands, but I've got a good friend who does, especially ones as good with a pistol as you are."

"Who might that be, Mr. Chisum?"

"His name's John Tunstall. He's not much older than you, 'bout twenty-four I suspect, but he and I are going into business together, and I know he'll need some extra men."

"How'll I find him?"

"You head on into Lincoln and go to the building marked Tunstall's General Store. I reckon he'll be there 'bout now. Tell him I sent you."

Bonney shook hands with Chisum. "Thanks, Mr. Chisum. I appreciate the help."

"Hold on there, Bonney," Falcon said. "Give me a minute and I'll ride into Lincoln with you . . . if you want some company, that is."

"Sure. Always nice to have somebody to talk to on the trail."

Four

As they rode toward Lincoln, Falcon and Bonney talked.

"You're a pretty fair hand with that short gun, Billy. Where'd you learn to shoot like that?"

"You can call me Kid, Falcon. Everybody else does. I learned to shoot 'cause I had to. I been on my own since I was fourteen or so. Hell, I worked sheep and cattle in Arizona, and even was a teamster for a while over at Camp Grant."

He gave a small smile. "You don't long survive doin' that kind of work less'n you can shoot, fast and straight."

Falcon nodded. He knew how hard life was on the frontier, and how it made boys grow to men in a very short time.

Before Falcon could answer the Kid his horse Diablo laid his ears back and nickered, shaking his head from side to side.

Falcon stiffened. Something was wrong for Diablo to act skittish like this. He casually reached down and slipped the rawhide hammer thongs off his Colts.

Bonney saw what he was doing and asked, "You see somethin'?"

"I think we may have some trouble up ahead, where the trail turns around that clump of mesquite trees. My horse is acting up, and that usually means company's coming."

Kid hooked his coat in his belt and slipped his hammer

thongs off. "Well, if they's thieves, they's gonna be mighty disappointed. I ain't got two coins to rub together. I was hoping for a grubstake from Chisum so's I could eat tonight."

As the pair approached the copse of trees, four riders walked their horses out of hiding and blocked the trail.

The leader of the group, a tall, skinny man with chin whiskers and a scar on his left cheek that drew his lips up in a perpetual scowl, held a short, double-barreled shotgun pointed at the sky, with its stock on his thigh. "You gents work for Chisum?"

Falcon reined Diablo to a halt ten yards from the group. "And what business is it of yours who we work for?"

"We're deputy sheriffs, working for the sheriff of Lincoln County, William Brady."

"That don't answer the man's question," the Kid said, his lips curled up in a grin that didn't reach his eyes.

"We been having some reports that other people's stock has been turning up in Chisum's herd. You boys know anything 'bout that?"

Falcon gave a slow smile. "I don't reckon Mr. Chisum would much appreciate being called a rustler, but I could be wrong. Why don't you men ride on up to his ranch and ask *him* your questions?

A shorter, fat man sitting to the leader's left said, " 'Cause we're askin' you gents. Now you tell us what you know or we'll be forced to arrest you, and you can spend some time in jail thinking over your answers."

The Kid's face paled at the mention of jail, but his grin didn't change. "I don't think I'd like that, an' I don't think you're man enough to take me anywheres."

"Why you little . . ." the fat man started to say as he went for his gun.

Before he got his pistol halfway out of his holster, the Kid drew and fired. His Colt exploded, belching a cloud of acrid-smelling smoke as it blew a chunk of meat out of the man's right shoulder and spun him around, knocking him off his horse to sprawl facedown in the dirt.

As the leader started to lower his shotgun and the other two riders reached for their pistols, they found themselves staring down the barrel of both of Falcon's Colts, hammers back. "Easy, boys. Just put those weapons back where they came from and raise your hands."

The men's eyes grew wide at the speed with which Billy and Falcon had drawn, surprised to find themselves at a disadvantage.

"Just keep them fingers off the triggers," the skinny man said. "You don't want to go shootin' no officers of the law."

"We didn't want to shoot nobody, 'til that tub of lard there tried to draw on me," the Kid said. "Now we're gonna ride on into Lincoln. If you galoots want to dance some more, you'll know where to find us."

Falcon and the Kid holstered their weapons and rode on toward town, while the deputies began to patch up the wounded man's arm.

The Kid must have noticed Falcon's frown, for he asked, "What's the matter, Falcon? You mad about something?"

Falcon glanced over at him. "We could have avoided gunplay back there, Kid. You didn't have to goad that man into going for his guns."

The Kid pursed his lips and nodded. "Yeah, I suppose we could have let them take us into town and stick us in that jail until the sheriff decided he wanted to talk to us."

"It wouldn't have gone that far."

"Damn right it wouldn't have. I'll tell you, Falcon, I've been in jail twice, an' I broke out twice. I can't stand bein' locked up, caged like some animal, not able to move around."

He shook his head, lips pressed tight. "No sir, I don't ever intend for that to happen again, and if 'n I have to kill somebody to keep from being locked up, then so be it."

Falcon watched the Kid as he talked, thinking he was right about the Kid's eyes. He was a stone-cold killer, never mind the boyish looks and the ever present grin. He would have to watch himself so he wouldn't get caught up in the Kid's messes.

Falcon and the Kid arrived in Lincoln about an hour later. The town wasn't overly large, consisting of a row of small adobe houses on the west side of the main street, and several larger, more impressive buildings lined up on the eastern side.

The first of the large buildings on their left had a sign over the door saying La Placita, J.J. Dolan & Co.. It was two stories high and had a large window in the front filled with all manner of ranching implements, along with saddles and boots and clothes.

"Damn," the Kid said, his eyes wide, "that's 'bout the biggest general store I ever seen."

Falcon glanced at the place as they passed it, thinking the Kid was right. It was a very large building for a general store. He looked up at the second-story, which had a row of windows across the front, showing either offices or living quarters above the store itself.

The next building they came to was the county courthouse. Since Lincoln was the county seat it, too, was large and impressive. Right next to it was the bank, with a sign over it saying Lincoln County Bank, J.J. Dolan, President.

Falcon looked farther up the street, wondering if there were any saloons. Chisum had said most of the men in the surrounding area went over to Fort Sumner to gamble. The upstanding citizens of Lincoln were not allowing any gaming houses in their city. The town was fairly busy, with dogs and children running up and down the street, wagons being loaded with supplies in front of stores, and horses being shod at the blacksmith's small barn farther down the street.

All in all, the city looked not much different to Falcon than dozens of others he had seen in his travels. It was a

more or less typical cow town which served the main purpose of supplying surrounding ranches with supplies, a
place for punchers to let off steam when the branding and
calving of the herds was done.

As they walked their mounts down the street, the Kid
said, "I'm so hungry my belly must think my throat's been
cut."

Falcon removed his hat and sleeved sweat off his forehead. "Me, too. What say we pull up to the hotel over there
and see if they've got any chow worth eating?"

The Kid cut his eyes toward Falcon. "Naw, I think I'll
just grab me some water over at the town well and see if I
can find out which direction Tunstall's ranch is from here."

"Kid," Falcon said, "it looks like we're both going to be
here for a spell. How about I treat you to some grub, and
you can pay me back from your first month's wages?"

The Kid shook his head. "Never did much like bein'
beholden to anybody. I can make my own way."

As they came up on the hotel, the smell of enchiladas,
beans, and rice cooking tickled their noses. The Kid
smacked his lips as his mouth watered at the delicious
aroma.

"Come on, Kid," Falcon urged. "I'm flush right now,
and like I said, you can pay me back later."

The Kid sighed. "Well, all right, but I'm gonna give you
my marker so's there won't be no mistake about this bein'
a handout or anything."

Falcon laughed. "Have it your way, Kid, but hurry up.
My stomach's beginning to growl at the smell of that food."

They dismounted and strolled into the hotel lobby,
paused a moment to get their bearings, then headed into
the main dining room.

There were six tables spread out across the room, four
of them full of cowboys with heads bent over plates shov-
eling in food and washing it down with pitchers of beer.

Falcon and the Kid took a corner table and sat with their

backs to the walls where they could see the entrance to the room.

A heavyset Mexican woman wearing a bright red apron walked over to their table. "What would you gentlemens like?"

"Bring us a couple of steaks, charred on the outside and bloody in the middle, a plate of enchiladas, some beans and rice, and a handful of tortillas." He looked at the Kid. "That all right with you?"

"Yeah."

"And a pitcher of some beer, if it's cold," Falcon added.

"We no serve it no other way, señor," the woman said, grinning and showing a dark gap where her front teeth were missing.

"You got any lemonade?" Kid asked.

"Si, señor."

After she left the Kid explained, "I don't hardly ever drink alcohol."

A few minutes later a young, black teenager brought a pitcher of beer for Falcon and lemonade for the Kid and two glass mugs to their table. After pouring the lemonade, Billy held his glass up and said, "To a new start in a new town, Falcon."

Falcon smiled and drank. The beer was cold and tasted good after their hours on the trail. He wiped foam off his mouth, and asked, "You don't like beer?"

"It's not that so much, Falcon. It's just that I've never seen it do no man any good. Most of 'em get a snootful of that stuff and think they're right handy with a gun. Usually just gets 'em killed."

"I hope you are able to settle down here, Kid," Falcon said. "It seems a good town to make a new start in."

The Kid's eyes grew serious. "Yeah, I hope so. I'm tired of moving from place to place. I been on the go since I was a pup, never staying in one town long enough to make no real life for myself. It's time I settled down and picked me a spot to take root."

Their waiter returned with a large tray covered with plates of steaming food, which he set down on the table in front of them. "Time to quit jawin' and start eatin'," Billy said.

As they ate, Falcon let his gaze wander around the room, watching the other cowboys at the surrounding tables. At a table in a far corner there were four men eating and drinking. The man doing most of the talking was tall, with wide shoulders, a barrel chest, and an ample paunch. He was wearing a black leather vest with a silver star on his right breast. He had a loud, strident voice which carried across the room, and his eyes were star packer's eyes— never still, flitting back and forth around the room as if looking for trouble.

His eyes met Falcon's, and he seemed to notice Falcon watching him. A slight frown creased his forehead as his mind worked, trying to recollect if he recognized the stranger.

As Falcon watched, the star packer nudged the lanky, gangling man next to him and nodded in Falcon's direction. The skinny man looked over with narrowed eyes, as if he were a bit shortsighted, then shrugged and went back to his beans and enchiladas.

Falcon broke eye contact and finished eating. He wasn't too worried about the lawman. He knew the Wanted Posters on him had been recalled after his brother had talked to the governor, so he was no longer a fugitive from the law. Still, it paid to be cautious in new towns. Some sheriffs took instant dislikes to strangers, especially ones who weren't cowboys working for the local brands.

As Falcon took his last bite of steak and drained his beer glass, the door to the dining room burst open and two men came running into the room. It was the tall, skinny galoot with the chin whiskers and scar on his face, one of the four who had braced Falcon and the Kid on the trail into town.

He and his companion walked straight to the table where the lawman sat and began talking in a rapid voice, too low for Falcon to hear what was being said.

He nudged the Kid with his elbow and inclined his head toward the group across the room. "We may have some trouble, Kid."

The Kid looked up from the last of his beans, wiped his mouth on his sleeve, and reached down to loosen the hammer thongs on his Colt.

Falcon noticed the movement and put his hand on the Kid's arm. "Easy, cowboy. Remember, you're here to make a new start. Getting into a shooting match with the sheriff is not a good way to begin your stay here."

"I'm not plannin' nothin', Falcon. But it don't hurt none to be ready, just in case."

After Scarface stopped talking, the man with the star nodded in their direction. The two new arrivals turned to stare at Falcon and the Kid, then pointed and nodded their heads.

Star packer pursed his lips, then got to his feet, hitching up his gunbelt and getting his hat from a nearby hatrack. He ambled across the room, followed by the six men with him until he stopped to stand in front of their table.

"Howdy, gents," he said, hands hanging near his pistol.

Falcon pushed his chair back, leaned back, and extended his right leg, with his right hand on his thigh near his Colt in case the sheriff gave him no choice.

"Good morning, Sheriff," Falcon said, staring at the man with the badge but watching his friends out of the corner of his eyes.

The Kid said nothing, but Falcon noticed he shifted in his chair so his pistol was within ready reach should the need arise. He, too, watched the group before them, a slight grin curling the corners of his mouth, his eyes as cold as a winter blizzard.

"My name's Sheriff William Brady. My men tell me you drew down on them, and shot one of my deputies."

Falcon cut his eyes to Scarface. "Then your men are liars, sheriff."

Scarface blanched at the insult, his hand falling toward his pistol as he leaned forward.

Falcon didn't move or take his eyes off the man. "Your man drew on my friend and me first, Sheriff, for no reason."

Falcon paused for just a second, then continued. "And if you don't control that one there, he'll be the next one lying on his back with a bullet in his chest." He inclined his head toward Scarface.

Brady's eyes narrowed as he studied Falcon and noticed the way his Colts were tied down low, and the way his hands were quiet, with no sign of nerves at facing seven men to their two. He chewed on his lip, considering his options.

"Well, whatever the cause I don't take kindly to strangers shootin' up my men."

Falcon shrugged. "I don't take kindly to tinhorn deputies trying to throw their weight around by hassling law-abiding citizens who aren't breaking any laws, Sheriff. Last time I looked, it was still legal to ride down a trail minding your own business."

"They was comin' from Chisum's, Bill," Scarface said in a whiny voice.

"That true, mister?" the sheriff asked.

"Yes. My father was an old friend of Mr. Chisum's, and I stopped by to give him my regards on my way to Fort Sumner."

"Then you don't work for him?"

Falcon shook his head. "No."

The sheriff turned his attention to the Kid. "How about you, boy?"

The Kid's grin faltered for just a second at the word *boy*, then returned, as insolent as ever. "Not me, neither," he said.

"That's the one shot Johnny Roy," Scarface said, pointing at the Kid.

"That so, boy?" the sheriff asked.

The Kid leaned back in his chair, his hand near his pistol. "If Johnny Roy is the name of the fat tub of lard who tried to draw on me, then I'm the one that shot him."

"What's your name, son?"

"The name's Billy Bonney, Sheriff, but I go by Kid."

"How about you, mister?"

"My name is Falcon MacCallister, Sheriff, and the Kid is right. As I said earlier, your man drew on us without provocation or cause, and we acted in self-defense."

Brady frowned. "If Johnny drew first, how'd you manage to put lead in him? He's pretty quick with a six-gun."

Kid snorted. "Quick? The man was slow as molasses in January."

Scarface said, "Johnny never ever cleared leather, Bill. He never had a chance."

Kid glanced at where Scarface held his hand on the butt of his pistol. "Neither will you, if you try to pull that hogleg," he said. "I'll drop you where you stand."

Brady shook his head. "That's mighty tough talk for someone outnumbered three to one, boy."

Kid smirked and started to stand up, but Falcon put a hand on his arm. "Sheriff, have we broken any laws?"

Brady glanced at Falcon and rubbed his chin. "I don't suppose so, not if the shootin' went as you say it did."

"Then I suggest you question all your men about the events on the trail before we start something here that might get someone else hurt."

Brady nodded. "I'll do that, Mr. MacCallister, and I'll also take a look at my posters, see if there's any paper out on you boys."

Five

As Brady walked out of the room Falcon noticed the Kid watching him with narrowed eyes and pursed lips.

"You worried about what Sheriff Brady might find among those wanted posters, Kid?"

Kid shrugged. "Not really. I done told you I was in jail a couple of times and broke out." He rubbed his chin, then felt the thin, wispy hairs of his sparse moustache, a thoughtful look on his face. " 'Course, that was under another name, so I doubt it matters what the sheriff does."

"What name were you using then?"

"Henry Antrim, but I was called Kid Antrim."

Falcon shook his head, sighing. "Well, I hope the sheriff is as dumb as he looks, and doesn't make the connection between Kid Antrim and Billy Bonney."

Kid looked surprised. "I never thought of that."

"Let's hope the sheriff doesn't either, Kid, or we'll both have some heavy explaining to do."

Falcon stood up, threw some coins down on the table, and said, "Now, let's see if we can find out where this Mr. Tunstall you're looking for lives."

The Kid raised his hand, summoning their waitress.

"Si, señor, may I help you?"

"Yeah. Can you tell us where to find a Mr. John Tunstall?"

The Mexican's face paled, and her eyes widened as she

looked over her shoulder to see if anyone was listening. "Not so loud, señor. This place not like Mr. Tunstall much."

She glanced around again, then whispered, "He has general store at other end of town. You cannot miss it."

When she finished, she picked up Falcon's money and hurried back through the door into the kitchen, casting a worried look over her shoulder at the Kid and Falcon before she disappeared.

"What do you suppose she meant by all that?" Kid asked.

"Only one way to find out, Kid. Let's mosey on down the street and look for his store."

As they walked down the wooden planks of the town's boardwalk, Falcon watched the townspeople as they scurried about their business.

"You notice anything funny about these people, Kid?"

The Kid glanced around, shrugging. "Naw. Why'd you ask?"

"It's just a feeling I get . . . seems they're all so serious, almost as if they're walking on eggshells, waiting for something to happen."

The Kid shrugged again. "Couldn't tell it by me, Falcon. They just look like ordinary folk doin' whatever it takes to get along."

He stopped and pointed up ahead. "There it is—Tunstall's Emporium, the sign says."

Falcon, more observant than the Kid, also noticed the pair of tough-looking gunhands hanging around the entrance to Tunstall's place. They were leaning back against the wall on either side of the door, thumbs hooked in belts with holsters tied down low on their legs. Though their posture was relaxed, he could see their eyes scanning the street, missing nothing.

"I wonder why Tunstall feels the need to have armed guards in front of his store" Falcon muttered to himself.

"What'd you say?" the Kid asked, impatient now to find Tunstall.

"Nothing," Falcon answered, "just thinking out loud."

They walked up the boardwalk and had started to enter the store, when one of the gunnies grabbed the Kid by the arm. Suddenly, he was staring down the barrel of a .44 Colt that appeared as if by magic in the Kid's hand.

"If'n I was you, mister, I'd let go of my arm, real gentle like," the Kid said through tight lips.

Falcon put a hand on the Colt, pushing it down. "That's all right, Kid. This man is just doing what Mr. Tunstall pays him to do, guard his establishment."

The Kid raised his eyebrows. "That right, mister? You work for Tunstall?"

The cowboy nodded, sweat running down his forehead to drip into his eyes, his gaze locked on the Colt in the Kid's hand. "Yeah. We're supposed to keep any of Dolan's or Riley's men outta here."

"Who?" the Kid asked.

"Never mind, Kid. I'm sure Mr. Tunstall will fill us in once we get to talk to him."

A voice from inside called, "It's okay, Roy. Let the gentlemen in, please."

Falcon and the Kid walked into a large room filled with all manner of ranching implements, clothes, and foodstuffs. There was a counter running along one side of the wall off to the right, and in a far corner sat a large, potbellied stove. Next to the stove was a table where four men sat drinking coffee.

One of the men was young, appearing to be in his early twenties, with a fair complexion and bright green eyes, wearing a brown jacket over corduroy pants. The other men were older. One wore a suit and vest with a gold watchchain hanging across it. The other two were cowboys, wearing jeans and shirts and Stetson hats which had seen plenty of wear. Like the two outside the door, the punchers were packing pistols tied down low on their legs, and looked ready to use them.

The Kid walked up to the older man in the suit and stuck out his hand. "Mr. Tunstall, my name's Billy Bonney and—"

The man held up his hand, grinning. "Hold on there, slick. My name is Alexander McSween. I'm Mr. Tunstall's lawyer."

He inclined his head to the younger man sitting next to him. "There's the man you want to talk to."

Tunstall stood up and held out his hand. "Mr. Bonney, I'm John Henry Tunstall," he said with an English accent. He looked at the other men, adding, "Alex McSween is my lawyer, Dick Brewer there is foreman of my ranch, and the chap next to him is his assistant, Charlie Bowdre."

The Kid tipped his hat, "Howdy, boys. This here is my friend, Falcon MacCallister."

Falcon nodded and Tunstall grinned, saying, "You any relation to Jamie MacCallister?"

"Yes. He was my father."

Tunstall frowned. "Was?"

"Yes. He died a while back."

"I'm sorry to hear that," Tunstall said. "I can't tell you how many times I've sat here next to this very stove during a blue norther and listened to John Chisum tell tales of how the two of them rode together, fighting Indians, rustlers, and seems like just about everyone else, in the old days."

Falcon smiled. "Probably the same tall stories I used to hear from my dad, and he had more than his share of adventures in his life."

"Well, maybe we'll get a chance to share some stories, if you plan to be around here long enough."

He looked back to the Kid. "What can I do for you, Mr. Bonney?"

"I spoke with Mr. Chisum, an' he said you could maybe use another hand. I'm lookin' for work."

Tunstall glanced at the way the Kid wore his pistol, low on his hip. "You any good with that six-shooter?"

The Kid grinned and shrugged. "Pretty fair. I usually hit what I'm aimin' at, if that's what you mean."

Dick Brewer growled through a voice that sounded as if he had eaten broken glass for breakfast, "You have any problem aiming it at other men?"

"Not enough so's you can tell it. Why? That part of the job?"

Tunstall laughed. "The way things are going, it's more than likely."

He turned his attention to Falcon. "You looking for work, too, Falcon?"

Falcon shook his head. "Not at the present time. I'm on my way to Fort Sumner. I hear there's a saloon there I might be able to buy an interest in."

"Oh, you mean Beaver Smith's place, The Drinking Hole?"

Falcon nodded. "John Chisum told me he might be interested in making a deal, if the price were right."

"It's a prosperous establishment. Gets a lot of trade from both the soldiers stationed at the fort, and from the surrounding ranches. Of course, old Beaver is getting along in years. He might be willing to take in a partner."

Dick Brewer and Charlie Bowdre stood up. "Sittin' here and jawin' ain't gettin' those cattle took care of, Mr. Tunstall. We'd better get on back to the ranch."

Tunstall nodded at the Kid. "Take Mr. Bonney with you and get him some clean clothes and set him up in the bunkhouse. Show him around and fill him in on what our situation is, so he'll know what we need."

"Yes, sir."

The Kid shook hands with Tunstall, then turned to leave. He grinned and touched the brim of his hat. "See ya' around, Falcon. I like to turn a card or two on occasion, so I'll look up your place on my day off. I still owe you for the meal."

"So long, Kid. You take it easy, you hear?"

After they left, Tunstall said, "You in a hurry, Falcon, or have you got time for some coffee?"

"Always time for *cafecito,* John," he said, and pulled out a chair. He just couldn't bring himself to keep calling someone his own age or younger mister any more.

Tunstall took a pot off the stove, poured a cup for Falcon, and freshened his own. While Tunstall was preparing their drinks, Falcon took the chance to study McSween. He was a typical western lawyer, with slicked back hair, a slight paunch that strained the front of his vest and bulged over his belt, and a face with a weak chin and expression that told Falcon he wouldn't be a man he'd want to depend on in a fight. He looked to be the type to cut and run at the first opportunity.

Tunstall, on the other hand, seemed to Falcon to have steely-eyed determination written all over him. His green eyes and fair skin and accent marked him as a man from a long way off, but he had a quiet strength, and Falcon bet he was a born leader whose men would go through fire for him if he asked.

"If you don't mind my saying it, John, it appears to me you're more interested in hiring guns than punchers," Falcon asked.

Tunstall nodded. "Yes, unfortunately that is the case. We're on the verge of a range war here, Falcon."

"Over what? There seems to be plenty of water and feeding ground to go around."

"There are two Irishmen, J.J. Dolan and John Riley, who are behind most of the trouble—"

When Tunstall mentioned the names, McSween scowled and muttered, "Bastards!" under his breath.

"These chaps own the large general store at the other end of town—used to be called La Placita before they bought it from Lawrence Murphey," Tunstall continued, ignoring the interruption. "Now they hold a virtual monopoly of the county's trade. In addition, they have close ties to influential territorial officials in the capital at Santa Fe, known as the Santa Fe Ring. Their bloody friends there have given them complete control of all government contracts for supplying beef to army posts and Indian reservations."

Falcon tasted his coffee, then said, "These two must have a sizable spread to be able to sell that much beef to the government."

Tunstall gave a bitter smile. "Not a bloody head. They buy every bit of the meat they sell from the other ranchers around here, at rock bottom prices, and then sell it to their friends in Santa Fe at a huge profit, which they then spread around to buy more power in the capital."

"Buy it, hell!" McSween interrupted, his face turning beet red, starting to wheeze. "Get their friend Jesse Evans and his gang to steal most of it, by my reckoning."

Tunstall shook a finger at McSween. "Now, take it easy, Alex. You know we can't prove that, and besides, you know when you get angry your asthma starts to act up."

"I can see how that would not make the cattlemen around here very happy," Falcon said.

"And, to add insult to injury, until I opened my store they were able to charge whatever they wanted to the ranchers for their supplies. The owners weren't able to complain, or they'd be cut off from buying from La Placita. They pretty much had things their own way in Lincoln County and the surrounding Pecos Valley until I decided to make a change."

"Oh?"

"John Chisum and I saw no reason why mere merchants, with little or no experience in cattle raising, should have a corner on the government contracts, or why we ranchers who owned vast herds should not deal directly with the government as beef suppliers. So, John and I hired Alex McSween here, a jolly good lawyer, and we organized a number of the smaller ranchers and farmers who were unable to get credit from La Placita, to go up against Dolan and Riley. I opened this store, and we began to try to get some of the contracts directly. John Chisum and Alex and I also opened a bank to help our cattlemen friends who need it."

"I can see where that would cause some hard feelings from the Dolan and Riley factions."

Tunstall nodded. "It certainly has. By spreading our own money around Santa Fe, we've been able to make some inroads into their business, and have gotten a few contracts of our own. The problem is they have Lincoln pretty much sewed up, and they control Sheriff Brady and his cronies lock, stock, and barrel. Falcon, it's a powder keg, just waiting to explode."

"So that's why you're hiring men who are handy with pistols as cowhands?"

"Yes. I'm afraid that sooner or later the whole matter will be decided by who has the greater firepower."

Falcon finished his coffee and stood. "Well, thanks for the drink, and good luck to you and Mr. Chisum. I know from things my father told me that he's a good man."

Tunstall rose and shook Falcon's hand. "He's one of the best, as was your father, to hear him tell it. Good luck, Falcon. When you come back to Lincoln, consider my house yours for as long as you need it."

McSween didn't stand, but tipped his hat. "See you around, Falcon."

"You can bet on it, Alex."

As Falcon walked out to his horse, he wondered just what kind of snake's nest he and the Kid were getting into.

"One thing," he muttered, "it sure as hell won't be boring around here."

Six

Falcon enjoyed the ride from Lincoln to Fort Sumner and took his time, letting Diablo find his own pace on the winding mountain trail. The fall air was crisp and clean, smelling of sage and cactus blossoms and pine needles from the trees that dotted the mountainsides. He could see milling herds of cattle off in the distance, and several small ranch houses were scattered across the countryside.

Along the small river that flanked the trail, some farmer had planted trees in thick orchards, and their limbs were heavy with fruit.

When Falcon arrived in Fort Sumner he found a cow town like many of the hundreds in the West. Small, without an abundance of citizens, it served the purpose of being a watering hole for cowboys from nearby ranches and soldiers from the adjacent garrison at the fort. There were more saloons and eating establishments than houses, and very few children could be seen playing in the dusty streets.

It was just what Falcon was looking for, a place where thirsty punchers and soldiers came to raise a little hell and spend hard-earned dollars learning the intricacies of poker and faro. He would be more than willing to teach them, and earn a few dollars for himself in the bargain.

After he got Diablo rubbed and fed and bedded down at the livery stable, he registered at the town's only hotel. Paying the desk clerk fifty cents for a hot bath, he cleaned up and changed into a fresh shirt and pants, had his coat and hat brushed clean by the Chinese attendant, and made his way on foot to The Drinking Hole saloon to appraise the situation.

Though it was early in the evening, the place was almost full. Along one side of the room was a long bar, backed by a seven-foot mirror and a painting of a reclining nude woman swathed in red silk sheets that didn't manage to cover much of her body. There were several kegs of beer, and a row of various brands of liquor, mainly bourbon and rye.

There were eight tables scattered across the room, and all had poker games going, with sweating, drunken cowboys and soldiers laughing and joking among themselves as they spent in one night what it had taken them thirty days to earn. In a far corner was a faro table, surrounded by a crowd of men "riding the tiger"—betting against the next card to come out of the box with the painting of a tiger on it.

Falcon felt right at home. Gambling was his favorite way to make money, and it was his favorite pastime. He never tired of the thrill of pitting his wits against men who thought winning at poker was a matter of luck instead of skill. And calling a bet with his last gold coin, knowing if he lost he wouldn't eat, was the kind of pressure he lived for.

He walked to the bar, squeezed in between two punchers, and ordered a whiskey. When it came he turned and leaned back against the bar as he drank, observing the room and its occupants. Picking the right game to enter was as important as drawing the right cards. He didn't play with men who looked as if they couldn't afford to lose. He wanted the kind of high stakes game only the prosperous could give him.

At one of the tables there were two men who were, like Falcon, wearing suit coats and white shirts, and two others

who were wearing jeans and leather vests but were too old
to be punchers—probably local ranchers out to get away
from their wives and children for an evening of fun and
games. Falcon figured the suits were professional gamblers
or merchants or bankers, men who could well afford to
play his type of game.

He drained his drink, got a refill, and ambled over to
stand watching the play at the table he'd picked out. After
a moment, one of the rancher types looked up, studied
him for a moment, and said, "Care to sit in, friend?"

"Don't mind if I do," Falcon replied, pulling out a chair
and taking a seat. "Playing five card stud?"

The man nodded, "Ten dollar ante, pot limit on bets.
Too rich for your blood?"

"Suits me," Falcon said, and pulled a stack of greenbacks
from his coat pocket.

One of the suits stared at the roll of money, glanced at
the other man wearing a suit and raised his eyebrows, a
slight grin curling his lips. Falcon kept his face straight,
noticing everything that went on at the table. One of the
secrets of his success as a gambler was his ability to read
other players, and he knew from the start the two to watch
out for were the men wearing suits, though over the years
he had found that most of the really good card players
acted as if they didn't know the difference between a
straight and a flush.

The man who invited him to sit down introduced the
other players.

"My name's Ben Johnson," the rancher said. Then he
inclined his head to the man on his left, also wearing ranch
clothes. "That's Johnny Albright, and those two are Louis
Longacre and Marcus Cahill."

Falcon nodded, "I'm Falcon MacCallister."

Ben riffled the cards, waited for the antes to be put in
the pot at the center of the table, then began to deal.

"You new in town, Falcon?" he asked as he passed out the cards.

"Just got in today."

"Are you here on business, or pleasure?" asked Louis Longacre.

When Falcon raised his eyebrows at the question, Ben grunted, a smile on his sun-weathered face. "Louis ain't being nosy, Falcon, he's the town banker. He's always hoping someone will come into town and buy up some of the mortgages he's holding paper on."

"Sure," Louis said, "no offense meant."

"None taken," Falcon replied. "As a matter of fact, it's a little of both. I'm looking to possibly invest some money here in Fort Sumner, maybe do a little business. As to the pleasure, that depends on how the cards fall in the next few hours."

Ben and Louis laughed, but Johnny Albright just scowled, staring at his cards. "Ben, just shut up and deal the damned cards. This ain't no ladies' society social. Let's play poker."

Falcon glanced at the pile of chips and money in front of Johnny. It was considerably smaller than the others'. It was always the losers who wanted to hurry the game along, often so they could lose their money even faster. He settled back in his chair and watched the others as the game progressed.

He was in no hurry. It would take him a couple of hours to figure out the other player's "tells"—the little unconscious motions and mannerisms most players make that can tell an experienced poker player how good their hand is, and whether they're bluffing or betting against strength.

Soon, Falcon learned that Louis Longacre owned the Fort Sumner bank and was a partner of Marcus Cahill in several other businesses in town, including the hotel and the livery stable. Ben Johnson and Johnny Albright were both ranchers, as he had figured, and owned two of the largest spreads east of town.

Of the group at the table, Louis and Marcus were better than average players, Ben was average, and Johnny was terrible.

Falcon played conservatively, betting only when he had a good hand, folding with anything less than a sure winner, while he learned the habits of his opponents.

He noticed that Louis picked at the corner of his moustache when he was bluffing or betting on a weak hand, while Marcus licked his lips and leaned slightly forward in his chair when he was on a bluff.

Ben had few tells, but tended not to push his advantage when he had good cards, rarely bluffed with any conviction, and folded several winning hands when pressed. He obviously played for the fun of the game, and not to make or lose any important amounts of money.

Johnny Albright, on the other hand, did everything badly. He sweated and blinked rapidly and nervously when he tried to bluff, and became boisterous and jubilant when he had a good hand, thus letting the others know they should bail out without letting Johnny make anything.

Falcon, for his part, played to stay about even, throwing in some winning hands so as not to make too good an impression on the other men. If he was going to be playing here for any length of time, he didn't want them to think he was a card sharp, or it would be hard to find men to play with him. The hardest thing about making a living at gambling was to let your opponents think you had won by luck, not skill. That way, they would keep coming back for more, hoping your luck would change.

It was a role Falcon had perfected over the years. He would take a little from each player at the table, letting each win a few big pots from him, but staying always a little ahead of the game. At the end of the night, most times, he won more than he lost and would leave the game richer than when he entered it.

It was well after midnight when Falcon stifled a yawn, figuring it was about time to call it a night. He was two hundred and fifty dollars ahead, Ben and Marcus were about even, and Louis had won over six hundred dollars, most of it from Johnny Albright.

Johnny didn't seem to mind overly much, other than cussing his luck and the damned cards that just wouldn't fall his way. Falcon noticed Marcus and Louis glancing at each other with tiny, tight smiles on their faces, and realized this was probably a weekly occurrence, with Johnny losing and the others winning. He hoped the man had a profitable ranch, because his poker playing was costing him plenty.

Falcon came fully awake when a man at an adjacent table shouted and jumped to his feet, knocking his chair over as he clawed for his pistol.

"You lyin' son of a bitch," he screamed drunkenly, his bleary, bloodshot eyes staring across the table.

He was a young soldier in uniform, and swayed unsteadily on his feet as he aimed the Colt army revolver at another player at his table, who sat with large eyes and raised hands.

"You been cheatin' me all night, Billy Bob, an' I'm gonna drill you fer it!"

"I ain't neither been cheatin' you, Joey," the terrified puncher said. "You're just a lousy poker player, that's all."

In one fluid motion, Falcon stood up, drawing his Colt and bringing it down on top of the kid's head so fast no one in the room could follow the movement.

The young man dropped like a stone, unconscious but unhurt, and then everyone was talking and moving at once.

"Goddamn, did you see that feller draw?" one of the players at the next table said to the man next to him.

"Damn, he moved quicker than a rattler," another said to no one in particular.

Falcon bent over the soldier, checked his head to make sure he was all right, then asked one of his soldier friends to take him out to the base and have the army doctor take a look at him.

A short, stubby man wearing a bright red plaid shirt, yellow suspenders, and sporting a full, bushy beard waddled over to the table. He looked at Falcon and stuck out his hand.

"Howdy, pardner. I'm Beaver Smith. I own this place, and I owe you a drink fer preventin' that young buck from killin' somebody."

Falcon took the hand and introduced himself. "Just let me collect my money and I'll take you up on that drink, Mr. Smith."

"Oh hell, son, just call me Beaver like everybody else."

Falcon shook hands all around at his table. "I enjoyed the evening, gents. I'd like to do it again sometime."

The others nodded, and Johnny Albright said, "Yeah, and maybe next time you won't be so lucky with them cards, Falcon."

Falcon smiled and shrugged. "You're right, Johnny. I was awfully lucky tonight. Maybe next time it will be your turn to have the luck."

Seven

Beaver Smith opened a door next to the bar and ushered Falcon into his office with a sweep of his hand. Falcon was impressed at the size and the opulence of the place. Though the saloon, like all of the other buildings in Fort Sumner, was nondescript and ordinary, Beaver's office was furnished and decorated very tastefully.

The entire floor was covered in a thick, woven rug, and the walls had dark wood paneling. There was a couch against one side wall, a small, well-stocked bar against another, and in the rear was a large, oaken desk with two heavy, easy chairs arrayed in front of it.

Beaver must have noticed Falcon's admiring gaze, for he said, "You like my little hideaway?"

Falcon nodded. "Yes, it's very nice, and rather unexpected."

Beaver grinned. "Yeah. When I bought The Drinking Hole more'n ten year ago, I decided if I was gonna spend half my life runnin' the place I wanted to make myself a room I'd enjoy bein' in."

He waved his arm at the chairs in front of his desk. "Take a load off, an' I'll get you a nip of some really fine bourbon—brought all the way from Kentucky it says on the label."

In a few moments, he had drinks for both of them and

he was settled in a plush, overstuffed desk chair, watching Falcon with appraising eyes.

"You don't strike me as the normal sort of travelin' gambler we usually get around here, Falcon."

There's more to this man than meets the eye, Falcon thought. "That's because I'm not a gambler. At least I don't make my living at it," Falcon replied.

Beaver took a long sip of his whiskey, wiped his beard with the back of his hand, and sighed. "Man, that's smooth." Then, he cut his eyes back at Falcon. "I didn't think so. Just what do you do for a livin', Falcon?"

"Oh, I've got my hand in several ventures. I own a ranch and breed some horses, and I own a saloon in Valley, Colorado, called The Wild Rose." He smiled and added, "And I do a bit of gambling to pass the time when I'm not otherwise engaged."

"So, you must know what I have to put up with, runnin' The Drinking Hole." Beaver shook his head, "Sometimes I think I'm gettin' a bit long in the tooth to be in this business. If it's not drunken cowboys shootin' the place up, it's pissed-off soldiers fightin' and throwin' chairs and breakin' furniture."

"Yes, it can be rather exciting, especially late in the night when the boys have gotten a snootful of whiskey and realize they've lost all their money for the rest of the month."

Falcon paused to take a drink of his bourbon, noticing it was a good brand, so rich and flavorful he could almost taste the redwood barrels it had been aged in. "That's why I'd like to make you an offer on The Drinking Hole."

Beaver's eyebrows almost disappeared in the mop of wild hair on his head. "You mean you want to buy my saloon?"

Falcon nodded. "If it's for sale."

Beaver shrugged. "Son, everything's for sale, if the price is right." He held his glass up and stared into the amber fluid for a moment. "Though I don't rightly know just what I'd do with myself if I sold out. It's true, runnin' the place gets a bit wearying, but I'm not the sort to go sit by a stream with a pole and fish the rest of my life."

"I realize that, Beaver, and I'm not the sort of man to settle down in one town for any length of time. So, how about this? I'll pay you a fair price for half ownership in The Drinking Hole, and for as long as I'm around I'll run it and you can take some time off to rest up or travel or whatever you want to do. When I get tired of Fort Sumner I'll be on my way, and you can send my half of our profits to my bank back in Valley, Colorado."

Beaver pursed his lips. "You'd trust me to do that, young feller?"

"I never enter into a business arrangement with a man I can't trust," Falcon said. "And in all my years I've never yet been disappointed in any of my partners."

Beaver thought for a moment, eyeing Falcon over the rim of his glass as he drank. Finally, he got up and poured them both another round.

"Well, if we're gonna make a deal, let's get down to some serious negotiatin'," he said with a wide grin.

It took almost two more hours and the rest of the bottle of bourbon before they agreed on a price for Falcon to purchase a half interest in The Drinking Hole.

As they shook hands and Falcon prepared to return to his hotel, Beaver said, "I told you I was a good judge of character. If you run the saloon half as well as you bargain, our profits are assured."

The next night, after Beaver had packed up a suitcase and gone to visit his daughter over in Roswell, Falcon began his first night as new owner of The Drinking Hole. He arranged with the cook at the hotel to provide a large tray of sandwiches and several jars of pickled eggs, which he placed on the bar next to a sign saying Free Food.

Roy, the bartender, asked, "Why are we giving the food

away for free, Mr. MacCallister? We could charge for it and make a profit on it."

"We're going to make a profit on it, Roy. The more a puncher eats, the more he drinks, and our real profit is in the whiskey and beer we serve. Those pickled eggs make a man mighty thirsty, and the more we give away, the more whisky we'll sell."

"What about the sandwiches?"

"A man with a full stomach is less likely to get dead drunk and start a fight, or shoot up the place. And the longer it takes a man to get drunk, the longer he can drink and the more whiskey we'll sell."

Roy smiled and shook his head. "I can see things are going to be a mite different around here."

"Not too different," Falcon said. "Beaver ran a nice place. I just want to help him out with a few minor changes to enhance our profit margin a little."

As the saloon began to fill up Falcon went to his table. He had set up a felt-covered table in a corner away from the entrance, and he sat with his back to a wall so he could observe everything that went on and could see who came in the door before they could see him. He wanted no surprises. It was a habit of carefulness he had acquired over the years, and it had served him well.

He had Roy bring him a cup of coffee and he sat there, watching the play at the other tables and the faro game, and dealt himself a game of solitaire to play until the heavy poker players arrived.

When he saw Billy Bonney and Dick Brewer, John Tunstall's foreman, walk through the door, he waved Billy over to his table. Billy left Brewer at the bar and pulled up a seat across from Falcon.

"Howdy, Kid. Would you like a beer?"

The Kid frowned. "You know I don't drink nor smoke, Falcon."

"Well then, how's the new job going?"

The Kid smiled. "It's all right, so far. Mr. Tunstall seems a right decent man to work for."

"He got you punching cows?"

"No, thank goodness. Dick's in charge of the cattle. My job is to stay next to Mr. Tunstall and make sure nobody shoots him in the back."

Falcon frowned. "Things getting that bad?"

The Kid nodded. "Yeah. The boss thinks Murphey and Dolan are getting right tired of him taking their business away from them with his store, and he said Mr. Chisum was working on gettin' some of those government contracts to sell beef to the Indians. Mr. Tunstall says if that happens the lead is liable to start flyin' sooner rather than later."

"Well, be sure to keep a close eye on your own back while you're watching out for Tunstall's, Kid."

The Kid patted the Colt on his hip. "I keep my holster greased and the hammer thong off all the time, Falcon. I'm ready for whatever those galoots want to throw my way."

"What are you doing out this way, Kid?"

"I heard you bought into the saloon here, and I wanted to come give you some business. Mr. Tunstall advanced me some pay, an' it's been too long since I've sat in on a good poker game."

"You any good at poker?"

The Kid shrugged. "I usually win more'n I lose."

"That's all that counts."

Falcon glanced over the Kid's shoulder and saw Ben Johnson, Johnny Albright, Louis Longacre, and Marcus Cahill coming through the door.

"You're in luck, Kid. Here come some gents who'll be glad to test your luck."

The Kid smiled. "Luck has very little to do with winnin', Falcon. It's all in knowin' who you're up against, and bein' ready to do whatever it takes to beat him."

Falcon waved the men over and introduced them to the Kid.

"You men ready to play?" Falcon asked.

"Deal 'em," Johnny Albright said, his voice slurred enough to show he had already started drinking. "I feel real lucky tonight."

The Kid looked over at Falcon and winked, making Falcon smile in return. In some strange way, the Kid was a man after his own heart.

Eight

In Lincoln, a late night meeting was being held in a back room of La Placita, J.J. Dolan's general store. Dolan had asked Lawrence Murphey, called the Major, John Riley, Jack B. "Billy" Matthews, Jesse Evans, and Sheriff William Brady to meet together to discuss their strategy in dealing with Chisum and Tunstall.

Dolan, holding a glass of Irish whiskey in his hand, paced the room as he talked to the others, who were seated around a large potbellied stove to ward off the autumn chill.

"Sheriff, you've got to crack down on Chisum and Tunstall more. Since they've opened their damned store and bank, they've started to get some support from the smaller ranchers in the area, and I even hear from our friends in Santa Fe that the army is considering giving Chisum some of our contracts to supply beef to the Mescaleros."

"Hell, J.J., I don't know what else I can do. Every time I see any of their men in town I brace 'em. I've thrown half of them in jail for drunk and disorderly, but Tunstall just bails 'em out and gets 'em back to work."

Murphey, who was well into his third drink, slurred drunkenly from the corner, "it was different when I ran things 'round here."

He waved his glass as he spoke, sloshing whiskey on his arm, "We didn't put up with no interference in our plans.

Those that didn't go along didn't get credit at the store. That kept those lily-livered ranchers in line, I can tell you."

Dolan frowned. "Things are different now, Major. La Placita is losing more business every day to that damned Tunstall store, and to make matters worse Tunstall has been writing letters to the army complaining about the quality of meat and flour we've been selling to the Mescaleros."

Brady nodded. "Yeah, and the bastard's even wrote the U.S. Attorney in Santa Fe tellin' 'em I haven't been sending in the tax money I've been collectin' here in Lincoln County. He's damn sure gettin' too big for his britches, all right."

"What about that new hand he's hired, calls himself the Kid?"

Brady shrugged. "I couldn't find no papers on him, or his friend MacCallister."

Leaning back in his chair with his boots on the table, Jesse Evans said, "I rode with him for a while, played some cards with him over at Fort Stanton 'fore he came to work for Tunstall. He talked like he had a past, some trouble back in Arizona, I believe."

"Arizona, huh?" Brady asked. "I'll wire the sheriff over there and see if he knows anything. Might be a way to get back at Tunstall, get rid of some of those gunnies he's been hiring."

"You do that, William," Dolan said, "first thing in the morning. Now, why don't you leave us to talk some business you're better off not knowing?"

Brady climbed to his feet and nodded. "I'll do what I can, J.J.."

"You'd better, or that percentage you own in the store and bank here that I gave you won't be worth a damn to you," Dolan said.

After the sheriff left, Dolan turned to Riley. "You said anything to Jesse yet?"

"No."

Dolan turned to refill his glass. "Then tell him what we want."

Riley leaned forward, his elbows on the table. "It's getting too expensive to buy our meat from the ranchers. Profits are down. We want you and your gang to start raiding Chisum's herd for cattle. We'll buy all you can steal, at good prices, and we'll make sure Sheriff Brady doesn't connect you to the rustling."

Evans pulled a toothpick from between his lips, made a cigarette, and struck a lucifer on his pant leg. After he lighted the cigarette and blew smoke at the ceiling, he looked over at Riley.

"John, I take it you wouldn't be too disappointed if some of Chisum's men were to get . . . slightly hurt during our raids on his cattle."

Riley's lips curled up in a sneer. "We'd be most appreciative for any assistance you could give us in lowering the number of gunhands Chisum has available."

Dolan turned from refilling his drink. "It wouldn't be amiss if you got some of the cattle from Tunstall's spread, too, Jesse."

Evans shook his head. "That would be a mite more difficult. His Rio Feliz ranch is down on the Pecos River, and it'd be mighty tough to drive stolen beeves across it in the darkness. Plus, it ain't near as big and spread out as Chisum's range is. His men would most likely catch us in the act, and I don't suppose you want a full scale war, do you?"

Dolan pursed his lips and shook his head. "Not just yet, Jesse, but soon . . . soon."

Evans smiled, hands resting on the twin Colts he wore on each hip. "Then, since I'm going to be in the cattle business, I guess I'd better get to work."

Murphey staggered to his feet and poured himself another drink of whiskey, spilling more than he got in his glass.

"Damn, Jimmy, things have been going to hell since I

sold out to you. Just haven't been the same since the colonel died."

Dolan frowned at Murphey. "Major, when Colonel Fritz hired me, you and he were barely making a profit off your meat contracts. If you'll try to remember, it was me who got the ranchers to take less for their beef or have their credit cut off at the store, and it was my idea to have the Evans gang steal cattle from Chisum so we could get it at an even lower price."

Dolan took a deep swallow of his whiskey. "So don't whine to me about the good old days. You're making more money now than you ever did before you sold out to me."

Murphey nodded. "I know, Jimmy. I just miss Fritz, an' wish the consumption hadn't eaten him up so fast."

"Be glad it did," Riley said, putting a cigar in his mouth and lighting it. "If it hadn't, you would never have sold out to Jimmy, and we'd all have to be working for a living."

He turned to Dolan. "Jimmy, you need to get in touch with Judge Bristol and William Rynerson, the District Attorney of Lincoln County, and tell them to squash these complaints Tunstall's been making. Let 'em know their share of our contract profits will end if the army starts listening to what he's saying."

"I'm already on it, Johnny. Our friends in the Santa Fe Ring are taking steps to make sure no one listens to anything Mr. Tunstall has to say. Tom Catron, District Attorney in Santa Fe, will make sure the contracts keep coming our way."

"What about McSween? He's been making some noises about a lawsuit over at the courthouse."

"You leave Mr. McSween to me. I've got plans for him that will get him out of our hair, too."

He looked over at Jesse Evans. "Jesse, you can take what I'm paying you to rustle those cattle for us, and I'll double it if you can help me get rid of McSween."

Evans smirked. "You want him shot in the back, or the front?"

"Neither. I want you to get with Brady and find some . . . ah, legal way to do it."

"You want it legal?"

Dolan nodded. "At least, I want it to look that way if anybody asks."

Nine

Falcon peered over the top of the cards he held in his hand at a grinning Billy Bonney.

"Come on, Falcon. It's a simple decision. Call the bet or fold," the Kid said.

The other four men at the table had folded when the Kid raised Falcon's twenty dollar bet by fifty dollars. Falcon held a pair of jacks. Kid had drawn two cards in the five card stud game, indicating he might have three of a kind.

As Falcon thought, the Kid chewed for a second on his bottom lip, then resumed his ever present grinning.

"I'll call the bet, Kid. I have a pair of Dukes, and I think you have a busted flush."

Kid shook his head and nonchalantly flipped his cards into the middle of the table.

"Take the pot, Falcon. You called it right."

"Thanks, Kid. I was getting a mite short over here for a while. Maybe this hand changed my luck," Falcon said as he raked in the pile of money.

"How'd you know what I had?" the Kid asked, his face serious, no grin on it now.

Falcon pursed his lips, thinking on it for a moment.

"If I tell you how, it will ruin the magic of it," Falcon answered.

Roy Young, a local puncher who was sitting in the game next to Kid, spoke up. "I'd kind'a like to know, too, Mr.

MacCallister. Otherwise, people might get suspicious you got these here cards marked."

Falcon sighed. He knew he shouldn't have said it the moment he'd told the Kid what he had. *That's what I get for showing off,* he thought.

"It's really very simple. The Kid did something that he always does when he bluffs. If he was bluffing, then he didn't have three of a kind, so the only reason to draw two cards instead of three or four, is to try and make a flush."

"What was the Kid doin' that told you he was bluffin'?" Roy asked.

"That I don't tell you. If you studied the game as I do, instead of trusting to blind luck, you'd know already. Now, are we going to play cards or chat all night?"

"Deal 'em," the Kid said, "I still got thirty dollars that I need to make into fifty to get me some new boots and chaps."

As Falcon started to shuffle the cards, Roy, who had been drinking enough whiskey to feel brave, stood up suddenly, a belligerent expression on his face.

"That's not good enough for me! I think you're a cheat, MacCallister, an' I want my money back."

Falcon stopped shuffling and sat very still. It was a common hazard of his profession to be called a cheater. Most men who played poker didn't study their opponents as he did, and resented the fact that he consistently won when they were losing. He didn't take offense at the suggestion, as most men would, since he knew it was testimony to his prowess at the game, and he could usually talk his way out of the situations without resorting to gunplay.

He leaned back in his chair, staring at Roy.

"I explained to you how I won the hand, Roy. Now, either ante up or get out of the game. Don't let that whiskey you've been guzzling all night do your talking for you."

Walter Gibbons, a saddlemate of Roy's from the spread they both worked on, also stood up. "I'm with Roy, Mac-

Callister. You been winning all night, an' nobody's that lucky."

"Luck has nothing to do with winning at poker, Walter. It is a matter of skill."

Roy's face got beet-red and he slapped at the pistol on his belt. A split second later, so did Walter.

Falcon threw himself backward out of his chair, hit the floor and rolled to his knees, hands filled with iron.

His Colt Peacemakers exploded, kicking back into his palms, shooting flame and smoke from the barrels.

His left hand gun sent molten lead into Roy's face, punching a hole in his forehead and blowing brains and blood out the back of his head, dropping him like a stone.

His right-hand gun spit a .45 caliber slug into Walter's chest, shattering his breastbone and imbedding itself in his heart, spinning him around to sprawl facedown in the sawdust on the floor, dead before he hit the ground.

Out of the corner of his eye, Falcon saw the Kid whip out his pistol and aim it in his direction. The Kid's draw was so fast that he fired before Falcon could swing his pistols around toward him.

The Kid's bullet passed over Falcon's head, striking another man in the upper shoulder and dropping him to the floor, where he lay moaning and crying in pain.

Falcon glanced over his shoulder and saw the man had a pistol in his hand. He was a friend of Roy's, and had been about to shoot Falcon in the back.

Falcon got slowly to his feet, his nostrils wrinkling at the acrid smell of gunsmoke and cordite which filled the room with a gray haze.

He nodded at the Kid.

"Thanks, Kid. I owe you one for that."

"Naw, it weren't nothin'. I can't abide a backshooter. Man wants to join a fracas, that's all right with me, but he ought to have the *cojones* to do it face-to-face, not from behind like some bushwhacker."

"Nevertheless, I'm in your debt."

As Falcon and the Kid stood talking, another rider from Roy and Walter's ranch stepped through the batwings and leveled a rifle at the pair.

A tall man with a handlebar moustache standing at the bar drew in a flash and backhanded the puncher in the face with his pistol, knocking his head back and sending teeth and blood flying into the air.

The cowboy staggered, shook his ruined face once, then fell backward over a chair, out cold.

Falcon and the Kid whirled, hands full of iron, crouching to face this new threat.

The tall man held his hands up, a half-smile on his face.

"Hold on there, gents. I'm not involved in this. I just don't like backshooters any more than the Kid does."

The Kid squinted, then grinned and holstered his pistol.

"He's all right, Falcon. That there is Pat Garrett, an old acquaintance of mine."

Falcon walked over to the bar and held out his hand.

"I'm mighty obliged to you, Mr. Garrett."

Garrett took Falcon's hand.

"Let me buy you a drink," Falcon said.

"Don't mind if I do."

"How're you doin', Pat?" the Kid asked.

"Long time no see, Kid."

As they bellied to the bar, Falcon got a bottle of his best whiskey and poured himself and Garrett a drink. "I guess you don't want any of this, huh, Kid?"

The Kid shook his head. "Nope, but I'll take a glass of that there sarsaparilla, if you're offerin'."

Falcon complied, then turned to Garrett. "Where do you two know each other from?"

Garrett smiled. "I met the Kid when I first came out here. I was trying my hand at buffalo hunting, and me and my partner had a little trouble, so we . . . split up. The Kid and me were both scrounging around, looking for just about any work we could find."

The Kid broke in. "Yeah, and me and Pat played a few

hands of poker together. He's hell on the faro table, I'll tell you that."

Garrett, who was at least six-foot four inches tall, laughed. "They used to call us Big Casino and Little Casino around the gambling halls, cause we were such a sight standing at the tables next to each other."

"What are you up to now, Pat?" Falcon asked.

Garrett shrugged. "Not much. I just got into town to-night, and I haven't gotten a job yet."

Falcon nodded. "You ever do any bartending?"

"I've leaned against my share, but always on this side. Why?"

Falcon inclined his head. "Roy here, my regular man, has been wanting some time off to go back east and visit some kinfolk. How about you take his job until he gets back? That way, when things are slow, you might even be able to pick up a little money playing poker."

"Take the job, Pat," the Kid said. "I need for you to earn some money so I can take it away from you at the tables."

Garrett shook his head. "That'll be the day, Kid. All right, Mr. MacCallister, I'll do it. When do you want me to start?"

"Tomorrow's soon enough."

Garrett stroked his moustache. "It looks like your game is a couple of men short. If I could get a small advance, I'd be willing to teach the Kid some lessons about poker."

"That won't be a problem," Falcon said.

"Then get somebody to drag these men outta here so we can get back to playin'," the Kid said, putting his arm around Garrett's shoulders and leading him toward the table. "I still need to win that boots and chaps money."

Falcon glanced at the bartender. "Call the sheriff and take that one over to doc's place," he said, indicating the wounded man.

"This round's on the house," he called, "and we have one more empty seat in the game if anyone's interested."

* * *

Two hours later, shortly after midnight, he walked with Billy out to his horse.

"I was serious in there, Kid. I never forget a debt. If you ever need me, I'll be there with you."

The Kid waved a handful of dollars. "Hell, Falcon. I got me enough for my boots, so I'm satisfied."

Falcon noticed the Kid was climbing up on a different horse than the one he'd been riding when he met him the other day.

"That's a fine looking sorrel, Kid. New bronc?"

The Kid turned to Falcon, his eyes excited. "Yeah. When Mr. Tunstall hired me, he saw I was down on my luck, so he made me a present of this here horse, a new saddle, and a new gun."

He pulled out a nickel-plated Colt Peacemaker with ivory handles. Looking into Falcon's eyes, he said, "It's the first time in my life anybody's given me anything. I'll tell you, Falcon, Mr. Tunstall's the best man I ever knowed."

Falcon nodded. "Yes, everyone I've talked to has said the same thing, that he's a right smart gentleman."

"He's every bit of that," the Kid said as he swung up into the saddle. "I'm privileged to be working for the man and ridin' for his brand."

"You take care now, Kid. Watch your back. I've heard there's real bad blood between Tunstall and Dolan and his men."

"Don't you worry none 'bout me, Falcon. I'll take care to see that nothing happens to Mr. Tunstall."

He pulled his horse around and walked it down the street in the direction of Tunstall's Rio Feliz ranch.

"You won't be sorry you hired Pat Garrett," he called back over his shoulder. "He's a real fine fellow."

Falcon smiled to himself as he walked back into The Drinking Hole. He was glad the Kid seemed to have found a good place to work, for a man that would treat him right and appreciate him. Maybe that would keep him from getting into more trouble.

Ten

Over the course of the next several weeks Falcon settled into the routine of respected citizen and business owner of Fort Sumner, and found he was actually enjoying himself for the first time in several months. He almost forgot the reason he was roaming the country, away from his home in Valley, Colorado—the horrible death of his beloved wife Marie. Almost.

He began to learn the names of the townsfolk, and they, in turn, began to frequent The Drinking Hole in greater numbers than ever. Falcon began serving light lunches of steak sandwiches and sliced tomatoes and canned peaches and such. Many of the townspeople began to have lunch at his establishment, doing deals and talking business while eating and drinking.

He also found that the Kid had been right about the stranger he hired to bartend, Pat Garrett. The man was a natural born politician. Tall, lean, handsome, he had a way of making people feel at ease, encouraging them to talk about themselves so they stayed in the Hole longer and drank and ate more. Business had never been better. Falcon even found himself liking the big man, and ended up telling him some of the story of his past over long conversations during slow periods.

Garrett never drank while on duty, and kept a pot of fresh coffee to drink while talking. Falcon found Garrett to be a shrewd judge of character, almost as good as he himself was at reading people. Perhaps that was why he was such a good gambler, making more money in his off hours at poker than Falcon was paying him to tend bar.

Falcon noticed that certain group of businessmen from Lincoln were making the long trip around the mountain to Fort Sumner several times a week, to have lunch or a late dinner huddled at a corner table, heads together, speaking in low tones.

He couldn't understand why they would travel all that way to eat and talk when there were several establishments in Lincoln that would have served their purpose just as well. He supposed it was because they didn't want to be seen together by the people of Lincoln. Like all good businessmen, he kept his suspicions to himself and his mouth shut, and listened whenever he could.

James J. Dolan, Lawrence G. Murphey, and Sheriff Brady were becoming almost regulars at the lunches, often accompanied by a man Falcon was told was a lawyer named Billy Matthews.

Murphey, who drank to extreme, often became loud during these meetings, and Falcon was able to overhear some of his comments. Tunstall's name was mentioned, along with Chisum's, and on several occasions, there were heated discussions with a known gunfighter named Jesse Evans.

On one of those days, Evans stayed behind after the others left and signaled Garrett for another drink. Falcon, who was standing at the bar, offered to carry it to the gunny's table.

When he handed the drink to Evans, the man said, "Your name be Falcon MacCallister?"

"Yes."

"I've heard of you, MacCallister. Word around is you're pretty handy with them six-killers you wear on your belt."

Falcon wondered where this conversation was headed. "I know how to use them if the need arises."

"I also hear you've killed so many men you've lost count of the actual number."

Falcon inclined his head at a chair, and Evans nodded for him to have a seat.

"You hear a lot for a man I don't know. Just what business are you in, Mr. Evans? You don't have the look of a cow puncher."

Evans laughed, a nasty, sarcastic laugh. "Me? I'm not a cowboy. I make my living with my wits, MacCallister, just as I've heard you do."

Falcon shook his head. "I've never hired my gun out, if that's what you mean. And to answer your earlier question, the only men I've killed have been those who have done me or mine wrong. I never shot a man for profit, or in the course of doing business."

"Well, if I was to make an offer, a very good offer I might add, would you consider doing some business for some friends of mine, if the need arose?"

"By friends, do you mean J.J. Dolan and L.G. Murphey?"

Evans frowned and his eyes narrowed. "What makes you say that?"

Falcon shrugged. "They seem to be the only people I ever see you in here talking with."

"Well, what if it was them? Would you take on a job if it was offered?"

Falcon shook his head. "I told you, I don't hire my gun out, to anyone. Besides, I already have a job."

Evans smiled—at least, his lips curled up—but there was no humor in his eyes. "Good, 'cause my friends were a bit worried that if push came to shove you just might stick your nose into something that ain't none of your business."

"Are you talking about their campaign against John Tunstall and John Chisum?"

Evans straightened in his seat. "What do you mean by that, MacCallister?"

Now Falcon smiled, also without any mirth. "Oh, I hear things now and again."

"What things?"

"Things like you've been selling a lot of cattle to Murphey and Dolan for their government contracts, cattle you say you've been buying in Mexico, but no one's ever seen you riding toward the border and these cattle look a lot fatter and bigger than the usual Mexican steers."

Evans' hand inched toward his hip. "Those are dangerous things to be hearing, MacCallister. A man could get killed for repeating accusations like that."

Falcon moved his chair a bit and leaned back, his hand loose on the arm of his chair. "Don't even think about drawing on me, Evans. You'd be dead before you cleared leather."

"You that good, MacCallister?"

"Like you say you've heard, there are more men than I can count who found out how good I am."

Evans put his hand back on the table, finished his drink and wiped his mouth with the back of his hand, his eyes worried. If they had been playing poker, Falcon thought, he would have had the look of a man drawing to an inside straight with his last dollar in the pot.

"As they say, MacCallister, curiosity killed the cat."

Falcon shrugged. "I'd be worried if I was a cat. But I'm not. I am, however, a friend of John Chisum's and John Tunstall's, and I will be very disappointed if anything happens to either of them. Do you understand me, Evans?"

Evans glared with hate as he reached in his pocket and threw a couple of coins on the table. He got up and stalked out of the Hole without a backward glance.

Falcon took the money and gave it to Garrett. "I couldn't hear what you said, bossman," Pat told him, "but I'd say you put a sizeable burr under Jesse Evans's saddle just now."

"I hope so, Pat. I gave him some advice that I hope he takes."

"That wouldn't be about him shopping for cattle on Chisum's and Tunstall's spreads, would it?"

Falcon looked at Pat.

Pat shrugged. "I've been hearing things."

Falcon laughed. "The way people have been hearing things around here, you'd think this was a ladies' sewing circle instead of a saloon."

Just then, the Kid walked through the batwings, looking back over his shoulder at the departing Jesse Evans.

"Howdy Falcon, Pat."

"Hello, Kid," Falcon said.

"I just saw Jesse Evans leavin' here with an expression like he'd been sucking on lemons."

"Yes. He's been meeting here regularly with Dolan and Murphey from over in Lincoln."

The Kid frowned. "What're they doin' over here? Kind'a long way to come for a drink, isn't it?"

"That's what I've been thinking, too, Kid. Seems those three and Sheriff Brady like to come over here to talk business, two, maybe three times a week."

The Kid scowled. "That Sheriff Brady is crooked as a snake's trail. Mr. Tunstall tells me he's been trying to serve some papers on him and Mr. McSween about some old cattle deal or something."

Falcon's gaze became thoughtful. "Kind of makes you wonder what a sheriff and supposedly respectable businessmen have to do with a known outlaw like Jesse Evans, doesn't it?"

"I don't care who they're dancin' with, long as they leave my boss alone," the Kid snarled.

"What are you doing here in the middle of the day, Kid? Aren't you supposed to be working?" Falcon asked.

"Yeah, but the boss is staying out at the ranch and doesn't need me to watch his back out there. He asked me to come in to town and invite you out for dinner tonight. He wants to have a palaver with you."

"What about?"

"Beats me. He just told me to bring you back, if you're willin'."

Falcon shrugged. "I don't see any reason why not. I haven't had a home-cooked meal in quite a while. Is the cook out at the Rio Feliz any good?"

"She's a Mexican señora, wife of one of the vaqueros Mr. Tunstall uses to herd the beeves. Weighs about three hundred pounds and cooks a steak so tender you don't need a knife to cut it."

"Then let's go. The sooner we get there, the sooner we eat."

The Kid hesitated. "Uh, Falcon, you might want to go and put on a clean coat, spruce up a bit."

Falcon raised his eyebrows. "For supper?"

The Kid shrugged. "It's some custom the boss brought over here from England. He says they always 'dress for dinner' over there."

Falcon shook his head. "The man has a lot to learn about life in the West," he murmured to himself.

Eleven

Falcon saddled Diablo and the Kid rode the sorrel Tunstall had given him and they set off for the Rio Feliz ranch about an hour before dusk.

As they rode, Falcon asked, "By the way, Kid, how did Tunstall's ranch come by the name Rio Feliz?"

"The ranch is bounded by the Feliz River, a small, spring-fed branch off the Pecos River. Since it's spring-fed, it has water in it all summer, even in times of drought, so they called it the Feliz, which means happy or lucky in Mexican lingo."

Falcon nodded. "That's certainly something to be happy about in this country." He glanced around at the desert-like sand and gravel, with its creosote and mesquite bushes and frequent low-lying cacti. "Hell, even a horned toad would have trouble finding a drink out here when the summer heat's on."

After a ride of forty-five minutes, they crested a small hillock and crossed the boundary of the Rio Feliz ranch.

The Kid reined his mount to a halt. "Hold on a minute, Falcon. Lookie over there." He pointed to where a small dust cloud was rising against the setting sun.

Falcon shaded his eyes with his hand. He could see a group of men cutting about fifteen steers out of a larger group. "Looks like some of Tunstall's drovers are moving some of his beeves."

The Kid shook his head. "Trouble is, ain't no one supposed to be in this part of the range today. All the punchers are workin' over on the eastern side, not the western one."

Warning bells sounded in Falcon's mind. He wondered if the trouble he had been expecting between Tunstall and Chisum and the Dolan group was about to start. "You think we're looking at some rustlers?"

"I don't see no other explanation," the Kid said, his face hard, covered with hatred.

Falcon reached into his saddlebag and brought out a pair of binoculars, focusing them on the riders who could be seen herding a small group of cattle in the distance. He saw that one of the men was Jesse Evans, wearing the same shirt he had worn in The Drinking Hole.

"I think you're right, Kid, unless Tunstall has hired Jesse Evans. That's him, and some of the men I've seen him hanging around with over in Fort Sumner."

The Kid's eyes narrowed. "Then, these are gonna be the last cattle that hombre ever steals from my boss!"

He pulled a Winchester carbine out of his saddle boot and looked over at Falcon, spitting in the dirt before speaking.

"Why don't you wait right here, Falcon? This ain't a job you signed on for."

Falcon pulled his own .4440 carbine out of his saddle boot and shucked a shell into the chamber. "Don't be dumb, Kid. I count at least ten riders in that group." He grinned. "That makes the odds about right for the two of us, but a bit much for one man."

The Kid's eyes took on a strange, feverish light, and his lips curled up in the grin Falcon had come to know meant danger. Falcon realized that the Kid seemed to enjoy situations where blood was likely to be spilled.

"Then let's ride, pardner," the Kid snarled out of the side of his mouth.

Instinctively, both men turned their broncs to the west, to circle around and come at the rustlers with the setting sun at their backs, seeking any advantage they could get against superior numbers.

When they were about two hundred yards from the riders Falcon pulled Diablo to a halt and brought out a short, doublebarreled Greener ten gauge shotgun. He broke it open and checked the loads, then snapped it shut and slung it over his shoulder by a rawhide strap affixed to the barrel and stock. He put an extra ten rounds in his coat pockets, unhooked the hammer thong on his Colt pistols, and nodded at the Kid. He was ready to do battle, to the death.

Falcon and the Kid both brought their carbines to their shoulders and aimed. "I'll take the left riders, you take the right," Falcon said.

Almost as one, the two carbines exploded, kicking back and sending foot-long spears of flame into the darkening light.

Seconds later, Falcon saw two riders throw their arms up, blown out of their saddles, to fall and be trampled by the milling herd of cattle.

The Kid and Falcon put spurs to mounts and charged, flicking the levers of their carbines as they rode to put fresh shells in the firing chambers.

Falcon leaned low over Diablo's neck, to make a smaller target when the return fire started. He could hear the big stallion snorting and grunting as he galloped as fast as the wind toward the rustlers.

Jesse Evans saw his men fall and whirled his horse to see what had happened. He recognized the charging riders and screamed at his remaining men.

"Yo! We got company comin'!"

He pulled his rifle out of his saddle boot, put it to his shoulder, and began to fire as fast as he could pull the trigger and jerk the lever.

Mack Maloney and Joey Jacobs, the two men closest to Evans, pulled pistols, leaned over the necks of their broncs, and rode at full tilt toward Falcon and the Kid, firing over their horses' heads.

A bullet tore through the shoulder padding on Falcon's suit just as he pulled the trigger on his carbine. His bullet sped through the air, entered Joey Jacobs' left eye, and blew out the back of his head, knocking him backward out of his saddle.

A moment later, the Kid's slug tore into Mack Maloney's chest, shattering his breast bone and ricocheting into his heart, stopping it before Mack knew he was hit. He grunted, spitting frothy blood from grimacing lips, and slumped in his saddle.

Evans pointed to Indian Bob, a half-breed Mescalero outlaw who rode with him, and yelled, "Kill those bastards!"

Indian Bob and Curley Monroe both whirled their mounts around and charged toward the Kid and Falcon.

Falcon's carbine clicked on an empty chamber. "Damn!" he muttered. He was out of ammunition. In one motion, without slowing his horse, he booted the carbine and swung the Greener express gun around on its strap to his shoulder.

Indian Bob's pistol fired from thirty yards, the bullet nicking Diablo's ear and scorching a shallow groove in Falcon's thigh. He eared back the hammers on the Greener and fired both barrels from the hip without aiming.

The big gun exploded, kicking back and almost unseating Falcon with the force of the twin 10 gauge shells filled with 00-buckshot. The .38 caliber size balls of lead flew in a deadly swarm toward Indian Bob. The molten slugs tore the left half of his horse's head off, then continued on and took off Indian Bob's left arm and leg at the joints, whirling him around and scattering bloody body parts into the desert sand. His body catapulted off his bronc to land in a *cholla* cactus, but he was beyond feeling any pain by then.

Curley Monroe's Smith and Wesson American pistol fired at the Kid from point blank range as the two riders closed on each other. Monroe's slugs tore into the Kid's Stetson, sending it flying from his head.

Without even ducking the Kid aimed and pulled the trigger on his Colt. The hammer fell on an empty chamber.

Closer now, Curley Monroe grinned, seeing the Kid's gun was empty, and slowed his mount as he aimed at the Kid's chest for another shot.

Faster than a striking rattler, the Kid drew with his left hand and fired two quick shots, snapping them off left-handed without aiming.

One of the slugs buzzed by Curley's head, making him jerk to the side just in time to meet the other bullet as it entered his jaw, tearing the bone from his face, leaving nothing below his upper teeth but bloody tissue. He tried to scream in pain, but his throat was no longer there to make a sound.

As he rode by Falcon, holding his ruined face in his hands, Falcon swung the empty Greener by the barrel, hitting Curley in the forehead with the stock, crushing his skull and putting his lights out for good.

Evans and his two remaining hands turned their mounts around and leaned over their necks as they ran for their lives.

Billy sighted on the back of Evans' head and pulled the trigger on his Colt, but the bullet failed, a misfire, saving Evans' life . . . for the moment.

Falcon took his bandanna off and wrapped it around Diablo's ear, which was oozing blood. The furrow in his thigh wasn't bleeding at all, the heat of the bullet having cauterized the gash.

He walked Diablo over to the Kid, who was resting his sorrel next to the bloody remains of Indian Bob, entangled in the cholla cactus.

Falcon took out a stogie and lighted it with a lucifer. After he puffed it to life, he glanced down at what remained of Indian Bob and shook his head.

"Tough luck, fellah. I suspect a thing like that'll ruin your entire afternoon."

Twelve

Falcon almost laughed at the expression on Dick Brewer's face as he and the Kid rode up to the Rio Feliz ranch house. Brewer was sitting on the front porch drinking coffee and smoking when they came within the light from several lanterns on the porch supports.

He jumped up and ran to the door. "Mr. Tunstall, come quick! It's the Kid, and he's got a whole passel of bodies with him!"

Tunstall came to the door, pipe in hand, and gave Falcon a quizzical look when he saw the horses with dead men thrown over the saddles strung out behind him.

"Good evening, Mr. MacCallister. You and the Kid have some trouble?"

Falcon smiled, thinking Tunstall was just like all the other men from England he had met . . . aloof, imperturbable, and prone to understatement. Well, he would beat him at his own game.

"Good evening, John," Falcon replied as he dismounted. "No, no trouble. Why do you ask?"

Tunstall took the pipe from his mouth and pointed it at Diablo. "I see you've wrapped your kerchief around your horse's ear, and I notice a tear in your right trouser leg. I suspect there's been foul play of some sort."

Falcon laughed. No one could best the British at being laconic.

"Well, John, I see what you mean. These men," Falcon said, pointing over his shoulder at the bodies on the horses, "were rustling some of your cattle. They had the misfortune to try and do it in front of the Kid and me."

The Kid swung his leg over the saddle horn and jumped to the ground, eyes bright with excitement.

"These galoots're part of Jesse Evans's gang, boss. He was with the rustlers and seemed to be callin' the shots."

Tunstall nodded, thoughtfully. "And Evans got away?"

"Yes," Falcon said, "along with two or three of his men. They weren't too happy about the welcome the Kid and I gave them."

"Dick, would you get Juan and some of the boys to take care of . . . this mess, please? And have Carlos come and take a look at Mr. MacCallister's horse's ear, if you would."

"Yes, sir," Brewer replied, looking at the Kid and smiling.

Falcon saw the Kid return the smile. He remembered the Kid telling him that he and Brewer had become very good friends over the past couple of weeks and had taken to spending their off days together, fishing and sparking the ladies of nearby towns.

"Falcon, why don't you and the Kid come into the house? Dinner is ready, and Marguerite will be very disappointed if we let it get cold," Tunstall said.

As they walked in he added, "I've asked Dick Brewer to join us, if you don't mind. I've some ranch business to discuss with you, and he can help apprise you of the situation we're facing here."

The four of them sat down to a huge feast of enchiladas, beans, steaks, sliced tomatoes, and corn on the cob. Tunstall forbade any talk of business until they had all eaten their fill.

Falcon noticed that the Kid was ravenous, and ate like he was half starved. It was a reaction to killing someone he had seen before, both in the war and afterward out west. Some men became nauseated after a gun battle, others became very hungry, while some sought out the company of women for furious lovemaking. It was as if, in the face of death, they sought somehow to reaffirm being alive, and the fact of having survived.

Falcon, for his part, felt a strange sadness at the wasting of precious life, no matter how worthless the men he killed were. The taking away of all a man was, or could ever hope to be, by pulling a trigger and ending his life was an experience he didn't much like, even if the men brought it upon themselves.

After dinner, as Tunstall called it, the men gathered in his study, where he passed out cigars and brandy to Falcon and Brewer, and lemonade and a plate of sugar cookies to the Kid.

Tunstall settled himself behind a large, oaken desk, fiddled with his pipe until he had it going to his satisfaction, then held up his brandy glass.

"I drink a toast to you, Falcon and Kid, for saving my cattle from those desperadoes led by Jesse Evans. You have my gratitude."

Falcon drank his brandy, then lighted his cigar and leaned back in his chair, waiting for Tunstall to come to the point of the meeting.

"Falcon, I think you know some of what has been going on between the Dolan faction in Lincoln, and John Chisum and myself."

Falcon nodded. "The way I understand it, Murphey and Dolan pretty much had things their own way here with their store and their government contracts to supply beef to the Mescalero Indian tribes until you and Chisum decided to go into competition with them."

"That is correct. Just recently, Dolan bought out Murphey when he became despondent over the death of his previous partner, Colonel Fritz. Fritz and Murphey, a few years back, were instrumental in getting Major William Brady, who served under them in the army, elected as sheriff of Lincoln County."

Falcon nodded. Now he understood why Brady was under obligation to the Dolan faction, and why he was a frequent guest of theirs for lunch at The Drinking Hole.

"What about the state authorities? Can you go to them for help?" Falcon asked.

Dick Brewer snorted. "Not hardly. In addition to having the sheriff under their control, the Dolan gang has widespread influence in Santa Fe, with a group known as the Santa Fe Ring. These are powerful money men who practically control the state government, especially as regards the awarding of governmental contracts."

Tunstall paused to relight his pipe and refill his brandy glass, motioning Brewer to continue.

"Besides having the Santa Fe Ring and all its power behind him, Dolan also has the backing of the judge of the third district Warren Bristol, and the district attorney, William Rynerson."

Falcon looked at Tunstall. "And against this group stands only yourself and John Chisum?"

Tunstall nodded. "And of course, our lawyer, Alexander McSween."

"What about the other ranchers around here? Won't any of them stand with you?"

Tunstall shrugged. "Some will, those who've been treated bad by Dolan's store, but most are afraid that if they go up against Dolan they won't have anyone to buy their cattle, and the very low prices Dolan pays are better than nothing."

"I see. Well, John, what is it you want from me?"

Tunstall leaned forward, his elbows on his desk. "We have an opportunity. Since Dolan bought out Murphey, he's taken John Riley, his old overseer, in as a partner and promoted Billy Matthews to his second in command. I think it is Billy Matthews who has hired Jesse Evans and his gang to raid my and Chisum's herds."

Tunstall reached across the desk to refill Falcon's glass.

"I want you to come in with Chisum and me against these cattle thieves and help us defeat them. We need every man who is good with a gun to stand alongside us."

Falcon shook his head. "I'm sorry, John, but this affair is none of my business."

He held up his hand as Tunstall started to protest. "Like I say, I'm just a saloon owner, and I don't know how long I'm going to be staying in the area. But I will say this if I'm ever in a position to help you out or to make things a little more even I will do all in my power to do so."

"Will you testify along with the Kid that it was Evans who tried to steal my cattle?"

"Absolutely. And I'll make sure Sheriff Brady arrests him for it. Perhaps if he faces enough time in jail he can be made to tell who hired him to rob you, and who he was selling the cattle to."

"With Judge Bristol on the bench, Evans will probably never be convicted, but I guess that's about all we can do."

Falcon stood up. "Thanks for the excellent dinner, John. I've been getting awfully tired of hotel food lately."

"Say, Falcon, that reminds me. There is a little spread over on the Ruidosa River. The owner fell off his horse a few months back and broke his neck. His widow, Mary Smithers, has been talking about moving to town if she can find someone to lease the place. She's got a wonderful Mexican cook working for her, a cousin to my cook, Marguerite."

Falcon smiled. "I'll certainly look into it, John. Anything's better than living in one room in a hotel."

He walked out and found Diablo tied to the hitching rail, a white bandage on his ear.

He stepped into the stirrup and climbed into the saddle, tipping his hat.

"Adios, John. I'll see you in town tomorrow, Kid, and we can go to the sheriff and tell him about Evans."

Thirteen

Though the autumn days were getting quite cool, Sheriff William Brady was sweating. Falcon thought he had never seen a man dance around a question so much.

Brady took off his hat and sleeved sweat off his forehead. "I don't think Judge Bristol will issue an arrest warrant for a man on such flimsy evidence," he said, as he sat at his desk and avoided meeting Falcon's eyes.

Falcon glanced at the Kid, who was standing next to him and becoming angrier by the minute. He winked, trying to get the Kid to cool off and not cause any trouble. He wanted the matter to be handled as diplomatically as possible.

"Sheriff Brady, I don't believe you need a judge to sign an arrest warrant in this case. After all, you have two witnesses who saw Evans commit a crime, and known friends and associates of his were killed during said crime. According to the law, that's evidence enough for you to arrest the man and put him in jail."

Brady shook his head. "I don't know. I'd better talk to the judge, or the district attorney, Mr. Rynerson."

Falcon narrowed his eyes, and his voice got hard. "I can see that you are not going to do your duty, Sheriff."

He turned to the Kid. "Come on, Kid, let's go over to the telegraph office and wire the governor's office like you suggested in the first place."

Brady looked up, eyes wide. "Now hold on, gents. You don't have to do anything like that. I didn't say I wouldn't do it."

The Kid spoke up from the doorway where he was standing. "Hey, Falcon, there's Evans's horse now. It's tied up down in front of Dolan's store."

Falcon unhooked the hammer thong on his Colts.

"Come on, Kid. Let's go have a talk with Mr. Evans. I don't rightly appreciate someone shooting at us while trying to rustle cattle on my friend's ranch."

Brady jumped to his feet. "Wait a minute! You two can't just go up and brace a man in my town. He's liable to go for his gun—"

The Kid snarled, "That's what we hope he'll do. Then we won't have to hang around waiting for you to get off your butt and do your job."

Brady stood there for a moment, and Falcon thought he could almost hear the man thinking. He was certainly between a rock and a hard place—he knew they would kill Evans if he didn't arrest him.

Finally, he shrugged and got his hat off a rack. "All right, gentlemen. I'll put Mr. Evans under arrest. But I doubt he'll be convicted on your testimony alone."

"Not in Judge Bristol's court. But we're going to see if we can get the U.S. Marshals to take him over to Ruidosa, to stand trial where he doesn't have so many . . . business associates," Falcon said, enjoying the look it brought to Brady's face.

Falcon and the Kid followed the sheriff as he walked down the boardwalk to Dolan's store. When they entered they found Jesse Evans and two other men sitting at a table in the back, talking to James Dolan and John Riley.

When Evans saw Falcon and the Kid with Brady, he jumped up and grabbed for his pistol. Before he could clear leather, he found himself facing the drawn guns of both Falcon and the Kid.

Brady stepped between the men, his hands in the air. "Now hold on. Everyone just calm down."

Dolan stood up. "What is the meaning of this intrusion, Sheriff Brady?"

"These two say they saw Jesse attempting to rustle cattle off Tunstall's ranch last night, Mr. Dolan."

Dolan stared at Falcon, a slight smile forming on his lips. "Why, that couldn't be true," he said. "Jesse was with me last night. We were talking business until late in the evening."

The Kid, his voice rising, said, "You're a liar, Dolan! We killed most of his men, and the yellow-bellied coward ran for cover like a scalded dog!"

"Why you—" Evans started to say, shutting his mouth when the Kid eared back the hammer on his Colt and raised it to point directly at his face.

"Go on, you lowdown cur. Give me a reason," the Kid said, his eyes blazing and his lips grinning.

Falcon stepped forward, a thoughtful look on his face. "I was there, Mr. Dolan, so I know you aren't telling the truth. I wonder why someone would deliberately lie to protect a cattle rustler, unless he was somehow involved in the matter himself."

"Are you accusing me of—" Dolan started to say, until Sheriff Brady interrupted him.

"Take it easy, Mr. Dolan. I've got to arrest Jesse and take him to jail. Then, we'll let Judge Bristol decide what to do about all this."

Dolan relaxed and sat back down at the table. "That's right, Sheriff. This is a matter best handled by the judge."

"I'm not goin' to let him put me behind bars," Evans said.

"Calm down, Jesse," Dolan said. "We'll take care of this. I'm sure the judge will realize there's been some mistake made."

"You're the one who's made the mistake, Dolan," Falcon

said. "I'm going to ride over to Ruidosa and see if I can get the U.S. Marshals to take a hand in this affair. You and your cronies on the bench and in the district attorney's office had better watch yourselves. One way or the other, justice will be done."

As Brady took Evans's pistols from him and walked him toward the jail, Falcon and the Kid could see the sheriff talking rapidly to the gunman, no doubt telling him not to worry that the judge would let him go.

"Kid, I'm going to ride over to Ruidosa and talk to the marshals over there, and while I'm in the area I'm going to see about leasing that ranchito Mr. Tunstall told me about. You head on back to the Rio Feliz and tell John what's going on."

"All right, Falcon. But if Brady lets Evans out of jail, I'm gonna kill him."

"Settle down, Kid. Don't go off half-cocked. We've got the law on our side, so don't do anything foolish."

The Kid nodded. "I'll see you when you get back."

Falcon was disappointed to find out the U.S. Marshals wouldn't intervene in a local matter of Lincoln County unless there was obvious malfeasance at the trial. They refused to move Evans to Ruidosa, but promised that if he were let go under suspicious circumstances, they would take action.

On his way back to Fort Sumner, Falcon stopped off at the Smithers' ranch. It was a small cabin, nestled in a grove of pine trees on the very banks of the Ruidosa River. He talked to Mrs. Smithers, a middle-aged woman who looked tired and worn out from trying to run the small spread without her husband.

She agreed to rent the place to Falcon while she tried to find a buyer for it. They settled on a price, and he asked if the cook would be willing to stay and keep house and cook for him. She said she would, so the deal was struck.

Falcon accompanied Mrs. Smithers into Fort Sumner and arranged to have his clothes and personal items sent out to the ranch.

Now, he thought, *maybe I can get back to running my saloon and doing a little gambling. I'm tired of mixing in other people's business, though it would be nice to see Dolan and his cronies brought down a notch or two.* He shook his head as he walked into The Drinking Hole. John Tunstall was a good man, but Falcon just didn't know if he was tough enough for the West, where might made right more often than not, and the rule of law was secondary to who had the upper hand.

Fourteen

Less than a week after Jesse Evans's arrest, James Dolan called a meeting of his friends and associates. They met in a back room of his La Placita store in Lincoln. Present were Dolan, John Riley, Billy Matthews, Sheriff William Brady, and Judge Warren Bristol.

"Bill, have you taken care of Evans yet?"

Sheriff Brady smiled and nodded. "Yeah. Earlier tonight, someone broke in the jail while I was over at the hotel having supper and busted him out."

Dolan nodded. "I assume he'll be at the usual place should I need him."

"Yes, sir."

"Good, 'cause I will have need of his services in the next few days."

Dolan looked over at Judge Bristol, who sat in a corner, quietly fuming.

"Warren, I need a favor."

The judge looked up resentfully. "Dammit, Jimmy, you shouldn't have called me to come over here. You know there'll be hell to pay if anyone finds out I'm working with you."

"Your share of the Dolan Enterprises money ought to make up for any trouble I cause you, Warren. Now quit your whining, I need some legal advice."

Bristol took a pipe from his suit coat and began fussing

with it, filling it with a wad of tobacco that smelled bad even before he lighted it. "Go on, I'm listening."

"I need some legal way to get at Tunstall. I need some excuse to serve a writ on him, something that will let me tie up his business for a while. His store and bank are beginning to really cut into my . . . I mean our, profits.

Riley, Dolan's second in command of his operation, snorted. "Hell, Jimmy, I don't know why you don't just send Evans and his gang out to Tunstall's ranch and burn the bastard out."

Dolan shook his head. "John, I know you favor the direct approach, but the days are gone when we could get away with something like that. First of all, Tunstall's hired too many good guns of his own. That Rio Feliz Ranch looks more like a fort than a cattle operation."

He paused to take a long, black stogie out of his coat and light it. As he trailed smoke from his nostrils toward the ceiling, he added, "Besides, too many of the smaller ranchers around here are beginning to side with Tunstall, and his letters to the Mesilla *Independent* newspaper about Sheriff Brady's diversion of some of their tax monies are beginning to get some attention in Santa Fe, attention we don't need right now. We need to try a more subtle approach."

Bristol lighted his pipe and sucked on it, blowing out pungent blue clouds of smoke as he thought. After a moment he looked up, a satisfied grin on his face.

"Say, Jimmy, didn't you tell me you once hired that lawyer that works for Tunstall, Alexander McSween, to collect on a life insurance policy of Colonel Fritz's?"

Dolan's eyes narrowed, "Yeah. He went up to New York and got a check for a little over seven thousand dollars. I told him I should get the money, as I was successor to L.G. Murphey and Company, but he put it in his account. He said he would pay it out when the legal heirs were determined."

Bristol sat back and spread his hands and smiled. "Well, there you are."

Dolan frowned. "I don't understand. How does my fight with McSween help me to get to Tunstall?"

"There is a little known law in New Mexico called joint and several liability. That means, if McSween owes you money and can't pay, and he is partners with Tunstall, you can attach Tunstall's property to pay McSween's debt. With that, and those notes you bought up that John Chisum owes on, you can tie up the entire Tunstall and Chisum operation."

Dolan nodded. "I'm beginning to see the light here, Judge. Now, here's what we're gonna do . . ."

On December twenty-first, Dolan took the affidavit signed by Judge Bristol to his business associate, District Attorney Rynerson, to effect the arrest of Alexander McSween on a charge of embezzlement and a note of summary judgment against John Chisum.

Dolan waited until McSween and his wife, accompanied by John Chisum, set out on a trip to St. Louis. Dolan then wired the sheriff of San Miguel County to detain the McSweens and Chisum. He wanted them out of the way while he took on Tunstall.

Chisum, who refused to answer the complaints, was jailed, receiving a sentence of eight days. McSween made bail and headed back toward Lincoln.

With Chisum and McSween out of the picture, Dolan had Sheriff Brady levy an attachment on Tunstall's bank and store, stating that since McSween owned part of them, they could take the two as part payment on his debt.

McSween arrived back in Lincoln and was immediately arrested and put in jail by Sheriff Brady, to be released only upon pledging of enough property to cover the amount he supposedly owed to J.J. Dolan.

Tunstall, with the Kid as his bodyguard, came to town

and pledged a number of cattle and horses, which he was to deliver to town the next day.

On their way back to Rio Feliz, Tunstall and the Kid stopped in at The Drinking Hole, and sat down with Falcon MacCallister.

Falcon ordered whiskey for Tunstall and sarsaparilla for the Kid.

"I hear you've been busy of late, John," Falcon said.

"Yes. That damned James Dolan is trying every sneaky legal trick in the book to start a war with John Chisum and me."

The Kid took a deep swallow of his carbonated drink, burped once, then said, "I say we give it to him, boss. Between us and Chisum's men, we got plenty of firepower to take on the whole Dolan gang."

"It may well come to that, Billy. But with John Chisum still in jail up in Mesilla, his brothers won't allow his cowboys to join in our fight until they get John's permission."

Falcon realized that the tensions he had noted on his arrival in the area were coming to a boil. There was going to be bloodshed before too long.

"So, John, what do you intend to do?" Falcon asked.

Tunstall shrugged. "I'll just have to play along for a while, until Chisum and I can get together and decide what to do. Meantime, I must take some cattle and horses into Lincoln tomorrow to try to get Alex McSween out of jail."

"I say to hell with 'em," The Kid snarled in his boyish voice. "We ought 'a give 'em lead instead of beeves."

"I will not have a single man killed over a few cattle," Tunstall said, firmly. "I will play along with their legal games, and pursue the matter in the courts. Dolan will not prevail if we can get the lawsuit heard in an impartial venue."

"Do you need some help tomorrow?" Falcon asked.

Tunstall smiled. "No, but thank you for the offer, Falcon. I plan to take Billy here along as my guard, and some other men from the ranch to herd the cattle. I'm sure it will all go smoothly."

The Kid looked at Falcon and grinned his dangerous grin. "I just hope they try and start some trouble. I'll be ready for 'em if they do, an' I'll make 'em wish they had never been born."

That same night, Dolan had Billy Matthews fetch Jesse Evans and some of his gang to his store. Evans arrived, along with Frank Baker, Tom Hill, George Hindman, Johnny Hurley, "Buckshot" Roberts, Manuel "the Indian" Segovia, and William "Buck" Morton.

"Boys," Dolan said after passing out bottles of whiskey to the hardened gunmen, "tomorrow, John Tunstall is going to be bringing in some cattle and horses to turn over to me to get his lawyer, McSween, out of jail."

Evans pulled the cork from his bottle and took a deep swig. "I hope the Kid is with him. I have a score to settle with that bastard."

"You'll get your chance. Tunstall never goes anywhere without Bonney. But whatever it takes, I don't want Tunstall and those cattle to make it to Lincoln. I intend to keep possession of his store and bank."

"What do you want us to do?" Evans asked.

"It would be worth a great deal of money to me if, by some happenstance, Tunstall were to suffer an accident and be killed," Dolan said.

Buck Morton grinned, showing yellow, rotten teeth. "Consider it done, Mr. Dolan."

"Of course, there should be no witnesses left who can testify to the matter."

"There won't be nobody left who can say we didn't act in self-defense."

Dolan stood and offered a toast. "Then goodnight, gentlemen, and good hunting tomorrow."

Fifteen

As the Kid helped drive the small herd of cattle and horses toward Lincoln he thought about how much he had liked working for John Tunstall at the Rio Feliz Ranch, although the Englishman had some peculiar habits. He was always stiff and mannerly, and his speech was so odd it made some of the other ranchhands laugh . . . men like Fred Waite, John Middleton, Charley Bowdre, and Dick Brewer. But this trouble between Tunstall and the Santa Fe Ring, headed by Jimmy Dolan and John Riley, was no laughing matter.

Kid knew Dolan had hired as many as twenty-two gunmen and outlaws . . . bad men the likes of Jesse Evans, Billy Morton, and Tom Hill, according to folks around Lincoln—and everyone, including John Tunstall, expected shooting to start at any time. Tunstall had warned all his ranchhands to keep their guns handy, even though he was a peaceloving man who did not want bloodshed.

Down deep, the Kid figured there was no way to avoid flying lead before the difficulties were settled. Changing his name from Antrim to Bonney after the shooting at Fort Grant in Arizona Territory had not changed his character. He was fiercely loyal to those who befriended him, and he was ready to stand with John Tunstall no matter the odds or the cost.

* * *

The Kid rode his best sorrel pony, the one John Tunstall had given him when he was first hired, flanking the horse herd along with Middleton, Dick Brewer, Charley Bowdre, Fred Waite, and Henry Brown. Tunstall rode at the front on a good bay stud, leading them toward the Penasco River crossing. This was rough, brushy country, hard on horses and men.

Waite rode up beside the Kid. He glanced over his shoulder and said, "Every now an' then appears we got somebody followin' us. Can't say for sure."

The Kid examined their backtrail. "Don't see a thing, Fred, only they could be tryin' to stay hid, whoever it is."

"You know damn well who it'll be. Jimmy Dolan an' Jesse Evans, prob'ly Billy Morton an' Tom Hill. They ain't nothin' but hired killers, every damn one of 'em."

"Mr. Tunstall acts worried," the Kid agreed. "He wouldn't be givin' up these horses an' beeves so easy if he wasn't scared we'll be in a war with them Santa Fe boys."

Waite looked backward again. "I can feel trouble comin', an' when I get that feelin' I ain't hardly ever wrong, like when my knee hurts just afore it rains."

"You sound like an old woman with the rheumatiz," the Kid said, grinning.

"I ain't funnin' you. All week long I've had this real bad feelin'."

"You worry too damn much. If Morton or Evans or any of that bunch shows up, we'll just shoot 'em down."

Waite looked at the Kid's pistol. "You any good with that thing?"

"I've killed a man or two, if that's what you're askin'. I shot this big-mouth horseshoer down in Camp Grant when he called me out."

"You did? You actually killed him?"

"Deader'n a gate hinge. He was big. Thought he was tough. I showed him otherwise. A gun is a funny thing, Fred. It ain't nothin' but a piece of iron, but if you use it right it makes all men equal."

"I never knowed you shot somebody dead, Kid."

"I ain't braggin' about it. Just made mention of it so you'd know I ain't just carryin' it on my hip for decoration. I can shoot, if the need arises."

Waite turned back again, scanning the horizon. "Looks like I seen 'em again just now . . . four or five riders. If you look real close you can see the dust from the horses' hooves risin' on the wind."

The Kid couldn't see any dust. "Quit you're damn worryin', Fred. We've got big John Middleton an' Dick Brewer with us. We can handle trouble if it shows up."

They heard a shout coming from the front of the herd. Dick Brewer was standing in his stirrups. "Wild turkeys, boys! Let's go hunt down our supper!"

Waite grinned. "A roasted turkey dinner does sound mighty nice. Let's see if we can down a couple."

"Suits hell outta me," the Kid replied, reaching for his Winchester .44 rifle booted to the front of his saddle.

They took off at a trot toward the tops of a string of low hills thick with brush, following Brewer and Middleton and Charley Bowdre.

The Kid jacked a shell into the firing chamber of his rifle and watched the brushy hilltops.

"Don't see a damn thing," Waite said, urging his horse to a faster trot.

"Me neither," the Kid replied, wondering what it was Fred had seen.

Waite pointed down to the horse herd and John Tunstall riding at the front. "You reckon the bossman won't mind if we leave him for a spell?"

"I'd imagine he'd be just as happy to have turkey as the rest of us."

They came to the top of the first rocky hills and saw John Middleton spurring his horse to a gallop.

"Yonder they go!" Bowdre cried, pointing the barrel of his rifle at a pair of wild turkey hens flying low over the tops of the sagebrush.

"Supper time!" Waite cried, asking his horse for a hard run over the hilltop.

The Kid had forgotten to look back at the horse herd for the moment, intent upon the turkey hunt. Only seconds later he heard a gunshot coming from behind him.

He jerked his sorrel to a sliding halt and turned back to the valley leading to the Penasco. What he saw made his blood run cold.

Four men on horseback were charging toward Tunstall from the rear, and seven more came galloping from the north, from the direction of the river. Rifle barrels and pistols gleamed in the late day sun.

"Hold up, Fred!" the Kid cried. "Look down there! If I ain't mistaken that's Jesse Evans an' that bastard Billy Morton, coming after Mr. Tunstall with drawn guns!"

"Son of a bitch!" Waite cried, swinging his horse around. "What are we gonna do, Kid?"

"We've gotta ride back an' help Mr. Tunstall."

"But look, Kid! They've got us outnumbered. We'll get our heads shot off."

The Kid saw riders coming from both directions. "We can't just leave him down there. They'll kill him for sure if we don't do something—"

"This ain't our fight, Kid. I say we stay out of it. Maybe Evans an' his bunch are only after the horses."

"They wouldn't have brought so many men," the Kid replied, squinting in the sun's late glare. "They aim to do Mr. Tunstall harm, or they wouldn't have needed to bring along a whole damn army."

"Let's stay out of it, Kid."

"I ain't made that way . . ."

Just as he said it, the Kid saw one of the lead riders coming from the north take aim at John Tunstall. The crack of a bullet resounded off the hills.

Tunstall fell off his horse, collapsing in the dirt as most of the horse herd scattered.

"Sweet Jesus!" Waite exclaimed. "They shot Mr. Tunstall down in cold blood!"

"Just like I figured they would," the Kid snapped, pulling his rifle to his shoulder. "We gotta do somethin' to help him or he's dead, for sure."

"They'll come after us," Waite warned.

"Let the sumbitches come," the Kid said as a strange calm came over him. "I ain't scared of Jesse Evans or Morton or none of them gunslicks."

Off to the east, John Middleton and Charley Bowdre were watching the affair. Dick Brewer was nowhere in sight.

The Kid saw Tunstall squirm in the dust and rocks, holding his belly. "He's gutshot. He's gonna die anyway, most likely, if we don't get him to a doctor."

"But there ain't no doctors this side of Mesilla, Kid. How the hell are we gonna get him there? First off, we'll have to shoot our way down there to run them bastards who work for Dolan off."

"We can do it. There's enough of us."

Waite looked around. "Where's Dick? He's foreman of this outfit. It's his job to tell us what to do."

The Kid wagged his head. "It's our job to help Mr. Tunstall, if we ain't too late."

"We're already too late," Waite protested, pointing down to John Tunstall's writhing form.

The Kid chewed his bottom lip. "We can't just sit here an' watch 'em do this."

Waite swallowed hard. "Jesse Evans is one mean hombre, an' he's got plenty of friends with him. I heard stories from up in Denver that Tom Hill is a backshooter."

"We won't give 'em a shot at our backs, Fred. Let's ride down. Give a signal to the others."

Waite seemed uncertain. Then he gave a wave to Middleton and raised his rifle.

John Middleton shook his head against it . . . he was a quarter mile away, but the Kid could see it clearly.

"The yellow bastard," he whispered. "Are the rest of us gonna let Evans an' his boys kill Mr. Tunstall without puttin' up no fight at all?"

"I ain't goin'," Waite said quietly, unable to look the Kid straight in the eye.

"Mr. Tunstall gave us all a job when nobody else would, an' now you say you won't help him?"

"This job don't pay enough."

Another pistol shot cracked from the shallow valley as one of the horsemen fired down at Tunstall.

"Goddamn!" the Kid said, grinding his teeth. "They're shootin' at a defenseless man."

One of the Dolan riders stepped down, aiming a pistol at Tunstall's head.

"Look!" said the Kid, his voice like sand. "They same as executed Mr. Tunstall. He ain't even got his gun out."

"Leave it be, Kid," Waite warned. "This ain't our fight in the first place . . . it's between Mr. Tunstall an' Murphy an' Dolan an' them boys in Santa Fe."

"The *hell* it *ain't* our fight! Look at what they's doin' to him . . . leavin' him lyin' on the ground, shooting him like he was a pig at butcherin' time."

"It's a job for the law, Billy Bonney, an' we sure as hell ain't no lawmen. We'll tell what we seen to Sheriff Brady when we get to Lincoln."

"Brady's as crooked as the rest of 'em," the Kid replied savagely. "He's the son of a bitch we oughta shoot."

"We'd go to prison, for sure."

"Not if we killed 'em all. Won't be none of the bastards left to testify against us."

Waite gave the Kid a strange look. "You've got a mean streak in you, Billy, if you mean what you say. You can't just go 'round killin' the law an' everybody else."

"Maybe," the Kid answered

Then a stocky cowboy standing over Tunstall did a

strange thing. He jerked Tunstall's pistol out of his belt and fired two shots into the air.

The Kid said, a question not really meant for Waite: "What was that all about?"

Sixteen

It sickened the Kid when he saw Dolan's men ride away with the horse herd, leaving John Tunstall lying on his back, as still as the rocks and scrub trees around him.

"He's dead for sure," the Kid whispered, heeling his sorrel off the hilltop to ride down to the spot where the Englishman lay in a pool of blood.

"We didn't have no choice, Kid," Waite said, his face the color of snow. "We'd be dead, too, if we tangled with them boys over a few head of horses."

The Kid turned quickly to Waite, anger tightening his jaw. "It wasn't over any damn horses, Fred. It was over a man's life, a good man's life, a man who gave us all a job an' a place to stay an' fed us good. I can't believe you're too dumb to figure that out."

"Don't get all riled up at me, Kid," Waite protested. "All I said was, it wasn't our fight. Besides that, it was up to Dick Brewer to tell us what to do. In case you've forgot, he's ramrod of this outfit."

"Not any more, he ain't," the Kid said quietly, riding closer to Tunstall's motionless form. "We're all out of a job on account of this."

"Leastways, we're still alive," Waite answered.

"To tell the truth, I ain't all that proud to be breathin' right now," the Kid said. "A man's gotta have loyalty to his friends or his life ain't worth spit. We damn sure didn't show no loyalty to Mr. Tunstall.''

Waite lowered his face, hiding his eyes below his hat brim as they rode up on the body.

The Kid swung down, squatting on his haunches to look at Tunstall's face. The Englishman's eyes were open, glazed over with death. His face had been smashed in by bullets at close range. Two bulletholes in his chest seeped blood onto the rocky soil beneath him. His curious derby hat lay in the dust a few feet away.

Suddenly the Kid noticed something, just as Fred Waite got down to stare at the corpse.

"Look here, Fred."

"I can see he's dead, Kid. Don't need to look no closer to be sure."

"That ain't what I'm talkin' about. Look at Mr. Tunstall's pistol. He's got it in his fist . . ."

"Don't see what's so all important 'bout that, Kid. He's got a gun in his hand. Ain't no big deal to me."

"The hell it ain't. You saw the same thing I did while we was sitting up on that ridge. One of Dolan's men bent down an' pulled out Mr. Tunstall's pistol, remember? Then he fired it up in the air two times."

"I remember," Waite said, scratching his beard stubble thoughtfully.

"Some rotten son of a bitch put the gun in Mr. Tunstall's hand after they killed him. They fired his pistol so it'd look like he was shootin' back."

"Hadn't thought of that," Waite agreed.

"That way," the Kid continued, "when Sheriff Brady rides out here to investigate what happened, it's gonna look like Mr. Tunstall was shootin' at Dolan's boys. Dolan may even try to claim Mr. Tunstall fired first. Jimmy Dolan can claim it was self-defense."

"But we seen the whole thing, Kid. Hell, nearly all of us

did. We can set the sheriff straight on how it really happened today."

"If he'll listen."

"I ain't sure what you mean by that, Kid. He can't help but listen to so many of us."

The Kid stood up, watching Middleton and Brown and Brewer and Charley Bowdre come riding toward them from the hills. "I'm convinced Sheriff Brady is in cahoots with Murphy an' Dolan an' Riley. I can't prove a damn thing, only I've seen 'em together too many times, talkin' real quiet. Sometimes that rotten lawyer, Billy Matthews, was with 'em."

"That don't make Sheriff Brady a crook," Waite said, with little conviction in his voice. "I've seen 'em together my own self a few times, over at Beaver Smith's old saloon, the one that stranger named MacCallister took over. The barkeep, a big, tall feller named Garrett, tole me they was in there quite often."

"I know Garrett," replied the Kid. "We're friends, sorta. I met him when he first came to this country. He was flat broke an' said he'd gotten in an argument with his partner somewhere down in Texas an' had to kill him. Claimed it was self-defense, just like Dolan's gonna say happened here today. They're all gonna swear Mr. Tunstall fired first, an' it'll be our word against theirs it didn't happen that way. If Sheriff Brady is an honest lawman, he'll listen to us. But if he's the crook I think he is, won't be no charges filed against Jesse Evans or Billy Morton or Tom Hill . . . none of them boys we saw commit the murder of our friend."

Brewer and Middleton and Bowdre rode up, halting their winded horses a few yards away. Dick Brewer's face was twisted hard.

"He's dead, ain't he?" Brewer asked, looking at the Kid when he spoke.

"Yeah. Me an' Fred saw the whole thing. They shot him down like a dog. Mr. Tunstall hadn't even pulled his pistol."

Brewer frowned. "But he's got it in his fist right now, Kid."

"Evans, or Morton, put it there. One of 'em jerked out Mr: Tunstall's gun an' fired it in the air two times."

"I heard the shots," Brewer remembered. "I was on the far side of them hills when the shootin' started."

"I seen what happened," Middleton said. "The Kid's tellin' it right. They rode up on Tunstall an' shot him off his horse, then one of the bastards shot him in the face an' swung down an' fired the Englishman's pistol twice, straight up in the air."

"They murdered him," Charley Bowdre said. "Billy Morton's gonna claim they was a legal posse, sworn in by Sheriff Brady, an' that Tunstall fired first."

Brewer gave the others a look as Henry Brown rode up on a lathered chestnut. "This is war, boys. Mr. Tunstall was my friend, an' he don't deserve to die like this."

"He sure as hell don't," the Kid agreed.

"I've got an idea," Brewer continued. "We'll ride back to Lincoln an' pay a visit on Justice of the Peace Wilson. We tell him what happened, an' ask him to swear us in as legal deputy constables of Lincoln County. Judge Wilson likes Alexander McSween. We'll ask lawyer McSween to go with us when we see the judge."

"Then what are we gonna do?" Fred Waite asked, hooking his thumbs in his gunbelt.

Brewer's jaw turned to granite. "We'll ask Judge Wilson to give us arrest warrants for Jesse Evans, Billy Morton, Tom Hill, an' anybody else who was with 'em today. Then we'll hunt 'em down an' put 'em in jail up at Mesilla."

"That's sure enough gonna start a war," Waite said. "Dolan an' Riley won't take it lyin' down."

"Who gives a damn?" Brewer snapped.

The Kid nodded his agreement. "We'll kill the sons of bitches who won't come quiet, an' it'll all be nice an' legal. We'll be representin' the law."

"Let's do it," John Middleton said. "As soon as McSween hears what they done to Mr. Tunstall he'll go with us to see Judge Wilson. If the judge will make us all deputies an' gives us warrants for the killers of John Tunstall, we'll make Mr. Jimmy Dolan an' Johnny Riley sorry they ever plotted to kill a good man like this."

Brewer looked around at the others. "Are we all in agreement on it?"

Heads nodded. Fred Waite was last to show his support for the idea.

"Let's head for Mr. McSween's house," Waite said. "If he agrees with us, you can count me in, too."

The Kid turned away from Tunstall's body to climb aboard his horse. He spoke to Brewer when he was in the saddle. "We gotta leave Mr. Tunstall's body just like we found it, so when Sheriff Brady shows up he can see for himself where it happened. But my money says Evans an' Morton are gonna claim Mr. Tunstall fired first."

"Some of us can swear otherwise," Middleton said. "I saw the whole thing. So did the Kid an' Fred."

"I'll swear to the fact it was cold-blooded murder," Waite said, mounting his horse.

Brewer took one last look at their dead friend and employer before he picked up his reins. "Yonder lays a good man, boys, a good friend. I want you all to remember what he looks like layin' in a puddle of blood, for when we go after Morton an' his yellow pardners."

The Kid rode over to Brewer and halted his sorrel. "If it's a war they want, let's give 'em one."

Henry Brown patted the butt of his holstered pistol. "We can give 'em a little dose of their own medicine, an' if Judge Wilson agrees it'll all be nice an' legal."

Brewer gave his companions another lingering look, passing his gaze across their faces. "We'll call ourselves the Regulators, 'cause we're gonna regulate some of the crooked dealin's in this county. We'll cover every inch of

Lincoln County if we have to, until every last one of 'em is behind bars, waitin' to stand trial for the murder of John Tunstall."

"I like it," Middleton said, shaking his head. "Regulators sounds good to me."

The Kid looked north, toward the township of Lincoln. "I don't much give a damn what we call ourselves," he said, speaking in a low voice. "All I care about is gettin' the men who killed our friend."

Brewer swung his horse around. "Let's ride for Lincoln, boys."

The Kid fell in beside Brewer as the others followed them away from the murder scene. Brewer gave the Kid a sideways glance.

"How come you an' Fred didn't ride down an' lend a hand when you seen what they was doin' to Mr. Tunstall?" Brewer asked.

The question struck the Kid like a knife. "We just sat up on that hill like we was froze solid. They'd already shot Mr. Tunstall off his horse before we realized what they aimed to do. I wish I could do things over, even as bad outnumbered as we was. We shoulda done somethin' . . ."

Falcon was sitting at his table, laying out a game of solitaire, when Pat Garrett walked over. Pat leaned down and whispered in his ear, "Falcon, one of the cowboys at the bar said John Tunstall has been shot."

"What? When?" Falcon exclaimed.

"Out on the road to Lincoln. The puncher said it was some of Evans's men that did it. There's a group of Tunstall's friends all gathering at Alexander McSween's house tonight to see what's to be done about it."

Falcon grabbed his hat. "I'd better get on over there and see what's going on. I have a feeling this may lead to a full scale range war."

He walked hurriedly to the livery stable, threw a saddle on Diablo and rode as hard as he could for McSween's house.

When he arrived shortly after dusk, he found a group of almost sixty men milling around in front of the house. He shouldered his way inside and found the Kid, Dick Brewer, Fred Waite, Bob Widenmann, and John Middleton sitting in McSween's living room. All of the men were quite excited and all were drinking whiskey except the Kid, who had a cup of steaming coffee in his hand.

The Kid smiled when he saw Falcon, but it was a sad smile with none of his usual jocularity in it.

"Howdy, Falcon," he said. "I guess you heard what them murderin' bastards did to the boss man."

Falcon nodded. "I heard John was shot by some of Evans's men. Is that true?"

The Kid stared down into his coffee for a moment before replying, then looked up and told Falcon the entire story, not leaving out how guilty he felt about not intervening.

Just as the Kid finished his tale, McSween approached the pair and handed Falcon a glass of whiskey.

"Alex, just what do you intend to do about this?" Falcon asked.

McSween shook his head. "I don't rightly know just now."

"Have you reported what happened to Sheriff Brady?"

Kid turned his head and spit on the floor. "Tell Brady? That son of a bitch won't do nothin'. He's in on this with the rest of that Dolan bunch."

Falcon was about to reply when someone knocked on the door and walked in. It was John Riley, and he was drunk as a hoot owl.

"I jus' wanted to say I'm sorry 'bout what happened to Tunstall." He slurred his words as he stood weaving in the living room.

"An' I wan' you to know I didn't know nothin' 'bout it."

As he talked, he took a kerchief out of his pocket to wipe sweat off his forehead. As he raised the kerchief to his face, a small, leather-bound book fell to the floor.

Falcon bent and quickly picked it up, putting it in his pocket before the drunken Riley could see.

McSween grabbed the Kid as he started toward Riley, with blood in his eye.

"You'd better hightail it on out of here, Riley, 'fore the Kid or one of the others blows you into next week."

Riley held up his hands, turning bleary eyes toward the Kid. "I tell you I'm not involved in all this, Kid. It was that outlaw Evans that shot Tunstall, not any of us."

When the Kid strained against McSween's grasp, Riley quickly turned and rushed from the room, fear on his face.

After he was gone, the Kid adjusted his holster and said, "I'm gonna go get some revenge for Mr. Tunstall. Anybody comin' with me?"

Falcon said, "Hold on, Kid. Let's see what Mr. Riley dropped before we go off half-cocked." He turned some pages, reading the handwritten notes.

"Jesus," he whispered to himself. *This is the dynamite that might blow this entire county apart,* he thought.

"Gentlemen, let me have your attention," he called to the group in the house.

When they were all listening he said, "This is a memorandum book that Riley dropped when he was here. Among other items, there is a record of the occasions on which stolen cattle have been purchased from the Evans gang, cattle stolen from the Tunstall and Chisum ranches."

McSween slammed his fist into his palm. "Goddamn! I knew those bastards were involved in the cattle thefts. Now we have proof!"

"That's not all," Falcon added. "Let me read you a letter, dated fourteen February, eighteen seventy-eight, from District Attorney Rynerson. It's addressed to Riley and Dolan."

He held up the letter to show the men, then began reading from it:

I believe Tunstall is in with the swindlers—with the rogue McSween. They have the money belonging to the Fritz estate, and they know it. It must be made hot for them, all the hotter the better—especially is this necessary now that it has been discovered there is no hell. Shake that McSween outfit up until it shells out and squares up, and then shake it out of Lincoln. I will aid to punish the scoundrels all I can. Get the people with control—you know how to do it, and be assured, I shall help you all I can, for I believe there was never found a more scoundrelly set than that outfit.

When he finished reading the letter Falcon saw that the men were riled up, ready to go immediately to find and kill the entire Dolan faction.

"Hold on, boys," Falcon said. He turned to McSween, "You know for certain now that you can expect no justice in Lincoln, so you'd better not let these boys head there with guns in hand. Even if they win the battle they will lose the war, for the law is on the side of Dolan and his men."

McSween nodded. "He's right, men. Let me think for a minute. We've got to do this right, or we end up losing in the long run."

After a few minutes spent pacing back and forth, his hands locked behind his back, McSween stopped and addressed the crew.

"All right, here's what we're going to do. First off, I want some men sent to locate Tunstall's body and have it brought into Lincoln. We need to arrange a proper burial for him on the Rio Feliz.

"As far as getting the men responsible for this atrocity and making them pay, here is what we're going to do . . ."

Seventeen

The next morning, the Kid and Dick Brewer and a few others accompanied Alexander McSween on a journey.

Soon, five somber-faced men gathered around a lamplit desk where a silver-haired Territorial Justice of the Peace of Lincoln County, John "Squire" Wilson, put pen to paper, granting legal authority to act as deputy constables within his jurisdiction to seven men: Rob Widenmann, Dick Brewer, Billy Bonney, Charley Bowdre, John Middleton, Henry Brown, and Fred Waite.

The Kid stood beside Brewer across the desk as Judge Wilson finished his paperwork. Tall, angular Alexander McSween whispered quiet instructions to the judge.

Outside the judge's small house at the outskirts of Lincoln township, Middleton and Brown stood guard with rifles, for Brewer had concerns that Jimmy Dolan might anticipate their move and try to stop it before it became official.

"Now for the warrants, Judge," McSween said. "You've heard the testimony of Billy Bonney, Fred Waite, and John Middleton, as to the murder. Three men who took part in the killing have been positively identified—Jesse Evans, Billy Morton and Tom Hill. If you'll complete those arrest warrants, Constable Brewer and his deputies can go about making the arrests. Unfortunately, we cannot be sure James

J. Dolan was present. However, it should be painfully clear he was responsible."

"I can't issue a warrant for a man who isn't identified," the judge croaked, clearing his throat. "You'll have to offer a Territorial Judge up in Mesilla some sort of proof as to Dolan's role in this."

The Kid looked down at the badge he held in his palm. In all his life he'd never dreamed of becoming a lawman. But to avenge the death of a gentle friend like John Tunstall the Kid was willing to pin a badge to his chest.

After the ceremony and with the arrest warrants in hand, the seven men all shook hands, somber at what they saw as their sworn duty, the avenging of John Tunstall's death.

While the others waited at McSween's house for the arrival of Tunstall's body, the Kid took a ride to Fort Sumner. He figured the early evening air would clear his head, help ease the pain he felt at his friend and boss's sudden death.

Falcon, seeing the Kid enter the batwings of The Drinking Hole, folded his hand and cashed out of his poker game. He greeted the Kid, got a bottle of whiskey and some sarsaparilla, and led him back into Beaver Smith's office.

After they were seated, the Kid folded back the edge of a leather vest he was wearing to show Falcon his badge.

Falcon nodded, having known of the men's plans to seek out Squire Wilson.

"So, what are your plans now, Kid?" Falcon asked as he lighted a cigar.

"I plan to kill the sons of bitches who murdered John Tunstall!"

Falcon leaned back in his desk chair, whiskey in one hand and cigar in the other, observing the Kid closely.

"You think pinning that piece of tin to your chest gives you the right to do that?"

"No. But my loyalty to my friend, who's lying in a coffin over in Lincoln with a passel of slugs in him, does."

Falcon nodded. "Kid, I'm not one to get up on a high

horse . . . hell, I've ridden the revenge trail myself for more years than I care to remember. But I want you to think this over very carefully. Right now, the majority of people in Lincoln County and the surrounding country are on your side. They know Tunstall was murdered, and they want the scoundrels who did it to pay the price."

Falcon paused to take a long drag on his cigar, easing the bite of the tobacco smoke on his tongue with a drink of whiskey. He tilted smoke from his nostrils and continued, "But if you and the others go off half-cocked and assassinate the killers, the tide of public opinion will turn, and you'll find yourselves the villains in this affair. Is that what you want?"

As he talked, Falcon stared deep into the Kid's eyes. He desperately wanted to reach this young man he had befriended. He wondered briefly what drew him to the Kid, finally realizing it was because he saw a lot of himself in him—a fierce loyalty, a desire to see wrongs righted, and a belief he could triumph against almost impossible odds to bring killers to justice.

The Kid's expression changed. He looked doubtful for the first time.

He took a gulp of his sarsaparilla, belched, and shook his head.

"Damn, Falcon. I know what you're sayin' is true, but I can't just sit around and wait for the law to do what it's supposed to. You know as well as I do that Dolan has the local law in his pocket. Sheriff Brady is up to his neck in this affair. Hell, he was leading the posse that went after Tunstall, an' it was him who allowed an escaped prisoner to shoot down the boss in cold blood. How can we expect him to do the right thing?"

Falcon blew smoke at the ceiling. "You're right, Kid. Brady isn't going to help you and your friends. But I can tell you now, if you try and serve those warrants on Dolan and Evans and the rest, there's going to be bloodshed, and that's a fact."

The Kid's face changed again, the wildness returning to his eyes as his lips curled in a grin with no mirth in it.

"Bloodshed is what I want, Falcon, long as it's Dolan's blood that gets spilled."

Falcon sighed. He was getting nowhere. The Kid was beyond listening to reason.

"Then you're determined to serve those warrants on Dolan and his men?"

"Yes, an' the sooner the better."

Falcon stood up and took his hat from the rack next to his desk.

"Well, do you mind if I ride along?" Falcon asked, hoping he could keep the Kid's murderous instincts from causing him to do something foolish.

"Naw. It's all right by me."

The Kid stood and pulled his hat down tight. "Let's ride, Falcon. They ought to have Tunstall's body at McSween's by now, an' I'd like to pay my respects 'fore goin' over to Dolan's."

The other six Regulators were gathered together in a group at Alexander McSween's house when the Kid and Falcon arrived. Tunstall's body was lying in a pine coffin in the parlor of the house, his face covered with a white kerchief.

The Kid stood next to the coffin and pulled back the kerchief, his face paling at the sight of his friend's ruined face.

He turned away, eyes glistening with unshed tears. "Damn, I hate that they shot him right in the face at close range."

McSween nodded. "It's going to be hard for even Sheriff Brady to call this self-defense."

The Kid looked at the others. "How about we take a ride over to Dolan's and serve these warrants tonight?"

McSween shook his head. "Not just yet, boys. Brady's got to have a postmortem done in the morning. Let's wait and see how he plays his hand. If he does right, and calls it murder, then we'll let him do his job."

The Kid spoke up. "And if he doesn't?"

McSween frowned. "Then the Regulators will have to do it for him."

The next morning, Sheriff Brady had the post surgeon from Fort Stanton, Dr. D.M. Appel, do the autopsy, paying him the unheard of price of one hundred dollars for the job.

Dr. Appel, in his official report, stressed that besides the two bullet wounds "no other bruises on head or body" could be found.

McSween and the Regulators were furious, having seen firsthand how Tunstall's head had been badly mutilated. They became further enraged when Brady officially said that Tunstall was killed after shooting at Evans and his men, and the killing was justified.

When he heard this, the Kid unhooked the hammer thong from his Colt and said to the others, "Let's go get those bastards!"

Falcon glanced at McSween. "Alex, don't you think it would be wise if you asked Atanancio Martinez, the county constable, to serve the warrants? That way no one can claim this is a vigilante group you're mounting."

McSween stroked his chin, thinking. Finally he nodded. "You're right, Falcon, and Martinez is sympathetic to our cause. We'll get him to go with us. That way everyone will know we're on the side of the law."

"I have another suggestion," Falcon said.

"What is it?" McSween asked.

"Don't send the entire group of Regulators with Martinez. Just have a couple of them go along to make sure the job gets done. After all, how much resistance do you expect from Jimmy Dolan?"

McSween nodded. "That's a good idea. Kid, you and Fred Waite go get Martinez and ask him to serve our warrants. The rest of us will wait here to see what happens."

The Kid nodded, slapped Waite on the shoulder, and said, "Let's go arrest that son of a bitch, Fred."

Falcon was disappointed. He had been trying to keep the hotheaded Kid out of this as much as possible. He knew the Kid was still very emotional about Tunstall's death and was itching to pull the trigger on someone, especially Dolan or Evans.

"If you don't mind, I think I'll tag along with the Kid and Waite," Falcon said to McSween.

"Not at all, Falcon, not at all," he replied.

After locating Atanacio Martinez and explaining they wanted him to help them serve warrants on Dolan, the four men made their way to Dolan's store at the other end of town.

The Kid glanced at Falcon. "You loaded up six and six, Falcon?"

Falcon shook his head. "I don't think we're going to need our guns on this trip, Kid. Dolan is no gunfighter, and Evans and his bunch wouldn't dare show their faces in this town right now, with the way everyone feels about Tunstall's killing."

"Maybe not, but we might get lucky and he might make a try to escape or to fill his hand."

Falcon stared at him. The Kid had changed with Tunstall's death. He seemed older, more cynical, filled with hate. Gone was the good-natured, funloving kid he had met out at Chisum's ranch. Falcon just hoped the old Kid would come back after all this was over.

When they walked into the store, several customers, seeing the expressions on the men's faces, hurriedly paid for their merchandise and made for the door.

Falcon hung back, pretending to shop as he watched the Kid and the others walk into Dolan's office at the back of the store. When the door opened, he could see Dolan sitting behind his desk, talking with Sheriff William Brady.

The Kid sauntered over to the desk and threw the warrants onto the desk.

"We're here to arrest you for the murder of John Tunstall, Dolan," the Kid said, his voice low but tight with hatred.

Without warning, Brady drew his pistol and pointed it at the Kid.

"Under what authority are you operating, Bonney?"

Atanacio Martinez explained that Squire Wilson, Justice of the Peace of Lincoln County, had appointed the Kid and the others special deputies.

Brady smirked. "That don't hold no water in Lincoln. I'm the only law around here, and I say what you're doin' is illegal. I will not permit you to serve any warrants in my town."

With that, he picked the papers off the desk and stuffed them in his pockets.

"I'm placing you three men under arrest for attempted assault."

The Kid's face turned red and his hand quivered, just above his Colt.

Brady smiled again, "Go on, Kid. Try for it. I'd love to put a window in your skull."

Falcon walked to the doorway. "Take it easy, Kid," he said.

Brady looked at him. "You takin' a hand in this, Mac-Callister?"

Falcon shook his head. "No, I'm just a citizen, watching you arrest men for no good reason."

He looked at the Kid, knowing he had vowed never to

go to jail again. "Kid, you and the others stay calm. I'll let McSween know what's going on. You won't be in jail long, I promise you."

Brady snorted. "We'll see about that. Now, you gents lay them pistols on the desk and let's mosey on over to the lockup."

The Kid turned worried eyes on Falcon, then walked with the others toward the jail.

As Falcon turned to leave, Dolan spoke for the first time.

"I'd keep my nose out of this, MacCallister, if I were you.

"Like I said, Jimmy, I'm just an ordinary citizen who wants to see justice done."

Falcon climbed up on Diablo and rode as fast as he could to McSween's office.

After Falcon left, Dolan grabbed his hat and started for the door.

"Where you goin' boss?" his clerk asked.

"I'm headed over to Fort Stanton to get Captain Purington to send some soldiers to guard the store from Tunstall's friends. Then I'm gonna take a ride over to Doña Aña County to see if I can persuade John Kinney and some of his men to come to work for me."

The clerk looked startled. "John Kinney, the famous outlaw?"

Dolan smiled. "One and the same."

Eighteen

On February twenty-second, Falcon stood in a drizzle of rain mixed with sleet and watched six men lower John Tunstall's body into his grave. He shivered, not so much from the cold, but from the realization that a full scale war was about to begin.

Brady had released Martinez after holding him for a few hours, but, two days later, the Kid and Waite were still in jail.

The soldiers that Dolan had gotten Captain Purington to send from Fort Stanton were now gone, and Lincoln resembled an armed camp, with gunfighters from both sides prowling the streets, just waiting for someone to start the shooting.

Some time after the funeral, Bob Widenmann arrived from Fort Stanton with a small detachment of troops, and Falcon accompanied them to the jail.

With the soldiers backing his play, Falcon stepped into the jail and demanded that Brady release the Kid and Waite.

Brady glanced out the window, saw the troops on their mounts, and unlocked the iron doors.

The Kid walked slowly over to get his pistol off a hook on the wall and strap it on. Then he turned toward Brady and stood there, an insolent grin on his face but his eyes cold as the February ice outside.

"Make your will, Brady."

Brady's face paled. "Is that a threat?"

The Kid turned to leave. "Nope. It's a promise."

Outside, the Kid paused and threw his head back and took a deep breath. "Jesus, it's good to be able to breathe free air again."

He looked at Falcon and stuck out his hand. "I owe you for gettin' me out of jail, Falcon."

Falcon shook his hand. "That's all right, Kid."

Bob Widenmann tipped his hat and wheeled his horse around, leading the soldiers toward Tunstall's store.

Falcon and the Kid followed Widenmann into the store, finding five men hired by Brady guarding it—George Peppin, Jim Longwell, John Long, Charley Martin, and a black ex-trooper named Clark.

Widenmann disarmed them, and with the soldiers to back his play he marched them over to the jail and forced Brady to arrest them for trespassing.

Brady kept the men overnight and then released them, vowing to kill McSween for forcing his hand in the matter.

That night the Kid invited Falcon to accompany him to a meeting called by Dick Brewer in Tunstall's store.

The room was filled with former Tunstall employees, including Waite, Middleton, a stock detective from the Hunters and Evans company named Frank Macnab, and others such as Doc Scurlock, Charlie Bowdre, Henry Brown, Sam Smith, and Jim French.

Brewer led the meeting.

After a fiery speech decrying the lawlessness of Dolan and his "hirelings" Brady and Evans, Brewer said, "Men, I want you all to join me in forming a group to right the wrongs that have been done. I propose we call ourselves Regulators, and that we clean up the town of Lincoln."

The men cheered and raised their pistols in the air, vowing to get Dolan and Brady and Evans for what they had done to their friend, John Tunstall.

Once the excitement died down, Falcon pulled the Kid aside. He wanted to try once more to get him to listen to reason, to reconsider what he was doing.

"Kid, this group you're set on joining is nothing more than a bunch of vigilantes, and being a vigilante is just one short step from the owl hoot trail."

The Kid shook his head stubbornly. "We're not vigilantes, Falcon, we're Regulators. And we're gonna regulate Dolan and Evans and his gang out of Lincoln."

"Whatever you call yourselves, Kid, doesn't matter. If you ride with these men it's going to set you on a course that can only lead to your death, either from the Dolan men, or from the law later."

"You got it wrong, Falcon. All of us Regulators swore an oath to remain loyal to each other no matter what happens, and we all promised our purpose was to arrest, not to execute, the wrongdoers and to bring them to Lincoln, where they will be held for trial."

Falcon shook his head. "Kid, no matter what they say, these men are out for blood. I count you as a friend, and I hope you'll reconsider riding with them."

"They're my friends, too, Falcon, and I swore an oath of allegiance." He looked sad. "I hate to go against you, Falcon, but I've given my word, and I intend to keep it."

Falcon sighed. "Then so be it, Kid." He stuck out his hand. "Good luck."

The Kid took it in a firm grip. "What we're doin' is right, Falcon. Later on, maybe you'll see that."

A couple of days later Falcon was in The Drinking Hole when an excited Kid burst through the batwings.

"Hey, Falcon! Some of the Evans gang has been sighted over near the Pecos, camped out. The Regulators are goin' after 'em. You wanna come?"

Falcon considered it. He had no desire to align himself

with a vigilante group, favoring a more personal approach to seeking vengeance, but he could see that the Kid was heading down the wrong path. If he didn't learn to corral his temper, he was a sure candidate for the owl hoot trail, with a hangman's noose waiting for him at its end.

He decided he'd give one last try at helping his friend stay out of trouble.

"Sure, Kid. Give me five minutes to throw a saddle on Diablo and I'll ride along."

He hesitated. "But only if you're riding out there to arrest those men, not gun them down without giving them a chance to surrender."

The Kid waved a dismissive hand. "Don't worry so much, Falcon. Everything will be on the up and up."

Falcon saddled his mount and joined the group of seven men. Dick Brewer seemed to have assumed the role of leader of the Regulators, which Falcon thought appropriate. He had been foreman of Tunstall's Rio Feliz Ranch, and was used to giving these men orders.

After a few hours ride, the Regulators crested a small hill and could see a campfire trailing a lazy plume of smoke into the crisp, clear air. There could be seen several men still lying under blankets near the fire, while a number of others were hunched over with plates on their laps and coffee mugs on the ground next to them. The horses were tied nearby to a rope strung between two cottonwood trees near the banks of the slowly moving Pecos River.

Brewer pulled a Winchester carbine from his saddle boot and jacked a shell into the chamber, causing several of the Regulators to do the same.

When he put the rifle to his shoulder and took aim, Falcon nudged Diablo with his knees and pulled up next to Brewer.

"Hold on, Dick," Falcon said loudly enough for the others to hear. "I understood you men were acting as county deputies, and were going to give those men down there a chance to surrender."

Brewer lowered the gun, glaring at Falcon.

"Those bastards didn't give John Tunstall a chance to surrender, so why should we?"

"Because you're wearing that badge on your chest. That makes you stand for something besides vengeance. If you want to shoot a sleeping man down in cold blood, fine. But take that badge off and do it as Dick Brewer, private citizen, not a county deputy."

Brewer pursed his lips, thinking on it for a moment.

"You're right, Falcon. In fact, I hope they do surrender, 'cause sittin' in jail waitin' for a necktie party is worse on 'em than being shot down sudden like."

Falcon nodded. "And you won't have to be looking over your shoulder for the rest of your life for a star packer trailing you, either."

Brewer twisted in his saddle and said to his men, "Load 'em up six and six boys. We're goin' in there and call the dance."

The men drew their weapons and Brewer led them toward the camp at a slow trot. When they were within a hundred yards, he halted the column and shouted, "Yo, the camp!"

Falcon could see a sudden flurry of activity near the fire, like an ant bed with a stick stuck in it. Several of the men bolted for their horses, while a couple of others rolled behind their saddles, still on the ground, and aimed rifles over them.

"Evans!" Brewer shouted again, "I'm County Deputy Dick Brewer, and I'm givin' you one chance to surrender and come out with your hands up!"

His offer was met with a volley of rifle fire, one of the bullets striking Henry Brown in the left shoulder and throwing him out of his saddle.

The Kid, his eyes wild with excitement, gave a rebel yell

and put the spurs to his sorrel, leaning over the bronc's neck and firing his pistol as he charged toward the camp.

"Damn," Falcon muttered to himself. Filling his hands with iron, he put Diablo's reins in his teeth and charged after the Kid, firing with both hands at the shooting outlaws.

As the Regulators rode down on them, one of the gang raised up on his knees behind his saddle, his Henry repeating rifle to his shoulder, and began to fire at the Kid.

The Kid's Colt misfired when he was twenty-five yards from the man, who grinned and took careful aim, planning to put one in the Kid's face.

Falcon fired twice, once with each hand, one bullet taking the man in the stomach, doubling him over. The second slug entered the top of his bowed head, exploding his brain in a fine red mist and dropping him dead as a stone.

The Kid reined to a halt and began to punch out his empties, giving Falcon a nod and wink of thanks as he reloaded.

Dick Brewer galloped by the Kid and Falcon toward where the rest of the gang were jumping into their saddles, firing his carbine as fast as he could work the lever.

One of the men whirled his horse just as Brewer's .4440 slug hit his mount in the neck. The horse stumbled, throwing its rider to the ground, where Brewer quickly drew down on him.

"I give up! Don't shoot!" the man screamed, holding both hands high, face contorted with fear, covered with sweat.

Brewer aimed the carbine, a nasty grin on his face, when Falcon rode between the two men.

"Hold on, Dick. He's surrendering," Falcon said.

Brewer lowered his carbine and leaned to the side to spit in the dust. "Somebody put a rope on this bastard," he said, and reined his mount around to give chase to the other fleeing outlaws.

Charley Bowdre fired a ten gauge, sawed-off express gun at a man riding by, who was shooting at him over his horse's head with a pistol.

The 00-buckshot loads tore the man's shoulder and half his face off, flinging him off the bronc to lie crumpled in a pool of his own blood, moaning for a moment until he died.

The last of the outlaws to get to his horse spurred the animal and galloped off toward the Pecos, leaning low over his mount's neck. Suddenly, his saddle, which he hadn't had time to properly tighten, came loose, and he spilled in the mud and reeds at the edge of the water.

John Middleton was close behind and aimed his rifle at the mud-splattered gang member, saying, "Grab some sky, or I'll drill you through and through!"

The man slowly got to his feet, limping on his left leg and raising his hands, his head bowed in defeat.

When the dust and gunsmoke finally cleared, the Regulators had two prisoners, William Buck Morton and Frank Baker, and had killed three of the Evans gang members, Charley "Toothpick" Jameson, Billy "Scarface" Robinson, and "Clubfoot" Jack McGee.

The rest of the men, probably including Jesse Evans himself, had managed to escape.

The Regulators gathered around the campfire, some drinking whiskey from pint bottles, others pouring themselves coffee from the outlaws' own pot on the fire.

Morton and Baker were tied back-to-back, sitting under a cottonwood tree a short distance from the campfire.

The Kid walked up to Brewer, his face angry and flushed.

"Dick, we've got two of 'em, and they are the worst of the lot." He pointed his Colt at the prisoners, "Buck Morton over there is the man I saw shoot John and then smash his face with a rifle butt. Let's avenge John Tunstall by killin' 'em right now!"

Brewer thought on it for a moment. Then, with a glance

at Falcon, who stood drinking coffee and smoking a cigar nearby, he shook his head.

"No, Kid. I think it'll be better if we take the sons of bitches into Lincoln and let 'em face a necktie party. That'll send a message to the others that we're gonna get them, too, sooner or later."

Charley Bowdre looked at the sky. "It's gettin' late, Dick. I don't think we can make Lincoln 'fore nightfall, an' I don't want to be out here with these galoots tonight in case Evans and his men decide to come back."

Falcon spoke up. "If we head a little due east, we could stop the night at Chisum's South Spring Ranch. Evans wouldn't dare try to attack us there."

Brewer nodded. "Falcon's right, boys. Let's saddle up and head east."

The next morning, after staying the night at Chisum's ranch, the Regulators saddled up and prepared to leave for Lincoln.

As they got the prisoners ready, one of Chisum's hands came galloping up to them, his horse lathered and blowing hard.

"Mr. Brewer, I just got in from Lincoln. Word there is Jimmy Dolan has got back from Mesilla and is organizing a bunch of men into a posse. He plans to take your prisoners and let 'em go, an' he says he's gonna kill any of you that try to stop him."

Falcon walked over to Brewer. "Dick, why don't you men take the round about way back to Lincoln, through Blackwater Canyon, over near Agua Negra, and I'll take the direct route. If I find out Dolan does have a posse I'll ride out and warn you, and you can take the prisoners to Roswell instead."

Brewer nodded.

"That's a right sound plan, Falcon. Much obliged."

He stepped up on his horse. "Come on, boys, we're headin' home the long way, to give Falcon a chance to warn us about what Dolan and his crew are up to."

The Regulators rode off to the east, while Falcon rode toward the northeast.

Falcon, who wasn't known to have joined the Regulators, hoped he could manage to keep things civilized and somehow prevent an all out range war. There had been too many deaths already over a feud between two men.

Nineteen

As the Regulators rode the winding road toward the entrance to Blackwater Canyon, Bill McCloskey spurred his horse to catch up with Dick Brewer at the front of the column of men.

McCloskey had joined the Regulators at Chisum's ranch, professing sympathy with their plans to capture Evans and his gang. He had occasionally been employed by Tunstall, and had been sent on an errand the day before Tunstall was killed, but the men knew he hadn't followed Tunstall's orders. In fact, they had been with the Matthews posse when they rode in to the Tunstall ranch and found Tunstall had already departed.

He had joined the Regulators only after Morton and Baker were captured, and he was increasingly regarded as a possible spy, especially because of his sympathetic attitude toward the prisoners and his concern over their welfare.

As he rode next to Brewer, McCloskey said, "Dick, the ropes on the prisoners are mighty tight, an' it appears to be cuttin' into their hands. You mind if I loosen them ties a bit?"

Brewer looked at him, his eyes narrowed. "What's goin' on, Bill? Why're you so concerned 'bout those outlaws?"

McCloskey flushed, and stammered, "Oh, no reason, Dick. just didn't want their hands fallin' off from lack of blood, that's all."

The Kid, who was riding on the other side of Brewer, leaned forward in the saddle so he could get a closer look at McCloskey.

"Bill, I noticed you been awful chummy with those bastards ever since you joined up with us at Chisum's. You got any special reason to be so close to them guys?"

"Uh . . . no, Kid. I didn't mean nothin' by it."

As the column rode farther into Blackwater Canyon, they came to a clearing next to the trail.

Brewer held up his hand. "Yo, boys. Let's pull off the road here and take a nooning."

After the men had all dismounted, they gathered in a circle around Brewer, waiting to see what his orders would be.

He looked over at the Kid, standing next to McCloskey. "Kid, get Bill's sidearm."

Before the startled McCloskey could react, the Kid reached over and pulled his Colt from its holster, stepping back from the suddenly isolated man.

Brewer pulled his pistol, casually aiming it at McCloskey's belly.

"Bill, I got a few questions I been wantin' to ask you."

Sweat began to run down McCloskey's forehead and drip into his eyes, though the March temperature was cool.

"What's goin' on, Dick? I ain't done nothin' wrong."

"Well, me and some of the boys have been wonderin' 'bout why you showed up at the Rio Feliz with Matthews' posse, when you was supposed to be runnin' an errand for Mr. Tunstall, an' we also been wonderin' why you been takin' such a special interest in the welfare of our prisoners. You got anything to say about that, Bill?"

McCloskey started backing up, his hands held out. "Now wait a minute, fellas, I done told you I ain't done nothin' wrong."

The Regulators closed ranks, standing in a line, staring at the sweat pouring off McCloskey's face. . . .

* * *

Falcon had Diablo in a full canter, whistling as he rode toward Blackwater Canyon. He was in a good mood, as he had found out that Dolan had been unable to mount any kind of posse that would pose a threat to the Regulators or their prisoners.

He wasn't so sure the prisoners would actually be held for any length of time or ever have to stand trial, considering Sheriff Brady's partiality to the Dolan faction, but that wasn't his worry. He just wanted the Regulators to act in a lawful manner and turn the men over to the sheriff. What happened after that didn't really concern him. At least the Kid wouldn't be riding the owl hoot trail, and the Regulators would have acted as true lawmen, not vigilantes.

Diablo jerked his head up and nickered at the sound of a gunshot up ahead.

Falcon pulled back on the reins, considering his options. Suddenly, a few minutes later, there was a flurry of shots, at least nine or ten in a row.

Falcon drew his pistol and put the spurs to Diablo, leaning forward and pulling his hat down tight as the stud kicked up his heels and began to fly.

He knew the Regulators were up ahead somewhere. Maybe the Evans gang had ambushed them.

He slowed the bronc as he entered Blackwater Canyon, knowing it was a perfect place for bushwhackers to hide and pick off a larger group of men.

As he rounded a turn in the trail, going slow, both hands filled with iron, he saw a gathering up ahead, and recognized the Kid's spotted sorrel among the horses tethered there.

"Yo, the camp!" Falcon called, wanting to make sure everything was all right before proceeding any farther.

A small figure stepped out of the crowd, shaded his eyes, then waved Falcon on.

"Yo, Falcon, come on in. It's me, Kid."

When he got to the Kid, he dismounted and walked over to join the others, who were standing over three bodies on the ground.

One of the dead men was Bill McCloskey, who was lying on his back with a bullethole in the middle of his chest. His eyes were open and staring, as if surprised to find their owner dead.

A short distance away were two other corpses, both lying on their stomachs, sprawled as if shot down while running away.

Falcon walked over to the bodies and knelt down, examining them. He saw that Buck Morton had eleven bulletholes, all in his back. Next to him lay Frank Baker, the back of his head blown off and three more holes in his back.

Falcon removed his hat and sleeved sweat off his forehead, stood and turned to face the Regulators.

"Dick, what happened here?" Falcon asked, frowning.

Brewer thought for a moment, then said, "Morton there grabbed a gun from one of the hands and plugged McCloskey, then he and Baker tried to make a run for it."

Falcon looked down at the bodies. The rope marks on their wrists were still deep and red.

Falcon nodded, "I guess they chewed through those ropes on their hands, snuck up on one of you and stole a gun, then shot and killed the only man among you who was halfway friendly to them?"

The Kid stepped forward, a stubborn cant to his jaw. "That's the story, Falcon. And you and everybody else can take it or leave it."

Falcon glanced back at Morton's body, seeing a pistol on the ground next to his hands, still purple from the ropes that had been on them.

He shook his head, "That's the first time I've ever heard of a dead man drawing a gun."

Later on, the site of this killing would forever be called "Dead Man's Draw."

Falcon walked over to Brewer and stood before him. "This won't look good, Dick. I have some more news, some good and some bad."

Brewer took out his fixings and began to build a cigarette as the other Regulators gathered around.

"Tell us, Falcon."

"The good news is that Dolan wasn't able to form a posse to come after you. Seems the good people of Lincoln are mostly on your side in this matter."

"What's the bad news?" Brewer asked, trailing smoke from his nostrils.

"Two days ago, Governor Axtell paid a brief visit to Lincoln. He stayed for three hours, all of it spent in the company of Jimmy Dolan."

The Kid snorted. "The leader of the Santa Fe Ring paying his respects, no doubt."

"After listening to Dolan's side of things, he issued a proclamation the next day, declaring that John B. Wilson's appointment by the county commissioners as a justice of the peace was illegal and void, and all processes issued by him were void. He said Wilson had no authority whatsoever to act as justice of the peace."

Brewer flipped his cigarette to the ground and stubbed it out with his boot. "Is that all?"

"No. He also revoked Robert Widenmann's appointment as a federal marshal, and he asked the post commander at Fort Stanton to assist territorial civil officers in maintaining order and enforcing legal processes, which consist only of what Judge Bristol and Sheriff Brady and his deputies say."

Bowdre stepped forward, his forehead wrinkled. "What's all that double-talk mean, Falcon?"

Falcon looked at him. "It means that you Regulators

have no legal authority to make any arrests or kill anyone with the law's blessing." He looked over at the dead men.

"Damn!" the Kid said. He glanced at Brewer. "What're we gonna do, Dick?"

"You boys head on up to San Patricio and make a camp. I'll mosey on into Lincoln and see what the lay of the land is, and whether we're wanted men or not."

He looked at Falcon. "Will you ride with me, Falcon? I don't relish ridin' into Lincoln without some back up."

Falcon nodded. "I don't agree with what you men did here today, Dick, but I'll go along to make sure you get a fair hearing."

Twenty

On the night of March thirty-first, the Kid, along with Macnab, French, Waite, Middleton, and Brown, rode into Lincoln. They went directly to the Tunstall store, fired up the big iron stove in the back, and sat around drinking whiskey and eating whatever they could find—all except the Kid, who drank only coffee and ate nothing at all.

They had received a message by a Mexican kid who told them Señor Brewer said to come to Lincoln on April one. There would be a trial and they would all be cleared of any wrongdoing.

As they sat around, most of the men getting alkalaied on the whiskey, they talked about what had happened to bring them to this point in their lives. The more they talked, the more they all became convinced that Sheriff Brady was as much responsible for Tunstall's murder and the disorder in the district as anyone.

They also became convinced he was shielding Tunstall's murderers, and they decided to ambush the sheriff the first chance they had.

They finally fell into a drunken sleep, vowing to do something about Tunstall's killing first thing in the morning.

It was going on nine in the morning when the Kid saw Sheriff William Brady and Billy Matthews, along with George Hindman, John Long, and George Peppin, walk out of the Dolan and Murphey Store. All were deputized or, as in the case of Matthews, officers of the county. Matthews was district attorney for Lincoln.

The Kid was concealed behind an adobe brick wall where a gate for wagons led into a corral behind the Tunstall Store. Six Regulators were with the Kid . . . Frank MacNab, John Middleton, Rob Widenmann, Jim French, Henry Brown, and Fred Waite. They had been waiting since dawn.

"Here they come," said the Kid.

"I'll take down Brady," Middleton whispered, jacking a shell into his rifle. "I owe the son of a bitch for what he done to our boss. I've been waitin' a long time for this. Killin' Morton an' Baker wasn't near enough satisfaction to suit me. I want Brady, the rotten bastard. He's bought an' paid for by Dolan, an' everybody in Lincoln County knows it . . . he ain't got nobody fooled."

"We all owe him," the Kid replied.

"Damn right," Waite said, cocking his single-shot Colt pistol.

Behind them, Henry Brown rushed up with a Spencer carbine in his hands.

"Do you see 'em?" Brown asked, barely raising his head above the wall. "Yonder they is . . . I see em now. Brady's got a rifle, and Matthews has a pistol . John Long an' Peppin are carryin' iron. Can't tell from here about Hindman, but he hardly ever goes without a gun."

"Get down," the Kid snapped.

"They'll see you," Middleton added. "Just wait 'til you hear their boots . . . wait 'til they're real close. One thing we can't afford to do is miss this opportunity to kill the sorry sons of bitches."

"I'm gonna kill that bastard Brady myself," Waite said around a cheekful of chewing tobacco. "This damn war has got plumb out of hand, an' Brady's the one who allowed it. He's all mine."

"Just make damn sure he's dead," Middleton whispered as the sound of feet moving across hard ground reached them. "Put eleven slugs in him, just like we done to Billy Morton, that no good bastard Baker, an' McCloskey. Eleven bullets, boys, so they know who done this. We want to make damn sure we put a signature on these killin's."

"Nobody's gonna be countin' bulletholes in dead men," the Kid said. "Just make real sure all of 'em are dead . . . 'specially Brady."

"I ain't real sure 'bout this," Henry Brown said, although he cocked his Spencer as quietly as he could. "Shootin' a damn sheriff could get us in a bunch of trouble. We could all wind up in territorial prison up at Fort Stanton."

"Brady ain't no real sheriff, anyhow," the Kid said. "He's a damn hired gun workin' for Murphy an' Dolan, just like he was some cowboy mendin' fences. The laws in the New Mexico Territory don't mean a damn thing to him."

"Quiet now!" Waite hissed. "I can hear 'em talkin'. When they get close, we all rise up an' start shootin'. I sure as hell ain't gonna count the bullets I put in Brady. All I'm gonna do is make damn sure he's dead."

The Kid recalled how John Tunstall looked the day they found him with two bullet holes in his gut. "Just don't forget how our friend Mr. Tunstall died," he said, his hand growing wet on the stock of his rifle. "Think about how Mr. Tunstall was layin' in a pool of blood that day below the Penasco. That oughta be enough to keep your trigger finger sharp."

Jim French, a new member of the Regulators, spoke in a soft voice. "What about that new feller in town, the big guy who bought into Beaver Smith's saloon? Somebody told me his name was Falcon MacCallister, an' that he was hell on wheels with a gun. We need to know where he stands in this . . . if he's gonna take a side."

"He's a good friend of mine, saved my life a couple of times," the Kid replied. "You heard right—he is downright handy with a six-shooter. But it don't appear he's takin' no side in this war yet. I been figurin' Jimmy Dolan would offer MacCallister his price to join sides with 'em, after what we done to Morton an' Baker. But word is, MacCallister told him he was a friend of Big John Chisum an me, an' that puts him on our side of things. Mr. Chisum wants this trouble stopped. Evans an' his boys have been rustling his cattle mighty often. Maybe that's why Falcon MacCallister came to Lincoln County in the first place, to help Chisum put a stop to all the cattle stealin' out at his ranch. Could be MacCallister's workin' for Chisum an' they been keepin' it under their hats."

"I've seen him, too," Waite offered. "Some men got a look about 'em, an' I sure as hell wouldn't be lookin' forward to tanglin' with MacCallister. Far as I know, he ain't took no side yet, but a man can't be too careful. I sure hope you're right about him bein' tight with you and Chisum. From the looks of him I sure don't want no part of him in a fight."

"If he joins up with Dolan," the Kid whispered as the sound of footsteps and muted voices came close, "friend or no friend, we won't have no choice but to shoot him down. Now get ready, boys. Don't let Brady escape. Or Matthews, neither. Them's the two that have been causin' us problems."

"What about ole' Dad Peppin?" Brown asked.

"If he takes a gun to us, kill him," the Kid answered with no hesitation. "If he stays out of it, leave him be. Got no quarrel with Peppin, but we gotta remember he's a lawdog an' he takes his pay from Murphy an' Dolan, so don't go gettin' too softhearted. If Peppin comes out with a gun, drop him an' make sure he stays there."

"George ain't no bad man, Kid," Brown protested. "He's caught in the middle, looks like to me. I heard him say the other day he wished the army would come down an' put a stop to all this rustlin' an' killin'."

"Kill him, anyhow," Middleton warned. "We don't need no damn witnesses."

"Where's that big feller, MacCallister?" Waite asked. "Wish we knowed where he was."

"Down at Beaver Smith's, most likely," the Kid responded, his trigger finger tightening. "Don't worry none 'bout him, I done told you, he's a friend of mine. It's Brady an' Matthews we want."

"Here they are," Waite said. "I can't wait no longer, an' I sure as hell can't miss from this range."

Waite rose up above the top of the wall and fired off a quick shot. The Kid came up at almost the same time, aiming for Billy Matthews.

Sheriff Brady let out a yell and fell over on his back. Billy Matthews, whirling, took off at a run in the other direction, making for Murphey's store as fast as he could.

The Kid sighted in on Matthew's right leg and triggered off a well-placed shot.

Matthews went down, shrieking and clutching his thigh as a sheaf of papers he had held in one hand went fluttering down the street.

Brown and French opened fire. Sheriff Brady sat up with his hands pressed to his belly, just as another bullet struck him full in the chest.

Brady toppled over on his back, groaning, twisting this way and that while blood pumped from two bulletholes.

The blasting of gunfire ended the quiet in Lincoln, and now the Kid could hear women and children screaming all over the town. As he watched Sheriff Brady, Billy Matthews came staggering to his feet and took off in a lumbering run. John Long got up and started running in the same direction.

But as they ran a fusillade of bullets came from the adobe wall.

Hindman was felled almost at once. Ike Stockton, owner of a Lincoln saloon, raced outside to help Long. A spray of bullets caught Long in his back and ribs. He slumped to the street, and Ike ran back inside his drinking establishment

The Kid and Jim French leapt over the wall.

"I'll get Brady's gun!" the Kid shouted. He ran over to the sheriff and picked up his Winchester.

Billy Matthews, watching from the Cisneros house across the road, took aim and fired.

The bullet punched through the Kid's thigh, and zipped through French's leg, as well.

The Kid dropped Brady's rifle, and he and French hobbled back to the protection of the wall.

More shooting ensued . . . Matthews was firing from the Cisneros home, and Long, although badly wounded, was shooting from the corner of Dolan's store with a repeating rifle.

Sheriff Brady lifted his head off the dirt. Clutched in his bloody hand were arrest warrants for most of the Regulators, and a writ of attachment for all of Tunstall's remaining property, including the ranch itself.

Someone—the Kid wasn't sure who—came over the top, of the wall and fired five shots into Sheriff Brady's head and body. William Brady fell back on the caliche, quivering as the last pieces of paper fell from his grasp.

"Let's get out of town!" Middleton cried above the roar of continuous gunfire. "We got Brady. Long is hurt bad, an' Billy Matthews has a few holes in him, too!"

Somehow, George Peppin had escaped the flying lead, and lay hidden behind a stone water trough . . . the Kid saw him lift his head above the stones for a glimpse at what was happening on the main road through Lincoln.

"Okay," the Kid said as gunshots became more sporadic, less frequent. "We did what we came to do. Let the bastards think on this a spell."

With their objectives mostly accomplished, the Kid led his men to their horses behind the Tunstall corral and mounted up to ride out of town.

But John Middleton saw something from the back of his horse and he raised a hand to halt the others. "Yonder's Matthews," he said bitterly.

Middleton shouldered his rifle and fired a single shot at the district attorney. The slug caught Matthews in the lower leg and sent him sprawling on his face.

"There, you sumbitch!" Middleton snarled. "Now you've got two bad legs!"

"You got him!" Waite exclaimed, helping French climb up on his horse with blood pumping from his leg wound. He looked up at French. "John just helped square things for what they done to you, Jim. He got Matthews."

But the Kid saw Billy Matthews struggle to his hands and knees to make a quick exit around a corner of the Cisneros house just in the nick of time.

"We'll get the rest of 'em later," the Kid promised, turning his sorrel away from the fence.

Waite rode up alongside him. "You know damn well this is gonna force Dolan an' Murphy to send up to Fort Stanton for the army to come after us."

The Kid merely shrugged. "I ain't scared of no black footsoldiers, so long as I got a good horse."

Waite nodded, for the soldiers at Stanton were mostly all infantrymen.

Middleton rode up, grinning, levering another shell into his rifle. "Did you see that sumbitch fall down, Kid? He went down like he was poleaxed."

"He sure as hell did," the Kid agreed, swinging his horse away from Lincoln. "That was one hell of a fine shot you made, only he kept on crawlin' after you shot him."

Middleton scowled. "Maybe the bastard will bleed to death, anyhow."

The Kid kicked his horse to a lope toward a stand of juniper pines. "Either way, we taught Murphy an' Dolan an' his boys a real important lesson. They'd better not mess with the Regulators or we'll come gunnin' for 'em."

"Damn right," French said, tying a bandanna around the hole in his thigh. "We showed them high an' mighty boys a thing or two."

The bullet wound in the Kid's thigh had begun to throb, and he was losing a lot of blood. He took a red scarf from his neck and tied it tightly around his injury.

"We ain't done with 'em yet," the Kid promised as they left Lincoln behind. "We haven't squared things with Jesse yet, or some of the rest of 'em. Now let's get hid on the Ruidoso some place 'til we get healed up."

With that, the Regulators vanished into the pine woods, and soon the sounds of their horses faded to silence.

Jeffery Gauss peered around the corner of the door-frame of his adobe hut, watching the last of the Regulators disappear in a dense forest. He watched silently for a moment.

"Is it over?" His wife asked, cowering in the kitchen near her cast-iron wood stove.

"Appears so. Them was John Tunstall's friends. Call themselves the Regulators now. Dick Brewer and McSween got 'em all sworn in as deputies, only they just shot Sheriff Brady so many times he's gotta be dead. Those boys sure don't act like lawmen, bushwhackin' our sheriff. That real young one, the boy they call Billy the Kid, is the feller who killed Sheriff Brady, an' I'll testify to it in a court of law. Far as I'm concerned they oughta hang that Kid. I ain't no authority on the subject, but he acts like a mean-natured killer. He shot Bill Brady like a man shoots a crippled horse. . . ."

Twenty-one

The Kid's leg was throbbing, and the freezing wind mixed with snow from the March norther blowing in wasn't helping any, though the cold had made the bleeding almost stop. When the Regulators split up after killing Sheriff Brady, the Kid told Jim French to follow him toward the Ruidoso, saying he thought he knew where they might get some medical help for the wounds in their legs.

French was losing a lot of blood and showing it in his pale face and by his weakened condition, slumped over in his saddle as if it pained him greatly to sit a horse.

Covered with snow, ice crusting French's moustache and the Kid's Stetson, they finally rode up on a cabin nestled in a thicket of piñon pines east of the river.

"You reckon we can get help there?" French asked weakly as he held onto his saddlehorn, his breath smoking in the frigid air, chills racking his body.

The Kid reached over to steady French as he swayed in his saddle. They remained hidden in some trees while they studied the cabin to see if it was safe.

Finally the Kid spoke through chattering teeth, "We can ride down an' ask. That cabin belongs to Falcon MacCallister, an' last time we spoke we was still friends."

He glanced at French, " 'Course, that was just after the Regulators killed Baker and Morton, so I don't rightly know how he feels just now."

He pointed at the cabin. "There's two horses in that corral behind the house, so somebody's likely there now. I doubt if Falcon would draw down on us, but he may have some company who's not so friendly. Keep your hand near your gun, just in case. Can't always tell who's friendly an' who ain't in these parts 'til it's too late."

They rode their horses down a gentle slope toward the cabin with as much caution as possible, ready for a challenge from the log ranch house that might spell trouble.

Suddenly the Kid saw a tall man wearing a brace of pistols come out on the cabin's front porch, watching them ride closer without reaching for either gun.

"Hello the house!" the Kid cried when he recognized the man as Falcon MacCallister.

"Ride in!" a deep voice shouted.

The tall gunman still made no move toward his weapons. He must have recognized the Kid's horse, even covered with ice and snow.

"We've had a spell of bad luck, Falcon," the Kid began when they reached the front of the cabin. "We've both got bulletholes in our legs. Wondered if you might know a thing or two about how to stop the bleedin' and such."

"I'm acquainted with bullet wounds," Falcon replied, keeping an eye on the Kid. His expression was serious, but not hostile or threatening.

"How have you been, Kid?" He glanced at the blood on Kid's leg, frozen now in spiculed, red icicles on his pant leg. "Still trying to get revenge for John Tunstall's killing?"

"That's a fact," the Kid answered, gingerly swinging down from his blood-soaked saddle. "This here is Jim French, Falcon. You met him a time or two at The Drinking Hole. Playin' Monte, I believe it was."

"I remember," Falcon said. "Tie off those horses to the corral fence over near the shed where they can get some shelter and come inside. I've got a fire built, some coffee on the stove, and some healing salve I can use to dress those holes with. Maybe it'll keep them from festering some, if you wrap them tight and stay off them for a while to let the healing begin."

"We're much obliged," French groaned, easing himself down to the ground, dusting snow and ice off his shoulders and hat. "Don't figure I could have ridden much farther than this in this norther."

Hobbling, they led their horses over to the pole fence and tied them under the overhang of a wooden shed. After dumping some hay from a trough on the ground for them to eat, Jim French gave the Kid a glance. "You were right. This MacCallister is okay. I think we can trust him."

The Kid nodded and started off toward the cabin.

"Good thing, too, 'cause he looks meaner'n a two-headed rattler," French said in a quiet voice as they neared the house.

They walked inside a small but neat and tidy cabin. There were curtains on the windows, woven rugs on the floor, what appeared to be hand-made furnishings, a woodstove, and a bullhide chair in one corner beside a hand-cut, pine table which was polished until it gleamed.

Falcon was opening a small jar. A pile of clean rags lay on the table. He gave the Kid and French a sideways look. "Take off your guns and pants, boys. Looks like the bullets went clean through, so you should mend without any problem, as long as we can keep infection to a minimum. Luckily, the cold should help out some."

"It was the same bullet," the Kid told him, unbuckling his gunbelt. He grinned, then groaned as he unbuttoned his pants. "Damn near anybody would call that a run of bad luck, when one bullet gets two men in the leg."

"I heard about the shooting in Lincoln," Falcon said. Hearing this, the Kid froze.

"Just what did you hear about it?" the Kid asked, wondering if Falcon was about to get the drop on them now that he and French had taken off their guns. He still wasn't sure Falcon didn't hold the killing of Baker and Morton against him. He had certainly been mad enough at the time. Even the Kid had begun to feel ashamed at what they had done when Falcon turned that disgusted stare on him, the bodies at his feet.

"Not all that much," Falcon replied with a small shrug. "Some of your bunch killed Sheriff Brady. A Chisum cowboy came riding through early this morning. He told me what he'd heard. He didn't see it, mind you. He said folks are saying the Regulators murdered the sheriff and wounded Billy Matthews. Also got a man named Long."

"It wasn't murder," the Kid protested, feeling more uneasy as Falcon continued to speak. "This has turned into a war, Falcon, a range war. Brady had it comin'. He's on the payroll of the man who ordered John Tunstall gunned down in cold blood."

The Kid paused, sorrow overcoming him for a moment. "And, as you know, I witnessed the whole thing. Jesse Evans an' Billy Morton did the shootin', along with Tom Hill. Mr. Tunstall didn't even have his pistol out when they shot him in the face."

"Kid, you know that isn't the official version going around," Falcon said quietly. "Sheriff Brady has been telling everyone two shots had been fired in John Tunstall's pistol."

The Kid bristled. "And I can tell you how that happened. After they killed him, Jesse Evans jerked out Mr. Tunstall's gun and fired it twice up in the air. Then they put it in his hand after he was already dead. I swear it's the truth."

"I believe you," Falcon said. "I know all about Evans and his gang." He looked up from examining the Kid's leg. "And, of course, you've already killed Morton for his part in the fracas."

"Damn right we did," French said, nodding once. "He had it comin', and so did that bastard Baker."

Falcon put the jar of wintergreen salve on the tabletop

and walked past the Kid and French to the cabin door, giving the hills around them a careful examination, watching the snow fall for a moment, as if thinking.

"You've got bigger troubles headed your way, if what that Chisum rider told me is the truth."

"How's that?" the Kid asked.

Falcon turned back to them. "Seems Billy Matthews has organized a couple of big posses to hunt all of you down. George Hindman is in charge of one posse."

"There's more'n one?" French asked.

"At least two. An old bounty hunter from down in Texas by the name of Andrew Roberts is leading the others. Folks call him Buckshot Roberts. Always uses a shotgun when he has a choice. And he's not above backshooting a man to earn his money, or killing him in bed while he's asleep if he gets the chance."

"I've heard the name Buckshot Roberts," the Kid said. "How many men will be after us?"

"Hard to say, son."

"But we were legal constables of Lincoln County when we arrested Baker and Morton, with legal arrest warrants. They can't just come after us an' gun us down."

Falcon shook his head. "I told you at the time, Kid, killing men who were your prisoners wouldn't sit well with people. Remember, Governor Axtell invalidated your appointments to the constables' positions, and he did the same to the warrants you carry. As you no doubt know, somebody with a lot of political pull whispered in the governor's ear."

"That'd be Lawrence Murphey or Jimmy Dolan," the Kid snapped angrily, glaring at French after hearing again the news Falcon just gave them. "They took away our badges. I can't hardly make myself believe it."

"They'll hunt us down like stray dogs," French said, a look of fear in his eyes.

"Most likely," the Kid said softly. "We'll be runnin' for our lives now, unless we stand up an' fight 'em like men."

"There ain't nearly enough of us," French argued.

"We'll find some more men," the Kid said, still boiling mad over what had been done to them. "We ain't backin' down from 'em just because they got to the governor."

Falcon chuckled, looking the Kid up and down.

"What was funny 'bout that?" asked the Kid.

Falcon hooked his thumbs in his gunbelt. "I guess you could say it's because I like your style, Kid. You've got two big posses headed your way and you haven't shown the slightest inclination to back down. I like backbone in a man." He hesitated, then added, " 'Course, it's got to be tempered with a healthy respect for one's enemies, or it becomes foolhardiness."

"I've seen how good you are with a gun," said the Kid, "and no one would ever question your backbone. Any chance you'd throw in with us?"

Falcon wagged his head. "Not officially, Kid. But I might be inclined to take a hand in things if certain circumstances come up."

"What sort of circumstances are you talkin' about?" French asked.

Again, Falcon chuckled. "If the odds got too long against you when I'm around, or it I can see it won't be a fair fight. I won't promise you anything. Could be some of Dolan's boys might turn up missing from time to time."

"Then you *will* help us!" the Kid exclaimed.

"I told you, not officially. This isn't any of my affair, and I can probably be of more use if I stay on the outside and not appear to take sides. Remember, Kid, all I said was, there could come a time when some of Dolan's gunmen don't show up for payday."

"You know," the Kid said, "Dolan's men are out to get Alex McSween, and John Chisum, too."

"Like I said," Falcon explained, "this isn't my war, and

unless it spills over to involve Chisum I'm staying out. But if anyone sends gunnies or outlaws after John without good reason, this Dolan is gonna start losing gunhands and partners."

"I wish you'd talk with Dick Brewer, Falcon. He seen and heard some things in Lincoln that might make you change your mind and ride with us after Evans."

"Nothing's gonna change my mind, son."

"Not even if Dick told you all the things Dolan an' his boys have done, includin' buying influence from the big wheels in Santa Fe so's we can't get a fair hearing?"

"I'll talk to Dick about what he knows, and maybe I'll pass the information along to some authorities who can do something about it, but I don't ride with anybody. When I work with a gun, I always work alone."

French was watching Falcon closely. "Must mean you're real good. Can't say as I've ever heard of Falcon MacCallister by reputation."

The statement brought a grin to Falcon's face. "A reputation doesn't mean all that much, Jim. Most times, it's blown up to make it sound better."

"I wasn't meanin' to say you weren't . . ."

Falcon halted him by raising his hand. "No need to explain. I know what you're meaning to say. There may be plenty of gun slicks who are faster than I am. I've just never met up with any of them yet."

The Kid could see there was no point in arguing with Falcon further. He limped over to the table and dropped his pants before picking up the jar of salve.

"Push it deep into your wounds as you can," Falcon said. "Then tie a bandage around it real tight."

The Kid did as he was told, feeling a fiery burning in his leg muscle when he pushed the pungent ointment into the hole in the front of his thigh. "Stings like hell," he said, "but not near as bad as a bullet."

"You boys are welcome to rest here a while. Hardly anybody knows about this cabin. I hired it from a widow lady a while back, to use while I ran The Drinking Hole. I only plan to stay in the area a short while longer."

"Sure hope you don't pull out now," said the Kid, tying a strip of cloth around his injury. "I have a feelin' we're gonna need all the help we can get."

"I never promised I'd help you, Kid," Falcon reminded. "I said there could come a time when I'd even things up for you and your friends."

"Anything'll be a help, Mr. MacCallister," French said.

"Call me Falcon. No need to be so formal."

French winced when he applied the salve to his leg wound, pushing it deep with the tip of his finger coated in medication. "We appreciate the offer to let us rest a spell," he said. "I don't think I can ride another mile without rest an' maybe a bite of food."

He looked over at the Franklin stove in the corner. "And that stove's mighty welcome, too."

"I've got plenty of fatback and beans, and a few tins peaches and pears," Falcon said. "Some Arbuckles coffee, too. I'll rustle you boys up something to eat while you tend to your horses. After they've eaten their fill and watered themselves, just put them in the corral with mine. The piñon trees will keep most of the cold off of them."

"We're mighty obliged, Falcon," the Kid said, glad he could still call Falcon his friend, and hoping there might be some way to convince this tall gunman to stay in Lincoln County for a spell. Having a man like him on their side might make one hell of a difference.

Twenty-two

After a couple of weeks, the Kid and French recovered from their wounds enough to ride toward San Patricio to meet up with Dick Brewer and the other Regulators, who were camped in the region.

On the way, the Kid met a young man named Tom O'Folliard, and the two became instant friends. O'Folliard was of the same age as the Kid. He had drifted into New Mexico from Uvalde, Texas. The Kid persuaded him to take a hand in the war against the Dolan forces, to become a Regulator.

When they met up with Brewer, the Kid found out he was plenty pissed-off about the killing of Brady, thinking it to have been a dumb move on their part.

"Kid, up until then we had the people of Lincoln on our side," he said over a campfire in the hills above San Patricio. "Now, a lot of the citizens think we're no more than outlaws, worse even than Dolan's men, who have been robbin' 'em blind for years."

He stopped talking long enough to drink his coffee, then turned his gaze back on the Kid. "Some of 'em are even callin' you a mad dog killer, a crazy man who shoots first and asks questions later."

The Kid stuck out his chin, too stubborn to admit Brewer was right in his assessment of their actions.

"Well, Dick, that kind of reputation don't do a man no harm, especially when he's got a pack of hound dogs on his trail. Might make 'em think twice 'bout tanglin' with him.''

Brewer nodded, " 'Course, even though what you done was stupid, what Dolan's doin' is even worse. I just can't believe he's put a two hundred dollar reward on any Regulator arrested or killed. Hell, that's more money than most punchers earn in a year. We're gonna have every hardscrabble cowpoke in the county lookin' to earn some of that easy money.''

The Kid's lips grew tight. "Then it's up to us to not make the money so easy to get.''

Brewer pointed over his shoulder to two men that the Kid didn't know sitting by the fire.

"Kid, I want you to meet Frank and George Coe. They joined up when they heard about Dolan taking Tunstall's cattle from the Rio Feliz up to San Nicolas spring. He plans to sell 'em to the government to feed the Injuns, an' keep the money for himself.''

The Kid shook his head. "That's what started this whole mess in the first place, Dolan stealing Tunstall's and Chisum's beeves.''

"Yeah, and the Coes have agreed to help us get them cattle back to where they belong.'' He paused and nodded at Tom, sitting next to the Kid.

"Who's that you got with you?''

The Kid inclined his head at Tom. "This here's Tom O'Folliard. He agreed to ride with us. He wants to be a Regulator, too.''

Brewer shook his head, grinning ruefully. "Can't say as I understand why anybody would want to join up in this fracas, but welcome, Tom O'Folliard. Glad to have any man who knows how to use a six-killer. We're gonna need all the help we can got to make it out of this alive.''

Brewer stood up, poured the remainder of his coffee on the fire, and said, "Mount up, boys. We got some distance to cover to get Mr. Tunstall's cattle back to his ranch.''

After riding all day without stopping to take a proper nooning, the men were much relieved to crest a hill and see Blazer's Mill in the distance.

"What's that place?" the Kid asked Brewer.

"That's Blazer's Mill. Old Doc Blazer leases it to the Mescalero Indian Agency," Brewer answered. "The agent's wife, Mrs. Godfroy, is known to serve a pretty mean dinner to passersby, an' my stomach's tellin' me it's time we took some food."

The Regulators rode down the hill at a gallop, whooping and hollering at the chance to get out of the saddle and put on a feedbag.

Once they had seen to their horses, the men were shown into a back area of the building, set up as a dining hall, with several long tables arranged along the walls.

Brewer told Mrs. Godfroy, "Bring us all the food you got, an keep it comin' 'til we're done."

"I've got a whole pig and half a calf on the fire out back. You think that'll be enough for you boys?"

The Kid laughed. "Hell, that's enough for me. The others can fend for themselves."

"Buckshot Roberts" wanted out of the New Mexico Territory, and to that end he had sold his tiny holdings above the Ruidoso River, meaning to leave the country as soon as he was paid for his property. The buyer was from back east, and a check for Roberts' land was in the hands of the mail service.

Riding toward Dr. Joseph Blazer's mills—a sawmill and a gristmill, he kept his favorite mule at a slow lope, hoping a check for payment had arrived at Blazers with the mail wagon, even though mail service in this part of the territory was notoriously unreliable.

But as Roberts topped a rise above the mills, he saw a collection of horses in the corrals out back. Aware of the troubles between the so-called Regulators and Dolan's men, he felt sure the horses belonged to one faction or the other. There could be trouble if Blazer had Regulators as visitors, since he'd been a friend to Billy Matthews and Jimmy Dolan after he'd come to the New Mexico Territory from Texas last year, not without good reason, following a shoot-out with a group of Texas Rangers in Goliad County.

"Hellfire," Roberts growled, urging his mule toward the mills, anyway. He wasn't going to let anything stand in the way of his way getting the money he was owed. This wasn't his fight, and it was better to pull stakes now, before things went any further. After the killing of Lincoln County Sheriff William Brady, it seemed like everyone was taking a side. All talk lately had been about how the fight would escalate and it would be hard to remain neutral in something like this, a cattle war pitting powerful men like Catron in Santa Fe and his boys, Lawrence Murphy and Jimmy Dolan, against a man like John Chisum and small ranchers. *It could get a man killed,* he thought. The time was at hand to go elsewhere, before he became embroiled in the controversy and was asked to employ his guns. Of course, he thought, if worst came to worst and he had to kill a few of them Regulators, the two hundred dollars a man would come in mighty handy.

As he rode closer to the two story house where Dr. Blazer practiced dentistry, he saw George Coe and Dick Brewer come out on the porch.

"Trouble," Roberts grunted, taking the hammer thong off his Colt .44, then drawing his Winchester from its saddle boot. He would show these Regulators he wasn't a man to be trifled with, even though an old shotgun wound left so many iron pellets in his left arm he was unable to raise it above his shoulder. He could still shoot.

"Hold it right there, Buckshot!" shouted George Coe, one of the latest area ranchers to join sides with the Regulators. "If you aim to come any closer, you'll have to leave them guns and walk the rest of the way."

"Like hell!" "Buckshot" snapped. "Don't no son of a bitch tell me when I can carry a gun!"

Charley Bowdre and Billy Bonney, the one everyone called the Kid, came out to flank Brewer and Coe. However, this did nothing to discourage Roberts. "You boys back out of the damn way," he cried, lifting the muzzle of his rifle. "I come to get my mail, an' by God ain't nobody gonna stop me. I'll kill the first bastard who reaches for a gun!"

It was as if Bowdre were intent upon obliging him. Bowdre's pistol came out.

Roberts fired his Winchester from the hip, sending a slug into Bowdre's belly, although it struck his belt buckle and ricocheted off into George Coe's hand, sending the gun he was holding spinning into the dirt.

In the same instant, Roberts jumped off his mule and ran for a corner of the building.

The Kid and Brewer jerked their guns and started firing at him. Every shot was a miss until he was safely behind the adobe wall.

"You boys lookin' for a fight?" he bellowed. "Then I'll damn sure give you one!"

Roberts swung around the corner, blasting his rifle into the men on Blazer's front porch while they were scattering to find cover. His first shot missed the Kid by inches.

Brewer ducked inside the doorway and peered around the doorframe . . . it would prove to be a fatal mistake.

Roberts fired. His rifle slug hit Dick Brewer above the eye and came out the back of his head, rupturing his skull. Blood and brains and a plug of his black hair went flying all over the porch.

Brewer slumped to the boards, dead before he landed, his head a pulpy mass of brain tissue and shattered bone.

"You boys want some more?" Roberts cried, jacking another shell into his rifle.

He got an answer, a .44 bullet blasting from the Kid's gun where he was hidden behind the far corner of the house. The slug struck adobe, bouncing off harmlessly, making a singing sound as it flew away.

Roberts leaned out again and fired. The Kid ducked back to safety, out of the line of fire.

Charley Bowdre poked his head around a rear corner of the house. "Throw it down, Buckshot, or I'm gonna kill you!" he demanded.

Roberts whirled for a shot at Bowdre. Bowdre fired first. A red-hot pain raced through Roberts' belly, and he staggered back from the force of impact, mortally wounded. While he'd tasted lead before, he never felt pain before like this from the hole in his gut.

An open window into a bedroom of Dr. Blazer's house gave Roberts the only chance he had. Almost blinded by pain, he made a feeble jump through the window, landing on the floor on his chest with a painful grunt.

He rolled over, attempting to reload his rifle, certain that more Regulators would be coming for him. When the Winchester's cartridge tube was fully loaded, Roberts came unsteadily to his feet and crept over to a bed, pulling the mattress off to serve as a shield from stray bullets when they rushed him.

Leaning back against the bedroom wall, half hidden behind a thick mattress, he waited, trying to stem the flow of blood pouring from his belly wound.

"I'm gutshot," he groaned quietly. He knew few men could survive a belly wound like his, but he vowed silently to take a few Regulators with him when he went. He'd already downed their leader, Dick Brewer. Maybe he could get a few more.

"Come out with your hands empty!"

Roberts did not recognize the voice.

"We got you surrounded!" another said. "You ain't gonna get out alive 'less you toss out them guns."

"To hell with you!" he shouted back. "Come an' get me, if you got the nerve."

A silence followed.

"We got your mule, Buckshot. You'll never get out of here! Give it up now!"

"Ain't my way of doin' things!" he answered. "You boys come for me. I'll take you with me to a grave!"

"You're bein' stupid, Buckshot. There's ten of us, an' just one of you!"

His stomach was killing him. Blood was pooling on the floor all around him.

"Never was one to worry bout the odds against me!" he said after placing a hand over his belly. "I can kill a bunch of you if you try an' rush me."

Another longer silence.

"We'll wait you out, you ole' bastard. After you bleed for a few hours, you won't be so damn disagreeable."

"Maybe," he answered, softer, feeling his head reel with the pains shooting through him. "Only way you're gonna find out is to rush me."

"Stop bein' a damn fool."

"Always was a bit of a fool," Roberts replied, taking his hand off the hole in his abdomen when he felt it grow wet with blood.

"You aim to die?" another voice asked from the back of the house.

"If I have to. You boys callin' yourselves Regulators ain't got me killed just yet."

A small man named John Ryan, a part-time storekeeper at the Murphy and Dolan store, was a friend of Roberts. He offered to take a white flag of truce close enough to the house for Roberts to see him, an offer Roberts heard through the open window.

Ryan took a handkerchief and came around one side of a barn near the sawmill.

"Hey Buckshot!" he shouted. "Dr. Appel from Fort Stanton is on the way here. I know you got a bullet in you. Stop shootin' long enough fer him to look at yer wound."

"Don't need no damn help from some army doctor," Roberts shouted back. "I'm killin' any son of a bitch who gets close to this window or the door."

"You gotta listen to me, Buckshot. These boys ain't gonna rush you. You done killed Dick Brewer. They ain't got the nerve to rush you."

"To hell with every last one of 'em. All I wanted was a letter addressed to me from Saint Louis."

The pain in Roberts' abdomen was worsening, and he feared he would lose consciousness. He moved a bit closer to the window frame and looked out.

Men with rifles were hidden all around Dr. Blazer's house. He could see the glint of their rifle barrels in the late day sun.

"Don't do this no more, Buckshot," Ryan pleaded. "Let the sawbones have a look at you."

"I'm gutshot, John."

"Maybe the army doc can help you, anyhow."

"Nobody lives through a belly wound. I'm gonna die, but I damn sure aim to take some of them Regulators with me when I have to go."

"That don't make no sense," Ryan argued. "What did Tunstall or these Regulators ever do to you?"

Blood came in shorter, thicker bursts from the hole in his gut, and he felt himself growing weaker he could smell the acrid scent of his body wastes leaking from his ruptured bowels onto the floor.

"Got nothin' to do with it. I ain't lettin' 'em take me."

"You gotta be sensible. No reason for you to lay there an' bleed to death."

"I done killed Brewer. Maybe one or two more. I couldn't get no fair trial in this Territory."

"It won't matter if you bleed to death, Buckshot. Toss out that rifle an' give yourself up."

"The hell with you. I'm stayin'."

"But you're liable to die," Ryan begged, crouching down with his white truce flag between his knees.

"A man's gotta die sooner or later," Roberts answered, his voice failing him due to weakness. "Let them Regulators come at me. I'll make 'em pay real dear."

"You right sure you're mind's made up?" Ryan asked, backing up a low hill to the safety of a stand of pinon pines east of the Blazer home.

"I'm damn sure of it. Get the hell away from here," was Roberts' reply.

Andrew "Buckshot" Roberts died before dawn the next morning, as Dr. Appel from the army post at Fort Stanton arrived. Dick Brewer was obviously dead. Frank Coe had a severe wound to his hand, requiring the amputation of his thumb and forefinger.

Dick Brewer and Andrew Roberts were buried side by side at Blazer's Mills the next day, two enemies who had never met.

And with the death of "Buckshot" Roberts came a new enemy for the Regulators: The United States Army from nearby Fort Stanton.

The Kid escaped without a scratch. However, more was to come his way before the Lincoln County War came to an end . . .

Twenty-three

For four days Sheriff Peppin's posse had Alexander McSween's house in Lincoln surrounded. The Kid was growing edgy, as were many of the others. Almost twenty Regulators had been recruited, gathering at McSween's to execute the warrants for Jesse Evans, Sheriff Peppin, and several more. Shortly after the killing of Sheriff Brady, George Peppin was sworn in as sheriff and granted warrants for the arrest of the Regulators by powerful men close to the territorial governor. Both sides claimed to represent the law.

"Doc" Scurlock had been named captain of the Regulators after the killing of Dick Brewer, although everyone listened to McSween's counsel.

José Chavez, a new Regulator, was standing near a front window when he announced, "Here comes trouble."

The Kid came to the window, peering out with his rifle in his hands.

More than fifty uniformed soldiers from Fort Stanton came riding and marching into Lincoln—a dozen cavalrymen and the rest infantrymen.

"Looks like the army's gonna take a hand in this," the Kid said.

"They got no authority against us," Scurlock said. "This is a civilian matter."

McSween opened his front door a crack. "With or without the proper authority, it appears Colonel Dudley has decided to take sides with Sheriff Peppin and Jimmy Dolan."

"They bring a howitzer cannon and a Gatling gun," Chavez remarked, frowning.

"A cannon will blow these walls to pieces," McSween said quietly.

"We'll shoot the first son of a bitch who tries to aim it at us," Jim French said, almost fully recovered from his leg wound.

The Kid watched Colonel Dudley direct his men to move into the hills around McSween's adobe home. Some of Dolan's men went with the soldiers, breaking up into small groups to take up stations against the house.

"Look at that, boys. Men from the posse are hunkerin' down with the soldiers. Guess they think we'll be afraid to shoot at 'em if'n they're next to a blue belly."

Jim French snorted. "Huh, then they got another think comin'. If them soldier boys didn't wanna get shot at, they shouldn't have come to Lincoln."

"They've got us cornered now," the Kid said. "We gotta keep 'em from cuttin' us off to the river. It may be our only way out."

"They can't do this!" Scurlock insisted. "We have the legal authority and the warrants to arrest Peppin and every son of a bitch who was in that posse."

The Kid recalled his conversation with Falcon MacCallister at the cabin. "My friend from up north, MacCallister, said the governor invalidated our warrants an' took away our authority as constables."

"No one has informed me," McSween said, watching Dudley's troops scatter, forming a semi-circle around his house. "The governor overstepped his bounds if he did something like that without good reason."

"He's in Murphey an' Dolan's pockets," Scurlock said

with anger filling his voice. "Tom Catron up in Santa Fe is behind every bit of this."

"We're gonna have to shoot our way out of here," the Kid remarked.

"The Kid is right," Chavez said.

Jim French was at another window. "Look yonder, boys. One of Peppin's men is tryin' to sneak up on this side where them trees are the thickest carryin' a torch. They aim to burn us out, looks like."

"It's adobe," Scurlock said.

McSween looked at the rafters above them. "But the roof is made of wood. It's dry as tinder. If they are able to set the roof ablaze, we'll have to come out or the smoke will surely kill us."

The Kid looked over his shoulder at McSween. "And you got your wife and the other women and children in the east wing of the house to worry about. The way this wind's blowin', fire would catch 'em 'fore they could get quit of the house."

Without waiting for instructions, French fired his rifle out the window.

"You got the bastard!" Chavez cried.

A deputy working for Sheriff Peppin lay writhing in the dirt with a burning torch lying beside him.

"Nice shot," Scurlock said, grinning.

"It was a good shot," the Kid agreed after he saw the wounded deputy.

Answering rifle fire came pouring from the hills around the adobe and from the fire tower of a nearby house where some Dolan sharpshooters were stationed, smashing glass windowpanes, thudding into adobe walls and the roof.

"Look!" Chavez exclaimed. "Three of them soldiers is tryin' to turn that cannon on us."

"Shoot 'em down!" Scurlock snapped, raising his rifle to his shoulder.

The Regulators blasted away at the infantrymen around

the howitzer. Two soldiers dropped to the ground while the other fled to cover.

Sue McSween, Alexander's wife, had refused to leave the house before the shooting started. She now pointed to a rear window and let out a scream.

"What is it?" McSween cried, rushing to the window to see what had upset his wife.

Another of Peppin's deputies stood near a low adobe wall running up to the back porch. The deputy threw an oil-soaked torch up on the roof and ducked down behind the wall.

"Fire!" McSween yelled. "They managed to throw a burning stick up on the roof."

The Kid could see things taking a deadly turn. Instead of a standoff, the tide was turning toward Peppin's forces with the arrival of the soldiers.

"What time is it?" the Kid shouted at McSween.

McSween, a puzzled look on his face, pulled his pocket watch from his vest and opened the face. "It's a quarter to eight. Why?" he asked.

" 'Cause it'll be full dusk 'bout eight o'clock. I say we need to make a run for the river out the back, 'fore that fire burns the place down around us."

McSween sank to his knees, kneeling and leaning against the wall. It was plain that his courage was failing, and he was becoming more apathetic by the minute. He seemed almost in a state of emotional collapse.

The Kid realized someone needed to take charge or they would all die in this house.

"We can stick it out until dusk," he told the others, "if the fire doesn't burn any faster than it is now. Some of us are certain to get hit, but most of us can make it across the river. It's only a few hundred yards, and if we run fast and shoot fast, we can hold off Peppin's crowd so they can't do us much damage."

He turned to Mrs. McSween, regarding her with sympathy. "I expect, ma'am, you had better leave first. A dress ain't very good to make a run in."

Mrs. McSween glanced over at her husband, cowering against a far wall, and agreed to leave early enough so that she wouldn't impede the others when the time to make their break came.

"I'll take a couple of volunteers with me, an' we'll run out first to draw the fire of Dolan's men and the soldiers." He looked over and spoke to McSween. "That'll give you and the others a chance to slip out undetected and get to safety."

Everyone in the room agreed, standing tall and proud and showing no fear, except Ignacio Gonzalez, who had taken to whimpering and crying since he had been wounded in the arm.

The Kid turned to him, his face red and flushed from anger. "You damn coward!" the Kid said contemptuously, "I've got a great mind to hit you over the head with my pistol. We are going to stick here until it's full dark. Brace up and behave like a man."

Finally, dusk and darkness came to Lincoln. The Kid realized it was now or never.

"Let's make for the river now!" the Kid shouted, as more rifle fire came at them from the hills. "It's nearly dark out there."

"They'll shoot us the minute we step outside," McSween said, peering cautiously out a side window.

"We've gotta try it," Scurlock said. "Otherwise we're gonna be burned alive in here."

"I'll go out first," volunteered the Kid. "The rest of you come behind me. We'll stay next to the wall and use it for cover as long as we can, until we can make a dash for the trees along the riverbank."

"It's about the only choice we have," McSween said as smoke from burning wood shingles began to fill the kitchen and some of the other rooms.

"I'll be right behind you," Chavez said, leaving the window to hurry over to the back door.

Scurlock and more than a dozen others carried rifles over to stand behind the Kid and Chavez.

"Go whenever you're ready," Chavez said, levering a shell into the firing chamber of his rifle.

"If we throw enough lead back at 'em, maybe they won't be so damn brave," the Kid said, opening the door an inch or two to take a look outside.

"There may be some deputies hiding on the other side of the wall," the Kid warned.

"We'll kill the bastards," French snarled, coming up beside the Kid with his rifle cocked.

The Kid glanced over his shoulder. Alexander McSween sat on the floor, sobbing softly. He carried no guns, and seemed to be in the depths of despair.

"Follow us, Mr. McSween!" the Kid cried.

McSween merely wagged his head.

"C'mon, Kid," French said, shoving past Chavez and the others to be first out the back door.

Next came Harvey Morris, then Tom O'Folliard, before José Chavez and the Kid made it out to the wall. Flames from the burning roof illuminated them as they crept toward the river, making them easy targets.

A commotion at the front of the house made the Kid stop in his tracks to look back inside the house, and what he saw made his blood run cold.

Three men rushed through the unguarded front door with guns leveled.

"Give up, McSween!" a deep voice shouted.

"I shall never surrender!" McSween yelled back.

Then guns began to explode.

Five bullets cut down McSween so quickly that he did not have time to shield his face with his hands.

The next to fall was a new Regulator making his escape

through the back door, Vincente Romero. He flew off the porch after two shots caught him in the back.

Francisco Zamora wheeled around with his rifle to come to the aid of McSween. A slug caught him in the throat and he fell back on the seat of his pants, dropping his gun to grab his neck with both hands before he fell over dead.

Young Yginio Salazar crumpled with a bullet in the back fired by one of the posse. He began crawling toward the back door as smoke poured through holes burning in the roof, filling the house.

Ignàcio Gonzalez cradled his wounded arm as he came after the Kid and the other Regulators. He screamed in pain as another bullet grazed his side, but kept on running toward the wall, gripping his shattered arm, leaving a trail of blood behind him.

Florencio Chavez dashed out the back, ducking down so low he made a difficult target. José Sanchez was right behind him, and they turned away from the river, racing toward a chicken house a few dozen yards behind McSween's. In a matter of seconds they were out of sight.

"Run!" French cried, leading the rest of the Regulators toward the river.

Suddenly, two shadows appeared in the trees along the riverbank. Henry Brown and George Coe were motioning them toward the thicket.

"Hurry!" George shouted as the shooting behind them grew louder.

"This way!" Henry added before ducking back behind the trunk of a cottonwood tree.

The Kid fired over his shoulder when a man raised up near the adobe wall. A man screamed and the figure dropped out of sight.

French and O'Folliard were the first to reach Coe and Brown while Chavez and the Kid covered everyone's escape from the rear with occasional gunshots.

"This way," the Kid heard Coe say.

"Stay in them reeds an' keep down," Brown added in a quiet voice.

"We got horses tied downstream," Coe said as the Regulators trotted away from McSween's burning house.

"I saw 'em kill Mr. McSween," the Kid said to Doc Scurlock as they came to the water's edge.

"Damn," Scurlock hissed. "McSween never even carried no kind of gun."

"We'll get the yellow bastards another time," the Kid promised as they ran among tall canes growing along the bank. "They murdered Mr. McSween just like they murdered Mr. Tunstall that time."

"Damn right," Scurlock said, trotting through deep shadows, his mouth in a grim line. "We'll get revenge on 'em. Just you wait an' see."

"I'll be right there to lend a hand," the Kid said after a glance over his shoulder to see if any of the posse were following them. Flames from the roof of the house licked high in the night sky.

"The shootin' stopped," French said, slowing until the Kid and Scurlock were beside him.

"I reckon they killed all the others," Scurlock said bitterly.

The Kid couldn't shake the memory of Alexander McSween, sitting unarmed on the floor of his burning house when bullets tore through his body.

He remained silent about it now, but as they neared a group of saddled horses in a cottonwood grove downriver the Kid swore revenge against the killers of McSween. Their day of reckoning would come soon enough . . .

Twenty-four

Falcon was sitting at his usual table in The Drinking Hole, drinking coffee and reading about the latest exploits of the infamous Billy the Kid in the newspaper.

As he put a lucifer to his cigar, the batwings opened and in walked the most talked about outlaw in the state, the Kid.

Far from sneaking in looking over his shoulder, the Kid strolled in with head held high, like he was on top of the world.

Falcon leaned back, blew a plume of blue smoke at the ceiling, and smiled. *One thing you can always say about the Kid,* he thought, *he has style.*

As he made his way to Falcon's table the Kid smiled and waved at the people in the saloon, most of whom greeted him fondly, some calling out, "Go get 'em, Kid, ." One of the Mexican *vaqueros* in the bar yelled, "Give 'em hell, *Chivato.*"

When the Kid got to the table he waved at Pat Garrett behind the bar and said, "How 'bout a sarsaparilla, Pat?"

Pat grinned, shook his head, and fixed the Kid his drink.

The Kid sat down, crossed his legs, leaned back in his chair, and said, "How're things goin', Falcon?"

Falcon laughed, signaling Pat to bring him a whiskey. He guessed a visit from the Kid was reason enough to celebrate.

"I'm doing just fine, Kid. I won't ask how you're doing, since I've been reading about you almost every day in the newspapers."

The Kid scowled. "Don't believe everything you read, Falcon. They've got me killin' everyone in the county who dies for almost any reason, an' stealin' every cow that wanders off in the brush."

He grinned again, and Falcon realized that Billy just wasn't the sort to stay angry at anything for very long. His temper was explosive, but it cooled just as fast, and then he'd be the old Kid again, everyone's friend, especially the ladies.

"Hell, I read the other day some woman in Ruidosa claimed I ran up to her and stole her purse."

"Was there much money in it?" Falcon teased.

"Hell, no, it was near empty," the Kid teased back, taking a deep drink of his sarsaparilla, then burping as he always did.

Falcon sipped his whiskey and took a drag on his cigar, unsure of how to begin. He had some things on his mind he needed to say, to clear the air between them.

"Kid, there's some things I have to ask you."

The Kid's face sobered and he leaned forward, his elbows on the table.

"Go ahead, Falcon. I consider you my friend, an' you can ask me anything you want."

"These stories in the papers, about you killing all those people, are any of them true?"

The Kid thought for a minute, then shook his head.

"Falcon, much as I'd like everybody to believe I'm the fastest, meanest gun in the West, it just ain't so. I ain't killed anybody, far as I know, since the night we had the fight at McSween's."

Falcon was relieved to hear that. He didn't know why, but he felt a strange kinship to this boy. Perhaps it was because without some lucky breaks in his life, Falcon could be riding the same owl hoot trail Billy was, for much the same reasons.

"Good," Falcon said. "So, tell me what has really been going on in your life, Kid."

The Kid waved at Pat for another drink, then pulled a toothpick out of his pocket and began chewing on it as he spoke.

"You heard those bastards burned Mr. McSween's body, then went over to Tunstall's store and tore it up, stole most of the supplies, and all of the money out of his safe?"

Falcon nodded. "Yeah, I heard. Only Peppin's story was they were chasing members of your gang out of there and that you and your friends did all the damage and stole the money."

"That figures. Peppin never did stand too close to the truth, him and lying being such good friends."

"What happened after you escaped from McSween's?"

"I rode on over to San Patricio and met up with what remained of the Regulators. They decided that I should kind'a take over leadin', since everybody else was killed or on the run."

"I heard they called you to testify at a hearing at Fort Stanton about what happened at McSween's."

The Kid frowned. "Yeah, an' I told 'em just like it was, only Peppin and Colonel Dudley twisted everything around to make it sound like we was in the wrong. The coroner's jury, appointed by Peppin, of course, finally said that McSween, Harvey Morris, Francisco Zamora, and Vincente Romero died while they were resisting arrest by the sheriff's posse with force of arms."

He chuckled. "Hell, Falcon, those men offered to surrender two or three times, and those bastards led by Peppin and Dudley wouldn't let 'em."

"The papers said you killed one of Agent Godfroy's clerks over at Blazer's mill after you testified."

"Another lie," said the Kid bitterly. "Hell, Falcon,

Atananacio Martinez done testified he shot Bernstein in self-defense, but Dolan went around claimin' it was me, so of course Judge Bristol laid that one on me, too."

Falcon shook his head. "I heard a group of soldiers almost caught you one night, but they said you just disappeared like smoke from a campfire in a storm."

The Kid threw back his head and laughed. "You want to know what really happened?"

"Sure."

"I was on the run from the soldiers, who said I killed some Injuns on the Mescalero reservation—which I didn't, by the way—an' a Mexican farmer and his wife let me hole up in their little 'dobe house. It only had the one room, and they was sleepin' on a mattress in one corner and I was layin' down on another mattress in the other corner. When the soldiers came knocking at the door, the Mex and his wife put me betwixt the two mattresses and laid down on top of me. Those stupid soldiers went around the room lookin' but couldn't find me."

The Kid paused, took another drink of sarsaparilla, and smiled. "Hellfire, Falcon, I 'bout smothered under those mattresses, but I got away again."

"So, what are you going to do now?"

He shrugged. "Don't have much choice. The Dolan forces have me branded as the worst outlaw in the land, so won't nobody hire me for any real work. Guess I'll just stay with the Regulators and try to somehow avenge Tunstall's and McSween's deaths."

"What about Jesse Evans and his men?"

The Kid looked up. "What about them? Last I heard Evans was in custody over at Fort Sumner, being held for the murder of Mr. Tunstall."

Falcon shook his head. "Well, he and his men are out now. With the help of Judge Bristol, Rynerson staged a mock hearing, and he was acquitted. Rynerson let him plead self-defense, and the hand-picked jury bought it."

The Kid slammed his hand down on the table. "Damn! I swear to you, Falcon, if it's the last thing I ever do I'll see Evans in hell for what he did. Him and the whole Dolan group."

Falcon leaned forward and put his hand on the Kid's arm. "Kid, take it easy. There's nothing you can do now, it's all over. The law has spoken."

"Not my law, the law of the gun!" The Kid stood up and put his hand on his Colt. "I'll see you later, Falcon. I got me some men to hunt."

Without a backward glance, the Kid stormed from the saloon. Falcon sat helplessly watching a good man throw his life away with no chance at all of coming out of this fracas alive.

Falcon closed and locked the doors of The Drinking Hole at two in the morning, climbed on Diablo, and headed home toward the Ruidosa River under a full moon.

The sky was cloudless and clear, the air crisp and cold, and Falcon was enjoying his ride, until Diablo shook his head and nickered softly.

Pulling back on the reins, Falcon studied the trail ahead of him as Diablo slowed to a walk. *Uh oh,* he thought, *there's company up ahead waiting in that copse of mesquite trees.*

Watching closely, Falcon could see the intermittent glow of a cigarette as someone smoked while waiting for him to appear.

He unbuttoned his heavy coat and pulled the sides back, hooking them in his belt so they left his Colts exposed. He loosened the hammer thong on the pistols, then drew a short-barreled, ten gauge express gun from his left hand saddle boot.

Laying the shotgun across his saddle horn, he let Diablo walk up the trail until he was about thirty yards from the trees. By now he could see the fog-breath of several horses among the trees, and dark shapes of the men riding them. He counted four riders.

Falcon pulled Diablo to a halt, and sat there on the trail, silently staring at where the men were hiding, letting them know he saw them and was ready for them to come out.

Finally, after a few minutes, the riders emerged. Jesse Evans came out of the trees, followed by Smokey Johanson, "Turkey Neck" Bill McGraw, and Jack Spears. They were all hard men, and were among those who had ridden with Evans from the first, assisting him in all the rustling and shooting he had been doing over the past year.

As they came toward him, Falcon used the noise their horses made to cover the sound of him earing back the hammers on his shotgun.

"Howdy, gents. What can I do for you?" Falcon asked, as casual as if middle of the night confrontations were an everyday occurrence for him.

"Hello, MacCallister," Evans said, pulling his horse to a halt ten yards from Falcon.

Evans sat back against the cantle of his saddle, tipped his hat back on his head, and glanced at the moon overhead. "Nice night, ain't it?"

Falcon nodded, his eyes fixed on the men in front of him. "Yes. It's a good night for dying."

Evans stared at him, his eyes cold as the night air, shining in reflected moonlight. "Who said anything 'bout dyin', MacCallister? We just wanna ask you some questions 'bout Billy the Kid."

"Yeah," "Turkey Neck" McGraw growled, "we wanna know where the little bastard's hidin' out. We plan to pay him a visit."

Falcon pulled gently on Diablo's right rein, moving the bronc a little sideways so the shotgun pointed at the group in front of him.

"I don't know where the Kid is, at the moment. I do

know he intends to kill you, Jesse, and all the men who ride with you, for what you did to his friend John Tunstall."

Evans emitted a harsh laugh. "Is that so?"

Falcon nodded. "Yes. However, I don't intend to let that happen. I'm reserving that pleasure for myself."

"Why you . . ." Smokey Johanson said, and Falcon saw his hand move toward his pistol.

Without another word, Falcon let the hammer down on the ten gauge, sending a load of 00-buckshot exploding out of the barrel toward Johanson. The molten pellets caught the big Swede in the chest, blowing a hole clean though his body and catapulting him backward off his horse.

As Diablo shied from the sudden noise, Falcon threw the shotgun to his shoulder, fired the other barrel at McGraw, and could see his head disappear in the flash from the barrel.

"God damn!" Spears yelled as his and Evans's horses reared and crow-hopped, trying to get away from the noise and smoke.

Falcon dropped the express gun and grabbed iron as a pistol appeared in Spear's hand and he frantically tried to get his mount under control to get a clear shot at Falcon.

Falcon fired both Peacemakers from the hip, one slug tearing off Spear's right ear as it cut a deep furrow in his scalp, the other bullet entering his left eye, putting out his lights and slamming him to the ground, dead before he hit dirt.

Evans was holding onto his reins with both hands, still trying to get his horse calmed down. After a moment, he managed to still the frightened animal, and sat looking around him at his men, all lying dead on the ground.

"Hell, MacCallister," he said, his eyes wide and scared, "why'd you do that? We just wanted to talk."

Falcon put his pistols in the holsters and faced Evans. "Jesse, you been calling the dance around here for some time, riding roughshod over anyone who got in your way. You've killed some good men, men who were doing you no harm."

Falcon stared into the killer's eyes. "Now, you're going to learn that he who calls the dance has to pay the band. Fill your hands, or die where you sit."

Evans licked his lips, eyes darting to and fro, looking for some way to escape. Finally, he took a deep breath, and grabbed for his pistol.

Falcon drew and fired before Evans cleared leather, his bullet hitting Evans square in the chest, punching a hole through his breastbone and in his left lung.

Evans grunted and slumped in the saddle, staring at the front of his shirt, where blood, black as coal in the moonlight, pumped out in small squirts.

"Damn," he muttered, frothy blood on his lips, "you've kilt me."

Falcon holstered his Colt, pulled Diablo's reins and walked his horse around Evans, breathing noisily as he sat dying in his saddle.

"Like I said, Jesse," Falcon said as he passed, "It's a good night for dying."

Twenty-five

The Kid was headed up to White Oaks, after being forced to steal a few horses to keep his small group of Regulators fed. Times had been lean lately, and a stolen horse or two meant money in the bank if they were driven over to Tascosa in Texas, where no questions were asked.

Riding with the Kid were Buck Edwards, Dan Cook, Tom O'Folliard, Billy Wilson, and Charley Bowdre. They came upon the whiskey-peddling operation of "Whiskey Jim" Greathouse, and stopped for a rest and to water their horses. Some of the men wanted whiskey, but the Kid didn't partake of strong spirits no matter how festive the occasion.

All day the Kid had been edgy, with the nagging feeling they were being followed.

"You keep lookin' at our backtrail, Kid," Bowdre said as he dismounted in front of the Greathouse adobe outside of White Oaks.

"Got this feelin' we're bein' followed."

"Nobody's back there," O'Folliard said, tying off his horse at the rail.

"We'd have seen their dust," Wilson offered.

Buck Edwards gazed across the hills. "I been havin' this feelin', too."

Cook headed for the steps. "I'm thirsty. You boys can argue out here all damn day for all I care, but my throat's sayin' it needs whiskey."

"Get your whiskey," the Kid said. "Then we're movin'
on to Coyote Springs."

As the Kid and the others were making camp at an old
sawmill near Coyote Springs, a posse of eight or nine men
led by Deputy Sheriff Bill Hudgens suddenly came galloping
over a rise with guns drawn.

"Head for cover!" the Kid shouted.

As Wilson swung aboard his horse a bullet struck it in the
neck and it collapsed underneath him, bawling with fear
and pain as blood poured from its wound.

Gunshots sounded from every direction as the Kid swung
up on his mare, only to have the animal shot dead with a
bullet through its brain, sending it tumbling to the earth,
almost trapping his leg underneath the horse's weight.

Cook and Edwards dove for cover behind the old mill,
and the Kid was not far behind.

"They're circlin' us!" Wilson shouted, "an' now we's
short by two horses!"

Blasts of gunfire thundered from trees and brush and
rocks around the millhouse. Billy Wilson, trapped behind
a rock, was the target of most of the gunfire. Bullets kicked
up dust and rock chips all around him. So much lead was
flying he couldn't raise up to get off a shot of his own.

But as the shooting died down while the posse reloaded,
Wilson made his way to the sawmill walls and safety, dodging
and darting until a rock and adobe wall protected him from
speeding lead.

"Give it up, Kid!" a voice shouted. "We've got you boys
trapped!"

"Like hell!" the Kid yelled back, firing his rifle at the
voice.

Again the gunshots resumed, both sides wasting lead
since there was too much cover for an accurate shot. Burning gunpowder filled everyone's nostrils. The noise from

so many rifles and pistols was like the coming of a spring storm.

"How the hell are we gonna get out of here alive?" Wilson asked the Kid.

"Don't worry. We ain't done fightin' yet."

Edwards blasted away with his Winchester, and a wounded man cried out.

"Atta boy!" Wilson barked, sending a wild shot over the head of a posseman hidden behind a rock pile.

For half an hour the posse and the Kid's men traded bullets back and forth. Then the shooting fell to an occasional pop from either side.

"Maybe they're runnin' low on ammunition," Bowdre suggested as he reloaded.

"We ain't in the best of shape ourselves in that department," the Kid said.

By slow degrees the shooting ended. An eerie silence spread all around the mill.

"Wonder what's goin' on?" Edwards said, peering around a corner.

Before the Kid could answer, a voice shouted from the top of a hill. "Come on out and let's talk, Kid! Nobody'll shoot while we talk things over. We've got you surrounded."

"It's a long way from bein' over!" the Kid yelled back. "We just got our guns limbered up."

"You gotta listen to reason, Kid! We can starve you out if you don't surrender."

"We've got plenty to eat. We can start eatin' them dead horses you shot if we run out of beans."

"To hell with 'em," Wilson snarled. "Let 'em try to come and get us."

For several minutes there was silence from the posse, and the Kid guessed they must be talking over their options. All they could do was wait.

Then a voice echoed from a brush pile. "Hey, Kid! It's me, Jimmy Carlyle. Let's you an' me talk, just the two of us without our guns."

Carlyle was a popular blacksmith from the White Oaks area, and the Kid liked him. He wondered what Carlyle was doing with a posse after him and his men.

"I trust you, Jimmy!" he cried. "It's the rest of those bastards with you I don't trust. One of 'em could put a bullet in my back."

"I give you my word," Carlyle said.

The Kid thought about it a moment. "I ain't comin' out, but I give you my word you can come down here an' we'll talk. Nobody is gonna take a shot at you."

Another lengthy silence passed.

"I smell a trick," Edwards said under his breath. "Some of 'em will sneak around behind us while you an' Carlyle have your little talk."

"Maybe," the Kid said, wondering.

"We can cover the back pretty good from here," Wilson said, after looking out a broken rear window. "Don't see how they'd get very close without us seein' 'em."

"Jim's word will be good," the Kid promised. "If he'll come down here, then we'll let him come peaceful."

A moment later, Carlyle yelled, "I'm comin' down, Kid. I got no gun."

"Come down an' we'll talk," the Kid answered. "You got my word nobody'll take a shot at you."

The blacksmith rose up behind a clump of brush with his hands in the air.

"Don't nobody fire a shot," warned the Kid. "I gave him my word."

Jimmy Carlyle came walking slowly toward the mill, and it was easy to see he didn't have a gun.

"So far, so good," Wilson whispered, glancing over his left shoulder at the back of the building.

Carlyle walked bravely up to the door and the Kid lowered his rifle when the blacksmith walked inside. His face was covered with sweat.

"Tell me what you've got to say," the Kid began. "I know

it was Sheriff Hudgens who sent you down here to try an' talk us into givin' up."

"It's the only way, Kid. We've got men all around this ole' place, an' I damn sure don't wanna see you or any of these boys killed."

"We didn't come lookin' for no trouble," Wilson said. "We camped here real peaceful."

"But the law has got warrants for your arrest," Carlyle argued weakly. "The sheriff says we've got a duty to bring you boys in."

"Tell the sheriff he can go to hell," the Kid snapped.

The blacksmith eyed Wilson's whiskey jug. "I sure could use a swallow or two of that corn squeeze. This has been real hard on my nerves."

"Give him a drink," the Kid ordered.

Wilson handed him the jug. Carlyle took several long swallows and then sleeved his lips dry.

"What the hell is takin' so long?" a voice shouted from one hilltop.

Carlyle turned back to the open doorway. "We're talkin' things over. Wait a damn minute!"

"Have another drink," Wilson offered.

"An' tell 'em we ain't done talkin' yet," the Kid added, one eye on a front window.

"We ain't waitin' much longer," another voice cried from a juniper tree. "Five minutes more an' we're all gonna start shootin'."

Fear twisted Carlyle's face. He shouted back up the hill, "You boys promised wouldn't be no shootin' while I was down here talkin' to the Kid."

"Lyin' bastards," Edwards said between tightly clenched teeth, bringing his rifle up to his shoulder.

"Don't shoot!" the blacksmith said to Edwards. "Not now. I'll go back up an' talk to the sheriff about this here situation an' see if he'll listen."

"He'll listen to a goddamn gun goin' off if he ain't real careful," Edwards replied.

"No shootin'," the Kid said. "I gave my word on it, and a man's word is sometimes all he's got."

Carlyle edged farther out the door. "Let me talk to Hudgens an' I'll come back down. Maybe he'll let some of you ride off, but I can't promise nothin'. I know he's gonna want to put irons on the Kid here."

"Nobody's puttin' irons on me," the Kid remarked.

"I'll tell the sheriff what you said," Carlyle replied as he walked out on the porch.

From somewhere on a hillside, a lone gunshot cracked. No one could be sure exactly where it came from, but with the sound of a gun all of the Kid's men opened fire. And from the hills, the possemen started shooting.

Jimmy Carlyle took off in a lumbering run for the safety of some nearby bushes. He made it roughly thirty yards unharmed, then the back of his sweat-stained shirt erupted in a shower of blood.

Carlyle staggered a few steps more, calling out for the men from White Oak to stop firing. Then another slug shattered his right knee, and he went down on his face in the dirt.

"Damn!" the Kid bellowed. "I gave my word nothing would happen to Jimmy . . ."

Carlyle began to crawl feebly toward the bushes, leaving a red smear in his wake. Blood squirted from his back, covering his pants and the ground around him.

"Makes me sick," Bowdre said between blasts of rifle and pistol fire. "He's gotta be hurtin' somethin' awful, an' he sure as hell wasn't no bad man."

The Kid was furious. "That does it, boys!" he bellowed out a window. "We ain't leaving this place until we've killed every last one of you rotten sons of bitches!"

Sometime during the night, after Carlyle died, the Kid's message must have struck home. The surviving possemen quietly crept back to their horses and cleared out, leaving the Kid and his followers a clear pathway to ride in whatever direction they wanted.

Twenty-six

When Pat Garrett approached him, Falcon was raking in his winnings at the end of a night playing stud poker.

"Can I have a word, boss?"

"Sure Pat, pull up a seat and let's talk."

"I'm giving my notice, Falcon. I've decided to run for sheriff of Lincoln County."

"Oh?" Falcon said, surprised.

"Yeah. George Kimball's up for reelection, but I don't think he can win. No one around here thinks he's got the *cojones* to kill Billy the Kid."

Falcon leaned back in his chair, eyebrows raised. "And you think you can? For the sake of a job, you'd be willing to hunt down and kill the Kid, who you've always counted as a friend?"

Garrett poured himself a glass of whiskey from the bottle on the table. "I know how that sounds, Falcon, but the Kid's changed. He's runnin' around the county, rustling beeves and killin' people every day. It's about time somebody put a stop to it."

Falcon stared at Garrett. "Pat, you and I both know the only men the Kid has killed have been the one's trying to kill him." He shrugged. "As for the rustling, it's the only way he can eat, since he can't find honest work with the warrants out on him."

Garrett stuck out his jaw. "That don't matter none, Falcon. I plan to campaign on the promise to bring the Kid in, dead or alive."

"Do you have the backing of either party, Pat?"

Garrett nodded. "Falcon, I understand the power structure of New Mexico. The future rests with Captain Lea, John Chisum, T.B. Catron, Jimmy Dolan, Judge Bristol, and Colonel Rynerson. These men have the wealth and influence to manipulate the power around the state. They have all agreed to support me, if I promise to bring the Kid in."

Falcon smiled, shaking his head. "You're getting in bed with some strange partners, Pat. Personally, with the exception of John Chisum, I wouldn't bother to spit on these men if they were on fire."

Garrett dropped his gaze. Falcon stood up. "Then good luck to you, Pat. I won't vote for you, but I wish you well."

After Garrett won election as sheriff, his backers wanted him to begin the manhunt for the Kid immediately and not to wait until he was to take office in several months. So, they pressured Sheriff Kimball to appoint Garrett Deputy Sheriff, in hopes he could find and arrest, or kill, the Kid as soon as possible. They also pressured the governor to have him appointed deputy U.S. Marshal, to give him authority to pursue the Kid outside Lincoln County.

Throughout the summer and fall Garrett and his deputies, along with dozens of citizen posses, searched for the Kid and his Regulators. Governor Lew Wallace upped the reward to five hundred dollars for the Kid, dead or alive.

Falcon was getting bored with the area and its people. Like the Kid, he prized loyalty over all things. He resented the way the citizens who had once called the Kid their friend and Dolan their enemy now switched sides as Dolan accumulated more and more power.

Falcon also became disillusioned with his father's old friend, John Chisum. Chisum refused to help the Kid with money and backing when he needed it, and he sided with Dolan and called for the Kid's arrest. Falcon knew this was just a ploy by Chisum, who was hoping to get out of paying taxes on the huge stretches of land he owned by becoming buddies with the Dolan faction.

It was about eight o'clock in the evening and The Drinking Hole was almost empty. Most of the usual customers were home having supper and wouldn't start their carousing until later.

Falcon was playing solitaire, drinking coffee, and smoking a cigar when the batwings opened and in walked Jimmy Dolan, John Chisum, Johnny Albright, and Louis Longacre.

The four men took a corner table, ordering a bottle of Falcon's best whiskey from Roy, who was once again full-time bartender.

Falcon took a drag on his stogie, tipped smoke from his nostrils, and wondered how men of such diverse characters and personalities could possibly manage to get along, let alone do business with one another.

After a moment, Chisum looked up and noticed Falcon staring at him. He smiled, and waved.

"Hey, Falcon, come on over and have a drink," he called, his face already flushed and red from the amount of whiskey he'd been drinking.

Falcon got up and strolled over to the table.

"Howdy, John." He looked at Albright, "Hello, Johnny."

Albright, also pretty far along in his cups, smiled drunkenly and tipped his hat.

Louis Longacre raised his glass and smiled. "Good evening, Falcon."

Falcon glanced at him. "Everyone says bankers will do business with the devil himself if the money's right," Falcon said, cutting his eyes at Jimmy Dolan, "I guess that includes skunks, too, Louis."

Longacre's face grew flushed and he scowled, "You got no right to talk to me like that, MacCallister."

"Yeah, Falcon," Chisum blustered, "we're just here having a drink. No harm in that, is there?"

Falcon stared down at him. "John, my father always said you were so mean and tight with a dollar as to be a skinflint. He never said you were a man who would turn his back on his friends if there was money involved. I guess he didn't know you as well as he thought he did."

Chisum opened his mouth to reply, thought better of it, and looked back down at the table, holding his whiskey glass in both hands, shaking his head.

Dolan narrowed his eyes, "You weren't referring to me when you used the word skunk, were you MacCallister?"

Falcon stared at him. "Yes, Dolan, I was, though I could think of lots of other words—like scoundrel, back-shooter, and all around bastard—that would apply equally well."

Falcon turned around and started to walk off. Out of the corner of his eye he saw Dolan reach under his coat and pull out a short-barreled Smith and Wesson .38.

He whirled around, but Dolan had the drop on him.

Over at the bar, Roy leaned forward and put his hand on the double-barreled American Arms twelve gauge shotgun, but he was too late. Dolan had his pistol pointed at Falcon's head.

Dolan got up and walked around the table to stand behind Falcon, his gun at Falcon's back.

"Nobody calls me names and gets away with it, not even you, MacCallister. Let's take a walk outside, and I'll see if I can't make you eat them words."

The customers in the saloon jumped up from their tables and moved to the far side of the room, out of the line of fire in case there was gunplay, leaving Falcon and Dolan alone in the middle of the room.

"Do you mind if I turn around and face you?" Falcon asked, his hands at his sides.

"Just do it slow and careful like," Dolan said, "I'd hate to shoot you in here and spill your blood all over the floor."

As Falcon turned, his hand reached under his belt buckle and he drew his belly gun, bringing it up and placing the barrel against the underside of Dolan's chin.

"What's that?" Dolan asked, sweat breaking out on his forehead in spite of the coolness of the room.

Falcon grinned with his lips, but his eyes remained as cold as a rattler's just before it strikes.

"It's a .44 caliber derringer, Jimmy, and both barrels are loaded and cocked. One twitch of my finger and your brains will be all over the ceiling."

"But . . . but . . . I got a gun at your gut."

Falcon's expression didn't change. "I've never been afraid of dying, Dolan, and if I can take a snake like you with me, I'd almost consider it a pleasure."

Dolan's hand began to quiver, then shake. He slowly let the hammer down on his Smith and Wesson and held it out for Falcon to take.

"All right, here's my gun. Now lower yours, and we can call it even," Dolan said, sweat pouring off his face to run down his cheeks and drip onto his silk shirt.

As Falcon took his pistol, Roy grabbed the shotgun and aimed it over the bar, cocking both barrels with a loud metallic click.

"All right, gents," he called, "everybody settle down. Its Falcon's play now."

Falcon threw Dolan's pistol over in a far corner and put his derringer back behind his belt buckle.

"Since you don't like being called names, why don't you do something about it, low life?"

Dolan looked around at the men at his table. "Don't just stand there, do something!" he yelled.

Chisum shook his head, a slight smile curling the corners of his lips. "You called the play, Jimmy. We're out of it."

"Are you going to fight like a man, or are you scared now that you don't have a gun in your hand?" Falcon asked.

"I'm . . . I'm not one for fisticuffs," Dolan stammered.

Falcon reached out and slapped Dolan's face with his open palm. "Come on, Dolan. I'm calling you out. Fists, knives, guns, it doesn't matter to me. It's your choice."

"I apologize for pulling a gun on you, MacCallister. Now, is that enough?"

Falcon slapped him again, snapping his head around and turning the side of his face a bright red.

"Come on, coward. You're awfully brave when you've got snakes like Jesse Evans to do your fighting for you. What are you going to do now that Evans is dead and buried?"

Dolan's eyes narrowed. "It was you that killed Jesse and his men, wasn't it?"

Falcon grinned. "It's said in the west, a man's got to saddle his own horse and kill his own snakes." He shrugged. "I just follow the rules."

He slapped Dolan again, making Chisum and the others wince at the humiliation he was inflicting on the businessman.

Finally, Dolan had enough. He screamed, "You bastard!" and swung his fist at Falcon's head.

Falcon leaned to the side, letting the punch slip harmlessly by, and buried his right hand up to the wrist in Dolan's stomach.

Dolan doubled over, both hands on his gut, and Falcon planted his feet and swung with all his might in a roundhouse uppercut.

His knuckles caught Dolan on the bridge of his nose, flattening it and splattering blood and mucous all over his face as the blow straightened him up and threw him backward to land spread-eagled, unconscious, on his back on a table.

Falcon walked over and wiped blood and tissue off his hand onto Dolan's expensive silk shirt.

He turned to the men at Dolan's table. "Get this garbage out of here, and when he wakes up tell him if he ever sets foot through those batwings again, I'll kill him on the spot."

He looked over at Roy, who still held the express gun in his hands, sweat pouring off his face.

"Take it easy with that shotgun, Roy. The excitement's over for the night."

Roy turned to put the gun away, muttering, "I hope so. My heart can't take much more of this."

Twenty-seven

Tom Pickett had come to Fort Sumner with Dick Bowdre. The Kid had argued there would be strength in numbers, and the more men the Regulators could get to ride with them, the safer they would be. O'Folliard and Bowdre, two of the original Regulators, the Kid, Tom Pickett, Dave Rudabaugh, and Billie Wilson congregated under the Kid's leadership and rode twelve miles out of town, to hole up at the Wilcox ranch.

Pat Garrett, trying to earn the reward the governor had put on the Kid's head, heard a man named Frank Stewart was up from Texas, leading a posse looking for stolen cattle.

Stewart had with him Lon Chambers, Lee Hall, James East, Tom Emory, Luis Bozeman, Bob Williams, Charles Siringo, and "Big Foot" Wallace.

Garrett convinced Stewart to quit searching for rustled cattle and to help him track down the Kid. Garrett explained to Stewart's men they would be pursuing the Kid because he had in his possession a stolen herd of panhandle cattle.

"How can that be?" one of the Texans asked. "I heard 'bout the shootin' over at Greathouse's tradin' post, and that the Kid had been left afoot."

"Don't know," Stewart replied, "but if you doubt my word about it, just ask Mr. Garrett there."

The Texans did doubt his word, and were well aware it was a put up job, to gain the reward.

Garrett led the men toward Puerto de Luna, a hundred miles northeast, riding single file through bitter cold. By a little past midnight on December eighteenth, Garrett and his posse were on the outskirts of Fort Sumner.

"You men stay here, and keep a sharp look out," Garrett said to the posse. "I'll take Barney Mason with me and go look for somebody that may be able to help us find the Kid and the other Regulators."

Garrett and Mason entered the town, and soon found Juan Gallegos, a Mexican-American who was known to be friendly with the Kid.

In the cantina where Gallegos was drinking with friends, Garrett put a pistol in his back and said, "Come on, Juan, you're under arrest."

The startled man turned, hands in the air. "What for?"

"The crime of knowin' Billy the Kid," Mason snarled. "Now get your butt on that horse outside and let's go."

When they rode up to the rest of the posse, Gallegos, reined in his horse, suddenly fearful.

"What is this?" he asked. "I thought I was going to jail."

As the posse gathered around him, Garrett said, "We want to have a little talk with you first, Juan. Then there may not be any need in your going to jail."

After being worked over with pistols and fists for over an hour, the bloodied man finally held up his hands. "All right . . . all right. I had enough. I tell you where the Kid is."

Garrett wiped blood and mucous off his leather gloves on Gallegos's shirt. "Where is he, Juan? And you'd better tell the truth, or I'll hunt you and your family down and make you sorry you lied."

Juan paused to lean to the side and spit a broken tooth onto the dirt. "The Kid and some Regulators they are out at the Wilcox ranch, but he will come into town for supplies soon, and to see Charlie Bowdre's wife. She's sick."

Garrett took the posse into town and took over the hospital where Bowdre's wife was staying. He stationed men at all the windows, and two men with long rifles up on the roof. He was going to ambush the Kid and any friends with him when he rode into town.

"Don't give 'em no warning," he said to the men, "just open fire and blow 'em outta their saddles when they get in range."

While Garrett was getting his posse set up in the hospital, Juan Gallegos, hunched over his saddle holding his aching stomach, rode a back way into Fort Sumner and made his way to The Drinking Hole.

He stumbled through the batwings, causing all the people inside to stop talking and stare at the Mexican standing in the door, his face and nose swollen and bleeding, his clothes covered with blood and vomit.

"I need to speak with Señor MacCallister," Juan said, unable to see clearly through eyes swollen almost shut.

The bartender, Roy, worried that the man meant trouble, put his hand on the shotgun under the bar, until Falcon signaled him it was all right.

Falcon got up and went to Juan, putting his hand around his shoulders. He knew the man was a friend of the Kid's.

"Roy, get Juan here a drink and I'll take him to my office for a chat."

In the office, Juan took a deep swig of the whiskey, wincing when it burned his open cuts in his mouth.

"Señor MacCallister, Sheriff Garrett from Lincoln is in town. He has with him many mens, and they are planning to shoot the Kid."

Falcon questioned Juan closely, learning the posse was set up at the hospital. He tried to give Juan a double eagle gold piece for his trouble, but he declined.

"The Kid is good friend to many mens. He helped Juan's family once, and I no forget. It is my pleasure to help."

He hung his head. "Please tell *el Chivato* Juan try not to tell them anything."

"Don't worry, Juan. The Kid will understand."

Falcon went to the gun cabinet on a far wall and got out his Winchester .4440 and a box of ammunition. Then he slipped out a back door and headed for the hotel.

As he made his way through dark streets, leaden clouds overhead let go, and it began to snow heavily.

Falcon went into the hotel, ignored the snoring desk clerk, and took a key to a room on the top floor.

In the room, he pulled a chair over to the window, lighted a stogie, and sat back to wait. He had a clear view of the hotel and the street leading up to it from his position. He had promised the Kid he would take a hand if he got the chance and even up the odds a bit, and he intended to do just that.

Around eight o'clock in the morning, with snow still falling in thick white clouds, the Kid and the five men with him returned to Fort Sumner.

They rode up the street, hunched over against the cold, strung out in single file.

Garrett poked his rifle through a window and opened fire, shooting Tom O'Folliard through the chest, knocking him almost out of his saddle. The horse, startled by the gunfire, reared and ran straight toward the ambushers, who then began to shoot at the dark figures in the street.

O'Folliard, clutching his chest, cried out, "Don't shoot any more, I'm dyin'!"

Garrett's next shot hit the Kid's horse in its right shoulder, throwing the Kid to the ground.

Garrett took careful aim, the bead on his rifle barrel centered on the Kid's forehead.

Suddenly, the stucco next to Garrett's head exploded,

sending fragments into his eyes and face. His shot went wild as he ducked back from the window.

Rapid fire from a building across the street began to pepper the hospital, and one of the men on the roof was hit and fell screaming to the ground.

The Kid, seeing his chance, vaulted up on the back of Billie Wilson's horse, and they hightailed it out of town, with Pickett and Bowdre close behind.

As they passed the hotel, the Kid looked up and saw a white face at the window. Though he couldn't make out any features, he thought he knew who had saved his life, and he waved his hat at the man as they rode past.

Twenty-eight

It was a bitterly cold December night as the Kid, riding behind Billie Wilson, Dave Rudabaugh, Tom Pickett, and Charley Bowdre made their way through spits of wind-driven snow to the Wilcox Ranch house near Fort Sumner to escape the storm.

They built a fire in the old fireplace, tied their horses behind the house, and got set to wait out the snow. The house had been abandoned for years, and the Kid felt safe there. He didn't think the ambushers would be able to find them in this weather. They should be safe to hole up there for a day or two, or until the weather broke.

Two days later, when the snowfall had slowed to mere sprinkles, the Kid and his men left the Wilcox house and rode all day until they came to an abandoned rock house at Stinking Springs.

Cold and hungry, the men stopped to fix some hot food and let the horses rest overnight.

When Bowdre went out at first light to feed the horses, he was met by a fusillade of bullets fired by Pat Garrett and a posse of more than a dozen men who had been tipped off by an informer who hoped to earn part of the reward.

The Kid and everyone else scrambled from their bedrolls to fetch rifles.

Bowdre, mortally wounded, staggered back through the snow toward the house, leaving a trail of blood.

"They've murdered you, Charley!" the Kid shouted when Bowdre was closer to the house. "But we'll get revenge. Turn around and start shooting. Kill some of the sons of bitches before you die."

Bowdre turned around, confused, dazed by pain and blood loss, holding his hands in the air as though in surrender. "I'm dying!" he cried, stumbling toward Garrett's hiding place before he fell face-down in the snow near Garrett's feet.

The Kid signaled his men to lead their horses into the house by the back door. He had run outside to untie his bay mare when Pat Garrett fired directly into the horse's chest, felling it so it blocked the entrance.

Two more horses had their ropes cut in two by bullets and took off before the Kid's men could reach them, dragging loose rope behind them.

Rifle fire began between both factions, a constant drone of blasting guns. Gunfire came from the rear of the house and from all sides, too many guns for four men without horses to make good their escape.

"They've got us cornered," he told Rudabaugh.

Rudabaugh cupped his hands around his mouth. "We want to surrender!" he cried.

"You go out first," the Kid snapped, "since givin' up was your idea."

Without hesitation Rudabaugh tossed out his gun, raised his hands in the air, and walked out into the snow. He came up to Garrett and lowered his head.

"We've got you, Dave," Garrett said.

"I know. The others will give themselves up if you promise to take us to Santa Fe to stand trial. We won't none of us have a chance if you haul us to Las Vegas."

"You aren't exactly in a position to make deals."

"Would you rather fight a while longer an' maybe lose a few good men on your side?"

Garrett appeared to consider it.

The Kid, listening from a window, spoke to Wilson. "Dave ain't got as much nerve as I figured. He's tryin' to make us a deal to go to jail in Santa Fe, like he's scared of them folks up in Las Vegas."

"One thing's for sure, Kid," Wilson said. "This time we ain't gonna be so lucky. There ain't no way to escape from this place."

The Kid knew Wilson was right. "Then I reckon we give up an' hope for a fair trial."

"Won't be no such thing, an' you know it."

"It's come down to choices. We shoot it out with Garrett until our guns run empty or until his boys kill us off one at a time, or we make the best deal we can."

"Then we're finished," Wilson said, sighing, resting his rifle against a wall. "They'll hang every damn one of us. We're as good as dead."

"Maybe not. Governor Wallace said we'd get a good lawyer to defend us."

"I don't believe a damn word Lew Wallace says. If you ask me, he's plumb crazy . . . writing books all the time. Hell, he's hardly ever in his office, so I hear."

"You got any better ideas?"

"Nope," Wilson said after a moment's thought. "I guess we toss out our guns an' march out there with Rudabaugh. Damn, but it sure sticks in my craw."

One by one the three remaining Regulators walked slowly out of the rock house to join Dave Rudabaugh.

Garrett looked the Kid in the eye. "You made the right choice. We'll take you over to Miz Wilcox and get her to feed you something."

Having chained them hand and foot to the floor of a covered wagon to preclude any possibility of escape, Sheriff Garrett escorted the Kid, Dave Rudabaugh, Tom Pickett, and Billy Wilson off to Fort Sumner. At the time, the Kid had no way of knowing the promise made to Rudabaugh would be betrayed . . . they would be taken to Las Vegas to stand trial, and the lawyer Governor Wallace promised to have defend them would not arrive.

At Fort Sumner the Kid asked if he could say good-bye to a girlfriend, the daughter of the Navajo woman who had worked for McSween.

Deputy Jim East didn't like the idea. "He might figure a way to escape, Sheriff."

But Garrett relented. "Leave 'em both chained together so they can't run off."

East pointed the Kid and Rudabaugh into the shack where the Navajo girl lived. The Kid smiled when he saw her and hobbled over to give her a kiss.

"They will hang you, Billy," she whispered.

"They ain't got me hung yet."

"But this time, maybe so you won't be so lucky as before, I think."

He chuckled. "Don't worry. It's freezin' cold in that wagon. Give me your shawl. I'll give you this tintype they made of me, so you'll have somethin' to remember me by until I'm free again."

"I am afraid you won't ever be free, *Billito.*"

He continued to chuckle. "I've got a few cards up my sleeve I haven't played yet."

"But all the others, the ones who would help you, are dead or in prison."

"Who says I need any help?"

"You are never serious, *Billito.*"

"Time to go," Jim East said from the doorway. "Get back in that wagon so I can chain you two to the floor."

Billy took the shawl the girl gave him and wrapped himself against the cold.

They were marched outside at gunpoint, then herded into the wagon as heavier snow began to fall.

But just as the driver was about to climb up in the wagon seat, a lone rider appeared through the swirling snow. The Kid watched him approach.

"I know that man," said the Kid a moment later. "That's Falcon MacCallister. He may have changed his mind and decided to help us."

But MacCallister rode over to Sheriff Garrett and stopped his horse, blocking the path of the wagon.

"I just heard you captured Billy the Kid," he said.

"Him and three more. This means the Lincoln County War is officially over," Garrett said. "I'm taking them up to Las Vegas to stand trial before Judge Fountain."

"That double-crossin' son of a bitch," Rudabaugh growled when he heard about the broken promise. "If I could get my hands on a gun, I'd kill him."

"This ain't the time or the place," the Kid said, watching MacCallister closely to see if he might come to their aid.

"I don't think the Kid shot Sheriff Brady," Falcon told Pat Garrett. "He told me his side of the story."

"That's up to a jury," Garrett replied.

Falcon looked back at the snow-covered wagon. "I hope it's a fair jury. Be a shame to hang an innocent man."

"I know the Kid," Garrett said. "One thing he isn't is an innocent man. He's done more'n his share of killing in this county. But all that's over now."

Oddly, MacCallister grinned. "I wouldn't be too sure of that, Sheriff."

"And just what do you mean by that, Falcon?"

Falcon shrugged. "Some men are just natural born hard to kill, either by a gun or a rope. I wouldn't start dancing on his grave or spending any of that reward money until you've got the grave dug."

"There are half a dozen witnesses who'll swear the Kid shot Brady."

"Half a dozen Murphey and Dolan men?"

"That's a false accusation. It will be citizens of the town who actually saw the killing."

Again, MacCallister grinned and wagged his head. "I'd be real sure of that before I took him to trial. He's got lots of friends."

"They won't save him from justice."

"From what I hear tell, Sheriff, it may not be justice, after all."

Garrett looked back at the wagon. "We're wasting time here, Falcon. You're entitled to your opinion, but a judge and jury will decide the final outcome."

"Maybe. Maybe not," Falcon said, swinging his horse away to ride to the back of the wagon where he halted his mount again.

He looked into the Kid's eyes. "You ride quiet up to where Sheriff Garrett's taking you, son. Don't try anything that'll give him a reason to gun you down."

"I didn't kill Brady," the Kid said, his teeth chattering in the cold.

"Never said you did. Just bide your time, and maybe things will change."

Falcon rode off at a trot, and soon his outline was lost in sheets of windblown snow. The wagon jolted forward, wheels creaking over frozen ground.

Rudabaugh asked, "What did he mean, maybe things will change?"

"Can't say for sure," the Kid replied, "but if there's one feller in Lincoln County who could make things change, that was him."

"He didn't come right out an' offer to change the circumstances we're in right now."

The Kid covered his freezing ears with the shawl the Navajo girl gave him. "From what I know about him, that ain't his way of handlin' things."

Rudabaugh made a face. "Looks to me like he's gonna ride off an' let us hang."

Tom Pickett spoke up. "He's supposed to be one bad hombre with a gun, but he didn't show much of it here today. He coulda got the drop on Garrett an' let us loose."

"He'd be breakin' the law," the Kid replied. "If we get any help from him, it'll come another way." He paused, then said in a low voice, "Like the other night at the ambush."

Rudabaugh's expression did not change. "My money says we'll never set eyes on him again. We'll be facin' a hangman's noose all by our lonesome."

The Kid rested against the side of the wagon, deciding it was no use to try to convince the others that Falcon Mac-Callister might offer them a way out. At the moment, even the Kid had no idea how the big gunman could help.

One thing the Kid was certain of . . . he wasn't going to let anybody hang him. Somehow, he'd find a way to cheat the hangman out of his chance to make him swing at the end of a rope.

Twenty-nine

Roy walked over to Falcon at his table and handed him the early edition of the *Las Vegas Gazette* and his morning coffee.

"Boss, there's a couple of pages 'bout the Kid in the paper this mornin'."

"Thanks, Roy."

Falcon poured himself a cup of coffee from the pot on the table, lit a cheroot, and leaned back with his boots on the table while he smoked and drank and read.

J.H. Koogler, editor of the *Gazette* had obtained an interview with the Kid in jail. Falcon read on . . .

Through the kindness of Sheriff Romero, a representative of the *Gazette* was admitted to the jail yesterday morning. Mike Cosgrove, the obliging mail contractor who often met the boys while on business down the Pecos, had just gone in with five large bundles. The doors at the entrance stood open, and a large crowd strained their necks to get a glimpse of the prisoners, who stood in the passageway like children waiting for a Christmas tree distribution. One by one the bundles were unpacked, disclosing a good suit for each man. Mr. Cosgrove remarked that he wanted 'to see the boys go away in style.'

Billy 'the Kid' and Billie Wilson, who were shackled

together, stood patiently while a blacksmith took off their shackles and bracelets to allow them an opportunity to make a change of clothing. Both prisoners watched the operation which was to set them free for a short while. Wilson scarcely raised his eyes and spoke but once or twice to his *compadres,* Bonney, on the other hand, was light and chipper and was very communicative, laughing, joking, and chatting with the by-standers.

Falcon threw back his head and laughed at this description. *The Kid will be grinning and joking with the noose on his neck and his feet over nothing but air,* he thought with some affection. The more he found out about the Kid, the more he realized they were kin in their souls. Now, if only he could help the Kid get out of this scrape and off somewhere to start a new life.

He shook his head. Wishful thinking, he thought, and began to read the rest of the article.

"You appear to take it easy," the reporter said.

"Yes! What's the use of looking on the gloomy side of everything? The laugh's on me this time," he said. Then, looking around the *placita,* he asked, "Is the jail in Santa Fe any better than this?"

This seemed to trouble him considerably, for, as he explained, "This is a terrible place to put a fellow in." He put the same question to everyone who came near him, and when he learned that there was nothing better in store for him he shrugged his shoulders and said something about putting up with what he had to.

He was the attraction of the show, and as he stood there, lightly kicking the toes of his boots on the stone pavement to keep his feet warm, one would scarcely mistrust that he was the hero of the 'Forty

Thieves' romance which this paper has been running
in serial form for six weeks or more.

"There was a big crowd gazing at me, wasn't
there?" he exclaimed, and then smilingly continued,
"Well, perhaps some of them will think me half a
man now. Everyone seems to think I was some kind
of animal."

He did look human, indeed, but there was nothing
very mannish about his appearance, for he looked
and acted a mere boy. He is about five-foot, eight or
nine inches tall, slightly built and lithe, weighing
about 140; a frank and open countenance, looking
like a schoolboy, with the traditional silky fuzz on his
upper lip; clear blue eyes, with a roguish snap about
them; light hair and complexion. He is, in all, a handsome looking fellow, the imperfection being two
prominent front teeth, slightly protruding like squir-
rels' teeth, and he has agreeable and winning ways.

A cloud came over his face when he made some
allusion to his being made the hero of fabulous yarns,
and something like indignation was expressed when
he said that our Extra misrepresented him in saying
that he called his associates cowards. "I never said
any such thing," he pouted, "I know they ain't cowards."

Billie Wilson was glum and sober, but from underneath his broad-brimmed hat we saw a face that had
by no means bad look. He is light-complexioned,
light hair, bluish grey eyes, is a little stouter than Bonney, and far quieter. He appears ashamed and is not
in very good spirits.

Falcon snorted. *Reporters,* he thought, *only one rung above
lawyers on the social scale, but sometimes they can write something
so dumb it defies description.* He smirked as he read on . . .

A final stroke of the hammer cut the last rivet in

the bracelets, and they clanked on the pavement as they fell.

Bonney straightened up. Then, rubbing his wrists where the sharp edged irons had chafed him, he said, "I don't suppose you fellows would believe it, but this is the first time I ever had bracelets on. But many another fellow had them on, too."

With Wilson he walked toward the little hole in the wall to the place which is no "sell" on a place of confinement. Just before entering he turned and looked back and exclaimed: "They say, 'a fool for luck and a poor man for children'—Garrett takes them all in!'"

We saw them again at the depot when the crowd presented a really warlike appearance. Out of one of the windows, on which he was leaning, he talked freely with us of the whole affair.

"I don't blame you for writing of me as you have. You had to believe others' stories. But then I don't know as anyone would believe anything good of me, anyway," he said. "I wasn't the leader of any gang. I was for Billy all the time. About that Portales business, I owned the ranch with Charlie Bowdre. I took it up and was holding it because I knew that sometime a stage line would run by there, and I wanted to keep it for a station."

[It was rumored that the ranch at Los Portales which the Kid had homesteaded with Bowdre was a rendezvous for stolen stock, but none was ever found there.]

"But I found there were certain men who wouldn't let me live in the country, so I was going to leave. We had all our grub in the house when they took us in, and we going to a place about six miles away in the morning to cook it and then light out. I haven't stolen any stock. I made my living gambling, but that was the only way I could live. They wouldn't let me settle down. If they had, I wouldn't be here today." He held up his right hand, on which was the bracelet. "Chisum got me into all this trouble, and wouldn't help me out. I went to Lincoln to stand my trial on the warrant that was out for me, but the Territory took a change of venue to Doña Aña, and I knew that I had no show, and so I skinned out. When I was up to White Oaks the last time, I went there to consult with a lawyer, who had sent for me to come up. But I knew I couldn't stay there, either."

The conversation then drifted to the question of the final round-up of the party.

"If it hadn't been for the dead horse in the doorway I wouldn't be here. I would have ridden out on my bay mare and taken my chances at escaping," said he. "But I couldn't jump over that, for she would have jumped back, and I would have got it in the head. We could have stayed in the house but there wouldn't have been anything gained by that, for they would have starved us out. I thought it was better to come out and get a square meal—don't you?"

The prospect of a fight (at the train) exhilarated him, and he bitterly bemoaned being chained. "If I only had my Winchester I'd lick the whole crowd," was his confident comment on the strength of the attack party. He sighed and sighed again for a chance to take a hand in the fight, and the burden of his desire was to be set free to fight as soon as he should smell powder.

As the train pulled out, he lifted his hat and invited us to call and see him at Santa Fe, calling out *"Adios!"*"

Falcon smiled, thinking that if the Kid's brains were as large as his *cojones,* he would probably be president some day.

He folded the paper and laid it on the table, taking out another cigar and lighting it. He knew he could do nothing to help the Kid unless he survived his trial in Santa Fe and was brought back to Lincoln to stand trial for the killing of Sheriff Brady.

He poured more coffee and sat there, smoking and thinking. It was a perplexing problem, but he would figure some way to help the Kid, whatever it took.

Roy walked over and took the coffeepot to refill it.

"You think the Kid's gonna come out of this all right, boss?"

"We'll see, Roy, we'll see."

Thirty

After their capture at the old house in Stinking Springs by newly elected sheriff Pat Garrett, the Kid and his comrades were still hopeful that a new governor, Lew Wallace, would soon release them.

The Kid, Dave Rudabaugh, Charley Bowdre, Billy Wilson, and Tom Pickett had been prisoners at Las Vegas, the New Mexico Territory, to be charged in Mesilla for various crimes. But the Kid, now known across most of the region as Billy the Kid, was set to stand trial for the murder of Sheriff William Brady at Lincoln and it was there where he was headed to be hanged, after his conviction for the murder in the territorial court in Santa Fe.

The Kid had come by wagon to Lincoln. He was chained to the floor upstairs at the Lincoln County Courthouse, guarded by two men, Bob Olinger, and Deputy James Bell. Billy was lodged on the second floor in the northeast corner of the building.

Olinger enjoyed taunting the Kid. "You're gonna die by a rope, Billy Bonney," he often said.

Bell, on the other hand, seemed less antagonistic. "I know you're a desperate character," Bell said on one occasion, "but it seems you have a good reason for nearly everythin' you've done in New Mexico."

Sheriff Garrett stated publicly that the Kid was "daring and unscrupulous, that he would sacrifice the lives of a hundred men who stood between him an' what he wanted."

A friend of Olinger's came by to give Bob a similar warning that would prove to be fateful. "You think yourself an old hand in this business. But I tell you, as good a man as you are, that if that man Bonney is shown the slightest chance on earth, if he is allowed the use of one hand, or if he is not watched every moment from now until the moment he is executed, he will effect some plan by which he will murder the whole lot of you before you have time to even suspect that he has any such intention."

Olinger simply smiled and said, "The Kid has no more chance of escaping than of going to heaven."

Two days after his arrival, Falcon walked into the Lincoln County Courthouse and asked Olinger if he might have a word with his old friend, the Kid.

Olinger sneered. "The Kid ain't receivin' no visitors today . . . nor any other day, MacCallister."

Falcon fixed Olinger with his cold, blue eyes. "You know, Olinger, the Kid still has a lot of friends around here. I'll bet if I were to go back to Fort Sumner and tell everyone that came into my saloon that the Kid was really having it rough over here, that you were mistreating him something awful, why, it wouldn't be too long before your horse would go lame, or your dog would get killed, or a rock would fall out of the sky onto your head. You get my drift, Olinger?"

A tiny sheen of sweat appeared on Olinger's forehead, and he shifted his gaze, afraid to look Falcon in the eye.

"Okay, gambler, but I'm gonna be standin' right behind you, listenin' to every word. I don't want no talk of escape, you hear?"

Falcon nodded, contempt for the man in his every look.

Olinger followed Falcon upstairs, after searching him and removing his sidearm. The man was so incompetent that he failed to find the derringer hidden behind Falcon's belt, but it didn't matter. Falcon had other plans for the Kid.

As they entered the upstairs room where the Kid was chained to a bolt in the middle of the floor, Falcon grinned and walked over to shake his hand.

"Howdy, Kid. How're things?"

As their hands met, Falcon slipped a folded piece of paper into the Kid's palm. The Kid didn't hesitate, just took it and stuck it in his pocket without looking at it.

"Why, I'm doin' fine, Falcon. How're you?"

"I'm well, also, Kid. Anything I can do for you, to make things easier while you're here?"

"Sure, Falcon," the Kid said, evidently in high spirits, "just grab and hand me Bob's gun for a moment."

"My boy," Olinger said, softening his tone at a sharp glance from Falcon, "you'd better tell your friend here good-bye. Your days are short."

The Kid quipped, "Oh, I don't know—there's many a slip 'twixt the cup and the lip."

Falcon took out a cigar and lighted it with a lucifer. "How'd things go up in Santa Fe, Kid? The newspaper reports were kind of sketchy."

The Kid gave Falcon his cocky grin. "They had two federal indictments against me, one for killin' Buckshot Roberts, the other for the murder of Morris Bernstein. I got off on both of those."

Falcon nodded, blowing smoke from his nose toward Olinger, who coughed and moved a slight distance away, his hand remaining on his pistol.

"Then Judge Bristol put me on trial for the killin' of Sheriff Brady, with a hand-picked jury and a defense attorney who was a member of the Santa Fe Ring, a lodge brother of Dolan's. It didn't take the jury long to figure out which way the wind blew in Santa Fe. They sentenced me to hang. And," he said spreading his arms, "here I am."

Falcon nodded again. "I figured it was something like that. By the way, Kid, you'll be glad to know your old friend Pat Garrett has been having trouble getting his hands on the five hundred dollar reward for bringing you in."

The Kid grinned again. "Oh? I'm awful sorry to hear that. Why?"

"The acting governor, Rich, said his claim was without merit because the reward was for delivering you to the sheriff of Lincoln County, and Garrett never turned you over to Kimball."

The Kid threw back his head and laughed, long and loud. "Ain't that a hoot? Garrett goes to all the trouble to help frame me for a murder I didn't commit, and it ends up costing him his blood-money." He laughed again. "I just love a story with a happy ending, don't you Falcon?"

Falcon tipped his hat. "Don't you forget to keep up on your reading, you hear, Kid?"

The Kid slipped his hand in his pocket and winked where Olinger couldn't see him. "You bet, Falcon. I'll get right on it as soon as you leave."

Olinger followed Falcon to the door, grinned, and said, "Your boy don't have much time left, gambler."

Falcon turned to stare at Olinger, making the fat man break out in a sweat again.

"Tell you what, jailer," Falcon said, pulling a hundred dollar bill from his wallet. "I'll bet you a hundred and give you two to one that the Kid outlives you."

Olinger's grin faded and he got a sick look on his face. "What . . . what'd you say?"

Falcon pursed his lips, shook his head, then said, "Never mind. You wouldn't be able to pay off if you lost, would you?"

After Olinger slammed the courthouse door, Falcon walked to his horse, took a folded newspaper out of his saddlebags and stuck it under his arm. Whistling, he strolled over to the outhouse next to the courthouse, opened the door with the quarter moon cut out of it, and entered.

A few minutes later, he walked from the outhouse to Diablo, climbed into the saddle, and walked the horse toward Fort Sumner.

Not long after that, the Kid decided to make his move toward freedom. He pulled the note from his pocket and read it, grinned, then read it again before tearing it up and swallowing the pieces.

Later, the Kid, wearing leg irons and wrist manacles, sat in a chair near an open upstairs window of the Lincoln County Courthouse.

Olinger got up, stretching, giving the Kid a baleful stare before he spoke to Bell.

"I'm goin' across the street to get some lunch. I'll bring back somethin' for you an' this babyfaced boy."

"Suits me," Bell replied. "I am gettin' kinda hungry right about now."

"Keep a sharp eye on Bonney," Olinger said, resting his big, twelve gauge shotgun in a corner. "If he moves, kill the son of a bitch."

"But he's all chained up, Bob," Bell replied, inclining his head toward the Kid. "How the hell is he gonna go anyplace like this?"

"Just watch him real close. If it was up to me, I'd kill him now an' claim he was tryin' to escape. Garrett would believe us. We could say he slipped out of them bracelets somehow an' made a play for a gun."

"That'd be outright murder, Bob. Hell, the judge's already set the date. They're gonna hang him for sure, over killin' Sheriff Brady."

"I didn't kill Brady," the Kid said quietly, smiling a one-sided smile. "Somebody else must have gotten lucky. I never even aimed at Brady."

Olinger glowered at him. "Tell it to the judge, little Billy boy. Keep sayin' it over an over again 'til they hang you by the goddamn neck."

The Kid continued to smile. "They'll never hang me, Bob. You can count on that."

"We'll see," Olinger replied, making for the stairway down to the street. He hesitated at the top of the stairs, remembering what the gambler had said, and gave the Kid another cold look. "You could be right, Billy boy. I may just shoot you dead before you get to trial. Me an' James will swear you was tryin' to escape."

With that, Olinger went down the stairs and crossed the road to a small eatery inside the Wortley Hotel.

The Kid's mind worked furiously on a plan to escape while Olinger was across the street. Bell was far less likely to take deadly action.

"I need to go to the privy out back," he told Bell. "Can't wait no longer."

Bell came over and unlocked the chain binding the Kid to the floor, although he left the leg irons and wrist manacles in place as he pointed to the stairs.

"Go ahead, Kid," Bell said, his right hand on his pistol butt. "I'll be right behind you, so don't try nothin' stupid."

The Kid was planning to jump Bell after they went back up the stairway, then get the drop on Olinger as soon as he got back from lunch and handcuff him to Bell, after disarming them both. The Kid had small hands and large wrists, and he knew he could slip the cuffs off by folding his double-jointed thumbs flat against his palms.

He made his way slowly downstairs, then to the outhouse, all the while thinking about his escape. He didn't want to shoot Jim Bell if he could avoid it . . . Bell had shown him some kindness during his stay on the second floor, and he seemed like a nice enough fellow.

After using the privy, the Kid plodded slowly back up the steps, hampered by his leg irons. With his back to Bell, he slipped off one handcuff and pulled the pistol he had found wrapped in newspaper, where Falcon had hidden it.

At the top of the stairwell, the Kid whirled around and swung the pistol down across the top of Bell's head as hard as he could.

Bell fell facedown on the floor, groaning.

The Kid held the gun out, pointing it at Bell's face. "Get up off the floor," he said, "and get these ankle chains off me."

Bell scurried forward on hands and knees, ignoring the pistol, and grabbed the Kid's legs at the knees, throwing him onto his back.

Bell scrambled to his feet and started running down the stairs.

"Stop, Jim, or I'll have to shoot you!" the Kid cried.

Bell continued leaping down the steps. The Kid fired once with Bell's Colt, shattering stucco next to Bell's head. The guard kept running, the Kid fired again, and the deputy tumbled down the stairs with a mortal wound.

Outside, Godfrey Gauss, formerly a cook for the Tunstall cowboys, caught James Bell as he staggered away from the building with blood pouring from his chest. He collapsed in Gauss's arms and died instantly.

The Kid shuffled his shackled legs across the floor to Pat Garrett's office door, where he scooped up Bob Olinger's shotgun before making his way to the northeast corner window.

Gauss ran from the spot where he laid Bell toward the Wortley Hotel, yelling for Olinger at the top of his lungs while pointing to the second floor of the Lincoln County Courthouse, where the shot had been fired.

"Bob!" Gauss cried. "Come quick!"

Olinger appeared in the front doorway of the hotel dining room. "What the hell was that noise?" he bellowed.

"It's the Kid!" Gauss called back from the far side of the road. "The Kid has killed Jim Bell!"

Olinger ran toward the courthouse until he saw a shape in the upstairs window. "Son of a bitch!" Olinger said, coming to a sudden halt. "Looks like the bastard has killed me, too!"

The Kid stuck Olinger's shotgun out the window and aimed down. Godfrey Gauss took shelter under the porch roof of the courthouse.

"Look up, Bob!" the Kid shouted. "Look up, old boy, and see what you get!"

Olinger froze. "How the hell did you break loose from them chains?"

His answer came in the form of twin loads of heavy buckshot which Olinger had loaded himself. Olinger crumpled, his head and upper body shredded by shotgun pellets.

The Kid wasted no time. "Gauss! Bring me that pickaxe up here so I can get these chains off my feet."

Gauss, still wary, swung a heavy pickaxe up to the second floor balcony.

But the Kid was not finished with Gauss. "Run saddle me a horse from Billy Burt's corral. Don't be too damn long about gettin' it done."

Gauss took off in a lumbering run toward the corral, looking over his shoulder.

The Kid took the pickaxe and began smashing links between his leg irons until one line finally broke in half. Looping the ends over his belt, he walked to the north end of the hall and appeared on the balcony, where a knot of men stood watching what was going on.

The Kid stared down at Olinger's bloody body. He lifted the shotgun and smashed it on the handrail across the front of the balcony, then he tossed it to the ground near Olinger.

"Here's your gun, goddamn you!" he shouted. "You won't follow me with it any longer!"

Several spectators gave the Kid a cheer. Some carried guns, but no one attempted to aim one at him.

Gauss was having trouble saddling a spirited horse from Burt's corral, but at length he led the bay over to the front of the courthouse and tied it to a hitchrail.

The Kid armed himself with a rifle and a pistol from Pat Garrett's office before he hurried down the stairs. Emerging from a back door at the foot of the stairway, he paused when he came to James Bell's body.

"I am sorry I had to kill you," the Kid said loudly, so many of the townspeople heard him. "I couldn't help it."

He then made his way around to the street, where he stopped at Olinger's corpse.

"You ain't gonna round me up again," the Kid snarled, nudging the body with the toe of his boot.

He came over to the saddled horse, where he hesitated long enough to speak to Godfrey Gauss. "Old fellow," the Kid said, "if you hadn't gone for this horse, I would have killed you just like the others."

It was with some difficulty that the Kid finally mounted the skittish bay. He swung the horse away from the courthouse steps and jerked it to a halt when he saw the townsfolk watching him closely.

"Tell Billy Burt I will send his horse back to him as quick as I can," he shouted. Then he turned the animal again and made off at a gallop.

He was leaving two dead men behind him, and he knew Sheriff Pat Garrett would come after him for killing two of his deputies and escaping.

"To hell with all of 'em," the Kid muttered as the bay took him swiftly into the rugged countryside.

His first order of business was to free his legs of the iron cuffs and chains. He headed for Salazar's place to get help with the blacksmithing he needed.

The Kid also felt sure the new governor, Lew Wallace, would issue orders to begin an all-out manhunt for him now. This part of the territory would be crawling with men trying to track him down.

He wondered if he might be able to rest up and lay low at the cabin of Falcon MacCallister. MacCallister had shown some sympathy for his plight the day he and Jim French showed up with leg wounds, and he had sure come through for him today by hiding that pistol in the privy.

The Kid made up his mind on it. After he got these chains off his ankles he would make for MacCallister's cabin, hoping the big gunman would hide him out for a spell.

If he did, the Kid vowed to himself to never mention it, for he didn't want the tall gambler to get in any deeper for helping him than he already was.

Thirty-one

The Kid rode Billy Burt's pony as fast as he could, heading up into the foothills of the Capitan Mountains. He came out of the dense mesquite and creosote bushes into a small clearing.

Up ahead was a small, adobe cabin with a tiny corral nearby with some scraggly looking horses standing in it.

"Yo, the cabin!" Kid cried, his hands near the pistol he had stuck in his belt.

A middle-aged Mexican stepped out of the door of the cabin, an old Sharp's rifle in his hands. It was José Cordova, a schoolmaster from Fort Sumner, a man Kid had known for some time.

"José, it's me, Billy Bonney. Can I approach?"

"*El Chivato!*" Jose cried, with a smile. He lowered the Sharps and said, "Come on in, *Chivato*. You are welcome at my little *hacienda* any time."

The Kid walked his sweating pony up to the cabin and dismounted with some difficulty, as he still had bracelets on one arm and shackles on one of his legs.

He released the horse, slapping it on its rump and sending it on its way, knowing the animal would find its way back to Lincoln and its rightful owner, Billy Burt.

"You got a hammer and chisel, Jose? I gotta get these leg irons off, they're chafing me something terrible."

"Sure, Billy."

Cordova went into the house and came back with a small sledgehammer and a metal chisel. Together they worked for almost an hour before all the rivets were cut and the irons fell to the ground.

"I have some beans and tortillas. Are you hungry?" Cordova asked.

The Kid grinned. "I could eat one of those broncs you got in your corral if you offered."

As the two men ate pinto beans and tortillas and washed them down with mesquite bean coffee, Cordova asked what the Kid planned to do next.

"If 'n you'll let me borrow a saddle and one of your mounts, I'm gonna head for Mexico, soon as I can get some *dinero* together to make the trip."

Cordova waved a hand in the air. "Take what you need, *Chivato.*"

The Kid grinned his thanks. "By the way, José, I been meanin' to ask. I speak pretty good Mex, but what does *Chivato* mean, anyhow?"

José laughed. "It is not strictly a word, but it comes from *Chivo*, which is a male goat, and *Chiva*, which is a female goat. So," he spread his hands, a wide smile on his face, *Chivato* means small, or young goat, what *Americanos* call a 'kid'."

Billy nodded. "Oh."

Cordova punched him in the ribs, a sly smile on his face, "It is also slang for one who is pretty good with the ladies."

Now the Kid laughed. "Well, *compàdre,* I guess it fits both ways, don't it?"

Later, the Kid saddled one of Cordova's horses and waved as he rode off toward the mountains.

Just after dark he came upon another cabin, nestled in some tall, live oak and pine trees. He got off his horse and walked around the corner of the cabin, entering through a side door with his pistol in his hand.

He found two men in the kitchen, cooking supper.

"Well," the Kid said, waving the pistol, "I got you, haven't I?"

John Meadows and Tom Norris looked up from their cooking.

Meadows said, "Well, you have, so what are you gonna do with us?"

"I'm gonna eat supper with you."

Meadows slowly let out the breath he was holding. "That's all right, long as you can stand them beans."

After supper, the three men sat around talking, Meadows and Norris smoking hand-rolled cigarettes, the Kid chewing on some peppermint sticks Meadows had in the cupboard.

"What are you goin' to do about Pat Garrett, Kid?" Meadows asked. "He's sure to come lookin' for you again now that you've broken out of his jail."

"I don't have nothin' against Pat. If I was lyin' out there in the arroyo and Pat Garrett rode by and didn't see me, he would be the last man I would kill. I wouldn't hurt a hair on his head. He worked pretty rough to capture us, but he treated me good after he got me. He treated us humane and friendly, and was good to us after he did get us captured. I have ever such a good feeling for Pat Garrett."

"How do you feel about Bob Olinger?" Norris asked.

The Kid looked up, the grin slowly fading from his face. "I expressed that pretty good a day or so ago, when I shot-gunned him to death."

Meadows and Norris looked at each other. That was the first they'd heard about the death of Olinger.

Meadows cleared his throat. "Well, Kid. When I was sick and down and out you befriended me, and there is two things I have never done—I have never kissed the hand that slapped me, nor went back on a friend. Anyway, I'm going to befriend you now. I have got fourteen head of old Indian ponies. Some of them ain't very much, but you go out and look 'em over, and if one of them does you any good, take it. And you are welcome to them all. But don't go back to Fort Sumner, for if you do Garrett will get you sure as you do, or else you will have to kill him."

"I haven't got any money," the Kid said. "And what would I do in Mexico with no money? I'll have to go back and get a little 'fore I go."

"Sure as you do," Norris said, "Garrett will get you."

The Kid shook his head, a sly smile on his lips. "I've got too many friends up there, and I don't believe Pat will get me. I can stay there a while and get money enough and then go down to Mexico."

The Kid stood and held out his hands. "Thanks for the grub, boys, an' the offer of the mounts. I got a friend I've got to go see, 'fore I think about headin' south."

Pat Garrett was sitting in a saloon in White Oaks with John Poe when he heard the news of the Kid's escape.

He looked down at the table for a moment, then up at Poe.

"Now I'll have to go do it all over again," he said.

He offered Poe and a mutual friend, Tip McKinney, the job of accompanying him back to Fort Sumner to look for the Kid. They both accepted the job offer.

On the way to Fort Sumner, Garrett and Poe and McKinney stopped off at Bob Olinger's mother's house.

"Mrs. Olinger," Garrett said, "I just want you to know I'm going to go back and get the Kid for killing Bob."

The white-haired lady shook her head. "My son was a murderer from the cradle until the moment he died. My feeling is he got his just deserts when Billy shot him."

Garrett looked over at Poe, who shrugged.

"Nevertheless, Mrs. Olinger, I'm gonna get him, and either hang him or kill him for what he done."

On the ride into Fort Sumner Garrett thought on what Mrs. Olinger had said, and his relationship with the Kid.

Though he still counted the Kid as a friend, he was in a tough spot. Dolan and his backers in Santa Fe wanted the Kid brought to justice, and fast. If he didn't do it, they would just hire someone else to get the job done.

At least, he thought to himself, with me the Kid has a chance of being brought in alive. Anybody else they sent would just shoot him down like a dog.

Thirty-two

Pat Garrett stormed into The Drinking Hole, his face red and his neck swollen like a bull in heat. He stopped just inside the batwings, his head swiveling back and forth, looking for Falcon.

After a moment, when he didn't see him, he stomped over to the bar.

"Roy, where the hell's MacCallister?" he almost yelled.

Roy ignored him for a moment, continuing to wipe a beer glass until it shone. He slowly cut his eyes up at Pat, and Garrett realized he was no longer counted among the friends at The Drinking Hole.

"Could you speak a little louder, sir? I'm afraid I didn't hear you," Roy said with more than a touch of sarcasm.

Garrett took a deep breath, removed his hat, and sleeved his forehead of the sweat that clung there.

"I'm sorry for yellin', Roy. Things haven't been goin' too well for me lately."

Roy eyed the sweat stains on Garrett's silk shirt. "Kinda hot for April, ain't it?" he asked, a small smile on his face.

Garrett shook his head, returning the smile. "Yeah, Roy, an' over in Lincoln it's really hot for the sheriff since the Kid escaped."

"Aren't you the sheriff, Pat?"

"Yeah, but I don't know for how long if I don't manage

to find the Kid 'fore somebody else does, or 'fore he kills again."

Roy nodded. "Kinda tough place to be in, ain't it?" He hesitated, then added, " 'Course, it ain't near so bad as sittin' around waiting for somebody to come jerk you by the neck 'til you're dead, is it?"

Garrett took a deep breath, trying to calm his temper. *It wouldn't do any good to get in a fight with Roy. It'd only make matters worse,* he thought.

"Please, Roy, can you tell me where Mr. MacCallister is?"

"That's better, Pat." He inclined his head toward the back of the room. "He's in his office. Go on in. He's expectin' you."

"I'll bet he is," Garrett muttered under his breath as he walked to Falcon's office and knocked on the door.

"Come in," Falcon called. He was sitting leaning back in his chair, his boots on a pulled-out desk drawer, a whiskey in one hand and a long, black cigar in the other.

When Garrett entered the room Falcon got a concerned look on his face. "Why, what's the matter, Pat? You look like a gelding remembering the good old days, and not liking the new ones much."

"You got that right, Falcon."

Falcon nodded at the bottle of whiskey and glass sitting in front of Garrett, as if he had expected him to come and was ready for him.

"What can I do for you, Pat?"

Garrett poured himself a tall glass of bourbon and downed most of it in one long, convulsive swallow.

He wiped his mouth with the back of his sleeve and stared at Falcon with narrowed eyes. "I come here to find out if you had anything to do with the Kid's escape."

"And what if I told you, and you alone, that I did? What would you do about it?"

Garrett slammed his hand down on the desk. "Dammit, Falcon, he killed two good men in that escape!"

Falcon shrugged. "One good man, maybe, and one other."

He took a slow, deliberate drink of his whiskey, then a long draw on his cigar. With smoke trailing from his nostrils, he said, "But be that as it may, this is a dangerous country, Pat. Men are getting killed every day for no good reason. And, you've got to admit Olinger was warned, several times, about the improbability of Billy ever being hanged, and the danger of taunting and humiliating him just because he was shackled like a dog and couldn't defend himself."

Garrett slumped in his chair and drained the rest of his drink, quickly pouring himself another. He took a readymade out of his pocket and lighted it with a lucifer he struck on his knee-high leather boots.

Falcon thought he looked quite the gentleman sheriff, with his cute little derby hat, long suitcoat, vest over a silk shirt, and fancy boots.

"Falcon, I'm askin' you straight out, did you help the Kid escape?"

Falcon laughed. "Pat, I'm surprised at you. You're the sheriff of this here county, and a United States Deputy Marshal to boot. If you think I aided and abetted a killer in a jail breakout, then it's your duty to prove it, and arrest me."

Falcon leaned forward, both his eyes and his voice suddenly becoming hard as tempered steel. "But don't come whining around here to me because you can't keep a teenager locked up in your jail, with two full-time guards on him and with him chained to the floor."

"I take it that means you're not going to answer my question."

Falcon shrugged again. "I will tell you this, Pat. If, and I say *if*, I had it in my power to see that the Kid escaped, I would have done it."

"But, Falcon, can't you see Billy's changed? He's no better than a mad dog running in the streets tryin' to bite people. Only the Kid's bite is fatal."

"You don't understand the Kid, Pat, because you're so unlike him. To the Kid, the most important thing in the world is loyalty to one's friends. He has proven over and over that there is not anything he won't do for a friend."

Falcon shook his head. "I feel sorry for you, Pat, because you lack that quality. To you, a friend is just someone to use to gain power or money or position. For you, loyalty is a one-way proposition. That's why you'll never understand why a man like the Kid would risk his life—and in fact will probably lose his life—simply for doing what he thinks a friend should do . . . take care of his *compadres*, his partners, or his saddle-mates."

"That may be, Falcon, but if I find out you helped the Kid I'll be forced to come back here and arrest you for it."

Falcon smiled, took a last drag off his cigar, and stubbed it out. He looked up at Garrett, "Bring plenty of help if you try, Pat, because you aren't man enough to do it alone."

"I won't have to ask far, Falcon. There's plenty of men in Lincoln who think you ought to be shot down in the street, without waiting for proof."

"Some of Dolan's lap dogs, I presume?"

Garrett nodded.

"Do you count yourself among them, Pat?"

"If I did, you'd be dead already, Falcon."

Falcon got up and said, "Come on, Pat. I'll walk you to the door."

As they exited the batwings, side by side, they found a group of men milling about in the dusty street in front of The Drinking Hole.

Four men stood in the forefront of the group, talking in loud voices to the people behind them.

A barrel-chested man with a full beard and the sleeves on his plaid flannel shirt rolled up to reveal massive forearms covered with thick patches of coarse black hair, yelled, "How long are we gonna stand for this? We all know Mac-Callister let Bonney out of jail. Let's put a rope around his neck and string him up 'til he tells where the Kid is hiding."

"Who's the loudmouth?" Falcon asked, slowly pulling his coat back and loosening the hammer thongs on his Colt.

"That's Bud Warwick, a friend of Bob Olinger's. He's a teamster, drives mule teams across the desert when he's not drunked up or fighting in a saloon somewhere," Garrett answered.

A rail-thin man next to him held a shotgun up in the air. "What do you say, citizens? Let's go in and get the gambler and make him talk."

"That's Olinger's wife's brother, Slim Watkins, another worthless hunk of nothing. He's mad 'cause Olinger was the only one who ever bothered to bail him out when he got arrested for drunkenness," Garrett said out of the corner of his mouth.

Suddenly, the crowd quieted and the two men turned.

"There he is now!" Bud called, putting his hand on the butt of his pistol.

As Slim cradled the shotgun in his hands, Falcon said, "Yes, here I am, big mouth. Just what do you intend to do about it?" Falcon asked, his eyes cold as February ice.

"We're gonna make you tell where Billy the Kid is hidin'," and then we're gonna string the two of you up side by side," the big man answered, glowering at Falcon from under bushy eyebrows.

"Not likely, friend," Falcon said in a low, dangerous voice. "You'd be dead before you took the first step."

"Now hold on," Garrett called, holding up his hands. "As long as I'm sheriff of this county, there ain't gonna be any lynchin' or mob rule, you hear me?"

"Get outta the way, Sheriff," Slim Watkins said, earing

back the hammers on the shotgun and starting to turn. "We ain't got nothin' against you. We want MacCallister."

"Take it easy with that scattergun, Slim," Garrett said, his own hand hovering near his pistol. "I've already talked to MacCallister, and he says he don't know where the Kid is."

"The son of a bitch is lyin'!" Bud yelled, "An' he got my friend killed."

"Bob Olinger was a mean, cantankerous ass, who probably got what he deserved," Falcon said, turning his body slightly to the side to present less of a target, for he knew gunplay was imminent.

"Why you . . ." Bud yelled, his hand going for his gun.

At the same time, Slim started to raise the shotgun to his shoulder.

Both Garrett and Falcon grabbed iron, Falcon getting off two shots before Garrett or Bud cleared leather.

The first slug took Bud in the throat, blowing a large-sized hole in the back of his neck and snapping his head back, throwing him with arms spread wide back into the crowd, spewing blood and bits of bone and flesh all over the men there.

Falcon's second bullet hit Slim in the forehead and blew the top of his head off along with his Stetson, which landed upside down on the ground and lay there with most of Slim's skull still inside it.

Slim's eyes got wide in the second he lived after the shot. Then he gave a loud sigh and toppled backward.

When his shotgun hit the ground butt first, it went off, blowing a chunk of meat out of a bystander's thigh. The man fell to the dirt with a loud scream.

By the time Garrett raised his pistol both Slim and Bud were lying dead on the ground. He turned to Falcon, who was still slightly crouched, his Colt extended should anyone else in the crowd want to take a hand in the fracas.

"God Almighty, Falcon! You drilled both those galoots 'fore I cleared leather."

A voice from the mob could be heard to say, "Jesus, he's faster'n greased lightnin'!"

"And he didn't even aim, just fired from the hip and hit both men dead center," a voice nearby added, with awe.

Garrett turned back to face the people in front of the saloon. "Someone go get the doc and take care of that wounded man on the ground there. And the rest of you go on home and let the law take care of Billy Bonney."

As the townspeople dispersed, Garrett cut his eyes back to Falcon, who was putting his Colt back in his holster.

Falcon looked at Garrett, and smiled "Thanks for standing with me, Pat. There may be hope for you yet."

"What do you mean?"

"Just that maybe you'll remember what it means to call a man a friend, and not go gunning him down without giving him a chance."

"If you mean the Kid, I've sworn to uphold the law, Falcon."

"Are you talking about the law of someone like Jimmy Dolan, or are you talking about justice? They're not necessarily the same, Pat, a fact I hope you'll come to realize before it's too late."

Thirty-three

The Kid approached Falcon MacCallister's cabin slowly with his hands in plain sight. He didn't want the gunman to shoot before he recognized him.

Falcon came out on the porch, a rifle balanced in his right hand.

"It's me, the Kid!" he cried, raising both palms as he guided his horse toward the house with his knees. "Just wanted to talk a minute if you can spare the time."

"Ride in and climb down."

The Kid wondered if Falcon might have changed his mind about helping him after hearing about the two deputies killed in the escape. He knew Falcon was a friend, but he also knew Falcon didn't much approve of his new life as a gunman on the run.

He was still a little unsure if Falcon would get the drop on him to earn the five hundred dollar reward . . . or worse, just shoot him down at point-blank range, since the reward posters for Billy the Kid, alias William Bonney, said Dead or Alive.

The Kid stopped his horse and stepped to the ground. A late afternoon sun cast shadows among the piñons surrounding the shack. "I got to ask you, Falcon. I'm takin' a big chance by comin' here, but I need to know if you've changed your mind 'bout our friendship, whether you've given up on me ever goin' straight."

"If I had, you'd be dead by now, son."

"I know you didn't mean for me to kill no one when I escaped, but there weren't no other way. I want you to know I appreciate your help, and that I tried to get away without any killin', but they wouldn't let me."

Falcon sighed, "I know that, Kid. Olinger wouldn't have hesitated to kill you if you'd given him half a chance."

"I've a mind to go after Murphey and Dolan, especially after all they done to our friend Chisum. They've hit his cowherds mighty hard lately."

"And I've made a few of 'em pay for it with their lives," Falcon replied.

"I'd heard some got shot."

"A few. The ones who were dumb enough not to toss down their guns and clear out of this country like I told 'em to. I never warn a man but once."

"I'm real glad to know you ain't out after me," the Kid said, trusting Falcon's words. "I sure as hell don't need no more enemies."

"Sheriff Garrett has hired two experienced deputies from down in Texas, John Poe and Tip McKinney. They're both good with a gun, so be careful."

"Garrett's gunned down or locked up most of my friends with the Regulators. I'm pretty much on my own now. Met a young feller named Billy Barlow. He's back at our camp keepin' an eye on things."

"It looks to me like the Lincoln County War is finished." Falcon said in a calm voice. "Your side took a helluva whipping. Politics were against you, and when they brought in the army, the deck was stacked."

"We was fightin' for somethin' we believed in, settin' things right for the way they murdered poor ole' John Tunstall an' then Alexander McSween."

"I understand, Kid, but that doesn't change anything."

"I'm findin' that out real fast."

"What do you aim to do? Seems foolish for you to hang

around this part of the territory. Sooner or later, with that reward posted, they'll hunt you down and kill you or take you to stand trial."

"Unfinished business is what's keepin' me here. There's a few more who have to pay for what they did to Mr. Tunstall an' Mr. McSween. Then I reckon I'll clear out an' head down to Mexico."

"You could get killed seeking more revenge," Falcon said in a matter-of-fact way. "You've settled a number of scores, you and your friends. Why not let it rest?"

"I ain't built that way, Falcon. When a man's a friend of mine, I believe in bein' loyal to him plumb to the end, if that comes."

"I admire that in you, son, but it could also wind up being a death sentence."

"I stared death in the eye before. I ain't scared to do it again."

Falcon grinned. "Things are a lot worse for you since your escape from the Lincoln County jail. You've killed a pair of deputies, and that's something they won't tolerate."

"Didn't want to shoot Bell. He ran for the stairs an' I didn't have no choice. Olinger, he had it comin'. You won't get much argument on that in these parts."

"He was a bully, all right, but he had a badge. That makes it a lot worse for you."

"Couldn't hardly have been much worse," the Kid said, remembering his escape. "They had me chained up like a dog, waitin' to stand trial for murderin' Sheriff Brady. I didn't kill Brady."

"They've got plenty of witnesses who'll say otherwise on a witness stand."

"I never even aimed at Brady. That's the honest truth of the matter."

"Truth is sometimes hard to find when powerful people try to hide it," Falcon said.

"I reckon I'm findin' that out, too."

Falcon gave him a lingering look. "If I were you, Kid, I'd head for Mexico, or damn near anyplace else. It's just a matter of time before somebody bushwhacks you for the reward money. I'd give moving on some serious thought."

The Kid toed the ground with his boot. "I have been thinkin' on it some. But like I said before, I've still got business with Jimmy Dolan an' Lawrence Murphey. Maybe a couple more."

"You're old enough to make up your own mind on it, but you won't be able to raise another army like they did when Brewer organized the Regulators. Folks are scared now."

"I'd stand a better chance if you'd throw in with me an' Barlow, even for just a little while. I've heard it said you're damn near a one man army yourself."

Falcon wagged his head. "I don't champion causes, and I never join organizations. I make it a habit to act alone."

"Sure would be a help if you changed your mind just this once."

"Sorry, son."

"Looks like I'll be handlin' it on my own, then. Thought I'd ask."

Falcon seemed to hesitate, pointing the muzzle of his rifle down. "I might still be of some help, if Dolan's men aren't smart enough to leave catching you in the law's hands. I don't much cater to vigilante justice—not by you, Kid, and not by Dolan and his friends. If his men continue to try and hunt you down to settle a score for Dolan, some of 'em are gonna pay for their mistake in blood. I've already sent word to Dolan and Murphey. If they ignore my warning, they'll lose a few more gunslicks who ride for 'em."

"I reckon that's a whole lot better'n nothing," the Kid told him.

"If you care to come inside, I'll boil coffee. It'll be dark soon and coffee will be a help against the night chill."

"I figure I'd better get back to camp. Barlow's gettin'

real jumpy lately. But I'm obliged for the offer. We've been livin' on beans an' fatback for quite a spell, an' our coffee's nearly gone."

"I'll send along a sack of Arbuckles," Falcon said, turning to go back inside his rented cabin. "Maybe I can rustle up a little something else to eat."

"Be mighty kind of you, Falcon. Trouble is, I can't pay."

"I didn't say anything about money." Falcon disappeared inside, leaving the Kid to his thoughts.

It would have changed things considerably if Falcon had decided to join them. He was deadly with a six-shooter and a rifle. Men with good sense feared him around Lincoln, since his reputation was more widely known now.

But MacCallister was firm about not joining the fight in an official way, and he wasn't the type to be argued with . . . the Kid knew him well enough to know that.

A few minutes later Falcon came out with a small burlap bag full of coffee beans and other foodstuffs. He handed them over to the Kid.

"We're much obliged, Falcon."

The tall gunman merely nodded

The Kid hung the bag over his saddlehorn and mounted his sorrel mare.

"You ride careful, Kid," Falcon said, "cause there'll be plenty of 'em out to hang you or shoot you in the back to get that reward."

"Sure wish you'll reconsider, after you think about it some," the Kid said, collecting his reins.

"Nothing to think about," Falcon replied. "My mind's made up."

The Kid turned his horse for the ride back to camp, but he held his horse in check a moment. "No matter how this turns out, Falcon, you've been a good friend and they're hard to find."

Falcon grinned, then his face turned serious. "You keep looking over your shoulder. Stay away from the towns, such as Lincoln or Fort Sumner. That's where your enemies have got the best chances."

"I'll remember what you said," the Kid replied, waving before he urged his sorrel to a short lope up a wooded hillside to the west.

Barlow was nervous, irritable. "We can't stay out in these woods forever, Kid. I'm tired as hell of beans and sleepin' on hard ground. I could stand the sight of a pretty woman, too, if you know what I mean."

"I know just what you mean," the Kid said, chewing a warm tortilla they made with some of the *masa trigo* flour Falcon gave them.

"Let's ride north," Barlow continued. "Maybe things won't be so hot for us up around Fort Sumner, or Mesilla."

"They could be worse," the Kid observed, chewing. "That's Sheriff Pat Garrett's jurisdiction."

"He won't be expectin' us to ride right into his back yard, will he?"

"Hard to say about Pat. He's smart."

"But you an' him was friends."

"That was before they hung that badge on his chest and before they offered that reward."

Barlow took a sip of his coffee. "Money sure can change a man," he agreed.

"We could ride up to Fort Sumner at night, maybe slip in real quiet. I've got plenty of friends there. Jesus Silva would hide us out for a day or so."

"That Indian slave girl, Deluvina Maxwell, is sure enough a pretty gal," Barlow said.

The Kid chuckled. "She's always been a little sweet on me. So has Celsa Gutierrez, Pat Garrett's sister-in-law."

"Let's stop talkin' about it and ride up that way, just to see the lay."

"I reckon we could, if we done it careful."

"I say we start first thing in the mornin'," Barlow said. "I sure could set my teeth into a chunk of good beefsteak."

"Sounds good to me, too," said the Kid.

"Then it's settled. We pull out at first light for Fort Sumner and slip in tomorrow night, after we make sure there ain't no signs of a posse."

"Garrett wouldn't be dumb enough to bring a whole big bunch with him. Falcon MacCallister said he'd hired two men from down in Texas with experience. John Poe and Tip McKinney were their names."

"I've heard of Poe," Barlow said. "Can't recall, but I think he was from down around the Pecos."

"Won't make no difference if we don't run into 'em in the dark," the Kid said, wondering how much truth lay behind his words.

Thirty-four

The Kid rode cautiously into Fort Sumner on the night of July twenty-fourth, along with his new partner, Billy Barlow. Folks who knew the Kid often related how much the two looked alike, the only difference being Barlow was shorter, a half-breed Mexican from the panhandle country of west Texas, and sported a close-cropped beard. He had become a Regulator when stealing cattle from Jimmy Dolan became too risky.

"We'll go to Saval Gutierrez's house," the Kid said. "He can give us something to eat besides beans. Maybe his wife has some fresh tortillas."

"I don't like it," Barlow said as they guided their horses into Fort Sumner.

"Don't like what?" the Kid asked. "Last night you was all hot and bothered about comin' up here to Fort Sumner."

Barlow shrugged. "I changed my mind. You know Garrett and his deputies are crawlin' all over the county lookin' for you an' any of the rest of us Regulators who ain't dead or in jail. Garrett has become a tool of those boys up in Santa Fe."

"I can ask my ole' friend Pete Maxwell if there's been any sign of a posse," the Kid replied, swinging his horse over to the rear of Saval's adobe house in the dark.

Off in the distance he could hear harmonicas and guitars playing, and the sound of laughter coming from the old fort headquarters building, which now served as the gathering place for sheepmen and cowboys who made a living from the area.

But Barlow had still had concerns.

"Gutierrez is Garrett's brother-in-law, Kid. He might tell somebody we're here."

"Not Saval. He's a friend, an' he damn sure ain't got no lost love for Pat since he became sheriff. There's some bad blood between 'em."

The Kid laughed softly in the darkness. "Besides, his daughter Celsa would gut him if he turned me in."

"I still don't like it," Barlow said, swinging down off his horse behind Saval Gutierrez's shack. "Somethin' about this don't feel quite right."

"You're too damn edgy, Barlow," the Kid said, tying off his horse at a corner of a shed behind Saval's. "Relax. There's a dance goin' on. Hear that music? We'll have some fun for a change instead of bein' on the run from the law every damn day, the way we've been living'. I'm tired of boiled beans and sleeping on hard ground . . . especially sleeping alone."

Barlow looped his reins around a corral post. "What makes you so damn sure the law ain't here, waitin' for us?" he asked, giving their surroundings a look. He paid particular attention to the center of the village, where they could hear the music being played.

"Garrett wouldn't come here. He knows I've got too many friends in Fort Sumner."

"I ain't so damn sure," Barlow muttered, his hand resting on the butt of his Colt .41, an older, single-action pistol he seemed to prefer.

"Let's walk over to Jesus Silva's house," the Kid suggested, listening to music coming from the dance. "Jesus will feed us good, an' we won't have no worries. Jesus will have some meat, at least somethin' besides beans. Saval is poor as a church mouse, an' we might starve here at his place."

"Sure seems quiet tonight," Barlow said, "in spite of all

that damn Meskin music coming from over yonder in the middle of town."

The Kid stopped in his tracks. "If it'll make you feel any better I'll go ask Pete Maxwell if he's seen Garrett or any of the posse before we eat."

Barlow looked at the Kid, his lips turning up in a small smile. "You sure you don't want to head over to Maxwell's just so's you can get a gander at his daughter, Paulita?"

The Kid smiled back, "Well, that wouldn't exactly be an unwelcome occurrence, now would it?"

"I'm hungry enough to eat a bear," Barlow said. "Let's just be real sure we go careful."

The Kid chuckled softly. "I ain't stayed alive this long in the middle of a war in the New Mexico Territory by not bein' careful when the need arises. You gotta quit worryin' so much about the wrong things, Billy."

"It's my nature to worry," Barlow replied.

They walked softly across a narrow roadway toward the dark outline of Jèsus Silva's adobe.

"Ain't even no dogs barkin'," Barlow observed.

"No reason why a dog should bark tonight," the Kid said, feeling sure of himself. "This ain't unfriendly territory. If there was trouble, Pete would have sent word."

Music from a tiny cantina caught the Kid's attention, and he halted. "Let's stop at the dance. Celsa might be there, an' I need to tell her where I've been. I figure she's been worried, since I ain't talked to her in a spell."

"But she's Pat Garrett's sister-in-law." Barlow said it with concern in his voice.

"Won't matter. She wouldn't say a damn word to that lawman Garrett. Let's go."

At the dance, the Kid swept Celsa Gutierrez and several other young maidens across the floor, including Paulita Maxwell. Billy Barlow stood in a corner of the cantina with his hand near his gun, scowling and looking over his shoulder at the slightest sound.

"I sure am hungry," Barlow said after the Kid was through making a few turns across the dance floor with Celsa in his arms while the music played.

"We'll drop over at Silva's place," the Kid replied, giving Celsa a kiss on the cheek. "He'll have something to feed us an' you can be sure of that."

"Be careful, Billy," Celsa warned, her face twisted with concern. "Someone say they see Pat Garrett and two more men ride through the peach orchard this afternoon. I don't see them myself, but I hear people talk about it."

"We'll be real careful," the Kid told her. "No need to worry none about me, because I was born a real careful man, an' I intend to stay that way."

"I *worry,*" Celsa said. "Pat is saying he will kill you."

"Pat wouldn't do that. Hell, we're friends from way back when he first came to New Mexico Territory, an' he knows I wouldn't double-cross him."

They left the cantina in the dark, a moonless sky giving them no light to go by. The Kid led the way to Jèsus Silva's back door and knocked softly.

"Quien es?" a gentle voice cried.

"It's me, *Billito,*" the Kid answered.

The door opened a crack.

"Is that really you, *Chivato?*" Jesus asked.

"It's me, an' a friend. Billy Barlow. We've been on the run so long I'd forgotten what it's like to knock on a friend's door without duckin' down."

"Come in," Jèsus whispered, "only be careful, *Billito.* I am told Sheriff Garrett and two deputies—John Poe from down in Texas, and Tip McKinney—have been in town earlier in the day asking about you."

"Are they gone now?" the Kid asked.

Jèsus gave the darkness a slow examination. "Who can

say, *Billito?* You know Garrett is after the reward posted on your head."

The Kid and Barlow stepped inside Silva's small adobe and hung their hats on a peg.

"When was the last time anyone seen Garrett or his deputies?" Barlow asked in a quiet voice.

"They came early, before sundown," Silva replied. "No one has seen them since."

"I can ask Pete Maxwell," the Kid responded. "Pete's been friendly to me during all this trouble. He's a friend of John Chisum's."

"Be careful," Jèsus warned. "The governor has posted a big reward for you."

"I know all about the reward," the Kid replied.

Jèsus added sticks of firewood to his stove.

"Have you got any beef?" the Kid asked. "We been livin' on beans and fatback so long I 'bout forgot what a good beefsteak tastes like."

"No. But Señor Maxwell has just killed a fresh beef, and it is hanging at the corner of his porch. He told me I can cut off as much as I need."

"I'll go," Barlow said. "Just give me a sharp knife, and I can get what we want . . ."

Pat Garrett, John Poe, and Tip McKinney had arrived at Fort Sumner well after dark, and it was near midnight when they crept across the peach orchard toward the Maxwell house.

Pete Maxwell, angered by the Kid's attentions to his daughter, Paulita, had sent a trusted vaquero into White Oaks to tell John Poe about the Kid's frequent visits to his house.

John Poe whispered to Garrett as they slipped through the darkness, "You know, Pat, I ain't never seen Bonney before. How'll I know it's him?"

Pat whispered back, "Don't shoot unless I give the word."

When they got to the Maxwell house, Pete was inside asleep, with no lights on.

Garrett turned to Poe and McKinney. "You boys stay out here on the porch and keep a sharp lookout. I'll slip inside and ask Pete about the message he sent concerning the Kid."

Soon after Garrett went through the door, Poe saw a shadowy figure crouched over, making his way toward the house in the darkness.

When he was forty feet away the man stopped, evidently seeing the outline of Poe and McKinney on the porch.

"Quien es?" the man whispered in a hoarse voice. *"Quien es?"*

Poe and McKinney weren't about to reveal their identities by answering, so they remained quiet.

The man then stepped abruptly up to Pete Maxwell's bedroom window.

"Pedro, quienes son estros hombres afuera?" the man whispered toward the Maxwell bed.

Pete Maxwell sat up in bed, startled, and called out, "That's him!"

Garrett, startled by the sudden commotion in the bedroom, drew his pistol and fired at the shadowy figure.

Two gunshots rang out, and the Kid jumped out of his chair at Jèsus Silva's table, clawing his Colt .44 free of its holster as he came to his feet.

"That came from Maxwell's," the Kid said.

Jèsus went to a window of his shack. "Yes. I can see a body lying on the porch. It must be your friend, Barlow.' "

The Kid edged to Silva's back door. "But who would shoot a man without a gun coming to Pete's back porch with a knife to cut off a slice of beef?"

"Maybe it is Pat Garrett," Silva warned.

"But why would he shoot Barlow?"

"He may have believed it was you, *Billito*. The two of you look the same in the dark."

"Damn," the Kid hissed, stepping out into the darkness.

He could hear voices coming from Pete Maxwell's porch, and he recognized one as that of John Poe.

"You've shot the wrong man, Pat. This isn't Billy the Kid. He wouldn't come to this place unarmed."

"It's him . . . I think," a voice the Kid recognized as Garrett's replied. "I *know* it's him."

"He don't even *look* like your description of him," Poe insisted.

"It sure as hell don't," another voice said, probably the voice of deputy McKinney.

"Pull the body inside Maxwell's bedroom," the Kid heard Garrett say. "We won't let nobody get a good look until we're sure. One of you boys light a lamp inside, once we've got the door closed. I know Billy the Kid. I'll damn sure recognize him when I see him."

"I'm tellin' you this is the wrong man," Poe insisted as he picked up the dead man's feet and began pulling him into Pete Maxwell's bedroom.

"It can't be," Garrett said. "I'm sure I recognized him even in the dark."

"But this feller's got a beard," McKinney's voice exclaimed as they pulled the body inside. "You know Billy the Kid ain't got no beard."

"Just shut up and close the goddamn door," Garrett snapped as a crowd of people came toward Maxwell's place, drawn by the gunshots.

The Kid edged closer to the house, wanting to see if Billy Barlow was in fact dead.

Suddenly, Garrett looked over his shoulder and stared directly at the Kid, his gun in his hand hanging next to his leg.

Instead of raising the gun and firing, Garrett shook his head at the Kid, then turned and walked into the house.

The Kid holstered his pistol and hurried back to his horse, wondering why Pat Garrett did not say publicly he'd killed Barlow, and why he didn't try to shoot him when he had the chance.

The Kid mounted and rode at a slow trot out of Fort Sumner toward Frank Lobato's sheep camp high in the mountains south of Fort Sumner, wondering what was behind the strange behavior of Pat Garrett. Surely he had immediately recognized his mistake, shooting down Billy Barlow when he was supposed to be after him. And why didn't he raise an alarm when he saw the Kid standing nearby? The Kid couldn't make head nor tail of what was going on in Pat Garrett's mind.

Two days later, as the Kid was resting up at Frank Lobato's sheep camp, a rider from Fort Sumner came through— Iginio Salazar, who was an old friend.

"Kid," Salazar said before he brought his horse to a full stop, "you won't believe what Pat Garrett do."

The Kid got up off his bedroll. "Tell me what you're talking about."

"Garrett shoot your young friend, Billy Barlow, an now he passes the body off as you. They bury him the next day, and Sheriff Garrett now tries with the territorial legislature for the five hundred dollar reward."

The Kid looked to the south, toward Mexico. "Maybe Garrett is doin' me a favor," he said under his breath. "Could be if I clear out of this country, everyone will believe I'm dead, an' that will be the end of it."

He shook his head. Damn, but life was strange. Here was the man sworn to hang him risking his own reputation in order to give the Kid a chance to make a new life.

Thirty-five

The Kid rode up on Falcon's cabin in the darkness. He halted his horse a safe distance away.

"Falcon MacCallister!" he called out. "Don't shoot. I'm a friend."

Moments later a shadow appeared at a rear corner of the house, staying back just enough to have cover in case trouble started.

"Who's there?" a familiar deep voice asked.

"It's me, Billy Bonney . . . the Kid"

"Can't be. The Kid's dead and buried at Fort Sumner," Falcon replied.

"Garrett shot the wrong man. If you'll give me a minute I can explain."

"It does sound like you, Kid. Looks a helluva lot like you, too, even in the moonlight. Swing down, only remember I've got a gun trained on your belly. If this is some kind of trick it ain't gonna work."

The Kid stepped down gingerly. "It's no trick, Falcon. Garrett shot Billy Barlow the other night, thinkin' it was me."

He ground hitched his horse and walked toward Falcon with his hands showing.

"It is you," Falcon said. "Come inside, quick, before anyone else sees you, and I'll light a lamp."

The Kid followed Falcon through the back door. Falcon

walked around the room, closing cloth curtains over all the windows before he turned to a table in the kitchen. A match was struck and quickly a flame came to life in a lantern.

Falcon turned down the wick so the light was dim. "Take a seat at the table. I'll boil a pot of coffee while you tell me the whole story."

The Kid slumped into a hand-made hide-backed chair. "Me an' Barlow rode to Fort Sumner. We went to the dance they was havin' there. Afterwards, we went to my friend Jèsus Silva's house so he could fix us somethin' to eat."

"Was Garrett at Fort Sumner?" Falcon asked, stoking the potbelly with sticks of firewood before adding a few dippers of water to a smoke-blackened coffeepot, then a handful of beans after he put the pot on the stove.

"We had a few folks warn us that Garrett an' two deputies were in the vicinity earlier that day, but I guessed he'd cleared out when we didn't see no sign of him."

"Go on," Falcon said, coming over to the table, examining the Kid's face in the lamplight.

"We was hungry for beef, since we'd been hidin' out in the hills for so long. Jèsus said Pete Maxwell had a side of beef fresh killed, hanging on a corner of his porch. I offered to go cut a slice off it, only Barlow said he'd go. He took a knife an' went across them dark streets to Maxwell's while me an' Jesus talked about things, about how bad it has gotten for us here in Lincoln County."

When the Kid hesitated, Falcon said, "Tell me what happened next."

"I heard two or three shots. I pulled my pistol an' went runnin' outside."

"The shots came from Maxwell's place?"

"That general direction. That's when I heard voices, only I didn't actually recognize but one of 'em."

"That'd be Pat Garrett."

"Right. Garrett said, 'that was the Kid, and I think I've got him'."

"But it was Barlow he shot?" Falcon asked.

"Yeah. Shot him dead. Then this voice I didn't recognize said, 'Pat, you've shot the wrong man!' real loud."

"What did Garrett say?"

"He said to pull the body inside so they could see him in the light, but he was sure it was me—the Kid—he'd killed."

"So they pulled the body into Maxwell's place, where they could see the dead man's face."

"Right, an' that's when this different voice . . . I figure it was Tip McKinney . . . said, 'He don't even *look* like the Kid, Pat. I think you shot the wrong man. Besides, the Kid wouldn't come to this place. It'd be too dangerous for him.' "

"What happened afterward?"

"That's the really strange thing, Falcon. I was havin' trouble making out what they was sayin', so I edged around the corner of the house I was hidin' behind, an' Pat looked up and saw me, plain as day."

Falcon's eyes narrowed before he turned to the pot on the stove and took it and poured them cups of steaming, black coffee.

Then he sat across the table from the Kid, pulled out a cigar, and lighted it. After a couple of puffs to get it going, he took a tentative sip of his coffee and leaned back in his chair and crossed his legs.

"Did Pat raise an alarm when he saw you?" he asked.

"No, an' that's the funny thing. He kind'a motioned me with his head to take off, like he'd almost expected to see me standin' there."

Falcon smoked thoughtfully for a moment, then leaned forward and put his elbows on the table, his fists together under his chin.

"So, you think by then he knew he shot the wrong man and was trying to hide it?"

Kid shook his head, eyebrows knit together. "No, I don't think that was it at all, Falcon. I may be wrong, but I kind'a got the idea maybe Garrett did it on purpose, to give me a chance to make a break for it and start a new life somewhere's else without John Law on my back trail."

Falcon nodded, slowly. "I see your point, Kid. Even if he shot the wrong man, he could always have said the two of you were together and still raised an alarm and come after you."

The Kid jerked his head up and down. "That's the way I figured it, too, Falcon."

"What did Pat do then, after he waved you off?"

"He told the other men to shut the door, an not to let nobody inside to view the body. That's when the door closed and I didn't hear no more voices."

"But you knew Garrett shot the wrong man. If anyone else in Fort Sumner saw you after the shooting, the whole town would know about Garrett's mistake."

"Jesus Silva knows, of course, from when I came runnin' back into his house. I told him to run fetch my horse, that it would be too dangerous out there for me. I made up my mind to clear out of town and lay low, 'til I saw what Garrett aimed to do about killin' Barlow, and to talk to you 'bout what I suspect Garrett's doin' by lettin' me go."

Falcon nodded. "I've seen Barlow. He looks a little bit like you."

"Except for the beard," the Kid explained. "And his skin is real dark, not like mine."

"I was told they buried the Kid . . . the body, early the next morning. Garrett himself had the coffin made and put Barlow in it and nailed the lid shut. He probably did that so anyone who knew you couldn't get a look at the body."

"That's the way I figure it. An' now Garrett's applied to the territorial legislature to collect the reward that was posted for me."

Falcon stared into the Kid's eyes, a slight smile tugging

at his lips. "Garrett gets the reward money, and you get away with your life. That's not a bad trade-off, Kid."

"I ain't got away yet. Somebody could still recognize me. That's why I been hidin' out up at Frank Lobato's sheep camp and only ridin' at night."

"You took a big chance coming here," Falcon observed. "You could have been followed."

"I made sure I wasn't."

"Do you trust this Frank Lobato? And how about your friend Jèsus Silva? Will they keep their mouths shut about what really happened?"

"They're good friends, Falcon, 'bout as good as you."

"But either one of them could challenge Pat Garrett's claim to the reward if they brought you in, dead or alive."

"I trust 'em not to do that."

"A trusting nature can get a man killed, son."

"Like I told you, they've been my friends through all this trouble. I'm bettin' my life, I reckon, that neither one of 'em will ever say a word."

Falcon got up to check on the coffee and pour another cup, a thoughtful frown creasing his face.

"I guess I wanted your advice on what to do," the Kid said when Falcon said nothing more.

Falcon added wood to the stove. "There are two possibilities, the way I see it. Garrett made a simple mistake in the dark and he's hoping to cover it up, figuring you'd be smart enough to head for parts unknown and never show back up here in the New Mexico Territory again."

The Kid added his own thoughts. "Me an' Pat were friends before this war started. I still believe he's doin' me a favor, lettin' folks think he killed me on purpose when he knew all along it was Barlow on that porch."

"Had you ever met John Poe or McKinney?"

The Kid wagged his head. "I believe it was you who first told me they came from down in Texas. I've never set eyes on either one."

Falcon came back to the table. "That way, Garrett could pull it off, collect the reward, and do you a favor all at the same time, providing you weren't seen leaving this part of the country."

"I'd like to believe me an' Pat were good enough friends so he'd do that."

"You heard both of his deputies say the body didn't resemble you physically," Falcon continued, "but in spite of that he tells his men to pull the body inside and close the door . . . not to let anybody see it."

"That's just about exactly what was said."

Falcon gave him a lopsided grin. "Garrett knew it was the wrong body. What we don't know is whether he made an honest mistake, or if he meant to let you live. I don't reckon it matters, unless somebody sees you who can identify you."

The Kid gave an uneasy glance out the cabin windows. "It's my idea to take off for the Mexican border. Maybe go down to Sonora for a few years, where I've got some Yaqui Indian friends in the horse business."

"I'd damn sure travel at night until I crossed the Rio Grande," Falcon said

"I'd aimed to."

"Later on, after you give it a few years for things to cool down, you could cross back into Texas some place. Only you'll have to go by a different name."

The Kid grinned weakly. "I've got a different name, a real one."

"What do you mean by that?" Falcon asked.

"All these years, folks thought my name was Antrim, or some said it was McCarty. Then I took to usin' Bonney for my last name, on account of it was my aunt's real name. She was from up in Indian Territory. But ain't none of 'em my actual birth name at all."

Falcon chuckled. "Just what the hell *is* your name, Kid? You've used about as many as there are ticks on a dog."

The Kid leaned back in his chair. "I was born William Henry Roberts, in Buffalo Gap, Texas, in eighteen fifty-nine. My daddy was called Wild Henry Roberts. My momma died when I was real young, an my daddy was meaner'n hell to me. So I ran off to live with my aunt Kathrine Bonney up in the Nations."

Falcon was still chuckling softly. "So there's nothing to that story about you being born in New York City?"

"I made it all up, 'cause I didn't want my real daddy to find me. He's powerful mean, an' he'd give me a terrible whippin' for runnin' away like I done."

"Then you're really William Henry Roberts." It was a statement, not a question.

"That's right, Falcon. You're the only one livin' who knows the truth about who I am."

The smell of coffee burning brought Falcon back over to the stove, where he poured two more tin cups of coffee. He put one in front of the Kid and tasted his own, blowing on it to cool it down a mite.

"Thanks," the Kid muttered. "I sure do hope my secret will be safe with you."

"It is," Falcon said. He shook his head, grinning again. "I could never make folks believe this county's most desperate outlaw was named Kid Roberts, anyway. They'd laugh me out of the territory."

"Things'll go better for me if everybody believes I'm Billy Bonney, an' that I'm dead an' buried at Fort Sumner. Garrett gets to collect the reward, an' I can start a new life down in Mexico."

"Just make sure you get there without being identified," Falcon said solemnly. "Travel the back roads at night until you strike that river. They call it the Rio Bravo down there, and there's plenty of shallow places to cross, especially this time of the year."

"That's just what I plan to do, only once again I ain't got any food, like the last time I came to see you."

"Food isn't a problem, son," Falcon said, walking over to a shelf laden with beans and flour and tins of peaches and tomatoes. "I can give you all you'll need."

"You've sure proved to be a mighty good friend, Falcon, and, God knows and I've learned those are few and far between."

Falcon began sacking up staples for the Kid's ride to the border. "Let's just say I was young and foolish once. I hope you've learned a lesson from this. When you take up a gun, it can be your own death sentence. This time, you got lucky on that score. Another man lies buried in your grave. Try to remember that before you give any thought to taking another man's life."

"I won't forget it," the Kid promised, meaning every word.

Once he had the Kid's saddlebags full of enough food for his upcoming journey, Falcon said, "Go on out there and feed and water your mount, then we'll get some shut-eye. You're going to need to be well rested before you start your trip."

"Well, I guess I'll sleep in tomorrow, and lay about here restin' up for the trip."

"Yeah, it's best if you take it easy and sleep tomorrow as much as you can. We can start out late in the day when the sun's low in the sky, so it'll be harder to get a fix on you if we come upon someone along the way."

The Kid crinkled up his forehead, "What do you mean we, Falcon? You ain't plannin' on headin' down to Mexico too, are ya?"

"No, Kid. But I've got some things I want to talk over with John Chisum tomorrow, and his South Spring Ranch is off to the south from here, so I can ride part way with you." He paused and scratched his chin, "Might be useful to be two riders 'til you get closer to the border. That way, if we do run upon someone I can distract them while you hightail it the other way."

The Kid gave a large yawn. "Sounds good to me, Falcon. It'll be nice to have some company, for part of the way at least."

He walked to the door, saying over his shoulder, "After I take care of my horse, I'm for gettin' flat. I'll see you in the morning."

The Kid and Falcon spent most of the next day seeing to Kid's horse's shoes and gear, making sure they would hold up for the several week trip down into the interior of Mexico. Falcon spent some of the time trying to teach the Kid something about life on the trail, since for most of his life he'd been a city dweller.

Finally, a couple of hours before dusk, they mounted up and rode south, toward John Chisum's South Spring Ranch.

The Kid took a deep breath and looked around as they rode.

"I'm sure gonna miss this part of the country, Falcon. The smell of pine and juniper, the creosote and sage blossoms in the spring, and the snow in the winter."

He laughed. "Don't 'spect I'll be seein' much of that down Sonora way."

Falcon snorted. "Just don't get to missing it too much, Kid. Not for a few years at least, until you can manage to put on a few pounds and grow some facial hair to hide your features."

"I don't intend to come back for quite a spell, and then I'll probably head on over to Texas and see what that part of the country has come to since I been gone."

Falcon nodded. "Glad to hear it, Kid."

Thirty-six

Deke Slaton and Roy Cobb led a group of twenty-three Apache renegades to the edge of a pine forest ending at a north pasture of John Chisum's South Springs Ranch. Dusk was spreading over a grassy expanse filled with grazing longhorn cattle. The young Apaches had slipped away from the Mescalero reservation to take the pay Slaton and Cobb were offering to rustle a sizable herd of Chisum's cows.

Slaton and Cobb were handpicked men working for the head of the Santa Fe Ring, Thomas Catron. Catron had grown tired of the way Lawrence Murphey and Jimmy Dolan were bungling the affair in Lincoln County. The object was to put John Chisum out of the beef contract business so Catron and his partners could have all the government contracts for themselves.

"This is gonna be easy," Deke said, sweeping the pasture with a wary eye. "No range riders. Nobody around. Hell, we didn't need all these damn Injuns, after all."

Roy glanced over his shoulder. The Mescalero Apaches were well armed with repeating rifles which Catron had sent down with Deke and Roy. Catron's impatience with Dolan and Murphey had reached a boiling point, and now he was taking matters into his own hands.

Flat, coppery faces framed by straight, coal-black hair were turned toward Deke and Roy. Most of the Apaches wore leather leggings and deerskin shirts this time of year, while a few wore ragged U.S. Cavalry coats and pants stolen from the worn garment piles at Fort Stanton. These young warriors were weary of reservation life and looking for excitement, and when the pay was right they were willing to do a little stealing or even killing in order to earn it.

"It won't hurt to have 'em," Roy said. "They can help us drive off damn near every one of them longhorns to Catron's packin' house west of Santa Fe. They'll be hung carcasses of beef before Chisum ever misses 'em."

"I was expectin' a fight," Deke said.

"The fight's gone out of what's left of them socalled Regulators since Sheriff Garrett killed Billy the Kid," Roy said, as if he was well-informed on the subject. "He was kinda their leader. Everybody thought he was bulletproof until the other night."

"Maybe now Chisum's pulled in his horns," Deke added, giving the cattle a final look before he signaled the Indians to spread out and start driving them north. The herd would easily number two hundred head.

Roy nodded. "Let's get this done, Deke. There's still one dangerous friend of Chisum's out there someplace, the big gent named Falcon MacCallister. He's killed off a bunch of Dolan's boys an' made it look easy. I heard he blowed Jesse Evans right out of his boots, and Jesse was one of the best with a gun I ever saw, next to you."

Deke prided himself on his reputation with guns, pistols or rifles. Because of his reputation, Thomas Catron was paying him very well to pull off this raid on Chisum.

"We was told this MacCallister hadn't really taken a side—only that he was a friend of Chisum's an' if he happened to be near where there was any trouble over Chisum's stock he'd use his guns to lend Chisum a hand. Besides, you can't believe half the stories these locals tell. Accordin' to them, this Falcon is damn near a killin' machine. Ain't nobody that good . . . not even me. I miss a few from time to time."

"I sure as hell hope MacCallister don't cross trails with us while we're drivin' off this herd," Roy said.

Deke grinned. "That's why we've got nearly twenty-five Injuns with us, Roy. If MacCallister shows up, we'll send 'em all after him. He'd need a damn Gatlin gun to stop this bunch of renegades."

"Let's go," Roy said. "It's gettin' dark."

Upon a signal from Deke, the mounted Apaches began to spread out south of the herd, to begin driving them north toward Santa Fe.

The sun dropped below the horizon, filling the hills and valleys with purpling shadows. The half-wild range cattle were reluctant to move in a bunch at first, until the Indians and Deke and Roy were able to get them settled and headed north in a strung-out group.

"Two riders," a young Apache named Gokilah said, pointing to a section of hilly country to the west. The Indian had galloped his pony over to inform Deke and Roy of the horsemen heading toward the slow-moving herd.

"Appears to be just a couple of cowboys," Roy said, for the light was fading and the men were hard to see.

"One of 'em's ridin' a big black horse," Deke observed. "The other guy is a little feller ridin' a sorrel. Damned if he ain't wearin' a battered top hat like them coach drivers do up in Saint Louis."

"Like the kind Billy the Kid wore, only he's dead now," Roy said. "Could be he's just some saloon drunk who found that ole' hat in a trash dump."

Deke turned to the Apache. "Take five or six of your warriors an' run 'em off. If they try to put up a fight, kill the sons of bitches."

Gokilah reined his pony away, beckoning to five more

Apaches for them to follow him. The six Indians took off at a gallop in the direction of the two strangers, levering shells into the firing chambers of their rifles.

"No sense in takin' any chances," Deke said. "Now let's keep this herd movin'. It'll be dark soon."

Deke and Roy could hear the Apaches screaming war cries as they raced toward the pair of horsemen. Roy was first to look over his shoulder.

"Them two ain't runnin' off," he told Deke.

Deke glanced that way, at once noticing the gleam of rifles in the hands of the two strangers.

A gunshot ripped through the evening quiet. An Apache flew off his pony's back, tumbling to the grass.

"Son of a bitch!" Roy exclaimed

The Apaches returned fire, rifles pounding, the crack of exploding gunpowder filling the air.

Answering fire came from the strangers, including a shot from the little man in the top hat that sent another Indian rolling off the side of his speeding pony.

"Damn," Deke snarled. "They both have got a hell of a good aim. Or real good luck."

Then both men jumped off their horses to the ground, kneeling as they held rifles to their shoulder. Two Winchesters fired in unison.

Gokilah shrieked and slid off his pony's withers into clumps of buffalo grass, rolling like a limp rag doll while his pony sped away.

A second Apache fell along with Gokilah, leaving only one Indian making a charge toward the strangers, a young renegade smart enough to know to turn his charging pony away from the pair of riflemen before he lost his life.

"Run get some more of them Injuns," Deke growled. "Bring 'em all. Let them cattle drift for a spell until we kill those two bastards."

Roy was watching the surviving Indian race out of rifle range. "I recognize that big feller by his description now,

Deke. That's Falcon MacCallister. They say he's a big son of a bitch, always ridin' a black horse, an' he's proved who he is by the way he can shoot."

"Ain't neither one of them missed," Deke said, "and a fast movin' target is a tough shot. Maybe it is MacCallister. We'll send every Apache we've got down on 'em, and see how good this Falcon really is."

"I've already seen he's mighty damn good," Roy said as he rode off to gather their renegades for an all-out rush toward the two riflemen.

Deke watched the pair mount their horses again and now they headed for the cover of some slender piñon pines just to the west of the valley the herd was in.

"They'll be harder to kill now," Deke grumbled, pulling his own Winchester from its saddle boot. "I may have to do this job myself."

Rifles roared from the trees and from the Apache warriors as the Indians raced back and forth near the pines, some hanging under their ponies' necks to make smaller targets for the men hidden in the forest.

Deke spurred his horse toward the fight. Roy was riding off to Peke's left.

"We'll circle them piñons an' get around behind 'em," Deke shouted.

Roy was watching three more Indians drop from their ponies' backs. "Those bastards sure can shoot, Deke," he yelled back in order to be heard above the gunfire and the thunder of racing hooves. "Now I'm damn near positive the big feller is Falcon MacCallister."

"I don't give a damn who he is," Deke snapped.

"We're liable to," Roy answered, a worried look on his face while he watched the wink of muzzle flashes coming from a section of pine forest. "If he turns out to be Falcon

MacCallister like I think, we could wind up with a few holes in our own hides."

The remark made Deke angry. "If you ain't got the nerve for this kind of work, get the hell into another profession. One man don't scare me . . . I don't care who he is, or how bad his reputation is."

"But there's two of 'em," Roy reminded, swinging his horse to the southwest to follow Deke in a circle around the spot where the pair of riflemen were taking such a deadly toll on the renegade Apaches.

"I can count, Roy!" Deke bellowed just as two more Indians were blasted from the backs of their ponies.

"Jesus," Roy said, watching the Apaches fall. "Whoever the hell them two fellers are, they damn sure don't miss very many shots."

Deke was furious, both at the reckless young Indians who charged straight toward the pines and at Roy for running out of nerve so quickly. When he got back to Santa Fe he meant to tell Thomas Catron never to use Roy Cobb on dangerous business like this again.

Another renegade let out a yelp as a bullet passed through his skull, sending blood and brains and hair flying into the darkening skies overhead as the warrior fell.

A badly wounded Apache with his intestines dangling from a huge hole in his abdomen rode blindly toward Deke and Roy, gripping his pony's mane with both hands, no longer carrying his rifle.

"Damn, look at that!" Roy exclaimed, as the young warrior rode past them, his face twisted in a mask of pain. "Them's his guts hangin' out."

"Ain't you never seen any blood before?" Deke snarled, more angry at Roy than ever. "It's gonna be your blood spilled on this grass unless we get behind those two sons of bitches and silence their guns real quick."

Roy wagged his head, still watching the wounded Indian until the Apache slid off his blood-splattered pony into the grass. 'I ain't sure we're bein' paid enough money for this," he said as he caught up with Deke, aiming for a place in the woods well to the south of the two riflemen.

"Just shut up and let's get these horses hid," Deke replied, trying to control his temper. "Then we'll start sneakin' up on Mr. Falcon MacCallister, and whoever the hell his little friend happens to be."

Thirty-seven

Deke crept forward, his rifle cocked and ready, weaving his way through a dark piñon forest. Roy was off to his left with his rifle ready.

"I can't see a damn thing," Roy whispered.

"Just keep listenin' to their guns," Deke replied, being careful to keep his voice low while he stepped cautiously over fallen pine cones and dry pine needles beyond the piñon thicket where they left their horses.

The pounding of rifles had slowed somewhat. Deke could see some of the Apaches out on the open prairie falling back to hold a conference out of rifle range. Less than a dozen Indians were still in the fight. The others were evidently dead, or badly wounded enough to retreat just beyond rifle range to talk about the deadly marksmanship of the men hidden in the trees. Deke saw them gathering in a swale, darker shadows among the dusky shapes of yucca and *cholla* dotting the valley.

The gunfire from Falcon MacCallister and his companion, if that was who was doing the shooting, had all but stopped. Every now and then, when an Indian got too close one of the men fired, and the result was usually fatal.

"It ain't far now," Deke whispered. "Watch out where you put your feet so's we don't make any noise. They ain't expectin' us from behind."

"I sure as hell hope they ain't," Roy said, crouching down as he moved from tree to tree.

Deke kept up his slow advance, determined to blow this Falcon MacCallister all the way to hell and back the minute he got the chance. He felt confident he could slip up on the men without being noticed.

A gun popped less than a hundred yards away.

"Yonder they is," Roy whispered very softly.

"Spread out," Deke replied in the same quiet voice. "Don't shoot 'til you're sure of a target."

"This ain't smart, Deke," Roy protested, although he kept on moving toward the sounds of rifles. "If this is Mac-Callister he ain't gonna be dumb enough not to watch his backside every now an' then."

"Shut the hell up an' keep movin'," Deke hissed, intent upon the direction from which the occasional rifle shots came, only they were far fewer now.

Roy hunkered down even lower and took mincing steps over fallen pine needles, his rifle to his shoulder. "Maybe we oughta use pistols," he wondered aloud, "seein' as we're gettin' this close."

Mad as Deke was at his partner, he didn't give a damn if Roy wanted to use a slingshot. Deke knew he could kill both men if he kept the element of surprise on their side. The only possible problem could come if somehow, Falcon MacCallister was anticipating an attack from the rear.

A rifle cracked sixty or seventy yards in front of Deke and he knew exactly where the riflemen were hidden now. "Gotcha," he said under his breath, inching closer to the spot, his Winchester pressed to his shoulder.

Another rifle shot sounded from the same place, and Deke allowed himself an unconscious grin. After these two bastards had killed so many of his Apaches, it would be pure pleasure to put a bullet through the backs of both men.

Roy stepped on a dry twig and the noise made Deke

flinch. He'd never really liked Roy Cobb, or trusted him to carry his share of the load.

"Be careful where you put your goddamn feet," he whispered.

"Sorry, boss, but it's dark as hell in here."

An idea struck Deke just then. "Stay where you are an' cover me. I'll slip up closer an' you keep your gun ready to back me up."

"Be damn glad to stay put right here," Roy answered in a tiny voice.

Deke crept onward, only a footstep at a time, staying in the shelter of piñon trunks wherever he could. Now, suddenly, all the guns were silent.

Them yellow-livered Apaches, he thought. *As soon as the fight got tough, they pulled back and refused to rush MacCallister's position again.*

He made his way on the balls of his feet to a thick pine trunk less than forty yards from where the pair of riflemen had been firing. Roy was twenty or thirty yards behind him, keeping an eye on his back.

I've got you boys now, Deke thought, slipping around the tree soundlessly.

A soft voice behind him did not alarm him at all, for he was certain it was Roy whispering to him.

"Can you see 'em?" the voice asked.

"Not yet," Deke replied. "Now shut the hell up so they won't hear us."

"I can see *you,* and I can kill you now."

Deke froze, for he quickly realized that the voice did not belong to Roy Cobb.

"Son of a bitch!" He snarled, whirling around toward the voice with his Winchester leveled.

A flash of bright light blossomed a few feet away, and with it came thunder like the noise from a spring storm. Something struck his breastbone, a hard lick like the kick from a reluctant mule being harnessed.

He fell backward, at the same time pulling the trigger on his rifle. Deke's ears were filled with noise, the report of his own gun and the shot that was fired at him.

Deke tried to keep his feet under him, staggering to remain upright. Red-hot pain jolted through his chest.

"You missed," the strangely deep voice said, louder than before.

As Deke was falling he heard another gunshot, and then Roy let out a yell for help.

Deke landed on his back, unable to draw a breath, his rifle falling from his hands. A curious ringing began in his ears, replacing the blast of gunshots he heard moments before the slug hit him.

"I'm shot," he gasped, struggling for just one mouthful of air.

"That's about the size of it."

Pain almost rendered Deke unconscious. He could feel blood leaking from the front of his shirt. "Who . . . the hell. . are you?" he asked, his mind gone numb with pain.

"What difference does a name make?" the voice replied.

Tremors shook Deke's limbs. He fought to remain awake long enough to reach for his pistol, unwilling to give up the battle so easily. "I gotta know," he croaked, sucking mightily for a breath.

"Not that it matters," the voice said quietly, "but I'm Falcon MacCallister. It won't matter because you'll be dead in a few minutes, either way."

Deke's trembling fingers closed around his pistol grips and with all the effort he could muster, he clawed the Colt free from its holster.

"You aim to take a shot at me with that pistol?" Falcon asked.

"I'm . . . gonna. . kill you, you son . . . of a bitch."

He could hear Roy wailing at the top of his lungs off in the distance.

"Plenty of folks have tried," Falcon said. "You won't be the first."

"How . . . the hell did you know . . . ?" Deke managed to say as he raised his Colt, thumbing back the hammer, lifting his head in spite of tremendous pain to search for a target among the piñon forest shadows.

"How did I know you'd be coming up behind me? I can't make myself believe you're stupid enough to ask me that sort of question."

Deke fired, and the .44 bucked in his fist. He'd only had a brief glimpse of something moving toward him in the forest. In so much pain, he couldn't wait any longer.

"You missed me again," Falcon said. "You aren't much when it comes to hitting what you aim at, are you?"

"You . . . bastard!"

Deke heard soft footsteps drawing closer to the spot where he had fallen.

"You've called me a bunch of names," Falcon said as the cries from Roy Cobb grew softer. "But you still can't seem to aim all that well, even though I'm letting you live long enough to take your best shot."

"I coulda killed . . . you," he mumbled as a gray mist began to surround his vision.

"I gave you every opportunity."

"You slipped . . . up . . . behind us."

"Wasn't that what you and your partner were trying to do to us?"

"Who's the . . . little guy?"

"You wouldn't believe me if I told you."

"Who is the son of a bitch?"

"He's Billy Bonney, or that's the name he's been going by since he came to Lincoln County."

"Like hell! Pat Garrett killed the Kid. He's already . . . in the ground at Fort Sumner."

"It won't matter if I tell you the truth, because you'll be

dead shortly, and you won't be able to tell anyone what really happened."

"What . . . the hell do you mean?" Deke asked, his mind growing foggy. Didn't everyone know that Sheriff Garrett shot the Kid at Pete Maxwell's the other night?

"Garrett shot the wrong man."

"What?" The notion wouldn't register in Deke's pain-ridden brain.

"He shot a man named Billy Barlow. The Kid is very much alive. He just shot your partner. We've been waiting for the two of you to show up."

"Can't be," Deke muttered, slipping closer to the blanket of fog swirling toward him.

"It's a fact," Falcon replied. "The trouble is, you won't be alive to see if I'm telling you the truth."

Off in the woods, Deke heard Roy cry, "Help me, Deke! I'm gutshot. My legs won't move!"

Now a darker shadow came in front of Deke's eyes, and a hand jerked his pistol from his trembling fist.

"So your name is Deke," Falcon said. "Can't say as I'm all that pleased to make your acquaintance, under the circumstances, but introductions aren't all that important when men are trying to kill each other."

"This . . . wasn't your fight," Deke groaned. "How come you to side with . . . Chisum?"

"He's a friend."

"That ain't . . . enough to be worth riskin' . . . your life over it."

"Depends on the man," Falcon told him, his voice with an edge to it now.

The pain exploding inside Deke's chest was too much to bear and yet he couldn't admit to himself that he was dying. "I'm gonna track you down an' . . . kill you, Mac-Callister." He barely managed to get the words out

"The only tracks you'll be making will be in an undertaker's wagon."

A rush of sudden anger gave Deke an extra ounce of strength and he raised his head. "I ain't . . . dead yet," he said through clenched teeth.

"I can help you with that," Falcon said, and Deke heard the cocking of a pistol.

There was a deafening noise. Deke felt his front teeth shatter, and something akin to a hot branding iron ran through his head.

Then Deke Slaton was surrounded by darkness, and silence.

Thirty-eight

Falcon walked over to where the Kid was standing above the man he'd shot.

"Got him right through the heart," the Kid said, "only he's still alive."

"Won't be for long," Falcon observed, for even in the dark of the piñon forest an inky pool of blood was spreading around the body, easy to see.

"He kinda whispered his name," the Kid went on in a quiet voice. "Roy Cobb."

"He called the other one Deke," Falcon remembered.

"Cobb said they didn't work for Jimmy Dolan or Murphey or any of the Lincoln County bunch. They came straight down from Santa Fe, bein' paid by Thomas Catron, the leader of the beef ring that started all this trouble. That's what this feller told me just before he blacked out."

"Somebody needs to pay a call on this Thomas Catron. Tell him what happened to his boys and his Apaches here tonight. It ain't over yet. There's still nine or ten Apaches out there and I intend to kill 'em all."

"How come, Falcon?" the Kid wondered. "They don't seem to want no more fight with us."

"It's personal, Kid."

"Personal? You've tangled with those same renegades before?"

"Not the same bunch, but they're renegades off a reservation and that makes 'em fair game."

"Fair game for a killin'? Mind tellin' me why you feel so hard-line about it?"

Falcon took a deep breath, gazing toward the open prairie where the renegades still sat their ponies watching the trees where the shooting had occurred. He was remembering the worst moment of his life, when a band of redskins came down on his place while he was away, slaughtering his wife, Marie, butchering her like a fatted calf, cutting her open, scalping her, leaving her alive to suffer horribly until she died slowly.

"You ain't gotta talk about it if you'd rather not," the Kid said.

"A band of renegades attacked my ranch while I was off on business. They took my wife with 'em. They had their way with her and then cut her open. Sliced off her scalp. My father told me when he found her she'd bled all over the place, so I know she suffered something awful."

"Was she . . . dead when he found her?"

Falcon merely nodded, turning away from the dying gunman from Santa Fe to walk to his horse.

"You're goin' after the others, ain't you?" the Kid said just as Roy Cobb let out his final breath.

"Sure as hell am," Falcon replied.

"I'll go with you," the Kid offered, hurrying to catch up to Falcon's longer strides.

"Nope," Falcon remarked. "This is my affair. Stay put until I'm done with 'em."

"You're gonna take all of 'em on by yourself?"

"Now you've got the idea," Falcon told him as he untied Diablo's reins and swung into the saddle.

He began thumbing cartridges into the loading tube of his Winchester rifle. Then he booted it and pulled one pistol at a time, opening the loading gates to check their loads.

"I'll damn sure ride out there an' help you," the Kid said again.

"I appreciate the offer," Falcon replied, reining Diablo away from the tree. "But this is my personal score to settle. It's been haunting me all these years. I can't sleep sometimes, picturing what my Marie must've looked like when Jamie found her."

"An' now you're out to kill every Indian renegade you run across. It don't matter what breed they are?"

Falcon halted his horse just long enough to answer the Kid's question. "Those are renegades, son. The law says we don't fight each other any more like we did in the old days, before the big treaty at Medicine Lodge. These Mescaleros broke their word to keep peace between us. They ran off looking for a fight with white men, and I aim to oblige 'em. Those renegades who killed my Marie ignored the treaty and went to war against me, against a defenseless woman. I'll make every redskin renegade I can find pay for what happened to my wife until I go to my grave. It's something I have to do."

At that, Falcon heeled Diablo through the piñons toward the open valley, where nine Apaches were gathered in a low spot with rifles balanced across their ponies' withers.

Falcon rode to the edge of the forest. He jerked his rifle free, jacked a load into place, twisted Diablo's reins around his saddlehorn so he could guide the trusty stud with his knees. At the last Falcon pulled the Colt pistol from his left holster, fisting it, then bringing the Winchester to his right shoulder.

"Move out, Diablo," he said soft and low, urging the big stallion into a run straight toward the Apaches.

The Indians did not move, watching him gallop toward them out of a setting sun as if they couldn't believe their eyes—one man charging toward nine armed warriors. Falcon knew they must believe he was crazy.

Hell, he thought, *they may well be right.*

The smooth running gait of Diablo did nothing to bother his aim when Falcon drew a bead on one Indian and pulled the trigger on his rifle, a shot of almost three hundred yards, impossible for all but the best marksmen.

A shrieking Indian twisted off his pony, flinging his rifle high above his head as he fell headfirst beneath the hooves of the other ponies.

Falcon gave the Winchester's loading lever a road agent's spin, twirling it around his outstretched hand, sending another brass-jacketed shell into the chamber. He was still too far out of range to use his Colt pistol, but he was sure the opportunity to use it would come.

Three Indians fired back at him, yet Falcon had anticipated their moves by kneeing Diablo to the left and right so the big horse changed leads with every stride. A zigzagging target was virtually impossible to hit without a stroke of luck. And if Falcon had anything to say about it, the Indians were plumb out of luck today.

Falcon fired his rifle again as two slugs whistled past him into the night sky, while a third plowed up dirt and grass many yards to the right of Diablo's run.

The shot from Falcon's Winchester found another mark when a Mescalero in a fringed buckskin shirt yelped like a scalded dog and rolled, ball-like, off the croup of his prancing pinto pony to land hard on the ground behind it.

Again, Falcon gave the rifle a one-handed spin, a practiced move he accomplished so smoothly it seemed like a fluid motion, not the working of a steel mechanism in a man's hand.

Four more shots thundered from the swale in Falcon's direction, and all were wide misses. The Indians' ponies were hard to control with all the shooting going on, rearing on hind legs or plunging against the pull of jaw reins.

Falcon aimed for an Apache and blasted him off his dappled gray. Blood flew from his ribs and back and it seemed the big .44 slug had all but torn the Indian in half.

Diablo continued his charge toward the milling Indians as the powerful horse dodged back and forth under the signals from Falcon's knees.

The remaining Apaches suddenly panicked, as if they realized this crazy white-eyes meant business, and swung their ponies away from Falcon's headlong rush, drumming their heels into the ribs of their mounts.

Their retreat did nothing to discourage MacCallister's grim determination to blast the Mescalero renegades to their happy hunting ground. He asked Diablo for more speed and singled out one Indian to ride down and kill. Six Mescaleros remained, and he meant to slaughter the entire bunch if he had his way.

He fired at the escaping Apache and blew the back of the warrior's skull apart, with blood, hair, and bone fragments flying high above the dappled pony until the dead Indian fell limply to the valley floor.

Turning Diablo after another target, Falcon aimed and fired twice with his Colt. Another warrior screamed in agony and went down hard.

Changing directions again, the scattering Apaches wanted no more of Falcon. Remembering Marie, he gave a mirthless grin. "Time for paybacks, you bastards," he growled, asking Diablo for all he had.

Falcon rested aboard the big black stud on a hilltop to survey the scene below. Diablo was blowing hard, covered with a thick coating of sweat and foam. Falcon leaned forward to pat the big stud's neck, for he had run as if he were chasing the devil for Falcon—which, in a sense, he had been.

Spread across a starlit valley, lying in patches of dark blood, nine Mescalero Apache renegades decorated the north Chisum pasture—men who had found all the excitement they could handle when they decided to leave the reservation and make some extra money by stealing.

He heard the Kid riding up the hill. As soon as the Kid got there he spoke.

"Never saw nothin' like it, Falcon." Kid removed his hat and sleeved off his face. Then he shook his head in awe, "You killed every one of 'em, like it was all in a day's work."

He glanced sideways at Falcon. "You know, I used to think I was a pretty bad hombre, but you just showed me something. There's always somebody over the next hill who's just a little bit badder."

Falcon gave the Kid a lopsided grin. "Now you know why I keep telling you to get off the hoot owl trail and go straight. That trail only leads to one conclusion, and it's always the same, being stood up in a pine box for folks to take pictures of and stand around gawking at."

The Kid nodded.

"You plannin' on goin' up to Santa Fe to have a talk with Catron?"

Falcon's thirst for revenge had lessened after the bloodbath and he turned to the Kid. "Maybe later, but right now I'm heading on down to John Chisum's to tell him what happened."

He stared out across the field, almost completely covered in darkness now. "He's probably heard the shots and is wondering who's gone to war out on his spread." He stuck out his hand. "It's time you started that long ride to the Mexican border."

The Kid leaned out of his saddle, taking Falcon's hand. "It's been a pleasure to know you, Falcon MacCallister. Thanks for all you did to try to help me an' my friends. We lost the war in Lincoln County, that's for sure, but we damn sure made 'em pay in blood to get it done."

Falcon didn't want more conversation right at the moment. "Best you start riding, son. And good luck to you. If you're as smart as I think you are, you won't ever show your face in the New Mexico Territory again. Let 'em all think you're buried up at Fort Sumner."

The Kid nodded and swung his horse off the hilltop, hitting a trot to the south. Crossing the dark valley, he glanced to his left and then his right when he rode past the bodies of some of the Apaches Falcon had killed.

Falcon watched the boy ride off, deciding the Kid's secret would always be safe with him.

He heeled Diablo off the grassy knob and headed for Chisum's South Springs Ranch, with a tale to tell.

Just once, he turned to watch the Kid ride out of sight over a ridge.

"Good luck down in Mexico, Kid," he said as Diablo carried him toward John Chisum's headquarters, *"Vaya con Dios, Chivato."*

Thirty-nine

After Diablo cooled down and was breathing normally, Falcon turned the big stallion's head north and rode slowly toward the South Spring Ranch house.

It was a grisly ride through all the Indians, their bodies scattered over much of the ground in the area Falcon had to ride through to get to Chisum's place.

He glanced at the dead men lying around him as he rode, and felt no remorse. The men had chosen their paths, and had died honorably. Most Indians wouldn't have asked for more from their gods.

He glanced back over his shoulder, saw the Kid give him a wave good-bye with his hat, and hoped he would someday meet up with the young man again—under different circumstances.

He snorted, thinking *The Kid has lived a fuller, more exciting life than most men three times his age. Now, if only he can learn from his mistakes and not keep on making the same ones over again.*

By the time Falcon got to the house Chisum and his men were out in the front yard, holding rifles, shotguns, and pistols. As he rode in Falcon held his hands high, showing the men he was no threat. He didn't want to get blown out of his saddle by an overly-anxious cowboy with something to prove.

Chisum, when he saw Falcon ride up, tipped his hat back and stood there with his hands on his hips.

"I should've known it was you, MacCallister. Hell, ever since you came to Lincoln County there's been a war on." He chuckled. "So why should tonight be any different?"

Falcon leaned forward, his arms crossed on his saddle horn. "Me and a friend was riding by when we saw about thirty Mescaleros trying to steal some of your beeves."

"You and one other man took on thirty Injuns by yourselves?" Chisum asked.

"Yeah, and two white men, who seemed to want your cattle for themselves."

Chisum pursed his lips as Falcon continued. "They said they worked for Thomas Catron, from up Santa Fe way."

Chisum's face flushed an angry red. "Where are these gents now, Falcon? I'd kind'a like to have a word with 'em."

Falcon grinned. "In hell, most likely. They didn't survive the fracas."

Chisum hesitated for a moment. Then he smiled and turned to walk back into the cabin. Without looking back he waved his hand, "Come on in and light and sit, and I'll buy you a drink."

Falcon smiled to himself. The old man was probably still pissed-off about him dressing him down in his saloon a while back. This promised to be an interesting conversation.

He stepped down off Diablo, stuck his Winchester .4440 carbine in the saddle boot, and handed his reins to one of the punchers standing nearby.

"Would you mind seeing that he gets some water and feed? He worked mighty hard for me out there this evening, and he deserves some oats, if you got any."

The cowboy said, "Sure thing, Mr. MacCallister. I thought we was fixin' to have to go to war when I heard all them gunshots over toward the south pasture." The puncher grinned, "It's gonna take a while for my heart to slow down to normal again."

The young man shook his head as he led Diablo toward the corral. "Yes sir, it's sure good to know it's gonna be a quiet night after all," he mumbled as he led Diablo toward the corral.

Falcon walked up on the porch and started to enter the house. Chisum's foreman, Mack, stopped him by putting a large hand on his shoulder.

"Falcon, I know you and the boss had some differences a while back, but I want to you know I'm much obliged to you for taking a hand in all this. The boss was mighty worried 'bout losin' the ranch 'til you and the Kid took Dolan's mind off him."

Falcon shrugged. "It wasn't so much, Mack. You'd of done the same for Mr. Chisum."

"Yeah, I would, Falcon. But the point is, most men when they seen what they was up against here in Lincoln County would've run for the hills, not stepped in to fight like you and that Billy Bonney did."

The big Irishman blushed. "Anyway, you got my gratitude, and my friendship." He stuck out his hand and stood there, his face still red and flushed, as if he wasn't sure Falcon would take it.

Falcon grabbed the hand, which swallowed his, and gave it a firm shake.

"You're a good man, Mack, and Chisum's lucky to have you as his ramrod. You take care now, you hear?"

Mack grinned and tipped his hat as he walked off the porch. Then he turned to his men and started hollering at them to get a move on out to the battle site before the Indians started stinking up the place.

Chisum stuck his head out the door, "You comin', Falcon, or you waitin' for this bourbon to age a little more?"

Falcon followed him into his study, thinking, *The bourbon*

*you serve could stand a little more aging, since it tastes like a cross
between kerosene and rubbing alcohol.*

Chisum poured them large glasses, opened a cigar box
on his desk, and offered one to Falcon before taking one
himself and sitting down.

As the two men got their cigars going, they studied each
other through the smoke, taking each other's measures.

Finally, cigars lighted and bourbon sampled, Chisum
spoke, pointing his cigar like a pistol, punctuating each
word with a jab of the stogie.

"Falcon, there ain't many men in this territory I'd let
talk to me the way you did the other day at your saloon
and not do something about it."

Falcon's face didn't change. He didn't come here to
apologize, and didn't intend to listen to the old man justify
himself.

"You took it, John, 'cause you knew I was right. I suspect
you've been more than a little ashamed of yourself for the
past few weeks."

The corner of Chisum's mouth turned up in a crooked
smile, and he shook his head.

"Damned if you ain't got more'n a little of your dad in
you, son." He chuckled, "Whenever we'd get crossways,
he'd sit there with that same expression on his face, like
he knew I was wrong and he was right . . . and damned if
he wasn't, most of the time."

Falcon smiled, remembering the same thing about Jamie
MacCallister. His dad had more than a little of an old fire-
and-brimstone preacher in him.

"By the way, son, who was the man who was out there
with you, killin' them Injuns right and left? He sure must've
had some sand in his gizzard to stand with you against them
odds, especially for someone else's cattle."

Chisum took a deep draught of his bourbon and sat
there, staring at Falcon, waiting for his answer.

"That's what I'm here to talk to you about, John."

Chisum waved his glass in the air, slopping a little over the side, and Falcon realized he must have already had a few that evening, even though it was barely supper time. Perhaps the rancher was drinking out of guilt at his recent alliance with Dolan and his Santa Fe Ring members.

"First, I'd like to know what's going on with you and the Dolan bunch. Just how deep are you in with those bastards?"

Chisum pursed his lips and stared at Falcon from under bushy eyebrows for a moment.

"I'm tempted to say it's none of your business, Falcon. But on second thought, I guess it is your business, since you've been a good friend to me and stood by me through this whole mess."

He reached over and took the bottle from his desk, poured another drink, held it up to see if Falcon wanted a refill, then noticed Falcon had barely touched his first drink.

"Let 'me explain a few things first, son. Not by way of makin' excuses, you understand, but just so's you'll know the lay of the land."

Falcon took a drag of his cigar and let the smoke trail from his nostrils as he said, "Go ahead, John, I'm listening."

Chisum swiveled in his chair to stare out a window at his ranch, extending as far as the eye could see.

"I got me over a hundred thousand acres, and more beeves than you can rightly count. The state and the county have been eatin' me alive with taxes, an' Dolan and his lawyers are bitin' at my heels with lawsuit after lawsuit like so many rabid dogs."

He shook his head. "Hell, I've already had to resort to puttin' the ranch in my brothers' names, tryin' to dodge their warrants."

"Did it work?" Falcon asked.

"So far, but it's a temporary solution. With Judge Bristol

in his pocket, Dolan can have damn near anything he wants in these parts."

He took another deep drink of his whiskey, his eyes clouded with remembered hate for Jimmy Dolan.

"So, that's what's behind your sudden change of heart, and why you abandoned the Regulators and Billy Bonney?"

Chisum turned rheumy eyes back to Falcon.

"That's about the size of it. When I realized Dolan and his friends weren't having to pay any taxes, I figured the best thing for me to do was swallow my pride and join in with them."

He sighed, stubbing out his cigar in an ashtray on the desk.

"Hell, it's the only way I could see to save this spread I've spent the last fifteen years building."

Falcon nodded. "I can see that, John, but the Kid and his friends could sure of used your help when they came asking."

"That was one of the hardest things I've ever done, Falcon, turning them boys down when they asked for my help." He looked down at his big hands, clasped in front of him. "I haven't slept a good night's sleep since I did it."

Falcon almost felt sorry for the rancher. He knew that when a man was between a rock and a hard place, he sometimes didn't always have the luxury of making the right decision.

"Well, John, maybe what I'm about to tell you will help make you sleep a little better. The Kid didn't hold any hard feelings toward you for what you did. He understood more than you think he did. He didn't know why you suddenly changed sides, but he knew you were an honorable man, and told me you must have had good reason."

"I liked that boy, Falcon. I kept hoping by my refusal to give him money to continue his fight, he'd have to leave the territory. I figured that was the only way he'd ever survive the Lincoln County war."

He pulled another cigar from his humidor and lighted it. Through blue clouds of smoke, he said, "I guess I was wrong about him leavin', but I was damn sure correct about him not surviving the fracas."

"Don't be too sure about that, John."

"What! What are you talking about, Falcon? The Kid's dead and buried over at Fort Sumner, didn't you hear?"

"My dad had an old saying, John. He used to tell me, 'Son, don't believe anything you hear, and only half what you see'."

Chisum leaned forward, his elbows on the desk. "Are you tellin' me those stories 'bout Garrett shootin' the wrong man are true?"

Falcon shook his head. "No, John, I'm not telling you anything, and I especially don't want you repeating those crazy tales of someone else being buried in the Kid's coffin."

Chisum leaned back with narrowed eyes, thinking over what Falcon was saying, and, more importantly, what he *wasn't* saying.

"So," he said, a small grin of relief on his face, "I guess that feller out there with you who was ready to take on the whole Apache tribe was a real fighter, someone who goes ahead no matter what the odds are? I bet he's kind'a small like, but fights like any two men?"

Falcon nodded, but held up his hand. "Let's say no more about that, John. There's already enough rumors going around, and, if I were you, and if you value your friendship with the Kid, I'd do everything I could to put a stop to that kind of talk."

Chisum nodded slowly, thinking about what Falcon meant.

"In fact," Falcon continued, "that's what I was coming here to talk to you about, when we ran into those Indians."

"What can I do to help . . . uh . . . put those ugly, untrue rumors to rest, Falcon?"

"Well, Pat Garrett has been trying to get the governor to authorize the payment of the reward for killing the Kid. So far, he's been stonewalled."

Chisum sat back in his chair, sipping his drink now instead of gulping it. Falcon thought he could almost see the worry wrinkles fading as the man realized his betrayal hadn't meant the death of the Kid.

"I thought, maybe, if you and some other prominent citizens got together and raised some money for the reward, the talk of the Kid still being alive might kind of die down."

Chisum considered it a moment, then leaned forward and slapped his hand down on his desk.

"I'll do it, by God! I'll give Garrett a thousand dollars of my own money, and I'll see to it that Dolan and his partners come up with some more."

"There's one more thing, John."

"Yes?"

"I know Pat's going to want to run for reelection to sheriff. It might be better if you could put a bug in Dolan's ear that he should perhaps support Kimball for sheriff."

"Why?"

"Because, the sooner Garrett's out of Lincoln County, the sooner the Kid and the Regulators will be just an old memory."

"Well, I don't think that will be too hard. Since Garrett's killed the Kid, he ain't been too popular around the area, anyway. For all the tales of the Kid running rampant through the countryside, most of the people of Lincoln County considered him a friend, and most of 'em don't have a lot of good things to say about the man who murdered him."

"Then we understand each other?"

Chisum stared Falcon in the eye, and Falcon could see that he'd lifted a tremendous burden off the rancher, who had evidently been blaming himself for the Kid's death.

"Completely. And I'll do everything in my power to squelch those rumors 'bout the Kid still bein' alive."

He hesitated, " 'Course, I'd be mighty embarrassed were the Kid to show up in these parts later."

"Won't happen, John. You have my word. If, and I emphasize the word *if,* the Kid were still alive, I can promise you he would become a new man and light out for parts unknown, under another name so no one would ever know he was still alive."

Chisum stood up and held out his hand.

"Falcon, I can't tell you what this visit has meant to me. For the first time since the burial, I can go around with my head held high again."

"You've absolutely no reason not to, John. As Shakespeare once said, "All's well that ends well'."

Forty

When Falcon approached his cabin after leaving John Chisum's South Spring Ranch, he saw three horses in his corral, eating hay and making themselves at home.

He eased off Diablo and walked to the back of the cabin, walking on his toes so as not to make any sounds. He doubted if his company was hostile—otherwise they wouldn't have left their horses in plain view—but he hadn't lived this long without being careful.

He filled his right hand with iron, pulled the back door open with his left hand, and stepped inside, immediately moving to the side with his back against a wall so he wouldn't be silhouetted against the open door.

One of the three men sitting at his table looked up, then turned to the others. "See, I told you he'd come loaded for bear."

Seeing the men sitting there, drinking coffee with their hands in plain sight on the table, Falcon relaxed and holstered his pistol.

The men's faces were vaguely familiar, but he couldn't place their names.

"Good evening, gentlemen. Mind if I join you in that coffee?"

"No, go right ahead," a tall, lanky man said. "We boiled plenty, an' it's good and strong."

Falcon poured himself a cup, tasted it, then added a little water with a dipper from the pail on his counter.

"Whew," he said, "this stuff's strong enough to float a horseshoe."

A second man, broad through the middle, with a beard and moustache, said, "Sorry 'bout that. We been on the trail a good ways an we needed something to keep us awake 'til you got here."

Falcon leaned back against the kitchen counter, his feet crossed at the ankles, sipped his coffee, and watched the men, waiting for them to explain who they were and why they were at his cabin in the middle of the night.

The tall, thin man built himself a cigarette, struck a lucifer on the heel of his boot and lighted it. Then he leaned back, coffee in one hand and butt in the other.

"Falcon, my name's Josiah G. Scurlock, but everybody just calls me Doc." He inclined his head toward his companions, "This here is Henry Brown and John Middleton."

Falcon nodded. Now he remembered. These men had been among the first group to join together and call themselves Regulators.

"Howdy, boys. To what do I owe the pleasure of a visit from the last of the Regulators?"

Scurlock smiled. Evidently he was to be the spokesman for the group.

"We hear you were a good friend to the Kid, always there when he needed you, an' we also hear rumors it was you took out Jesse Evans and a couple of his boys."

Falcon smiled and sipped his coffee, watching the men over the rim of his cup. He wondered where this was leading.

When Falcon didn't answer, Scurlock continued.

"When John Tunstall was killed, a group of friends and former employees of his joined together, to avenge his death."

He took a deep drag on his cigarette, then tipped smoke out of his nostrils as he talked. "When Bob Widenmann, Dick Brewer, Charley Bowdre, Fred Waite, the Kid, and us joined up, Falcon, we took a blood oath. We swore an oath to remain loyal to each other no matter what happened, and to make sure whoever killed John was punished."

Falcon began to see where this was heading, but he just nodded and listened.

"Now, we ain't exactly proud of what we done back when things were getting hot and heavy. When the Kid got indicted for killin' Sheriff Billy Brady I was in Kansas, and both Middleton and Brown here were out of town, also."

Falcon stepped over to the stove and refilled his coffee mug, not adding water this time. He realized this was going to take a while, and he was bone tired from a long day.

"Go on," he said, taking out a cigar and lighting it.

"Well, by the time I heard the news 'bout the Kid's arrest, he was already out of jail and on the run, so I didn't figure I needed to come back here and tell the truth." He looked down at this hands, folded on the table. "Falcon, it was me put those slugs in Brady, not the Kid."

Falcon stared at Scurlock. *So the Kid was telling the truth when he told me he didn't kill Brady,* he thought.

"Now, don't get me wrong, all of us, the Kid included, did plenty of things we could 'a gone to jail for, but we was acting as deputies, duly sworn and appointed."

"Cut to the chase," Brown said, looking as tired as Falcon felt. He looked over at Falcon, "What Doc is tryin' to say in his typical long-winded way is that we're all feelin' mighty guilty that we took an oath to stick together and then, when the going got rough, we lit out and left the Kid to do our work, an' he got himself killed for it."

Falcon kept his mouth shut. No matter how good friends these were of the Kid, too many people already knew he was alive, he wasn't about to tell anyone else the truth.

John Middleton nodded, his knuckles white where he was gripping his tin mug. "Yeah, so now we're back and we want to finish what we started, and make those that killed Tunstall, and the Kid, pay."

Falcon, his legs and butt aching from too many hours in the saddle, joined them at the table.

"And just how do you boys intend to do that?"

Scurlock crushed out his cigarette in a dish. "We're gonna kill Dolan an' the hired killers he's got with him."

Falcon shook his head. "I don't think that's such a good idea."

"Why not?" Brown said.

"First off, he's too well-connected, and too well-protected. If you did manage to kill him, his friends in Santa Fe and the army would never stop until all you men were hunted down and killed, or hanged."

"We're willin' to take our chances," Middleton said. "We owe it to the Kid, and the others who got killed tryin' to do what we all promised to do."

Falcon wagged his head again. "No, I think there's a better way."

"What's that?" Scurlock asked.

"Why not go after the men who did Dolan's dirty work for him? The Seven Rivers gang and the Doña Aña bunch, led by John Kinney."

Scurlock nodded, thinking on it.

"Those men are all known outlaws, and no one would mind overly much if you took them out. You could hit fast and hard and get away clean, and you wouldn't have John Law on your trail for the rest of your lives."

"Would that hurt Dolan?"

"In the worst way. He'd no longer have them to do his bidding, and he'd lose all the cattle these men have been stealing to fulfill his government contract to supply beef to the Mescaleros. It would cripple his operations here in Lincoln County."

The three men looked at each other for a moment, then Scurlock turned to Falcon. "Would you be willin' to ride with us?"

Falcon pursed his lips, then sighed. "I don't usually join causes, but in this case I might make an exception. These gangs have been riding roughshod over the entire county, and it's time someone took them down."

"How will we go about it?" Brown asked.

Falcon leaned forward, "I've got a plan. Here's what we'll do . . ."

The next evening, just before sunset, Falcon and the other three were on a ridge overlooking an area near Mesilla where the Seven Rivers gang was camped. There were close to two hundred head of stolen cattle the gang was preparing to drive to Santa Fe to sell to the government for Dolan.

Falcon put his binoculars down and looked at the other men.

"I count about twenty men. That makes it about four to one against us. You boys ready?"

Scurlock pulled his pistol out, opened the loading gate and spun the cylinder, checking his loads. "Ready," he said.

The men climbed on their horses. "We'll ride in fast and hard, out of the west so's the sun'll be at our backs," Falcon said.

He wrapped Diablo's reins around his saddle horn, pulled his Winchester .4440 carbine out of his saddle boot, levered a round into the chamber, and loosened the hammer thong on his Colt sidearm.

Henry Brown put his reins in his teeth and pulled a Greener ten gauge, short-barreled shotgun from his saddle boot, filling his pockets with extra shells.

John Middleton filled both his hands with pistols, and stuck a third in the front of his pants, behind his belt for quick access.

They were ready to ride.

Scurlock looked at the others. "For the Kid," he said.

Falcon smiled and nodded. "And for all the other men these bastards have killed."

They leaned forward in their saddles and spurred their

mounts, bounding over the ridge to ride out of the sun straight into the outlaws' camp.

As the four horses raced down the hill, several men in the camp, sitting around the fire drinking coffee and whiskey, looked up.

John Beckwith, the leader, said, "What the hell?"

Wallace Olinger, the brother of the man Kid shotgunned to death in his escape from jail, dropped his coffee cup and grabbed for his rifle, leaning against a nearby tree.

Falcon, pistol in his left hand and rifle in his right, raised the carbine to his shoulder and fired. His first shot took Billy Matthews in the left shoulder, spinning him around and knocking his pistol from his hand.

Brown veered his horse to the left and fired his Greener from the hip. The 00-buckshot loads tore into Matthews' chest, ripping it open and blowing his lungs to pieces, catapulting his body into the campfire, where it lay smoldering.

Scurlock rode toward Olinger, who began to fire his rifle as fast as he could lever the shells into the chamber. His second shot hit Scurlock in the side, cutting a shallow groove through his flank.

Scurlock didn't flinch at the burning in his side but took aim and thumbed back the hammer on his Colt Army .44. He fired once, missing, and then again, this time hitting Wally Olinger in the chest.

Olinger staggered back, but continued to fire until a bullet from Falcon tore through his lower jaw, shattering it and sending teeth and blood flying. Olinger fell to the dirt mortally wounded, to lie moaning and trying to scream for help, but only managing a garbled gurgling through his ruined mouth.

Brown twisted in the saddle and fired his second barrel at a man running toward his horse. The molten lead buckshot hit John Beckwith just below his buttocks, tearing his left leg off at the thigh and shredding his right leg down to the bone. He sprawled, screaming in pain, on his face, to be trampled as Brown's horse ran right over his writhing body.

Two more men, trying to climb aboard bucking, dancing horses, were cut down by Falcon as he rode past, his .44.40 slugs hitting one mid-center in the back, and the other in the neck.

Scurlock saw John Long—the man who had set fire to McSween's house—and fired into him as he was trying to jump on a horse and ride away, shooting back over his shoulder with a pistol.

Scurlock gave chase, firing his Colt Army .44 until it was empty. Unable to reload with his mount galloping at full speed, Scurlock rode up next to Long and pulled a Bowie knife out of his belt. As he pulled his horse right up against Long's, he slashed out backhanded with the razor-sharp blade, cutting a long gash in the side of Long's neck.

Long grabbed his neck with both hands, blood spurting from between his fingers, and finally fell to the ground, his eyes wide, with foamy blood running from his mouth and nose.

Middleton rode through the middle of the camp, straight at Buck Powell, who was crouched near the string of horses at the edge of the clearing.

Powell fired as fast as he could with both hands at the charging figure riding down on him. One of his bullets hit Middleton in the left shoulder, sending his pistol spinning out of his left hand. He drew another from his belt, thumbed back the hammer, and fired as he rode past Powell.

His shot hit Powell in the left temple, blowing a piece of his skull the size of his fist into the air, snapping Powell's head back and putting out his lights for good.

Middleton used his right hand to stuff his useless left arm into his belt so it wouldn't flop around as he rode, and whirled his horse to head back toward the camp.

He rode down one man who was running as fast as he could toward a distant grove of trees, trampling him under his horse's hooves, then shot another in the chest as he was putting a rifle to his shoulder to shoot at Falcon in the distance.

Falcon, his carbine empty, booted it and filled both hands with iron, firing with both as Diablo raced in circles around the camp.

Falcon blew three more men to hell, taking a bullet in his calf. Ne slowed Diablo long enough to wrap a bandanna around his leg to stop the bleeding, then continued his killing rampage.

Brown cracked open his Greener and was reloading when a black man rode right at him, firing a pistol over his mount's head. Brown looked up, staring death in the face, until the man was blown out of his saddle by Middleton, who grinned as he rode by.

Finally, it was quiet, except for the moaning and crying and shouting for help from the wounded.

Falcon, Middleton, Brown, and Scurlock gathered together at the edge of camp in the increasing darkness.

Falcon's nose wrinkled at the acrid stench of cordite and gunpowder, and the smell of blood and death was everywhere.

"You men had enough for now?" he asked.

Scurlock wheeled his horse around and surveyed the scene. There were at least fifteen dead, and four or five severely wounded. A couple of men had managed to make it to their horses and had escaped, riding leaned over their mounts as fast as they could.

"Yeah," he grunted. "I've got no stomach for shootin' wounded men."

Brown nodded. "Let 'em live or die on their own. I ain't plannin' on puttin' 'em out of their misery."

"Let's vamoose," Middleton said, his right hand over the hole in his left shoulder. "Our work here is done."

Forty-one

Falcon and the Regulators spent the next day resting and recovering from their wounds. Falcon had dressed Middleton's left shoulder wound—using a hot iron to cauterize the hole, then packing the wound with a poultice made of boiled herbs he had learned about from an old Indian medicine man.

His own leg wound was more a laceration than a through-and-through injury, so it merely required meticulous cleaning and application of the same poultice used on Middleton.

Scurlock's bullet wound was a small, shallow hole punched through the skin and fat of his right flank. He waved Falcon off, saying he was too mean to get an infection and would take his chances and let nature take its course. He did, however, consent to Falcon's washing the wound and putting a clean cloth on it as a dressing.

As they sat around, eating enchiladas, beans, and tortillas prepared by the Mexican cook Falcon had hired, they discussed their various options.

"Far as I can tell from what I've heard, John Kinney and the Doña Aña bunch hangs out most nights at the Palace Saloon in Lincoln."

He shook his head, "It'll be pretty dangerous to brace them there, 'cause Dolan's got the town sewed up tight."

"What about Sheriff Garrett?" Scurlock asked. "I'd love to put a window in his skull for what he did to the Kid."

Falcon thought a moment before replying. He had to be careful not to let on that the Kid was still alive because of Garrett's friendship.

"Men, you're gonna have to trust me on this, but Garrett's on our side."

He held up his hand as they started to protest. "Just believe me, Pat Garrett is not to be molested. I know for a fact the Kid would want it this way."

Scurlock pursed his lips. "You're askin' a lot, for us to take your word on this, Falcon."

"How about if I prove to you that Garrett is a friend? I'll go to him and make sure when we're ready to take out the Kinney gang, he'll be out of town with his deputies."

"You think he'd do that for us?" Brown asked, a skeptical look on his face.

Falcon nodded. "I can almost guarantee it."

"All right," Scurlock said. "If Garrett and his men are gone when we ride into town, I'll take that as a sign he's a friend of the Regulators and I'll pass the word that he's not to be bothered by any friends of the Kid."

"Good," Falcon said, leaning forward, "now here's what we'll do. We'll wait until after midnight, when the boys'll be liquored up as much as possible, and then we'll enter the saloon, front and back at the same time . . ."

It was close to midnight when the four men rode into Lincoln. Garrett had been contacted, and had taken his two deputies with him to go to the site of the Mesilla massacre of the Seven Rivers gang, to "investigate" the killings.

Falcon and the Regulators hitched their horses in the alley behind the Palace Saloon, ready for a quick getaway should the need arise.

Brown and Middleton stationed themselves next to the back door and would await Falcon's signal to enter.

Falcon and Scurlock went through the batwings, their pistols loaded up six and six and loose in their holsters.

They stopped just inside the door and surveyed the situation. John Kinney was standing at the bar, his back to the door, his arm around a saloon girl, a half-full bottle of whiskey on the counter in front of him.

Andrew Boyle and Joey Nash were in a poker game off to the right side of the room, while John Jones and James, his younger brother, were entertaining two women at the left side of the room.

There were three or four other men in the hall that Falcon didn't recognize, and he didn't know if they were members of the gang or not. He supposed he would find out soon enough.

He noticed that the bartender had a double-barreled shotgun on a rack behind the bar, and nudged Scurlock to show him its location.

Gradually, the room became quiet as the patrons noticed the two gunmen standing in the doorway, staring at Kinney's back.

He glanced up, catching sight of Falcon and Scurlock in the mirror over the bar. He took his arm from around the girl, motioned with his head for her to leave, and slowly turned around, leaning back against the bar on his elbows.

"Well," he called out in a loud voice, slightly slurring his words, indicating he had more than enough whiskey in him, "if it isn't Doc Scurlock, and the tall gambler from Colorado."

He grinned and took another drink of bourbon from his glass. "You boys here to get drunk and cry about your baby-faced friend that Garrett killed?"

Falcon and Scurlock didn't answer, but stood there, hands hanging at their sides, waiting.

"I want to tell you boys something," Kinney continued.

"I went out to boot hill today and pissed on Bonney's grave. What do you think about that?"

"I'm glad," Falcon said, his voice low and hard. "A man shouldn't have to die with a full bladder. It makes such a mess when he wets his pants."

Kinney frowned, his eyes narrow. "You think you're man enough to take me, MacCallister?"

"It don't take much of a man to kill a back-shooting coward, Kinney, which is what I hear you are. It also ain't much of a man who'll desecrate a man's grave but didn't have the *cojones* to stand up to him when he was alive."

Kinney stabbed his thumb in his chest. "I weren't afraid of nobody, least of all the Kid."

Falcon grinned insolently. "That's not what the Kid told me. He said when you were guarding him on his way to jail in Lincoln, he called you out and you turned white as a sheet and almost started crying. He said if he hadn't been shackled hand and foot, you would have turned tail and run away."

"That's a goddamn lie!" Kinney shouted.

"Well, coward, I'm not shackled, and my back's not turned. Show me what you're made of, if you've got the sand."

Kinney sleeved his mouth with the back of his arm, his eyes shifting to his men on either side of Scurlock and Falcon. Then he grinned.

"Oh, and your hired guns are welcome to join the dance," Falcon said, "long as they remember somebody's got to pay the band."

Kinney stepped away from the bar, his right hand over the butt of his gun. Suddenly, he grabbed iron.

Falcon's hand moved so fast it was almost a blur. His Colt was leveled, cocked, and fired before Kinney cleared leather. His slug took the gunny in the stomach, doubling him over and driving him to his knees.

The barman reached for his shotgun and Falcon shot

him through the hand, changing the bartender's mind about entering the fracas.

John and Jim Jones jumped to their feet, slinging the girls away from them as they clawed for their pistols.

Scurlock whirled, drew, and fanned the hammer of his Colt Army .44. The big gun kicked and exploded, sending flame and smoke belching from the barrel. His first slug took John in the neck, punching through and blowing out the man's spine, dropping him like a rag doll to the floor.

His second bullet hit Jim Jones in the right shoulder, spinning him around to where Scurlock's third bullet entered between his shoulder blades, throwing him facefirst onto the table, spreadeagled and dead.

Andrew Boyle and Joey Nash and the other three men at their table on Falcon's left all jumped up, drawing their pistols.

Middleton and Brown stepped though the back door and opened fire.

Brown had his Greener ten gauge leveled at his hip, and let go with both barrels. Andy Boyle was hit at the waist and cut almost in half, his guts and blood spraying out to cover the men next to him.

Middleton had pistols in both hands and was thumbing back the hammers and firing without aiming. Two of his bullets hit Joey Nash at the same time, lifting him off his feet to fly backward through the plate glass window in the front of the saloon, dead before he hit the ground.

Falcon killed two of the other men at Boyle's table, but held his fire when the third man held up his hands, shouting, "I quit! I'm not part of this—don't kill me!"

Falcon walked through the smoke and cordite of the room to stand before the frightened man.

"When Sheriff Garrett gets here, you be sure to tell him Kinney drew first, and the others joined in. You hear?"

"Yes sir, I sure will," he said.

Falcon stuck a finger in the man's chest. "You be sure

to tell it right. Otherwise my friends and I will have to pay you a visit. Do you understand?"

"Yes, sir. I promise, I'll tell it just like it happened."

Scurlock glanced at the bartender. "Tell Dolan the Regulators business in Lincoln is finished, unless he wants to try killing another innocent man."

Brown pointed the shotgun at the bartender. "And if he sends anyone after us, then we'll be back to have a talk with him, *comprende?*"

The bartender nodded quickly. "I'll make sure he gets the message."

Minutes later, the sweating bartender stood in front of Jimmy Dolan in the parlor of his house. Dolan was wearing a nightshirt and was rubbing sleepy eyes.

"Falcon MacCallister and them three Regulators just plumb blowed Kinney and his men to pieces, Mr. Dolan. Kinney didn't even clear leather 'fore MacCallister gutshot him and folded him up. He's still alive on the floor of the saloon, and he's sufferin' something awful."

Dolan poured himself a glass of whiskey and drank it down in one convulsive swallow.

"He's gonna die a hard death, Mr. Dolan."

"And you say they told you to give me a message?"

The man nodded. "They said if you didn't let the whole matter drop, or if you sent anybody after 'em, they'd be back to have a talk with you."

Dolan thought a moment, then poured himself another drink, sweat forming on his forehead.

"What're you gonna do, Mr. Dolan?"

Dolan shrugged, downed his drink, and said, "Why, I'm gonna take their advice. There's been enough killing in Lincoln for a while."

* * *

At the outskirts of Lincoln Falcon shook hands with the three Regulators.

"What are you boys going to do now?" he asked.

Doc Scurlock shrugged. "I'm headin' back to Kansas, probably to Abilene."

John Middleton removed his hat and sleeved sweat off his forehead. "Henry and me's gonna head on down to Texas. I hear there's plenty of work for a man who knows how to use a gun down around Fort Worth."

Henry Brown asked, "What about you, Falcon? What're your plans now?"

Falcon looked toward the north. "I'm going to take a trip up to Santa Fe, and have a word with Thomas B. Catron. It's time we put an end to the Lincoln County War."

Forty-two

Falcon had his mind made up. Before he left the New Mexico Territory to return home he meant to deliver a message to the political power behind one side of the range war, the powers who had opposed his friend, John Chisum. He was sick and tired of seeing Chisum and other honest ranchers in Lincoln County losing cows to rustlers and outlaws. It was time to issue a warning to men in high government circles, the so-called Santa Fe Ring.

It was to deliver this warning to greedy men, powerful men behind the scenes that he came to Santa Fe. He was directed to the office of Thomas B. Catron, United States District Attorney for the New Mexico Territory. Considered by many to be the most influential man in New Mexico, he was also making a huge profit with his contracts to provide beef to the army posts there, and to the Indian reservations.

This was a mission that would not likely require the use of a gun, as it had when Deke Slaton and Roy Cobb and their Mescalero Apache renegades struck the herd in Chisum's northern grazing country a few days earlier, or as it had when he took out the Seven Rivers gang and the Doña Aña bunch of John Kinney.

The job at hand was more the delivery of a promise of what would happen to Catron and his allies if anything else happened to John Chisum and his cattle ranching enterprise or the good people of Lincoln County.

He rode past the expansive governor's palace on the town square to the adobe brick building where a small sign indicated that the U.S. District Attorney had his office. A plaza at the center of Santa Fe was crowded with shoppers and travelers.

Falcon swung down and tied off Diablo at an iron ring affixed to a hitching post in front of the office building where Thomas Catron and other territorial officials kept their offices.

Santa Fe was busy this time of year, its streets filled with wagons laden with trade goods and families headed farther west to claim homesteads. A few Navajo tribesmen sold their hand-made silver and turquoise jewelry around the town square. The city appeared peaceful, as if its citizens were unaware of the bloody war going on in the southern section of the Territory in Lincoln County that had claimed so many lives, including the lives of innocent ranchers.

He walked into the district attorney's office wearing his pistols, poorly concealed by the tails of his tailored suit coat. He carried a pair of gunbelts over his left forearm, heavy with the two Colts stuck in their holsters.

A man in shirtsleeves looked up from a ledger as Falcon entered the front office. He gave Falcon a look of irritation over the intrusion.

"What may I do for you, sir?" the balding man asked in a rather impatient tone. He seemed annoyed by MacCallister's presence, although his gaze did stray to the six-guns Falcon carried and his eyes rounded a bit when he saw them hanging in an unusual spot, from Falcon's arm.

"I need to see Thomas Catron." Falcon said it in a voice leaving no doubt about his resolve.

"Do you have an appointment?"

"Don't figure I need one, mister. You tell him Falcon MacCallister is here, and I've got a couple of deathbed messages for him from two men who worked for him . . . Deke Slaton and Roy Cobb."

The man scowled. "I've never heard of either one of them. However, it would make no difference. Mr. Catron is busy at the moment. He does not see anyone without an appointment, no matter what it is about."

Falcon leaned over the desk, staring the clerk in the eye as he said, "Tell him, anyway. And tell him if he refuses to see me now, I'll go to all the way to Washington, to the Department of Justice, with these special messages. I'm sure your boss doesn't want me to do that. It has to do with these guns and holsters I'm carrying. Them, and the men who wore them, were hired by Mr. Catron, and he'll want to know the outcome of his little business venture down in Lincoln County. You might mention the South Spring Ranch of John Chisum to him, just in case he needs to refresh his memory."

"Mr. Catron cannot be disturbed right now."

Falcon swept his coattail away from the pistol he wore on his right hip. "Tell him. When he hears the reason I want to talk to him, he won't be nearly so busy that he can't spend a few minutes talking to me. Whatever he's doing, he'll stop long enough to hear what I have to say, before I send that wire to his bosses in Washington."

"Are you threatening me in the office of the United States District Attorney?"

"I'm just giving you the facts. You tell Catron what I said, and I assure you he'll end whatever business he's attending to in order to hear me out."

The clerk glanced at Falcon's gun again. "I'll tell him, Mr. MacCallister, but he's very busy at the moment. You'll have to come back when he can grant you an appointment. The United States Attorney can't simply cancel what he's doing to talk to some stranger about things he knows nothing about. He's a very busy man."

"I doubt it'll take that long," Falcon said. "If I was a

gambling man I'd bet big money he'll see me right away. Be real sure you remember those two names I gave you . . . Deke Slaton and Roy Cobb."

"Slaton and Cobb," the man muttered, climbing out of his chair with a deeper scowl on his face. "I may be forced to send for the city marshal if Mr. Catron refuses to see you immediately. I can have you thrown out of here, or arrested. You can't simply barge in here like this, demanding an appointment with Mr. Catron while he's conducting government business."

"Go ahead and send for the marshal now," Falcon snapped, his patience growing short. "I imagine the law would like to hear why I'm here to talk to Catron about his two hired gunmen, and the gang of renegade Apaches he sent down to John Chisum's South Springs Ranch to rustle his cowherds."

The clerk backed away toward a closed door behind him. "You must be mistaken," he said. "Mr. Catron would never be involved in anything illegal. This is all a mistake. Thomas Catron is the U.S. District Attorney for the federal territory of New Mexico."

Falcon gave him a slight grin. "No mistake, mister. Thomas Catron hired two gunmen and a band of renegade Apaches to steal a part of John Chisum's herd, and I can prove it. I have statements from the men he hired, in front of a witness. Unless Catron is interested in seeing what the inside of a jail cell looks like, he'll talk to me right away."

"Are you accusing the United States District Attorney of an illegal act?"

"I'm not only accusing him of it . . . I can prove it. Go tell Mr. Catron what I said, and tell him I'll give him exactly five minutes to see me. Otherwise, I'm headed to the telegraph office to contact some friends of mine in Washington."

"There must be some misunderstanding."

"No misunderstanding, you bald son of a bitch. Now tell

Catron that Falcon MacCallister is here to see him and that
he's got five minutes to make some time available to hear
what I have to tell him. If I don't get to see him in five
minutes, I'm headed for the telegraph office to send what
I know to Washington."

"This sounds preposterous, but I'll give him your message," the clerk said, heading for the closed door behind
him. "I can assure you that our city marshal will arrest you
it these charges you made are groundless."

"There are plenty of grounds," Falcon said, the muscles
in his jaw tight. "There's blood all over the ground down
at John Chisum's spread, and some of it belongs to men
hired to rustle his cattle by Thomas Catron. The leaders
of the rustlers told me who hired 'em."

"I don't believe you."

"Catron will. Now walk through that goddamn door and
tell him I'm here to see him."

The clerk knocked softly on Catron's office door and
then walked in. Moments later, a young woman carrying a
parasol came out, a pink flush brightening her cheeks.

Thomas Catron was a small man with a pencil-thin moustache, dressed in an expensive, brown business suit and
bow tie. He was chubby, his stomach straining the buttons
on his silk vest. When Falcon walked in his office, Catron's
eyelids slitted. He allowed his gaze to fall to the pair of
gunbelts dangling from Falcon's forearm.

Falcon closed the door behind him and came over to
Catron's desk.

"I'm told you have some ridiculous story about men who
you claim worked for me raiding Mr. Chisum's ranch in
order to steal some of his cattle." Catron said this with a
note of arrogance in his thin voice.

Falcon tossed the pair of gunbelts and holstered pistols
on top of Catron's desk, making a loud, thumping noise.

"Do you recognize these?"

"No," Catron answered. "Why should I? They are only two pistols. They could belong to anyone. Half the men in Santa Fe carry guns."

"They belong to a couple of boys you hired to lead a band of Mescalero Apache renegades off the reservation to rustle some of John Chisum's cattle."

"Absurd." Catron's spine stiffened and his eyes became hard and dark.

"It's the truth," Falcon told him, unmoved by the district attorney's rigid pose.

"You can't prove a thing, Mr. . . . ?" Catron said, almost spitting out the words.

"MacCallister. Falcon MacCallister. And I can prove every damn word I just said."

"Utter nonsense. I wouldn't have anything to do with such an endeavor. I am a United States District Attorney, and I uphold the law. I don't break it."

"It's like this, Catron. You hide behind your official title while you hire others to do your dirty work. You're in the beef contracting business with the government."

"There is no law against that."

"There is if the beef you sell to the Indian reservations and the army posts is stolen."

"Once again let me state for the record . . . I am a United States District Attorney for the New Mexico Territory. I do not break the law. It is my job to enforce it."

"You've done a damn poor job, Catron, and you've got your dirty hands in the stolen beef business up to your fat little neck."

Falcon pointed to the guns and gunbelts. "These pieces of iron belonged to Deke Slaton and Roy Cobb. They're both dead now, along with about twenty-five Apaches who worked for them the night they tried to steal John's cows. I just happened to be riding along when it took place."

"You killed them?" Catron asked.

"I sure as hell did."

"I could have you charged with murder. I can send you to the gallows."

Falcon wagged his head. "Not this time, Catron. Before Roy Cobb and Deke Slaton died, they confessed to be working for you, robbing John Chisum's ranch."

Catron snorted. "You can't prove a thing, MacCallister. Now get out of my office."

"I *can* prove it. I have witnesses, and a pile of dead bodies to show a judge and a jury."

Catron slumped against the back of his chair. "What is it you want from me, Mr. MacCallister?"

"Some sign that you've got good sense. If you send just one more raider down to John's pastures, or steal another single head of beef in Lincoln County, I'll take what I know to the governor."

"He won't believe you," Catron said defiantly.

"I reckon we'll both have to wait and see about that," Falcon said, leaving the guns on Catron's desk as he turned on his heel and walked out the office door.

Forty-three

Twice-convicted murderer Luis Valdez listened patiently to Thomas Catron's instructions. Standing beside Luis was another hired killer, Ramón Soto. Both gunmen served as bodyguards for Catron, often handling special assignments for him which sometimes included killing people who knew too much, or got in the way.

"Deke and Roy bungled it," Catron said, his office door tightly closed and locked after Luis and Ramón came in through the back way.

"The tall man who just left my office killed them both and all of the Apaches, or so he said." Catron pointed to the pair of gunbelts on his desk. "He delivered these guns, saying they belonged to Slaton and Cobb, and then he gave me a warning—unless John Chisum's and everyone else's cattle in Lincoln County are left alone, he will take what he knows to my superiors in Washington and to Governor Wallace. He claims to have witnesses to confessions telling of my complicity from Slaton and Cobb before they died. I can't run that risk. His name is Falcon MacCallister. He is not from this city. You will have no trouble recognizing him by the description I give you. I want him dead."

"I will kill him for you, Señor Catron," said Luis, a big man with a barrel chest. A pair of cartridge belts hung from each shoulder. He carried a modified Colt .44/.40, a Mason conversion known for its speed and reliability, a favorite of many gunfighters. "Tell me his name, what he looks like, and where I can find him. Ramón and I will bring you his head."

"I'm sure he's still in town. He left less than an hour ago. He's riding a big black stallion. He wears two pistols. He is unusually tall. He wore a dark suit coat and a flat brim Stetson hat."

Luis bowed politely and turned for the back door. "We will find him, señor."

Ramón followed Luis to the doorway. Ramón had a pair of Walker Colt .44s buckled around his waist. "If it is not important to you, Señor Catron, one of us will shoot him in the back and it will be finished . . . unless you want us to do it some other way."

Catron's expression hardened. "I don't care where you shoot him. I don't give a damn how it gets done. Just don't leave any witnesses."

Luis twisted the doorknob. "He is as good as dead right now, Señor Catron."

Catron smiled as the gunmen prepared to walk out. "I will be very generous," he said.

"You always have been, señor," Luis replied with a grin that showed a gleaming gold tooth in the front of his mouth.

Luis Valdez led the way into an alley behind the district attorney's office, to a *grulla* horse. Ramón Soto mounted a red sorrel with a flaxen mane and tail. The sun was low in the sky, casting deepening shadows behind the row of buildings.

"Where we look first?" Ramón asked Luis as they reined their horses away from the office.

"Split up. You ride the west side, and I will take the east side of town. If you find him, and if it can be done easily with no one watching who can identify you, then kill him at once. If shooting him where he is will be more difficult, come looking for me. We will follow him, and choose the right place to earn our money."

"Señor Catron looks worried," Ramón said as they came to the corner of a side street. "Is it possible this Falcon MacCallister was good enough to kill Deke and Roy without ambushing them in the dark, or killing them while they slept? Deke was very good with a gun—"

"I do not care, Ramón," Luis said, turning his horse east. "This time, Falcon MacCallister will be the hunted instead of the hunter. He will not be expecting us. The advantage will belong to us."

Ramón rode his sorrel at a jog trot past the slaughter-house owned by Thomas Catron and his partners. Stacks of curing cowhides gave off a rancid smell outside the butchering plant where the carcasses were hung and then quartered.

He spied a black horse tied to a fence near the pens where live cattle awaited the sledgehammer and the bleeding knife in a squeeze chute inside.

A lanky man in a dark coat and flat brim hat was peering over the fence examining the cows.

"That is him," Ramón said softly. "I bet he looking for the brand of John Chisum among the cattle."

He reined over toward the fence, appearing casual about it as he neared the corrals. And as Señor Catron had described, the man named MacCallister wore two pistols underneath his coat. He did not seem to notice Ramón's approach.

At a distance of twenty or thirty feet Ramón drew his right hand Walker Colt, for there was no one else around and this would be a perfect shot in MacCallister's back. He pulled rein on his sorrel and thumbed back the hammer on his single-action .44. Then he took careful aim at the center of MacCallister's spine.

In a blur of motion, MacCallister whirled around with a gun in his fist. Ramón pulled the trigger, surprised by how quick the stranger was.

Twin pistol blasts spooked Ramón's horse and cattle grazing on stacks of hay in the corrals.

It felt as if a gust of mighty wind had struck Ramón in the chest, sweeping him backward out of his saddle at the same time that his pistol exploded. He knew he was suspended in the air for a moment as his sorrel wheeled and lunged out from under him. What was happening did not make any sense. How could he hang in the air this way? Blood was flying before his face, covering his arms and belly.

And then he fell, landing flat on his back with a spearhead of unbearable pain knifing through his chest, spreading through him like chains of lightning across a stormy sky.

"Dios!" he gasped, closing an empty fist that had been holding a gun.

A shadow fell across his face. Blinded by pain, he could barely make out the features of the man looking down at him.

"You aren't much good as a backshooter, amigo. You made too damn much noise," a voice said.

Ramón's mind refused to work properly, although he heard the words the stranger said. "No," he protested weakly. "I did not mean to . . . shoot you . . ."

When his lungs emptied he found he was unable to speak or draw in another breath.

"Die slow, you backshooting bastard," MacCallister said as warm blood pumped from a hole in Ramón's ribs.

Ramón could feel broken bones grinding inside him when he tried to move. "No," he whispered, as the shape above him turned fuzzy, indistinct. He opened his mouth to call for his mother the way he did as a child when something hurt him, but no words came out, only a final, bubbling sigh as he closed his eyes.

Luis heard the crack of gunshots coming from the

slaughterhouse and he scolded himself for not thinking of
the most logical place for MacCallister to go—to the cattle
pens, to look for the brands of stolen beeves.

He spurred his *grulla* into a headlong run down a narrow
road leading to the Santa Fe Packing Company's butchering plant, where Luis was sure he'd heard at least two gunshots, fired almost at the same instant.

His horse pounded down hardpan caliche. Luis jerked
out his Mason Colt, ready for anything. If Ramón had killed
this tall stranger, he would need help getting the body away
before the city marshal came to investigate the noise.

Racing out of the business district, he swerved toward
the long adobe building and cattle corrals a quarter mile
away, set off by itself because of the smells green cowhides
and entrails produced as they began to dry.

Almost at once he saw Ramón's horse wandering rider-
less in a vacant field south of the killing plant. He wondered
if Ramón had gotten off his horse to slip up on this Mac-
Callister . . . or had Ramón met with the same fate as Deke
Slaton and Roy Cobb?

Slowing his *grulla* to a lope, Luis rode straight toward
the packing plant without a trace of fear in his heart. He
had shot down some of the West's most notorious gunmen,
in face-to-face duels, or by stealth. MacCallister would be
no different, no better than some Luis had put in their
graves. All he had to do was find him.

He jerked his horse to a halt when he saw a body lying
next to a corral fence. Blood encircled the still corpse of
Ramón Soto; flies had already begun to swarm around him,
feeding on the crimson feast.

Luis looked around him, his jaw clamped angrily. He saw
a big black stallion tied to a corral pole farther to the north,
but there was no sign of MacCallister.

Tightening his grip on his .44./.40, he heeled his winded
horse forward to begin a search for the man who would
earn him a generous reward from Señor Catron, a reward

he would now not have to split with his friend. Ramón had failed, but Ramón was sometimes fearful and careless. Luis had never tasted fear in his life, and, as now, he was always very cautious.

But no matter where he looked, riding past stacks of stinking cowskins, he found no sign of MacCallister. Some of the butchers from inside the slaughterhouse, clad in bloodstained aprons, were standing in an open doorway watching him after hearing the shooting.

"*Donde esta?* Where is he?" Luis cried.

As one butcher was raising a hand to point to a spot, Luis heard a deep voice behind him.

"Right here, *cabrón*. I reckon you're looking for me."

Luis swallowed, certain that as he turned around the man would shoot him. He decided to try to buy some time until he could catch MacCallister unawares.

"I am not looking for anyone, señor," he said. "I heard a gun and came to see if someone was in trouble." He still held the Mason in his right fist, partially concealed from anyone who stood behind him.

"You make a lousy liar, amigo. You came to kill me. Thomas Catron sent both of you, just like I figured he would."

"But you are wrong, señor," Luis protested. It was time to make his play, while MacCallister was talking instead of shooting.

Luis twisted in the saddle, aiming for the sound of the voice, catching sight of a man standing between two big piles of cowhides. He fired three shots as quickly as his finger could pull the trigger, the pistol's blast frightening his horse.

A fourth shot exploded from the stacks of hides. Something flattened Luis's nose, tunneling through his brain, exiting out the back of his head, taking his sombrero with it. He was driven off his horse, jerked out of the saddle before he slammed into the side of a corral fence, landing on his rump.

He dropped his gun, his skull wracked by pain, feebly reaching for his nose with a trembling hand. His nose wasn't there . . . His forefinger entered a large round hole draining blood over his lap. Blood filled his mouth, and when he tried to speak it spilled from his lips like water pouring from a bucket.

He saw someone coming toward him, a man with a pistol aimed down at him.

"Too slow," MacCallister said. "You gave me enough time to light a cigar before I shot you."

Luis could not speak, for when he tried he only spat more blood.

"If Thomas Catron aims to stay in the cattle rustling business, he'd better hire some men who can shoot in a hurry."

Suddenly, Luis Valdez understood that he was dying. For the first time in his life, along with the coppery taste of blood, he tasted fear.

"I reckon I'll be moving on now," MacCallister said, holstering his gun, talking as casually as if he were discussing the weather. "I've been thinking about riding over to the Arizona Territory. I hear some of those desert mountains west of Camp Grant are real pretty, and they're full of Apaches I can kill if I take the notion."

Luis felt himself floating away from his body. he could see himself resting against a fence with a hole through his head. He noticed that his eyes were open, glazed, staring at MacCallister.

Luis wondered if the mountains in Arizona were as pretty as the gunman said.

As Falcon crested a hill, he slowed Diablo and looked back over his shoulder at the bustling town of Santa Fe.

Such a lovely town. It's a shame the beauty hides so much corruption, he thought.

He wheeled Diablo around and started his journey toward the Dragoon Mountains—his brother had wired him the renegades who killed his wife had headed there.

As Diablo loped down the trail, a lone bald eagle soared overhead, shrieking its mournful song.

Falcon glanced up at the magnificent bird wheeling across an azure sky and was reminded of some words in a poem by Alexander Smith called *Dreamthorp*. He repeated them softly to the back of Diablo's head, as he felt all poetry should be said out loud: "I would rather be remembered by a song than a victory."

He leaned forward and patted Diablo's neck. "You think anyone will remember Billy the Kid in a song, old feller?"

Author's Note

This is a work of fiction. Falcon MacCallister and his role in the Lincoln County War are creation on my part. I have tried, for the most part, to remain faithful to events in Lincoln County during the conflict, and most of the main characters were real figures, depicted as recorded history portrays them.

The ultimate fate of one major figure, Billy the Kid, is open to debate. Most historians believe that he was killed by Pat Garrett in or near Pete Maxwell's bedroom at Fort Sumner on the night of July 14th, 1881. A surprising amount of evidence, including sophisticated computer photo comparisons of a tintype of the Kid and a photograph of an old man living under the name William Henry Roberts, who died in Texas in 1949, suggest otherwise.

In a book entitled *Alias Billy the Kid* by Dr. C.L. Sonnichsen and William V. Morrison (University of New Mexico Press, 1955), a strong case for Roberts being the Kid was presented. *The Return of the Outlaw Billy the Kid* (Republic of Texas Press, 1997) presents a statistically valid computer comparison of Roberts' face with the only known tintype of the Kid, and the similarities made them a statistical match. The claim made by Roberts that Barlow was killed in his place has been examined on the television programs *Prime Time Live* and *Unsolved Mysteries*. The movie *Young Guns II* depicts events as William Henry Roberts described them in 1948, with the Kid surviving in Texas long enough to see the Atomic Age.

Did Garrett knowingly bury another man as an act of

friendship for the Kid? They were friends before, and during, the first days of the Lincoln County War. Or did he simply make a mistake in the dark and try to cover it up in order to collect the reward being offered for the Kid? The debate continues to this day.

Falcon MacCallister knew the truth, but after he left the New Mexico Territory for the Dragoon Mountains of Arizona he refused to discuss his brief association with Billy the Kid with anyone.